TO THE CRY OF
THE SAND'LING

Tom Binnie

Polebrook Cottage Press, England

To my wife, Chris, and daughter, Nats.

CONTENTS

PREFACE

Cupar (1730): The Inn, the School and the Kirk

The long marketplace in Cupar runs north-to-south down Crossgate. It is wider at the north end where it is marked by the Mercate Cross. The coaching inn faces south on Bonnygate which runs east-to-west, crossing Crossgate like the top of a 'T'. There is a small, single-storey schoolhouse beyond the marketplace at the south end of Crossgate. The parish church is on Kirk Wynd, half-way down Crossgate, opposite the school. In 1730, the marketplace itself was lined by places of trade: the butcher's, the bakery, the linen weaver and dressmaker, general goods and candlemaker, the saddlery and tanner, and the public notaries. Farm goods, wheat, corn, rye, root vegetables and fruit in summer, were available from the market on Thursdays and Saturdays. As were hay, wool and livestock: chickens, geese, goats, pigs and occasionally cows and horses. Although the town men regularly sup at the Inn, particularly on market days, it is primarily a resting place for travellers. Apart from the East Tolbooth, the inn was the only two-storey building directly on the marketplace. It is a popular stopping place for the carriages, coaches and carts travelling to and from the ports such as Earl's Ferry on the south coast of Fife. The roads in general were not well maintained; their condition depended solely on the obligatory labour of local workers. A handsome stone building with mullioned windows and a slate roof, the inn had a carriage entrance allowing shelter for the departing and embarking passengers and a place where the horses could be unhooked and stabled. To the rear of the inn, alongside the stables, was the smithy and a kitchen garden with a path through it, leading to two fields for the horses. The stable building was quite extensive with stabling for sixteen horses topped by a hayloft and accommodation for the boys.

The parish church on Kirkgate, with its tall tower, was the centre of the parish administration, schooling, social communication and charitable work within the town. The order of seating at the Sunday worship aligned with the social hierarchy; the lairds and landowners' families at the front and the members of the parish council behind. Then came the masons, merchants and craftsmen followed by tradesmen, journeymen and farmers, lastly the agricultural workers and labourers. The mill owners' families sat beside the merchants. By law, families had to register with the church, usually by birth or marriage, to be considered and welcomed as a member of the parish. Any member of the parish in poverty or ill health, would be looked after. The mill workers who attended were mostly poor and many were not registered in the parish. Those that came usually stood at the very rear of the church which was now too small for its purpose.

The school was a stone-built, thatch-roofed, single classroom attached to a lower, three-roomed master's house. There was a small, walled, stone yard between the classroom and the road. Only boys aged between five and fourteen years, were admitted into the school. The school was managed by the parish council as mandated by the Education Act of 1694. The master's stipend of 180 Merks and any other expenses were funded - somewhat grudgingly - by a burden on the local landowners, the heritors.

The housing and care, or lack of it, of the mill workers and their families was fully the responsibility of the mill owner. Their legal status was that of a vassal or serf. The children of the mill workers, who worked long days in the mill from the age of five, did not come to church and could not attend the school. These children led a different existence to Rosie and the boys in the school. One which seemed to be without hope of betterment in their circumstances. The schoolmaster was permitted to take in some poor boys to the school, at his own discretion, but not many wanted to attend and any attempts to change this were usually frustrated by the parish council, the boys' parents or the mill owner's autocracy. It was to be another sixty years before some mill owners in New Lanark thought it would be of social benefit to educate the children of their workers.

PROLOGUE

W earing her white linen Sunday smock, Rosie heard her handful of grit sputter on the rough wood of the coffin lid and softly recited her mother's parting words, 'We are earthly souls but for a short time, use the gifts that god has bestowed on you with kindness and grace.' As the shovels of damp earth slowly began to fill the grave, her mind began the transformation from a brooding sense of painful loss to one of rising determination, accepting her mother's challenge to embrace this life she had been gifted and to fight for the values she believed in. The year was 1732; Rosie was eleven years old.

Rosie's friends, Jessie and Cora, stood a few yards back, on the damp, autumnal morning by a chestnut tree in the churchyard. Wearing their cassocks, the trio had sung a psalm as part of the short service in memoriam in the small presbyterian kirk.

> *There is a Stream whose gentle Flow,*
> *Supplies the City of our God;*
> *Life, Love and Joy still gliding thro',*
> *And Watering our devine Abode.*

Many from the town attended to pay their respects, which gave David, a teacher in the local parish school, great comfort. Their heart-felt sympathies emphasised his wife's importance and contribution to the community, but added to his sense of loss. A well-dressed older couple, whom Rosie did not recognise, was talking with her father. He beckoned her to come over.

'Rose, this is Mr and Mrs Grieve. They knew your mother when she was your age.'

Rosie curtsied; the woman spoke.

'Rose, I am so sorry,' she touched Rosie's cheek, brushing her hair as she did. 'Bless you child, you are just as she was, you have her beauty.'

'Thank you, ma'am.'

Her father nodded for her to leave.

Rosie, sniffling, walked toward her red-eyed friends. 'Oh Rose,' said Jessie, using her Sunday name. The three linked arms, forming a small circle. 'We're here,' said Cora squeezing her. 'We won't leave you', said Jess. They smiled sadly for each other and, standing under the tree on the still-frosted autumn leaf-fall, they allowed themselves to softly cry.

CHAPTER 1

Cupar, Fife, Scotland 1732

The *Bletherin' Bairns*, Rosie, Jessie and Cora, could barely remember a time when they did not have one another as friends. When the *Bairns* were younger, they were forever tearing nosily and noisily, around the small town where they were *weel kent*. Jessie was slightly older, Cora younger. Their mothers never had the one child for Sunday supper, they had three or none. Jessie was the innkeeper's daughter, with a stepbrother and stepsister who were older. Cora was a farmer's only daughter; she had four older brothers and one younger. Rosie was David and Janett Miller's only child. Jessie or Jess was the conventionally pretty one, slightly taller than the other two, fair-haired and fair-skinned. She could convincingly act gracefully, with charm, when she wanted to, unless when Cora and Rosie were around; then she was easily reduced to giggles. Cora, the smallest, had an all-year-round tanned skin and mid-brown hair. She had a lovely soft face but was firmly built. She could be very direct, even coarse at times, but was always cheeky and funny. Rosie had wavy brown, almost black, glossy hair, translucent skin and attractive angular features. She was scholarly by nature and was the voice of moderation in their antics until she was outvoted. Rosie loved the excitement and vibrancy of the other two but was usually the last to join in. They were a well-balanced gang.

They first met at the parish church as toddlers in the Nativity procession, as their parents gathered outside the church door after the Sunday morning service. As they grew older, they each extended their domestic boundaries. Rosie lived in the schoolmaster's house, which was attached to the single classroom. You could walk straight into the classroom from the hall of the house. On warm days, Rosie could be found sitting on the low school wall, often with a book in hand. Jessie was always buzzing round the inn, and Cora contrived a little freedom when accompanying one of her elder brothers into town; a venture which inevitably involved a visit to the inn. Whereas little groups of boys would be treated with suspicion, and shooed away or even *skelp'd*, the three girls were welcomed or at least tolerated. Sometimes they felt invisible, as they learned that walking purposefully was the best way to avoid attention. Rosie was the one that had difficulty leaving the school grounds and gaining freedom. She eventually got permission from her mother to play with Jessie as long as Jessie's mother agreed, she stayed by the marketplace, and she returned by an appointed hour, 'Not one minute after!' The church clock timed her day. Once, absorbed in activities at the inn, Rosie was ten minutes late back to the school. She was kept indoors, given extra duties and banned from reading any book but the bible for two weeks. The lesson stayed with her all her life.

All three were fascinated by the comings and goings

at the inn. The inn had four boarding rooms at the rear. These had no fire, but they were above the kitchen and were warm enough in winter. They were meant for single travellers but were often shared. On the first floor at the front were two well-furnished rooms for those that required more comfort and could afford it. It was these rooms that provided a good income for Jessie's family. Most of those staying were merchants or on church business. Cupar was a staging post for those arriving at the port of Earl's Ferry and travelling to and from the burgh of Perth and beyond. Should they disembark from the ferry in the morning, Cupar was the most convenient overnight stop. It also lay on the longer routes from Queensferry (Edinburgh), Dunfermline and the west to St Andrews, Dundee and the east coast. Longer journeys tended to be taken by sea rather than road. Pilgrims often arrived on foot or with a mule or donkey, and if there was room, they would be accommodated if they paid for their meal. Merchants travelled on horseback, singly or in pairs.

It was often just Jessie and Rosie who met, as Cora's visits into town were constrained to once or twice a week, and the days could not be predicted - more so in winter. There was always activity around the inn: the market supply to the kitchen, arriving and departing guests, horses and hay in and out of the stables, and the smithy, a place of warmth in winter, black, smoky and violently noisy. The girls were usually chased away when the blacksmith or his apprentice were busy, but in quieter times they could sit on the hay-bales and play with the cats that were drawn to the fire. At the rear of the inn, there was always shouting, laughter and humour, little of which was understood by the girls.

As they got older the two girls helped, sweeping, wiping, taking messages or running errands, and received a slice of cake or a piece of fruit in reward. Around four in the afternoon, their attention always directed to the mail coach that stopped four times a week. These travellers were often on a longer journey and commonly wore unusual garments and talked in strange accents and languages. Jessie and Rose watched as if it was a play and made up stories about who they were and where they were from. This invention would involve them for days, especially if there was a rare single woman traveller. The entire life of the town lay between the kirk and the inn.

One just-another day, Rosie and the girls were sitting on the Mercate steps, not doing very much, when two gentlemen each leading a horse approached them. As they neared, the girls saw they were very well-dressed and maybe not as old as they had first thought.

'Hello,' one of the men said in an unusual accent, 'and what are your names?'

'I'm Bluebell,' said Jess, 'and I'm Cowslip,' said Rosie,

'Tumbleweed,' said Cora, which made all five laugh.

'Would you please tell us where the inn is?'

'Oh yes,' said Jess, 'I'm the innkeeper's daughter, it's not far. I'll take you there.'

And turning on the charm, she led them off in the direction of the inn. She came back a short while later. 'They're not visitors. They said they live in the big house.' was all she was prepared to say. The girl's nicknames stuck, and their brief interaction with the interesting young men took a while to die down.

Not every day was bucolic. The butcher's daughter Ruth, a few years older, never took a liking to the girls who seemed spoilt and idle to her. Jessie seemed to suffer most of her outbursts, spits and swipes, and they avoided her whenever they could. Ruth was large, red-haired and strongly built. She brought the daily meat and fowl to the inn's kitchen wearing an apron covered in blood. She would bark insults at the girls and kick out at any dog or cat that showed an interest in her burden. Cora fell badly on the wrong side of her on one visit to town. Cora's brother was supping an ale at the inn, and the girls were sitting outside. Ruth called Jess, 'a little tart,' just because she had absent-mindedly stared as Ruth walked past. In response Cora said, '*At least her mither's no a heilan' coo.*' Rosie and Jessie looked shocked and did not laugh for fear. Ruth walked on toward the kitchen with her butcher's load. When she came out, it was with stealth. She grabbed Cora from behind, pulling her hair, forced her to the ground, and caught her with three or four hard punches to the face. Cora was strong but on this occasion was easily out powered. Ruth stopped. It was over in a moment. The lesson was controlled, clinical, violent and frightening. Jessie, who broke from frozen, said, 'I'll get your brother.' Distraught, Rosie bent down to comfort and assist Cora. She helped her up. 'No, no, don't tell him, no!' shouted Cora after Jessie, and Jessie stopped. Cora sobbed a while. Getting up she said, 'I'm fine, I'm right.' The girls tended to her, her nose was blooded, and one eye was yellow and closing, it would turn black. There was a terrifying amount of blood over her clothes, but they quickly found it was from Ruth's apron, not from Cora. Cora's brother came out. The incident must have been observed and Sam was already coming over.

'Shit, Cora what have you done!'

'I'm sorry, Sam,' she said.

'I'll finish my beer, then we'll go home. You'd better think of something.'

The girls did not understand. Cora was surely not to blame for her bruises. As they walked away, Cora's brother came back and addressed the girls in a firm voice,

'*Dunnae tell o' this. Tae onyone, right!*'

The girls nodded and said they wouldn't.

'Jess?'

'I won't Sam,' said Jessie.

There was also 'Titch'. Titch was, unsurprisingly, very small. He looked to be aged around four or five, but his stature had not changed in the last two or three years. Titch lived, although it is stretching the meaning of the word to use it herein, with an elderly lady in a damp, squalid, isolated cottage, down a dirt track by the River Eden. It was just within the parish boundary. Was she his mother, grandmother? Nobody knew. Nobody cared very much.

Walking into town, the girls would almost inevitably spot Titch. He hung around the stables or the smithy looking for warmth or scraps of food from the kitchen. He would often go to the mill cottages where he tried, with little luck, to beg a meal or a bed for the night. He wandered in the wood, gathering sticks, although this was a punishable offence. The old woman in the cottage was thin and bent. She was slow of mind and volatile when approached. She would grab at anything offered, but there was no gratitude. No sense could be made of any attempted conversation with her. She tried to grow vegetables at the back of her cottage and Titch could be found working the patch, planting turnip and kale, and stealing manure and hay from the stables to cover the ground in times of frost. He had rags bound on his feet instead of shoes. He wore an adult's filthy clothes, which were often freshly soiled. Titch stank of poverty and deprivation.

Titch did not speak, but he would usually nod affirmatively and look-up expectantly if addressed; but that was all. As Titch had, in the girls' minds, always been there, they accepted that he was as much a part of normal town life as, say, the parson or the fish lady. But they were just reaching that age when they were beginning to question things. In late spring, early summer, when the girls would sit on the steps at the cross, Titch would hover nearby. If they walked somewhere, he would follow. They shooed him away, but he always reappeared, and they didn't mind him, really.

It was Cora who started to play with him: playing catch, which he could, skimming stones on the river, handstands and skipping. If you tried something, Titch would copy. They made him laugh, and saw he had no teeth. Nobody knew his Christian name; he may not have had one. He did understand what the girls said and began to respond to their prompts.

Rosie questioned her parents as to why the church did not look after Titch and the woman. Her father replied that they were seen to be heathens and the church only looked after the godly. Her mother once gave her a pack of bread and dried fruit, which she took to the cottage. She picked a sunny day to walk with trepidation to the edge of the town and down the muddy track. There was damp in the air even then. The thatch was worn through, the windows boarded up, the turf roof rotting, a blackened hole took the place of a chimney.

After several knocks, at the point of giving up, the door opened, and Rosie wordlessly proffered the package. The woman snatched it out of her hand and quickly closed the door, disappearing back into the dark of the fetid house.

Later in the year, as the days got colder, the girls did not sit outside as often, and Titch stayed near the fire of the smithy if he could. Rosie raked in an old cupboard and found what she was looking for, an old pair of small leather boots which had been passed down to her that she had worn when she was younger. She got some saddle polish from the stables and worked hard on the boots to soften the leather. Jessie charmed the saddler into repairing some of the stitching and giving her string leather for laces. They were pleased; the boots looked fine.

The three girls found Titch near the stables and gave him the gift. His eyes opened wide. He grabbed and hugged the soft, black, shiny boots, responding to the girls' gift with his toothless smile. He made no move to put the boots on, despite the girl's excited instruction, and Rosie demonstrated by taking her own boot off and putting it on again. They then tried to grab his feet. Rosie and Jess wouldn't go near. Cora got the closest, but he squealed like a scalded cat and ran away. Over the next few days when they saw him, he smiled and nodded as he walked past in bound feet, hugging his new boots.

The following winter was hard. In December, the snow had fallen deep and then the frost arrived; the cold did not let up for weeks. It was just after the turn of the year, when the blacksmith's apprentice found Titch curled up at the back of the hayloft, stiff and dead. He may have been there for some time. The cats barely looked up from their place at the fire as he carried the diminutive body down the ladder.

The blacksmith and the stable-hand dug a shallow grave, needing a pickaxe and sharp-shovel to break into the frozen soil. They buried the emaciated body along with, as the girls insisted, his boots. They put him as near the churchyard as they could risk. Rosie found two good sticks and bound them together with the laces from the boots to make a small wooden cross. The girls stood as the men filled the pit and said a prayer. The next morning, the cross was gone from the small mound of earth.

Rosie's father, David, was committed to the education of his boys. It would be some time before he questioned why they were all boys. He tried to find a half-an-hour or so for Rosie each evening, before he sat and wrote letters at his desk in the schoolroom. Rosie supplemented this teaching by sometimes sitting outside the classroom door, and also by sneaking into the classroom and looking at the chalk-board work-slates when her father was out.

Then, importantly, two related events happened as Rosie and the girls were reaching the age of ten or eleven.

Jess and Cora became more aware of Rosie's habit of reading books; something they had hitherto ignored. They had naively assumed that you were gifted with the ability to read and write, or not, and that Rosie just could. Just as Jess had charm and looked pretty and Cora could run and fight, Rosie could read and write. But Rosie explained that anyone could read; you just had to try. So, occasionally, when the town was quiet or the weather was poor, Rosie would sit with the girls and go through the alphabet and coach them to read stories.

This occupied the girls over the winter months when they gathered together after their chores were finished. They had fun trying to read and write in odd places around the town: the barn, the inn, the stable yard, any place where Rosie could scratch something on a wall or in the dirt. Flat slate was not easy to find, but over a few weeks they scavenged three good sized pieces to use. Jess already knew quite a few words from the business of the inn, and she had no problem counting in her head, she just couldn't confidently put it down on paper. Cora barely recognised a word, but she could count too, cows and sheep and chickens, bales of hay and she knew furlongs, chains and acres.

Around the same time, David was aware he was not fulfilling his parental responsibility for Rosie's development. He was unable to overcome Rosie's reluctance to spend enough time singing, studying music, doing needlework, and reciting poetry and passages from the bible. She also seemed uninterested in learning how to run a house. These practices would be admired within his social circles and were necessary if she wished to marry well. Without them, her dowry would be ruinous. She always had her nose buried in one of the few books he had managed to acquire during his time at university. On occasion, he considered banning her from this habit, but an instinct acting against his logic overcame this urge.

The second event happened several months later, on the day when David was sent to St Andrews on behalf of the parish council to discuss the school curriculum; the school day was cancelled. Rosie's mother had gone out to do some charitable visits. The girls would often accompany her on these visits, but two families in the mill cottages had recently lost two young children and another was sick. Janett wanted Rosie, Jess and Cora to keep well away.

The girls were left on their own at the schoolhouse. They grabbed the opportunity and Rosie assumed the role of teacher on the raised stone platform at the front of four rows of tables. Cora and Jessie enthusiastically occupied two of the seats at the front table. They got carried away. Rosie even tried, in fun, to whack Cora with the cane when she kept looking out the window. Jess and Cora could do the sums more quickly than Rosie, which delighted them. They sang psalms, practised writing, read stories, and then took turns at being the teacher. Cora's mocking of Rosie's father's manner reduced the other two to giggles. David returned early and walked in. His fury rose, the girls froze, but just as he was about to rebuke them, a thought struck him so hard his fury switched to being directed at his own stupidity.

He had barely noticed recently that, despite receiving minimal tutoring, Rosie's educational attainment in most subjects was on a par with the best of his boys. There was no godly reason why these three, or any other girls, should not attend the parish school.

Recently returned from a visit to St Andrews University, David was to address the Parish Council regarding proposed curriculum changes. He added a second item to the agenda. He had been in post in the town school long enough to realise he had to use a bit of tact and diplomacy to get the majority of the council's support. The first item to be considered by the council was a longer teaching day. This would allow the incorporation of Latin and Greek into the teaching curriculum. These subjects were required by students who wished to enter a grammar school or a university. The universities were advocating this change in schooling. And the second item he now wished them to consider, was that girls would be allowed to attend the school for three hours a day, on the same terms as the boys.

The council members on the issues of education were the minister, the council leader and the local landowners, Sir Peter Rigg of Tarvit and John Melville of Barony. Each of these had a group or three of four councillors, who would usually follow their vote. John would never agree, and the minister would abstain unless it was a clerical issue. Sir Peter Rigg and the council leader were key to getting the support he needed. The leader would normally go with the status quo and would only support a major change if there was a clear majority. This was not an unreasonable approach. David knew he had to get Sir Peter on his side.

Sir Peter Rigg was the Laird and the major landowner of the town, collecting feu duties from most of the properties and the tolls at the gates. He attended church regularly, but his family did not accompany him. There was a small chapel at the house. Not very much was known about his wife and family. The family travelled often and did not often mix socially when they resided at Tarvit. The sons were occasionally seen at the inn. His family lost some of its wealth in the recession at the end of the 17th century, but Peter's fortunes were beginning to recover in the early 18th. He took an interest in the town and invested where and when he thought it was prudent. He had schooled as a lawyer and was well read. David's infrequent contact with Peter left David with the impression that he was an astute, clever and interesting man, but his strategic thinking could be hard to anticipate. Peter and his wife had a daughter, Adeline. Peter's two sons were from an earlier marriage. Adeline was a year or two older than Rosie. David sent a message to Tarvit House requesting an audience, *perhaps this week,* with Peter to discuss *local matters of education.* A reply came within the hour saying he would be welcome to visit tomorrow after one pm. There was an odd footnote, in a different hand, adding, '*Be it please you Sir, attend with your dauchter.*'

Rosie's father was pleased to receive a quick and positive response to his note to Sir Peter. This was a serious, indeed a vital meeting for his planned changes; he was uncertain about taking Rosie. These days, her tongue was not known to stay still for any length of time. Janett pointed out that if he wanted Sir Peter's support, he should consent to the request. Rosie was told, but not until the morning. Rosie listened attentively to her father about the importance of his visit and the requirement for her to attend. When he dismissed her, she left the room quietly, closing the door behind her; there was a long pause. Then a yelp, and she burst back in. 'I'm getting to go to the big house...the big house!' in a voice of rising pitch. She saw her father's frown and quickly retreated and closed the door as carefully as was possible at that moment, singing *enroute* to find her mother, 'The big house, the big house, I'm going to the big house!' She had never even been in the grounds of Tarvit House.

Her mother had boiled water and prepared a bath, she scrubbed Rosie who was slightly less effervescent but still singing, got her out of the tin bathtub then put her back in and scrubbed her again. Rosie began to worry about her appearance which had the beneficial effect of calming her down. 'Mother I have nothing suitable.' It also began to dawn on her that she did not know why she was going. Asking her parents did not shed any light. Janett brought her white Easter dress down and found a piece of bright floral linen which she quickly cut and formed into a belt and head scarf for Rosie to wear. Rosie, always fascinated by her deft, quick sewing hand, was pleased with the result. David requested a horse and cart from the inn and Jess's father was pleased to provide this at no charge. The cart arrived with Jess on board, expecting to visit Rosie. She was quite astonished to find Rosie dressed up and stepping up into the cart. Fit to burst with questions that would have to wait, Jess just smiled and waved as Rosie and the cart moved away. She did not know its destination and was hoping Rosie was not going far away or for too long.

They set off to arrive at one of the clock. The gatekeeper came out when he heard the cart. After quick nod to David, he opened the gates to let them through and told the driver to take the left fork on the main drive to the house. The drive was the smoothest road Rosie had known and the four-storey house was like an illustration in a story book. It had a central part with stone steps up to an entrance, which was on the first floor, and two wings each with three floors and long windows to the front.

The house was on raised ground and would have been visible from the town had there not been so many trees. Deer in the parkland looked at the cart curiously. At the bottom of the entrance steps, two men awaited, one helped Rosie and David alight and the other held the horse. A maid, just inside the door, invited them to sit on a dark, pew-like seat by the unlit fire in the reception hall, and she would inform Sir Peter of their arrival. Rosie sat and gently shook with nerves. After a few minutes a pretty, young girl in a beautiful dress came quickly down the stairs and skipped toward them offering her hand.

'*Bonjour, je suis Adeline.*'

'*Bonjour, mademoiselle,*' said David, '*Je m'appelle Mr Miller et voici M'elle Rose.*'

This gibberish did nothing to calm Rosie's trembles.

'I shall take you to meet papa.'

The three walked along the hall to a large double door passing the maid coming in the opposite direction who looked slightly puzzled. Knocking and putting her head round the door, Adeline said,

'Papa, Mr Miller and Rose are here.'

'Thank you, Adeline,' Peter Rigg said, inviting them in.

'Welcome, welcome. Adeline, would you please take Rose for a walk in the garden'

'*Oui papa,*' she replied, and she took Rosie's hand and pulled her gently away from the shutting door.

'It is so nice to meet you. Shall we get some cake first?'

She was charming like Jess can be, but ten times more so, Rosie thought.

'I hope you don't mind me asking you to come?'

'No,' said Rosie, 'but how?'

'I'll tell you in a minute, would you like some cake?'

They went through a door in the wood-panelled hall, which didn't seem like it was going to be a door, and then down some stairs and through another door into a corridor. There were lovely food and baking smells wafting along the corridor. Adeline looked at Rosie expectantly, but Rosie could still not conjure up a sound, never mind a sentence. A third door took them in to a large, very warm kitchen. Rosie had only felt such warmth at the smithy. The kitchen was lit by a large double window and a roaring fire. It had many wooden shelves of copper pans, ironware and white bowls. The black stove and the fireplace were huge, with many ovens of various sizes. The chimney breast, above the fireplace, held blackened chains, wheels, spikes, rods and gears. The chains rose up the wall and were attached to more rods and gears, which went into the wall above the fire. There was a huge, black kettle and an equally sized black pot on the stove. There were two large tables; one had some meat, flour, a wooden platter and a few white bowls on it. The other was a sitting table with eight unmatched, well-worn chairs set around it.

'*Bonjour Madame P*. can we please have some cake, this is my friend, Rose.'

'Hello Rose, and there's no cake for you, but you can have warm scones, lemon butter and red berries, will that do?'

'*Oui, oui, merci, Rose?*'

Rosie didn't say anything. Then the cook said,

'Does she speak?'

'I'm…not…quite…sure,' said Adeline, pausing between each word, and they both giggled.

And Rosie relaxed, 'Yes, please,' she said, and they sat expectantly at the long table. While they waited, Adeline began to explain how and why she had invited Rose to the house. You and your friends, Jessica and Coraline I think, met my two brothers a month or so ago in the town. They talked to Jess, is it, and she told them who you all were: the schoolmaster's daughter and a farmer's daughter plus herself, the innkeeper's daughter. She didn't tell them your real names. My brothers came back and Peter, the elder brother, told me there were three nice girls about my age in the town. It wasn't difficult to find out who you were; you three are quite well known! I'm not allowed to go into town at all, it's quite solitary here, and I longed to come and meet you and perhaps play. But that was impossible. Then, quite by chance, I saw the message your father sent, and ran to find my father to ask if the schoolmaster was coming, and if so, to invite you too. He said he'd already replied in acceptance and had sent a boy with the note. I ran to the entrance hall, and the note was still on the table, waiting to be collected, so I added an invitation for you.

'Did you tell your father?' said Rosie.

'No, but he was not too surprised to see you,' she smiled.

A kitchen maid brought over the scones. Adeline put a huge spoonful in her mouth; this action was not at all delicate. Rosie took a small bite and thought she had arrived in heaven.

Peter was sitting at a large desk in the beautiful wood panelled drawing room with high, painted ceilings, and a small lit fire in a large fireplace. There were tapestries and candle holders on the walls, a few ornate oak chairs and tables and well-worn rugs on the floor. On a long oak dresser, there was silverware, a candelabra and some ornamental glassware. Three portraits adorned the wall opposite the fireplace, two of men and one of a woman. One side wall had two sets of French windows which overlooked the rose garden. Peter stood and walked toward David with a welcoming handshake. 'I hope my daughter's impertinence did not upset you.'

'She was delightful,' replied David.

'I think I have an inkling of why you wished to see me. I saw the minister yesterday, and your two proposals for a change in schooling is causing quite a stir amongst the members of the parish council.'

'I think I understand both issues and your motivation, which I find enlightened and admirable,' he continued, 'however, I am also aware of the counter arguments.' He paused to allow David to substantiate his reasoning.

David responded, 'I believe, the inclusion of Latin and Greek is not just the learning of the language, but it also a means to learn about the nature of man in society, a chance to examine his motivations and behaviour along with values of good and bad, and right and wrong.'

'An experience that you and I have greatly benefited from,' added Peter.

'Yes, exactly.'

'It also provides an opportunity for the brighter boy to enter a university or the church.'

'But, if I may point out,' Peter responded, 'these are great benefits for a small number.'

'The merchants who fund the school, a few somewhat reluctantly, only see a need for the teaching of reading, grammar and accounting. Most accept this as important as it prepares their sons with the necessary skills for apprenticeship, clerking and trading.'

Sir Peter continued. 'Outside this narrow band of vocational education, however, they perceive little need. Even geography, history and physic they see as trifles and they would rather the children of the burgh were put to work, learning their trade, *on-the-job*,' pausing for a moment, 'they have a keen and not unreasonable awareness of lost time, lost resource, lost profit. Add in the inclusion of a few girls with the boys and they would only see them as a distraction in the class and a potential for a weakening in discipline. As I said, this is not my view, but the view that must be overcome if you are to succeed in your request.'

'I see the difficulty. I did not fully realise the opposition would have such motivation,' said David.

'I don't think you should give up hope,' Peter interjected.

'You still have a few weeks before the formal meeting, perhaps you can reconsider your approach in the light of what I have said.'

'You are welcome to come back and discuss it with me if you wish.'

'Thank you, I'm very grateful for your counsel.'

David did not resent the clear message that Peter was putting across. He was several years his senior and in a respected and powerful position, but what came across from the Laird was that he was impartial, pragmatic and trying to be supportive. David understood that here was a man of great experience in political matters. His approach was now beginning to look a little principled and naïve. David wondered if he was being manipulated, but if that had been the case, what purpose in granting him an audience; he could have been left to be fed to the dogs.

The maid knocked and entered with a tea tray.

'Now, would you like to take a seat by the fire and join me for tea, and perhaps a slice of our cook's cake? I see the girls seem quite happy in the garden. I would talk with you a little more about your views.'

'Thank you, Sir,' said David glancing out the French windows.

The gentlemen sat and talked more generally about scholastic values and their own university experiences. As the clock chimed three times, Sir Peter rose.

'I must not detain you any longer, but I have a small favour to ask.'

'Anything I can do; I would do gratefully.'

'Adeline is the only child of my second marriage; her mother is French. Adeline visits Tarvit for around one month perhaps twice a year. The rest of the time she is in our London house or with her mother's family in France.' Peter paused. 'My wife and Adeline follow Rome. I am a Presbyterian, as you know, and the boys are Episcopalian.'

'You all follow the same god.' David interjected, making Peter smile.

'In these turbulent and unpredictable times, I try to keep knowledge of Adeline's presence here to a minimum. I would hate for her to become the target of any unpleasant behaviour or worse.'

'How can I help?'

'Could you possibly ask Rose not to say anything about Adeline's presence? She can say she has been to the house and garden, of course.'

'I understand completely and will instruct Rose accordingly.' David replied, 'if you don't mind my asking, do the servants not chatter?'

'They reside here, are well chosen and well rewarded. So far, I've had confidence in them. Two servants and a maid are employed to accompany Adeline at all times to ensure her comfort and security.'

'I will impress on Rose the importance of this without giving details. I believe she can be trusted,' responded David.

'On that note we must part. If you wish to come again, Adeline would be delighted if you brought Rose, and indeed I would like to meet her too. And do come prepared to discuss the education of girls. I have some issues you may not be in accord with.' Sir Peter said with a smile.

At that he rang a hand bell, and a footman entered. 'Can you find the girls and bring them to the entrance hall and see that the gig is readied.'

The footman nodded and left. Peter showed David to the door and bade him goodbye.

As they headed through the corridors to the garden, Rosie's stomach cramped with all the excitement and the effect of the three buttered scones she had eaten. She stopped and whispered to Adeline that, 'She needed to go.' Puzzled at first, Adeline then caught the meaning and took Rosie upstairs and showed her to a low, panelled door off the hall.

Rosie opened the door and went in. Her anxiety increased. The room was the size of a bedroom. There was a side-table with a basin and jug of water, plus a bowl with, what seemed to be, sweet herbs. There was another smaller table with cloth towels. The only other thing in the room was a large wooden armchair. She wasn't sure what to do. Well, she knew what to do, but where to do it! There was no bucket. Rosie opened the door to the hall and peeked outside, but Adeline was no longer there. Miserably, she sat on the edge of an armchair and held her groaning stomach. What could she do; it was too far to run outside? Looking down in discomfort, she noticed that at the back of the chair seat was a hinged lid. Getting up, she lifted the lid. Another smaller wooden seat, also with a hinge, but this seat had a round hole in the middle of it, oh relief! A bucket below. She was going to take the bucket out but found she could comfortably sit on the holed-seat instead. She sat for a little while, she finished, stood up from the seat and put the top lid back down. Rosie rinsed her hands in the bowl of water, used a small cloth to dry her hands and decided that she liked this big house very, very much.

Adeline reappeared when Rosie went back out into the corridor and the girls skipped on their way to the garden. Rosie was still, for her at least, quite quiet. Filled with curiosity, she really just wanted to look around this wonderful house – with which Adeline was, unbelievably, bored.

In the garden they wandered around, chatting occasionally tig-tagging, and running in bursts.

'Adeline, do you speak two languages?'

'Yes, I speak English with my father when I am here or in London, and French with my mother or her family in France.'

'That's very clever.'

'Not really, I just grew up with it.'

'Don't they get mixed up?'

'Yes, when I change houses, and when I do it deliberately to annoy my father.'

The habit of annoying your father for fun was not one Rosie approved of nor even considered.

Rosie wanted to ask many more questions, but thought it was impolite to do so. Adeline had no such inhibition and was dying to know all about the life in the burgh and Rosie's friends. Rosie told funny stories about the three girls, using their nicknames, and then talked about the kirk, the school and the inn. Adeline also asked, more persistently than was polite, about boys. Rosie, at the age of ten, had no idea how to answer this. She had no brothers; there were boys around the town, but the ones her age she only saw in church, coming and going to the school, or going about with a journeyman. The most interesting ones were the boys from out-of-town, with strange accents, who arrived at the inn by coach. For Rosie, there was not much opportunity for conversation. Occasionally there was banter between the girls and local boys on market day or at the summer fair, but Cora and Jess, it seemed to Rosie, to be very rude and laughed at the boys.

'But don't you like boys?' Adeline said.

'I've no idea,' she replied, 'I haven't really noticed them.'

Adeline was disappointed with the reply, and Rosie thought she would ask Cora and Jess about this and try to come back with something Adeline would find more interesting, but she did not know what that would be.

To escape the subject, Rosie ran up a small hill to a nearby copse; she found a tree and tried to climb it. Her own mother would have strongly disapproved.

The company of Adeline and the excitement of the day had made her lightheaded. She was second in athletic ability of her gang, a long way behind Cora. Jessie, although not physically strong, had long legs, and could run at pace when she got going – an avoidance strategy she used regularly when her father was calling. Adeline watched Rosie and encouraged from below. The first branch was easy, and hearing 'Higher, higher!' she climbed onto the second. 'Higher, go higher!' She needed to move along the branch to perhaps reach a third. On reaching for the next branch her support snapped, and she struggled to maintain balance. She was nervously looking to the ground for a potential soft-landing spot, when she had a worrying flash-back to Cora's experience of a broken arm last year. She then felt herself defying gravity - she floated breathlessly upward. The two strong arms of the liveried footman had lifted her, firmly but gently, and deposited her on the ground. Embarrassed, she hung her head. Adeline was also quiet. The footman said in an English accent,

'Don't worry girls, I won't tell if you won't,' and he smiled, as the girls laughed.

'Your father is waiting for you in the hall, Miss Rose. Miss Adeline, your tutor is waiting for you to practise piano.'

'It's *Mademoiselle*,' said Adeline, under her breath.

Adeline hugged Rosie, and neither of them found any words, as the footman escorted Rosie back into the house by a quicker route. Adeline watched Rosie for a while, waved, then skipped away in the direction they had come.

David was waiting by the fire in the hall when the footman brought Rosie along.

'Hello, father,' said Rosie brightly.

'Hello,' he replied, less brightly, 'you have a tear in your dress.'

Rosie hadn't noticed. 'Oh, I'm sorry, father,' she said and nothing more. They got onto the open cart; it took around twenty minutes to get back to the schoolhouse in Cupar.

David had enjoyed the visit and was not cross with Rosie but used the journey to tell her of the confidentiality required regarding Adeline's presence in the house. In her guilt, she took the instruction without question, and then asked softly.

'Not even Jessie and Cora.'

'No one, except your mother; so only the three of us will know. Adhere to that, and there is a good chance we may be invited again.'

This pleased Rosie although she could not guess at the reasoning.

'But the girls know I went to the house.'

'You can talk about the visit to the kitchen and the garden, even the tree climbing–' Rosie looked up wide-eyed. '–just that you were on your own.'

'I promise, father,' she replied.

Rosie was puzzled but vowed to keep her promise. She then sat quietly for the journey home and smiled to herself as she recalled the details of her visit, trying to write everything into her memory, every part of the big house, every one of Adeline's antics. She would not tell anyone, but she was not going to forget. As they neared Millgate Port, a memory of Titch fleetingly crossed her mind; odd she thought, then thought no more of it – well at least for a few years.

CHAPTER 2

Edinburgh & the Dutch States 1709

Tom Miller, David's father, was an Edinburgh merchant who had risen to the status of burgess by the time he fatefully sailed on a ship to the Dutch province of Zeeland. Tom chiefly traded in textiles, buying imported cotton for the manufacture of linens, and exporting Scottish wool.

Tom first met David's mother, Margaret Lockhart, a councillor's daughter, by happenstance in the market, rather than by introduction. Margaret, nineteen years of age, pretty, socially accomplished, sensitive and quietly intelligent was being courted by Edward James Clerk, a member of a prominent and influential family. Margaret's father, James Lockhart, pressed for her to encourage Edward's entreaties but Margaret was not at all keen. Edward was a privileged fifth son, well above the Lockhart's societal status. He was charming and attentive, but Margaret sensed a quality, hidden in his nature, that she did not trust. He *disappeared* from time-to-time and could be evasive when challenged. Initially forgiving of Edward's mood swings, she enjoyed the generous and amusing side of his nature. It was not clear to her where the financial security of his future lay, despite the apparent wealth of his background. Her parents were blind to this, and saw only the possibility of a connection, albeit remote, to an honourable and influential house. Her resistance to becoming engaged to Edward was weakening, but during one of his times away from Edinburgh, she bumped into Tom. She realised immediately what she desired in a husband, and Tom was it. She firmly stood her ground against the family's shock and disapproval at her change of heart. Margaret happily became engaged to the enterprising merchant. The family were wary of Tom, as they had not been of Edward. Tom was honest, hardworking, trusting and trusted. He had also accrued more wealth in trade than many of the burgh's more eminent burgesses. The grounds for the family's suspicion were not helped by the fact that Tom's mercantile status and prospects would improve considerably on their marriage. After a few tense months, however, Margaret's father and mother became more familiar with Tom, and they allowed the marriage to proceed, welcoming him into the family and the business.

The Lockhart family lived in south-facing rooms on the second and third floors of a land in Edinburgh's High Street, between the castle and St Giles' kirk. Tom and Margaret moved into two rooms below them, and they virtually lived as one household. Above the stench of the street, the streaming warmth of the sun through the rear mullioned windows could be felt in the afternoons at most times of the year. The views of the countryside out to the Pentland Hills invoked echoes of Tom's rural upbringing. Tom had not seen a domestic interior of such richness before: the solid, if crudely fashioned, oak dresser and tables; thick rugs and tapestries of such detail he could identify the biblical parables and classical scenes they depicted. When the rays of the setting sun came in, the rooms were highlighted by the reddening reflections of silver and copper. It was the silver that impressed the most: goblets and plates and cutlery. Glass vases, ornaments and candle holders added to the sparkle that contrasted the deep reds and greens in the wall hangings. Tom also had to adjust to having maids and a cook attend to the functional duties of the household. But it was the air and the quiet that such an elevated residence brought that Tom enjoyed the most, even though his own pleasure brought a degree of moral conflict. The helpless poor who roamed the streets and lived in closes to the rear of the street-facing houses, in low, dank, stinking rooms, could not easily be forgotten.

The offices of the Lockhart family's business lay further down the High Street, between St Giles and the Tolbooth. A couple of years after his marriage, Tom was appointed a Burgess of Edinburgh with all the entitled merchant rights and benefits. Tom, sponsored by his father-in-law, James Lockhart, became a member of the Guild. He could now conduct foreign trade. Tom had understood his wife's family's initial concerns about their marriage and was determined to demonstrate his merit. His motivation was more for his own peace-of-mind than any real family pressure. Even after enjoying several pleasant years of marriage and the birth of his son David, he was still aware of, and perhaps too sensitive to, cynical gossip about his good fortune amongst the burgh's chattering classes. In his mind it was not just imagined insecurity, he felt this small-talk affected his social status and thus his political influence. He wanted to be respected and valued for his own sake, not just tolerated, because he had a powerful father-in-law.

Yet his drive for advancement was not primarily for greater wealth and self-importance. Tom has been charitably educated in a small parish by his local minister and the powerful influence of the bible readings and the wider knowledge of theology and religion that the parson instilled in him, moulded his character during his formative years. He realised in retrospect that he would not have been able to live within the society he had married into, nor conduct business, had it not been for this education. This wisdom he passed on to his son David at an early age.

What surprised him at first, was that, when he was involved with trade deals and latterly at burgh council meetings, the educational background of his peers and fellow merchants was often found wanting. He would speak out in frustration, and only to his wife, that he would rather to deal with the quick-thinking skills of a true craftsman rather than those of a bumbling burgess. As he had to work to make a living, he pragmatically realised that you had to gain the confidence and support of those around you. You could only effectively better things such as improving the lot of the poor if you had political power and influence. Trying to effect significant social or educational change without Council support was not something he saw as workable.

Through Tom's connections and trading knowledge, he came across an opportunity through John Coutts of Montrose for his father-in-law's company to make a significant commercial profit in an international trade. Tom found that tobacco imported to Bristol, England, from the Americas, was in plentiful supply and of a higher quality than could be obtained from Glasgow. Due to the recent Act of Union, it was now available tax-free, and could be re-exported to the Netherlands via the Scottish tariff free Staple port of Campveere.

Over a period of six months, by a variety of agreements with merchants in the English port, he accumulated, what he considered to be, a *goodly amount* of American tobacco. Acting for the company, he supplemented this light load with wool, to be readily brought from the Scottish Borders, human hair, coal and salt from East Fife, and lastly Scottish silverware. He leased a merchant ship from a shipyard near the port of Culross. The trade on the return journey would be dunnage of Dutch pantiles and the import to Edinburgh of finished linen, rugs, tapestries and art works for which there was a growing market in the newly unionised Scotland. He had to lay out a substantial sum with the backing of his father-in-law. The company borrowed from fellow merchants and the banks secured by the promise of a substantial profit.

It was a time of stability, peace, commercial growth and enterprise. Oddly perhaps, Edward Clerk who had never acknowledged Tom, in business nor socially, took a non-financial interest in Tom's plans. Edward had, apparently, financial contacts in London and offered his services to assist Tom in underwriting the trade. Although he was slightly suspicious at first, Edward's advice and contacts proved invaluable. When he received the letter of confirmation of insurance through Lloyd's of London, Tom felt the trade deal could be safely signed. This type of trade was uncommon in Scotland's mercantile economy, and it required all Tom's charm and persuasive nature to get the backing he had received.

The undertaking of such a trade impressed many of the Council members in Edinburgh and elsewhere and raised Tom's esteem, but more were keen to stand and watch, albeit with great interest. The inevitable delays in organising and financing such a venture, and the logistical operation in conveying the goods in the correct quantities to the ship, crewing the ship, and obtaining customs clearances led to a delay in casting-off. The date slipped from a relatively benign August to a wet November. Tom knew, with interest accumulating on the loans and potential deterioration in the goods, he could not wait; it was *early* November. Only as the sailing date neared did Tom realise that he must go; he must board the ship.

Margaret pleaded with him not to go to sea. Tom explained that only *he* could travel to Dutch State to choose and verify the quantity and quality of the paintings and other goods to be imported back to Scotland. The high value trades were not bulk items. In the social circles in which he now moved, many were setting up small estates with houses outside the burgh. He had learned the fashionable tastes and knew the viable prices of the market he was to trade into. Margaret was not placated.

Margaret loved Tom for his knowledge, practical intelligence and drive, but despite her social accomplishments, she felt she could not engage him as she would like. When she heard him talk quietly to their son and respond to David's questions, she was jealous of their conversation. Yet she knew that it would be wrong to act as an apprentice within a marriage, and she did not ask for an explanation when she had not understood an issue or point of view. Tom, on the other hand, loved Margaret for her latent passion which he sensed when she sang and played the harpsichord, yet it rarely surfaced in the everydayness of their partnership which was always under the supervision of Margaret's mother.

Tom promised Margaret that on his return, they would try again for a second child and pray for a daughter; he had been a dutiful rather than an attentive husband. He told her the profit from the trade would easily allow them to purchase their own *land* to the east, away from her family, in the cleaner air, near to the Holyrood crags.

The need to take the journey was more than that to him; he had invested too much in this. He could not patiently sit and wait for one or two months for his *ship to come in*. The energy and toil he had invested over the year had occupied pressed on his mind, virtually to the exclusion of everything else. It had left him no room for doubt. Now the arrangements were complete, small doubts crept in, especially when awakened, deep into night.

On November 17th, 1709, Tom, along with his two clerks, boarded The Reward at Leith, and headed for the Dutch port of Campveere, or Veere for short, in the Dutch province of Zeeland. After a day of sickness, when he stayed below deck, Tom settled into his first sea voyage. There was little material comfort in his small, dark, shared berth: a small shelf for a candle, a niche in the wall for papers or a book and a couple of hooks to hang a coat or jacket. Separated from the walkway by a single curtain, he found it difficult to concentrate sufficiently to read. He spent most of his time keeping his journal in the mess room or walking the deck and enjoying the hubbub of merchant navy life. The ship's officers provided agreeable company while eating the hot, meaty fare presented at supper. They enjoyed having a new and receptive audience for their well-worn tales.

On deck, Tom, not a religious man, found he had never experienced the wonder of such an example of God's powerful forces of nature. It saturated all his senses. The noise of the heavy swell crashing over the ship's bow, the groaning of the masts and snapping of the sail cloth, the smell of the salted sea, the violent buffeting of the wind, the flashing of acute sunlight through the low cloud base, acted in synergy to over-whelm him. He could be found standing high on the fo'c'sle, both hands tightly gripping the guard rail and letting the splattering sea-spray thrash over him. He became momentarily forgetful of everything else in his life. This state of mind was new to him; he found it stimulating. The Captain, when he became aware of his habit, had two of the deck hands drag him away, and later soberly reprimanded Tom for his carelessness.

On the fourth day the atmosphere on-board changed: the sky was dark, the sails came down, went up, then came down again. The swell was so high, on its ebb it felt like the ship was being sucked into Poseidon's bowels. Even the seasoned sailors were sickening. It became hard to tell which way the ship was travelling. Night fell. The ship tossed and turned as flotsam, and the sailors' endeavours could not influence its orientation nor its direction. Their lives were in other hands, and they knew it.

Tom spent the anxious night rolling fitfully on his

cabin-bed, but dawn broke to a calm sea. Screeching seagulls had found the ship and the call 'Land Aye' from the morning-watch removed the last of their fears. The first mate ordered a few small sails to be raised. The Captain had gone up on deck before dawn to catch the light of the last stars in the night sky. He used his experienced eye to quickly get a bearing on the part of the coast they could now see. A favourable northerly breeze took them south, down the coast of South Holland toward Zeeland. *The Reward* anchored in the Oosterschelde estuary to await the pilot and customs boat.

As the ship approached the harbour, the ship's captain joined him at the rail.

'Thank you, Captain for this safe arrival,' said Tom.

'It had its moments, Tom. You have not travelled to Veere before?'

'No, this is my first sea voyage.'

'It is a pretty and welcoming place.'

The captain pointed out the *Toren,* an old tower at the harbour entrance, now an inn, the *Stadhuis,* which had tall thin tower dominating the skyline, and a pretty row of five large houses on the *Kaai* facing the pier. These were *de Schotse Huizen.* There was another inn for the Scottish merchants where the *bier* was tax free. There was the *Conciergerie.* The Concierge or Conservator looked after all legal and tax matters and had the power to declare on matters of dispute. There was also a Scottish trading bank, a surgeon's house, and the manse for the Presbyterian minister. Behind these houses was a small courthouse and a gaol.

The Scottish merchants who live in Campveere had properties throughout the town. Behind them, he pointed out a large church which seemed to be still under construction. This was a Presbyterian church for the Scottish sailors and residents. Tom did not feel so far from home.

As they berthed at the wet, cobbled, mooring pier Tom saw it full of people and life. He guessed at their employ: harbour men at the mooring ropes, horses to pull and release the loading lift, barrowmen to move the baggage and smaller goods, two very large carts for the main load. Several well-dressed men were grouped together: customs officers, the harbour master, or merchants awaiting their valuable load. And there were shoremen and women, wives of sailors, women of the street, some with trays and barrows selling food and clothes, and at the harbour end of the pier, a fine coach.

Transactions in the port were tariff and tax free, and trades took place under Scottish, not local, legislation. Pre-selling and taking orders were illegal, so Tom had to take the goods to the markets or be approached by potential buyers in the vicinity of the port. This was a common process, and Tom had sent word to buyers in the port, in advance of his arrival. Tom was familiar with the procedures. He had spent many of his trading days on the docks in Leith and enjoyed the excitement of a berthing ship, the sport of the negotiation and the social camaraderie among the merchants and sailors.

Tom had prepared well, and several of the port merchants approached and welcomed him as he disembarked. It seemed incongruous that most of them were Scottish. Tom was not as uncomfortable as he had anticipated. He was a very experienced tradesman; he had chosen his goods carefully and knew the value of his inventory. The buyers seemed to realise this, and trades were readily made at a price that Tom judged acceptable; each trade ending with a handshake and a visit to a quayside inn. These trades made high margins and were good business.

When the majority of the sales were agreed, Tom became a buyer for the return load. This was not as straightforward as he had hoped. He filled *The Reward* with red pantiles and finished linen easily, the problem lay in the sale of the higher value goods. He found few buyers for his silverware, none with an offer he would accept. There were no serious art dealers in the vicinity of the port for any side of a trade.

The weather worsened and did not let up. The days were dark, the metalled streets glistened in the lamp light. Viewed though the damp air, the bright houses of the quayside lost some of their attractive lustre. The wind and rain seemed to push at Tom from all directions as he walked in the town between the ship, the inn, and the merchants' houses. He found that it was unlikely he would close a good deal for his silverware, nor would he find a reasonable selection of art works for him to view in Veere. He was advised, several times, to travel to Delft, where he would find a more productive market.

The captain of the *Reward* told him, he would leave the port at an opportune break in the weather, he could not wait for Tom to return. Tom was informed he had to stay in Veere or accept that the ship would leave without him.

Tom wished he had some counsel, as he could not sense the right decision. Sailing with the ship, returning now, would constitute a good trade for Tom, but it would just be a conventional trade. There would have been little point to his journey. Joseph, the senior clerk, could have managed such a trade. There would be no real credit nor acknowledgement nor admiration, if he returned without completing the high value trades; the trades he hoped would bring a social as well as an economic improvement to his Edinburgh world. It was the reason he borrowed, the reason he bargained, negotiated, cajoled; the reason he came. It was still possible for him to achieve his goal. The high value items were not bulky. He could easily find passage back to Scotland on another ship once he completed his transactions. Yet he felt uneasy about this too and was not sure why.

Tom sent his junior clerk back with the ship, collected and packed the silverware for overland transport, and arranged a horse and cart so that the journey to Delft could start early the next day. It was not an easy route, but they would cope with the conditions better on-land. He actually hoped that the storm would continue and keep the ship in port until they returned from Delft. The winds still battered the port the next morning as Tom and Joe battled to load the cart, lashing down the crates securely against the buffeting wind and squalling rain.

Joseph Greive, Joe, Tom's senior clerk, was five years older than him. As a tall, robust, gruff Scotsman from Leith, Joe presented an unlikely figure for an accounts clerk. Tom admired his scrupulous attention to detail and his willingness to take on unfamiliar tasks. They dressed in the sealskins they had worn on the sea voyage. Although cumbersome, they kept Tom and Joe dry and warm. The roads were wet but generally smooth, in better condition than those throughout Scotland.

There was less mud and a firmer base. But it was the landscape that seemed unusual; not a hill, not a mountain. It was disorienting. If you couldn't see the sun nor the stars, how did you know your direction? At the same time, it had a beauty of its own and Tom recalled the exhilaration he had felt at sea. In better weather, you would see for miles. In this weather, you were aware of God's power.

The trip to Delft involved a minimum of three ferry boat trips, dependent on the route taken over a number of inlets between Veere and Delft: Oosterschelde, Gevelingenmeer and Haringvliet. Schovwen was a low-lying island which they needed to sail round or cross on foot. They intended to get the packed cart on to the ferry boats, leaving the horses, then obtaining replacement horses at the jetty where they alighted. They would reverse the process on the return journey.

In Veere, Tom had trouble finding a willing driver, and he had to pay well above the basic rate for an elderly driver, Henrik, to take them to Delft and return. Sailing from another port was not an option which could be arranged in such a short time. They set off from Veere by the ferry boat mid-morning, the winds forced them to Noordbeveland rather than all the way to Schovwen.

There were no horses for the load, so they crossed the small island, wheeling the cart slowly by hand and spent an uncomfortable night at the ferryman's cottage. The next morning was calm and clear. Tom was relieved as his journey would be easier, but also troubled as he felt the *Reward* would likely sail. They took the short ferry to Schovwen and started north toward Brovwershaven where they hoped to catch a ferry across Haringvliet and then travel by land to Briel.

The ferry journey went well, and they reached a small port called Hellevoetsluis where they found two horses to take them to Briel. The land journey over wet ground, indistinct roads and mud was hard going. That second night was more comfortably spent in a warm and welcoming inn. Their driver, Henrik, turned out to be quite an affable fellow and they had entertainment in trying to understand his tales spoken in heavily accented, broken English. Tom felt better about his decision and the journey.

The Reward had set off as Tom had expected, but another storm was approaching from the West and the ship steered to head North in the heavy seas. The captain wanted to stay close to the coast hoping to find night shelter for the ship during the storm.

As the storm hit land, the wind got worse, especially in the open, and the rain was constant. The locals had said the sea level was unusually high, even for this time of year.

Tom opted for the short ferry trip to the island of Rosenburgh. The two horses accompanied them. The crossed the island and found someone to take them across the short straight and landed near Maaslandluis. It was now overland to Delft, but the storm and rain were getting worse.

As night fell, they found nowhere to stay, and they coaxed the horses in the dark along the muddy track. Joe led the pulling horse, the driver sat up, and Tom walked alongside the rear horse, looking for a place to shelter in the dark.

Crossing Maasland, Tom spotted a thin light and they headed towards it. As they approached, they saw it came from a small country house, not a cottage. There was no gatehouse and the three men, two horses and the laden cart approached the main door. There were a few lights on, and Tom banged on the heavy oak door at the front of the house. It was after the hour of ten. Joe and Henrik ventured round the side to see if there was any stabling, they could make use of. Eventually the door opened; it was a servant or footman. Tom quickly explained their distressed situation as best he could. Surprisingly, the servant spoke in broken English and left them outside while he woke his master for instruction. Joe and Henrik returned. A few minutes passed. The door reopened, an old man appeared in, what looked like, a wool coat.

'English, you say?' said the old man.

'Yes, sir, I'm a burgess from Edinburgh, Scotland.'

'Well, well, don't stand there, come in, come in.' he said, in good English. He then said something in Dutch to the servant who looked surprised and then, with more prompting, left them.

'Your coachman can take the horses round the back to the stables and wait there. He will be attended in the kitchen. You will have something to eat with me and I will have a fire lit upstairs. You cannot go out again in this dreadful night.'

'We have no wish to trouble you, sir,' said Tom

'Nonsense, come into the drawing room and take some wine.'

Tom had Henrik bring in their small personal bags before taking the horses and the cart to the stables.

Although a small house, it was old, and the room had an atmosphere of great richness. The walls were painted with ornamentation and covered in paintings with large gilded frames. In the semi-dark Tom could not see the paintings well; he could make out some details in the finely crafted landscapes and seascapes. This sparked his interest. The old man put several dry logs on the fire, which rekindled and lit the room.

'Forgive me,' said Tom, 'Thomas Miller, and this is Joseph Grieve, my senior clerk.'

'And I am van Reit. I had a Christian name once, but it's long since forgotten. Sit please sit.'

'I'm admiring your walls,' said Tom looking around the room.

'I am a collector, you see, a lifetime's penance.' Van Reit was smart, small and sprightly despite his apparent physical agedness.

A dishevelled maid came in carrying a tray of glasses and a decanter of wine. The Dutchman asked why they were journeying at night in this remote part of Zeeland and Tom briefly told of their voyage and the reason for the quest to quickly trade in art and high value goods. The maid brought in a tureen of warm broth, a loaf of bread, cake with dried fruit and some cured meats and cheese. These were gratefully received by Tom and Joe, who were invited to sit informally by the enlivened fire. Van Reit assured he was happy to stay up and enjoy some conversation. He did not get many visitors. They paused at the harsh sound of the rain and the wild wind which rattled the windows. The trees around the house could be heard creaking, and there was a loud crack which could have been a tree or lightning. The sounds of the storm drowned out any following thunder. Tom sent Joe to retire but he was keen to stay, to ask his host about the paintings on his walls, to see if he could obtain any guidance in approaching the art dealers in

Delft.

Settling by the fire, opening another bottle of wine, van Reit told Tom that he had been a merchant like himself trading under the Dutch East India Company, mainly in bulk shipping of spices. That is where he picked up the English language. It was a risky business, but the protestant work ethic, map-making, and the bank credit arrangements, were world leading at that time. Van Reit said he had never sailed, and applauded Tom's commitment. Tom asked about his family and van Reit said his wife had died some time ago, and he had lost his only son at sea during the time of the Third Anglo-Dutch War.

'Oh, I'm sorry,' said Tom.

'It was not in conflict, just an accident on board a merchant vessel.'

They sat talking, neither of them tiring. Van Reit took Tom through the paintings on the wall. Three small paintings, of ships at sea, were displayed as a group. At first van Reit avoided giving details but Tom pressed and discovered that van Reit had painted them himself.

Tom checked to see if the old man wanted to retire.

'Not at all, Sir. I can sleep tomorrow and all the days thereafter,' and he asked if Tom would mind putting another log or two on the fire.

Tom rose, 'First, I require something from my bag in the hall.'

He startled the footman, sleeping in the hall.

'Do not trouble yourself,' he said, pointing to his bag, and the footman caught his meaning.

Tom returned to the drawing room with a glass bottle full of amber liquid.

'Have you ever tried Scotch whisky, Sir?'

'No,' said van Reit with a smile, 'I've been waiting for the right occasion.'

Standing with glasses in hand, van Reit said, 'Follow me, if you will, I would like to show you something.' He gave Tom his glass and picked up one of the candelabra before leading Tom along the hall. He led Tom into a small library with two walls shelved with books, and a third wall with three medium sized paintings.

Holding up the light, van Reit said, 'And this is my Rembrandt.' Tom saw a dark portrait. 'It is a self-portrait, one of many,' said van Reit. Tom was aware of the reputation Rembrandt's work and its value, but he had never viewed an original. Van Reit moved on, 'and this might be a Van der Meer.'

'Might be?'

'Van der Meer is not so well known,' van Reit answered, 'and there are many paintings which are similar in style. I'd wager that this one is, and I think Van der Meer's time will come.'

The painter was unknown to Tom, but he appreciated the precise brushwork and the acuity of the artist's eye in his representation of a domestic scene. It was a beautifully executed and detailed painting of a maid in the kitchen of a fine house.

Lastly, there was a winter landscape by van de Velde. Tom liked this one the best and thought he could easily trade this style of painting back in Edinburgh. Van Reit said that Tom needed to be careful and clear about his market. The most popular is not necessarily the most profitable.

Tom and van Reit talked long into the night. When they eventually decided to retire, the Dutchman took and held Tom's hand in both of his, and said he would not rise with him in the morning, but he asked Tom, forcefully, if he would promise to call in again on his journey from Delft back to Veere. Tom said he would.

In the morning, Tom was tired, and Joe had to prompt him to rise and ready himself. The servants offered victuals and packed a basket with provisions for their journey. The driver brought the horses and the laden cart to the front of the house. The weather was dry and warmer, but the wind was still blustery and strong. Tom asked after van Reit, but the footman said he was not to be disturbed. He handed Tom a sealed envelope. Keen now, to get going, Tom put it in his pocket, and they departed through the gates of the yard.

Their journey across open moorland was not too arduous. They were well protected from the biting cold, and the country road improved considerably as they approached the town of Delft.

The *Reward* had set off the previous day, as Tom had expected. The storm was approached from the west and the ship steered north in the heavy seas. The captain tried to stay close to the coast in the hope of finding night shelter for the ship during the storm. Early in the morning, before sunrise, The Reward ran aground near the West Frisian Islands. Slipping its resting anchor, the heavily laden ship foundered in the storm with the loss of all hands but one. Tom, of course, knew nothing of this. The survivor was an oriental mate of lower rank with no English nor Dutch. He made it to land but was in poor condition.

CHAPTER 3

Delft, Zeeland 1709

The cart drew up at the high walls of Delft in the early evening. Tom, Joe and the driver, Henrik, waited at De Sunt Poort until they were allowed to enter the town on payment of a small tariff. Even in the low moonlight, Tom and Joe were impressed by the cleanliness of the streets and the majesty of the darkened buildings. Tom had been given a recommendation of suitable accommodation and Henrik found it directly. They were taken to two large comfortable rooms on the second floor of a tall house overlooking Oude Kerck. Tom's room was quite like his own in Edinburgh: dark-panelled with a fireplace and oak furniture, a good-sized bed and a cupboard to hang clothes, a cushioned fireside chair, a desk and chair, and a small chest. Exhausted from the journey, Tom and Joe took supper in their rooms and retired. Henrik unloaded the cart into storage nearby. Tom paid for security. The load of Scottish silver was valuable; its sale would provide the funding for their prospective, high-value purchases.

Henrik was released for a few days to visit some of his kin who lived in the town. After supper, Tom remembered the envelope from van Reit, and retrieved it from his pocket. There were four sheets of handwriting on thin paper: two were part-English part-Flemish, the third was solely in English, and the fourth Flemish only. Van Reit must have stayed up for some time the previous night in order to write these letters. The bilingual letters were introductions to two art dealers, giving their names and addresses in Delft. The third letter, in Flemish, was headed by a single name and an address. The fourth was written only in English and was for Tom. This letter contained a list of painters who produced work with a style and subject matter, van Reit thought Tom would like. Van Reit also thought these were in demand and would appreciate in value. Additionally, he included a shorter list of dealers and painters, he thought Tom best avoid.

I have one last note of general advice. Err on the cautious, the hard-earned profits of honourable trade are easily lost when dealing in the capricious Dutch art market.

Van Reit signed it at the bottom and added a footnote. *I greatly enjoyed our meeting. Pray that you indulge the whim of an old man and, if it please you sir, visit me again on your return. I have something that may be of interest to you and serve our mutual benefit.*

Tom did not sleep well after reading this and, coupled with the nervous excitement of being in this town, he rose before dawn and ventured out to check on the silver and explore his surroundings.

As the sky lightened, the first direct light he saw was reflected from the ornate spire of De Nieuwe Kerck. Tom was struck by the elegant beauty of the town. The variety in the colours of the brick-built houses, the small wood-shuttered windows, each street a muted spectrum of autumnal tones. The steep roofs host to warm-red pantiles and dormer windows, common to almost all buildings. Stepped gables, stucco and pargetered rendering made every house distinctive.

The thoroughfares were not streets; they were gently curved canals crossed by small bridges. There were few carts with horses on the red-bricked pathways. Payloads to the houses and businesses were conveyed on Dutch barges or *schuyts* then hand-carted to their destination. Without the trundle and clopping of road traffic, it was a quiet, clean and peaceful place. Tom heard the lapping and shlopping of the canal water, the long creaks of the *schuyts'* hulls and the clinking of the mooring chains, the shouts of the market traders, the chatter of other passing travellers, the rustle of trees which lined the main canals, and their incumbent birdsong. Without a stench of rot, Tom was aware of sweeter smells as he walked in Delft on that calm December morning: roasting hops, yeast, boiling oats, the fragrance of flowers, coffee. This aroma contrasted with his recollection of the noise and smell from man's industry around the Cowgate and the *Grafe Mercate* in his home streets in Edinburgh. Tom, for the first time during this voyage, missed his wife. She would love this place. If he did nothing else, he would find her a painting. Tom followed a familiar smell to find some unusual fresh bread at a local bakery. It was a house on the Market Square, with two shuttered windows on the ground floor, which opened to make it into a shop front. He had managed to communicate his purchase by gesture. He bought two loaves to back to the lodgings to share with Joseph.

After breakfast Tom copied out the names of recommended artists and sent Joe with it to visit art deal-

ers and tour markets for other goods of interest . Tom
had been impressed by how much language Joe had
acquired during their brief time in Veere. Tom himself was not so accomplished, and their host offered
her English-speaking daughter to accompany Tom. She
would help with any language and social difficulties.
Apparently, her father was English, but Tom was not
aware of his presence in the house. It was clear she expected to be paid.

Her name was Doortje. He would start with the two
dealers' names he had been given by van Riet. Tom
and Joe agreed to meet later that day at the Sailors'
Inn at der Koft. Tom and Doortje did not speak much
at first; she acted as servant and he the master. Tom
could not tell if Doortje was fourteen or twenty years.
She seemed like a grown woman but was very girlish,
unfettered in her nature. She was tall, fair, long-limbed
and angular, she had the proportions of a young maid
but in a larger form. He did not ask her age; she was
a servant. When Tom did ask a few general questions,
as they walked, Doortje took it as permission to practise her language skills by chattering in English. Tom
found he enjoyed this light interaction. Her spoken
English still retained the melodic vibrancy of her own
language. It offered him some relief in his mind from
his suppressed tensions and the importance of his purpose. She was forward in questioning him about Scotland and other details of his life.

He struggled with her name. 'Just name me, Doo,' she
said. The first address to visit was in the south-west of
the town. They first went south as Tom had expressed
a desire to see the interior of Nieuwe Kerck. It was
smaller than St Giles but had a warmer ambiance. The

interior walls were adorned with ornate wood carvings, and the quietness that made you feel that you had taken one step from earthly sin toward heavenly peace as you entered and the door closed behind you. Doortje came in too. Tom sat on a pew and bowed his head, saying a few words in prayer to himself. Doortje sat quietly a few rows behind. Leaving the church, they headed north to the first art dealer's address.

It was a calm day, with occasional glimpses of low sun when the gap in the clouds aligned with a gap in the houses. To Tom's eye, the redness of the light enhanced the beauty of the buildings. They meandered along the canal side path and over the humped footbridge. Tom liked the orthogonality of the street layout; it was easy to find your way around. He had not sent word as he did not wish to sit anxiously waiting for replies; he wanted to act. Tom wanted to walk the town, to see, hear and smell and touch; he wanted this experience.

Arriving at the address, Tom gave Doorjte the letter and took a step back. The door of the large house in Vaandelstrat was answered by a woman. After a short conversation with Doortje, the woman took the letter and closed the door. Doortje said the dealer was in the house and they were to wait. The woman came back promptly and asked if they would return on the hour. Doortje suggested they find a *koffiehuis*. Tom was unsure but felt adventurous. They quickly found one nearby and went in.

Tom looked at Doortje quizzically, 'Are women allowed in coffee houses in Delft?'

'*Ja*, it is common,' she replied smiling.

As they entered to the pretty timber-clad house, they found it a little unkempt but homely inside.

There were a few small groups at the tables; they were all male. There was an increase in the level of conversation and a few men glanced at them as they entered. Doortje confidently sat down and they were quickly attended by a girl. At least there is one other female, thought Tom. They ordered coffee and pastry. All seemed ordinary apart from the cheerful disposition of Doortje which she was trying, not very hard, to hide.

Returning to the dealer, they were welcomed by a man who introduced himself to Tom and appeared pleased to receive them both. The dealer spoke English and Tom sent Doortje to join the servants in the kitchen, which quelled her buoyancy. The art dealer knew van Riet well, and the content of the letter made him well disposed toward Tom. The men sat in a room with a few chairs, a large table and two cupboards with thin drawers. Framed paintings filled the magenta coloured walls. Tom said he was interested in fine art to sell in Scotland and England, and he gave the artists' names from van Riet's list as examples. Tom said he would pay a fair price, but he had a budget, and that he needed to ensure a profit on the sale back in Edinburgh. The dealer explained that, in house, he did not hold the quality paintings of the heritage that Tom was hoping to view. He knew of four or five suitable paintings that were for sale, but he would need two or three days to collect them from their owners. Tom asked about the paintings on the walls and any others he might have. The dealer said Tom was welcome to spend time viewing them, and the more recent paintings which were kept in the drawered cabinets. These were considerably cheaper than those of the artists van Riet had listed. Tom had well over an hour before the rendezvous with

Joe, so he decided to send Doortje home, and he used the time to look through the dealer's paintings.

Tom and Joe enjoyed a tankard of *bier* and venison pie at the inn. Joe had located other art dealers, but he was more impressed with the quality of the tin-glaze pottery he had found.

'There are a good number of potteries manufacturing this porcelain here in Delft,' said Joe. 'There is a wide range of pieces, from white, household earthenware to elaborately decorated vases, jugs and tiles. These are good imitations of Chinese porcelain.' Joe had brought a few examples and taken note of the prices.

Tom agreed with Joe that these would likely prove popular in the Scottish markets and warmed to the opportunity.

Tom and Joe decided to visit the potteries and look at the porcelain together in the afternoon. They had planned to look for a buyer for their silverware; it would wait until the next day.

Doortje served an evening meal in the dining room as they sat at a small table by the fire. Tom found her pleasant and attentive but more formal than earlier. She had prepared a tasty meal of duck, grain and kale, followed by a dried fruit pudding. Joe made a joke about taking Doortje back to Scotland which, although probably unheard by Doortje, Tom thought was ill-mannered and said so. Tom retired early to write his journal, which he had not kept up-to-date over the recent busy days. Tom had kept a journal since his youth; today, there was much to write about.

The next morning's weather was calm and bright. Having sent a note in advance, Tom headed to the second dealer alone. Doortje was clearly disappointed she wasn't required; if Tom had been honest with himself, he would have admitted that he was too. It was a similar experience to the previous day's visit. He was pleasantly received, and Tom would return to view paintings in a few days' time.

After meeting Joe for coffee in the *huis* Tom and Doortje had visited, Tom sent Joe to collect samples of the silverware from their storage, and to see if he could obtain a sale agreement at an acceptable price. Joe was the senior clerk and had Tom's authority to agree a trade. If he was concerned about the language, he could ask Doortje to accompany him. Joe was confident, the dialogue of trade was universal. Tom then went alone to visit the address on the fourth letter.

The house was not far from the lodgings. The door was answered by a maid who, after asking Tom to wait in the hall for a few minutes, showed him into a small sitting room at the front of the house. Tom was becoming accustomed to the colours, style and ornamentation of the rooms in Dutch houses. It was the combination of simplicity and space: a few pieces of elegant wood furniture, a sparse adornment of tasteful objects, and landscape and seascape paintings on the walls. There was not the dark tapestried, heavily rugged, overly furnished, rich abundance of the Jacobean style he was used to in Castle Hill Street. He found beauty in this spartan arrangement. The owner of the house, Janssen, was not surprised by the call, and did not require any further explanation from Tom. Janssen was van Reit's solicitor and a very old friend of his. He explained that van Reit had liked Tom very much and had asked him to assist Tom in any way, if Tom wished.

He could scrutinise any legal documents and notarise credit transfers, bills of sale and so forth.

'That is very useful, thank you, but what is your fee?'

'Van Reit has written to instruct me that he would cover all costs, with no obligation.'

Tom was taken aback, and not sure how to respond to such generosity. Tom was not an inexperienced merchant.'

'And the proviso?'

'None. Unfortunately, van Reit is in ill health and is housebound. He has considerable wealth and age has brought him a charitable nature. Van Reit looks after the local farmers and the poor. He has built dykes to provide arable land and makes regular contributions to the local church, the school and the university library. Perhaps he is trying to ensure a place beside God, I don't know, but believe me there is no ulterior motive. Do feel free to decline, and we will say no more about it. Van Reit himself would understand.'

In silence, Tom considered this for a few moments.

'Tom,' said Janssen, 'if you would like to hear more, please join me for supper and we can just talk informally, you need not make any decisions.'

'Thank you, I would appreciate that,' said Tom, and he chided himself to relax, 'I will need to send a note to my lodgings.'

'By all means.'

After the glass of red wine served before the supper, Tom did relax. They sat in an upstairs dining room, at a table that would seat eight. Janssen passed on the advice from Van Reit.

'Van Reit wrote me that you have not fully understood the vagaries of the Dutch art market and suggests

I advise on the risks and pitfalls. Although I do not know the specific market that you are addressing, I can inform you of the professional background and offer general guidance.'

Janssen explained, 'The best artists are sponsored. Most artwork is commissioned for very specific purposes.'

Janssen continued, 'The secondary market is volatile and prone to changes in taste. There are very many good, young artists producing *pretty* paintings of subjects which are popular. The artists van Riet has recommended are unlikely to lose value, but their paintings are over eighty years old and are hard to obtain at a reasonable price. The young artists copy their styles and subject matter. I can show you ten paintings by van Rijn which were painted in the last thirty years. What is the difference in value to a buyer between a well-painted copy and an original work?'

Tom explained that he wanted to sell into the merchant classes in Scotland. They are beginning to achieve the wealth to afford small country houses and, in a sense, are trying to emulate the aristocracy.'

Janssen laughed, 'An ideal market to sell ten new Rembrandts.'

Tom smiled in response. 'I am an honest trader and would not misrepresent the provenance of a work.'

Tom confessed, 'I am beginning to doubt my own ambition. To make a good profit on the art, I would have to take the risk of investing a large outlay, and the selling prices are uncertain and may be beyond the comfort of Edinburgh's merchant classes. I understand now, that I can find appealing paintings for a more modest outlay, but they would only have a cosmetic value and a lower margin.'

Janssen added, 'Bear in mind that many of the lesser paintings would not travel well, especially by sea in winter. The quality of the paint and the canvas may not be high and peeling and cracking are common problems with immature work.'

'I have two dealers who are seeking paintings on my behalf, do you think they can be trusted?'

'These names will not knowingly falsify provenance, but they are well-established dealers, their paintings will not be cheap,' replied Janssen.

'Janssen, I greatly appreciate this opportunity to talk through my position.'

So many of these thoughts had been unstructured in Tom's mind, yet his goal was clear. The *Reward,* which would be docking at Leith harbour within a few days, would cover all costs and bring a net profit, ten to twenty percent. This alone would make the venture worthwhile, but it was not a remarkable achievement. Add in the sale of the silverware and make a good margin on the reverse trade, he could buy that house for Margaret, and gain the confidence of a higher level of commercial backers. That is what he desired. They ate eggs, then fish, then venison and drank the best wine Tom could recall tasting. Tom then told Janssen about the porcelain,

'I am reconsidering my risk in buying fine art. I hear porcelain is a safer option. I do not know the home market well, but many merchant houses in Edinburgh still serve food on wooden platters and in pewter bowls. I've looked at my clerk's figures, this could produce a good profit.'

Janssen approved of his thinking. Delft had gone

through a similar social development, three decades earlier.

'The benefit of trading in porcelain is, it breaks. It does not deteriorate and there is always demand,' Janssen said. 'Have you taken into account the excise duty on porcelain?'

Tom said, 'At twelve and one-half percent, it is reasonable.'

'Let us end our supper by talking about other things.' Janssen smiled. 'Would you tell me of your family?'

'Gladly,' said Tom.

Tom told Janssen of Margaret, his son David, and the company, and his rise to becoming a burgess of the town of Edinburgh; he did not tell of the tensions he left behind in his household.

It was after midnight when he made to leave. They parted with Tom saying he would take a few days to look over the paintings offered.

'I will take some risk and buy a few quality paintings, even if I end up keeping them for myself. I will need to view and confirm the trade in porcelain.' He would ask Joe to press on the price for the silverware and obtain the shipping cost for the porcelain.

After too many glasses of wine, Tom rose unsteadily, from his chair and shook Janssen's hand. He expressed his profound gratitude for the evening's hospitality and his advice on the trade. He agreed to visit again in three days.

Reaching the bottom of the stairs, Tom saw Doortje sitting by the door, nodding sleepily.

'Doo, what on earth are you doing here?'

'I'm sorry, Sir, I thought you might get lost. I was worried. I brought your hat, coat and boots; it is snow-ing heavily.'

Janssen's housemaid opened the door and Tom looked out. The paths were white. The canals were white. Tom felt the icy blast and stepped back in.

The housemaid took the coat as Doortje sat Tom down and helped with his boots. The housemaid then tried to put Tom into his coat and hat. This was not as easy as it should have been. Doortje and the maid teased and laughed at Tom's fumbling incapacity and unintentional lack of cooperation. Tom smiled to himself at his circumstance. He never quite felt in control here; a sensation he was beginning to get used to and finding not wholly unpleasant.

Outside the ice had formed. First, on the brick pathways, then on the narrow canals. Only the river Oude was free of ice. What fowl there were on the frozen canals crowded on the still, dark water under the low bridges. On top of the iced paths, snow had fallen. Not damp clagging snow, but light, small-flaked, swirling snow. It sparkled when caught by the moonlight. Treacherous underfoot, the unstable Tom, supported by Doortje, teetered and slid his silent way back to the lodgings. On the flat paths, there were no bruising falls, just a stumble and a slip or two. One soft bump on the path, cushioned by snow, led Tom into a wrestle with Doortje to find his feet. It was unusually quiet, no lapping water, no creaking hulls, just the crump, crump, crump of their own footsteps.

Tom, who naturally had a deep, loud voice, started to sing a hymn.

Doortje shooshed him, 'Quiet, quiet!' she scolded. But then, on a short path, where there were few houses, in a voice trained in heaven, it seemed to Tom's ears,

Doortje started to sing a Danish folksong:

Mitt hjerte alltid vanker
i Jesu føderom,
der samles mine tanker
som i sin hovedsum.
Der er min lengsel hjemme,
der har min tro sin skatt;
jeg kan deg aldri glemme
velsignet julenatt.

Tom wiped his moistening eyes. He felt the closeness of her body and the comfort of her supporting arm linked though his.

Stumbling into the hall of the lodgings they were met by Joseph who was not pleased. He could not admonish Tom despite being ten years older. Joe did not understand why Doortje was with Tom, and he frowned questioningly at her, as they both managed Tom, who was now trying to sleep on his feet, up the stairway to his room. Joe dismissed Doortje and undressed Tom sufficiently to put him to bed. Joe retired.

A short while later, Tom woke partially; he needed the chamber pot. There was a quiet knock on the door which then opened slowly. Doortje, in her nightgown, stood framed in the threshold.

'Do you need your bed warming sir?' she said, quite matter-of-factly.

Tom paused just long enough to find the sobriety to ignore her ambiguity.

'No, I don't need a warming pan, Doo. The fire is lit. Thank you for fetching me tonight. Goodnight.'

Doortje withdrew. 'Goodnight, master.' she said, having not used that designation for him before.

In the morning, Tom was left to sleep and came down late to breakfast, where he was joined by Joe. Sore-headed, he tried to piece together his memory of the previous evening.

'Did you gain any benefit from your visit to the art dealers, Tom?' queried Joe.

'Joe, can we wait till after breakfast. There is nothing planned so we can go to the coffee house and look at the accounts and our trading situation. It would be useful for us to go over what I have discovered, and I can tell you of my discussion with Janssen.'

Tom hesitated, 'Joe?'

'Sir.'

'Last evening, Doortje came to find me out of concern and brought me back. I was not at my best and I was grateful. She was not complicit in my indulgence.'

Tom's confession was more to protect Doortje's reputation than any embarrassment he might have felt.

Doortje came in to clear up.

'I haven't seen your mother for a while?' enquired Joe.

'She has gone to visit her elderly mother, *mijn grootmoedar*. She lives two hours outside of town,' Doortje replied.

'Is there anything wrong?' she asked.

'Not at all, you are looking after us very well.'

Tom spent an hour in thought before meeting with his clerk at the coffee house. The snow had almost dis-appeared and there was a steady rain. Tom gave Joe a summary of his counsel with Janssen. Joe told him that he had managed to get a few more guilders for the silver but it required a response by the end of today. Tom explained his thinking.

'I've thought about it, Joe. I have decided to mitigate our risk and put half of the money from the sale of the silver into pottery. I shall look to buy a few paintings, but I will keep the remaining funds in notes or bullion; I will buy English pounds or gold, directly on the foreign exchange market.'

They spent the rest of the day touring the potteries, looking at the designs, completing the sales, and confirming the delivery

'To take the pottery to Leith,' he continued, 'we will first need to get the porcelain to Veere, and the cart journey is not suitable.'

Joe said he had anticipated that and found that there were many coastal *schuyts* that would take loads for a reasonable price. Also, that the ships from Veere would take the pottery at almost no cost because, as it is heavy, it can act as ballast for their lighter cargo.

'Excellent,' said Tom, 'We will make a good profit on this venture, Joe, and I hope that this is only our first together.'

'I would be happy to join you again,' replied Joe, 'but, next time, would you please choose a warmer time of year...and a calmer sea.'

Joe was to arrange the delivery of the porcelain to the pier at de Kolk then proceed to Campveere. He would arrange to ship the goods from Veere to Leith, three days hence. Tom, meanwhile, would complete the paperwork, go back to the art dealers and then return to see Janssen. The driver would then, the following day, take Tom, their trunks and any paintings back to Veere, calling into see van Riet if time allowed. Joe was instructed to leave on the same ship as the porcelain, even if Tom had not arrived. Delays were possible and Tom would follow when he was able.

'And we will dine out tonight!' said Tom.

The next morning the rain was still falling. Joe set off early finding their selection of porcelain had been delivered as arranged, to the port for loading onto the barge. He had quickly gone through with Tom, the process of finding a ship for the cargo in Veere and arranging due payment. If he had to board, and leave without Tom, he would leave a note at the customs house. They wished each other good fortune and good journeys, both looking forward to getting to Leith safely.

As Tom put on his oilskin before setting off on foot to visit the two art dealers, Doortje was waiting at the door,

'Will you be wanting supper tonight, sir?'

'Thank you, Doo, yes. Are there any other guests?'

'No sir, you are the only one tonight.'

'Please don't go to any trouble. I will be back before six.'

Doortje raised an eyebrow.

'I promise,' said Tom.

Tom had indicated his preference for seascapes, landscapes and interior scenes. The first dealer had obtained seven older paintings of domestic scenes by artists such as Metsu, Molenaur, Sorgh, and Henriks. He had also found a larger winter landscape by Joos de Momper, which Tom thought was stunning and one other, a view of Delft from the canal, attributed to van der Poel. These were privately owned but they were for sale at a *good price*. Of the paintings the second dealer had obtained, Tom liked two domestic and several street scenes, by Jacob Vrel and a seascape by Jan van

Goyen. Both dealers had given Tom an idea of price and, having spent time viewing, Tom left to consider his options in the coffee house. He promised to return to the dealer's studios with his decision, later in the day. The rain still fell.

He then went to call on Janssen who welcomed him warmly. Tom greatly appreciated Janssen's support and advice. Janssen offered food which Tom accepted, and they talked more informally over a glass of wine. Janssen asked if he still intended to call in on van Reit and Tom told him of his intention to finalise the purchase of the paintings today and set off by cart early tomorrow, heading to Vaandelstrat where he would stay the night.

Janssen then confessed that van Riet had asked his opinion of Tom. He told Tom that he had sent a good report. It struck Tom that he seemed to be more welcomed and appreciated in this alien country than he was at home, even amongst his own kin. Perhaps it was the novelty of being a foreigner, but there are traders from many countries in Zeeland. It had the most advanced foreign trading market in Europe. The experience of travel in a different land had made him more reflective in nature and he wondered if that would change when he returned.

Tom left with Janssen saying he hoped he would return soon. Tom shared the expectation of his return.

As Tom headed back to the dealers, he passed near the lodgings. He called in to find Doortje, who was surprised to see him.

'Are you busy?' he asked her on a whim.

'No, the work is done for the day and I have no new guests.'

'Would you be interested in coming with me to look at some paintings? I would value a second opinion.'

Doortje's face lit up. 'Can I?'

'Yes, of course.'

'But I know nothing about art,' said Doortje.

'That is the point, I'm looking for artwork that would appeal to a young person from a good house. Not an expert. What they might like to have on their wall.'

'Oh, thank you,' said Doortje.

She went upstairs to change, taking longer than he expected, and reappeared looking very smart. He was not sure about the social etiquette, but he had sensed an informality which was far from the niceties of Edinburgh's austere engagements. The rain lessened and Tom explained what he was thinking in regard of choosing the paintings.

What baffled Tom about Doortje is that for a girl who was not born nor brought up in a formally educated environment, she had an innate awareness and intelligent curiosity. This, he admitted to himself, he found attractive, but he worked to ensure he viewed her as a child, a pupil, and not someone of equivalent age nor status. The more she bounced around in her girlishly playful manner, the easier this was.

Back at the first dealer, Tom introduced Doortje as a friend and she was deferred to by the dealers who were happy to show her the artworks and persuade her of their merits and provenance. He had had to ask for her surname quickly when they were received at the studio door. She was to be addressed as Juffrouw Veenstra.

Doortje was quiet but appeared interested and attentive to the paintings, preferring to stop and give her preferences to Tom in English rather than engage in much dialogue with the dealer.

The first dealer worked hard for the sale, mistakenly thinking she might be the benefactor of any purchase. Tom decided to purchase the view of Delft at the price offered and two other paintings. For the winter scene he thought the price was too high and offered a lower price. The dealer said he would take his offer back to the client; he had not been given any leeway on the price.

At the second dealer Doortje had quickly gained confidence in the task and in manner. She was clearly enjoying the role. Tom agreed to purchase one of the Vrel street scenes; the quality looked better to him, and he also made an offer for the seascape by van Goyen. Doortje discussed the details with him and the rationale for this choice. He also bought two miniatures by Cornelis Pronk, a more recent artist, one of a windmill and one of a sailing barge.

If the offers for the winter scene and the seascape were accepted, he would call again on Janssen and ask for his help in securing the transactions and forwarding the paintings. Tom did not want to delay his due departure the following day.

He was about to dismiss Doortje, it felt more natural to take her with him, why not? Doortje was surprised, but confidence up, she gamely accepted his invitation and followed on.

Janssen was pleasantly surprised to see them and joked that it was not possible to conduct a journey to Scotland and back in three hours. He was equally delighted at Tom's female companion and ushered them into the drawing room, calling for wine. Tom went through the details, and Janssen was pleased to assist with the transactions. The two men agreed the arrangements for the finance and shipping of the paintings.

'Now we should have a little wine.' Janssen turned his attention to Doortje, and despite being Dutch, they conversed amicably in English.

Janssen then exclaimed, 'But if you have no other appointment tonight, you both must join me for supper.'

Tom looked to Doortje but Janssen would accept nothing other than compliance.

Tom and Janssen discussed many issues during the evening and Doortje mostly listened. She did, however, interject when she was strongly in disagreement, and would not be easily placated. Tom stayed on the right side of the wine and Doortje was moderate in her consumption.

At a reasonable hour they took their leave. They walked back quietly, without the alcohol fuelled liberation of the previous visit. She did link her arm through Tom's without making it seem anything but normal. No snow nor ice, the rain had started again.

Tom said that he hoped he had not been too presumptuous in including Doortje in his business and she replied that she had enjoyed the day and the evening very much. She said that it was unusual for her, as a young woman, to be treated with such respect and for her opinion to be considered. 'For that, Sir, I am very grateful. It is something I shall not forget.'

Doortje had a few chores to do and Tom said good night, directly going to his room. It wasn't too late in the day, so he wrote a letter to Janssen and kept his journal for a while, before putting a log on the fire and retiring. Just as he put on his night garment, the door opened and Doortje walked in slowly wearing her nightshirt, closing the door behind her. Tom looked, and as he was about to say something, Doortje moved her gown parially from one shoulder then fully from the other, revealing her breast. Tom moved towards her, 'Doo, No, I...' He reached out, with his hands toward her shoulders to lift her nightgown carefully back up, but she moved to the side and his hand met flesh. Doorjte stepped forward and put the forefinger of her right hand to his lips and the palm of her left down to his crotch. She manoeuvred him clumsily; he stumbled backwards toward the bed. Still standing, she held him and gently squeezed. He had no option but to sit on the end of the bed. She pushed his chest firmly, so he lay back, his feet still on the floor. She then climbed to kneel on the bed astride him, and looked straight into his eyes, 'Shush, shush, oh Tom,' she sighed.

She raised her nightshirt and gently rubbed against him. She found him aroused. Tom moved his hands to her thighs; she raised them to her breasts. She pulled up his shirt and moved some more. She put her hand down and, raising herself, helped him in. 'Master,' she said quietly, still looking at him. She leant down toward him and, for the first time, they kissed, abandoned kisses.

She moved off him to the side and they lay kissing and caressing for a long time until her hand again moved to hold him. The candles had gone out and the room was fire lit. She said things quietly in Flemish. She pulled him on top and they made caressing love for a long time before she felt him ready. His rhythmic movement increased. She grabbed his buttocks and held him in. They slept in each other's arms till dawn.

Doortje was not there in the morning when he woke

late. He washed, dressed and went down the stair. There were two new guests eating at the dining table. Tom felt an astonishing wave of jealousy which he fought. Doortje came in with a tray of food and said a smiling good morning. Tom was forced to sit and eat and exchange pleasantries with the two men. Tom looked at Doortje, she avoided his eye and just tended to the breakfast. Tom needed to get going, he was late already. Henrik was coming to collect his trunk. They would go to the art dealers, to pack and load the crates. He wanted to be away before eleven fore noon to arrive at van Reit's in reasonable time. He was disappointed to see it still raining. Before he went, he desperately needed to see Doortje for a few moments alone.

Henrik was already there. He quickly packed the trunk and sent the driver to the first dealer. He would follow. He left a note for Doortje in his room along with a gift of the miniature of the Dutch sailing barge. He waited in the hall and Doortje came out. He moved toward her.

'Doo, I...'

'Shush, master.' She held her finger to her mouth and looked over her shoulder.

'I...'

'Shush, don't make promises you cannot keep.'

'Doo, I will come back.'

'I hope so,' she said, and she moved forward and kissed him in a way that showed him she shared his emotion.

'You must go now.'

'I am sorry.' He did not want to leave her this way.

'Do not ever be sorry. *Let op jezelf liefste.*'

Another small kiss and he left. He looked back and

she waved from the doorstep and turned to close the door. For a moment he felt his life empty.

The dealer and the driver were packing the paintings. The second dealer had delivered his paintings to the first. The paintings in themselves were not heavy, but Tom had asked for a tin-lined crate to ensure that the paintings were not damaged during the voyage. There was no decision on the two larger paintings yet. They set off at mid-morning, Tom asked about the weather and Henrik said that it was common for the roads to have patches of water up to your knees, but the horses and the cart should have no problem. However, it would not be a quick journey. It was important to Tom to catch up with Joe and get back to Edinburgh. They stopped at an inn at the dock to pick up the second horse, and Tom went to get a coffee, a stimulant for the journey. A sailor who was drinking beer, picked up his accent and asked in English where he was heading. Tom, not really wanting to talk, replied abruptly,

'Campveere thence to Scotland.'

'Oh well, I hope you have better fortune than those poor souls on the *Reward*.'

Tom hesitated as he digested what he thought he had heard. His stomach dropped.

'What!' He grabbed the man.

'What are you saying?'

'Last week,' the man said, 'A Scottish ship went down, all but one soul lost. A tragedy if there was one. You hadn't heard?'

'Are you sure? The name, what was the name, *The*

Reward?'

'It was the *Reward* alright. I am sorry to have startled you sir.'

Tom went numb and just sat. Henrik came in and found Tom silent. The stranger explained what had happened and was keen to know why Tom had reacted so, but the driver just shepherded Tom out and on to the cart seat.

The driver spotted two men by the dock, one suited, and one in uniform, probably the harbourmaster. He got down from the cart and went to speak to them. After a few words the two men looked over at Tom. After a few more they shook hands and the driver returned.

'Is it true, Henrik?'

'I'm sorry, sir, yes. Shall we go on, sir?'

After a moment, Tom nodded. Tom's first instinct was to go back to Doortje. Then he remembered all the crew, the captain and first officer, his junior clerk, the characterful seamen, and their families.

'All hands for god's sake, all hands.' Tom swore inwardly. He needed to get home. He could not think. He imagined it, too clearly. He had just sailed on that ship in a storm. He could see it. He could see it. He wanted so badly to be there, with them. The ship, the lives, the money, Doortje, Margaret, the boy, his boy. His failure, it did not seem important, that is not what he cared about. He needed to think. He couldn't think.

The rain started. It was slow going. There was flood water on both sides of the raised polder road. Tom just sat staring forward as the driver took them carefully through Maasland towards van Reit's house. Tom was silent as they drove through patches of water. The wind got up and the rain turned to sleet, the light was poor. Tom and the driver were protected in their oilskins, the cart load covered by sailcloth. Tom's thoughts were an incoherent sea which he let wash over him.

Possible consequences and actions began to occur to him as the full weight of the dreadful news sank in. The going was getting harder and the driver said he would harness the spare horse in front and asked Tom to help. Their boots were ankle deep in water as they got down. It took almost half an hour to get the horse round and manage the harness. Tom wondered about turning back, but the driver said they were more than halfway, and Tom was motivated to move forward and not go back. The temptation to return to the comfort of Doortje would be too great if he went back to Delft. It bothered him hugely that he could still think of Doortje in the light of everything else. Was he not a good man?

They drove for another hour in silence, passing a copse by the water free road. Tom realised that Joe would have heard the news of the ship's fate. Tom did not know how Joe would react in thought nor in deed, but he had more thoughts, thoughts of dread: the news would reach Scotland. His family, Margaret, the boy, they would think him dead.

Tom tried to distract himself from this emotional torment by thinking about the financial consequences. Although all profit was likely lost, the boat had been insured and Tom and Joseph still had considerable goods, money and credit with them. Financially the loss, although large, was mitigated. He would need to go through the detail. If he could just get to Joe in Veere and get home. The driver kept the cart going, surely they must be near.

The road was suddenly water again and it seemed higher. You could only tell that you were on the track by the high poles that marked the edges. The horses were struggling. Tom stayed quiet for a while, but he then put his hand across to gain the attention of the driver. The driver didn't respond. 'Henrik!' he said pushing him. The driver jerked and talked incoherently. Tom looked at him and pulled on the rein to stop the cart. He was clearly not well. Tom got down, the water was above his knees and it was flowing across the track. 'Henrik, we need to turn. We need to go back,' he shouted. The driver said, 'No,' but Tom was not sure he had understood the direction.

It was now bitterly cold, Henrik got down to help Tom turn the cart. It was difficult, the wheels had slipped off the edge of the track and Tom only just managed to get it back. The driver got back up front and Tom, wading, led the horses. The light was fading. Tom looked for options. Those trees on the high ground were not too far away, he thought they could make it there. They may need to spend the night. The horses could hardly pull. As Tom led, he felt the water rise. They got near the trees; the trunks were underwater. The water was up to Tom's thighs. Tom did not panic, but for the first time he saw the possibility of not surviving this. Strangely, he felt calm. The horses were very agitated. He had to release the horses. Perhaps they could use the cart as a raft.

Tom struggled with the panicking horses. The driver just sat in the cart as if suspended in time. The horses, once released, stepped off the track and swam off together. Why did they go in that direction? Tom saw his error, should they have got on the horses and trusted their animal instincts. Too late now. The cart load was now vulnerable, water was lapping at the height of the tailboard. Tom took his satchel. It was important; it contained the money, a pistol in an oilcloth, a waxed box of shot, powder, barrel rod and oil, the other miniature painting, his journal and the letter to Janssen, which he had forgotten to leave with Doortje. He took time to strap the bag to the strongest high branch he could reach in the tree. Waist deep in water now, he did not understand how the water could rise so quickly.

The cart did not rise. It did not float. The metal box and the heavy wheels kept it grounded. Tom's hands and feet were numb now. Water had got past his oilskins. The driver just sat, water up to his knees.

'Henrik, we need to move the crates, I need your help.' Tom pulled at him from the side of the driver's seat, but he fell comatose into the water. He was still alive; he wordlessly shook his head. Tom then got into the cart to pull him up into the back of the cart. He sat him up and covered him with a sail cloth to protect him from the wind and the sleet. It was all he could do. Tom tried to push the trunks and the heavy crate off the back of the cart, but the water was up, the cart was submerging. The water kept rising. He could not move the crate. He looked up and could not see Henrik. He felt the cart begin to slide down the side of the track. He left it and tried to make it to the trees. The waters were swirling. Weighed down by his waterlogged clothes, he saw he wouldn't make it. A stray log hit him hard. He had no feeling in his hands or feet, but he managed to get his arm around the log and cling on to it. He waited in freezing hope that the swirling current would take him to the trees. That night, in striving to survive, Tom knew one thing. He wanted to live, not to avoid failure, not to make amends for the deaths to which he felt he had contributed, not for mercantile success, nor money nor recognition, not even, ashamedly, for Margaret and the boy. All that was raw and real in Tom's mind, as he fought for his life, was Doortje.

CHAPTER 4

Edinburgh, Scotland 1710

The Miller family heard the news of the *Reward* a week after the sinking. Word of the loss of a merchant ship travels as fast as the chatter at the port, the voyage of the next ship, the speed of a horse, but only when there is a survivor. The loss of a ship is the talk of the port towns for many years. Without a survivor or the sight of the wreck, there is a long period of worry, heartache and faint hope, before the inevitable conclusion is reached.

Tom's family had not been worried about his journey. In the world of seafaring, the voyage from Leith to Campveere was routine. Thus, they were stunned when they heard the news of the tragedy. In disbelief, for a time they still held on to hope. If one sailor survived and made it to the shore, there may have been others who survived. They had to wait. The details were unclear to them: Was the ship sunk? What of the cargo? They were not even sure if the ship was lost on the outward journey or the return. They had to wait patiently for more information. The tragedy left Tom's wife, Margaret, distraught. Putting her faith in prayers and God. Her hope held good in the days after they received the news. She held on to the belief that Tom would never leave her, that somehow, *he* would have been spared.

The Lockhart family's mortgaged investment in *The Reward's* valuable cargo, however, had been lost. Tom had unwittingly underinsured. The outgoing load was insured at cost, but the return load had not been accounted for. It was a blow from which the business would find it difficult to recover. The family had strong social connections, and, initially at least, they were treated warmly and sympathetically by their friends and associates. Only Margaret's father, James, was fully aware of the full financial implications for the business and for the family. The effect of this was held in abeyance until the formal notification of the loss of the ship was officially registered and thus attained legal foundation.

With no further news of the sinking other than that the wreck had been found and bodies had been washed ashore, the Lockhart family began to painfully accept that Tom had gone. Margaret held on as best she could and prayed for the strength to support the boy who was now without a father. Sadly, as weeks passed, she became victim to an illness of the mind, and was taken into her family's rooms to be cared for by her parents and their staff. She had shared Tom's dreams. She saw the achievement of the venture to Zeeland as liberating for them both. She shared with him the hope of a less constrained social life, free from her mother's overbearing influence, and that Tom be less dependent on her father and the family business. With Tom, she shared ambitions that could only be explored with autonomy. She felt that the loss of his life was the loss of hope in hers. She fell into melancholia.

Tom's senior clerk, Joseph Grieve, who was also believed lost, had been a long-standing and valued employee. Although his business was struggling, James Lockhart went to visit Joe's family to express his sympathy and promised to support them, in so far as he was able. He would ensure their rent and give them a small allowance until the children were old enough to work.

The Grieve family lived in rooms on the ground floor of a house to the north of the High Street. Not far from the Nor' Loch. James was invited inside and was surprised to find a normality, even a lightness, in their countenance. Not at all the sobriety of a house in mourning.

'But Joseph was not on board' Joe's wife, Mary, exclaimed in surprise, when James gave the reason for his visit. She then was quickly worried as if James' visit left room for doubt.

'Did you not bring us good news?' she said.

'All hands, one sailor got ashore, but they now say all hands,' said the old man.

'But not Joe and Tom, we received a letter.'

Joseph had sent two letters as soon as he heard the news of the sinking on reaching Campveere. One was sent via Leith on the next ship and the other to Tom at his lodgings in Delft.

'Not Tom! Are you sure? Not Tom?' he shouted, crossly in his anguish.

'I'll fetch the letter.' James lost his balance and grabbed the armrest of a chair.

'Oh, please be seated, sir. I'm sorry. I thought you knew.'

'Would you like some water?'

'Yes, please.'

The letter did not say much other than he, Joe, *and* Tom had not boarded *The Reward*. They had stayed behind to finalise additional business, and they expected to return to Leith within a week or more. They would soon travel from Campveere, but he did not know, as yet, the name of the ship.

'Mrs Grieve, I need to return home. Would you be so kind as to bring the letter, and would you come with me?'

'Yes, of course, sir.'

They walked in silence, taking the news to his wife, Margaret and the boy. Mary calmly read out the letter. James tried to moderate Margaret and her mother's initial disbelief and their consequent exuberant response. He still felt uneasy, even after rereading the letter. Margaret had no such reservations. Her prayers, for there had been many, had been answered.

David had seen his grandfather's reserved demeanour, and asked him, 'Is it true, sir?'

'It is only a letter, boy. And we have had no letter. Best wait, we can hope, but best wait. Aye?'

'Yes, sir. Thank you, sir.'

Margaret could not be calmed. She started going down to the dock early every morning to wait for the arrival of ships. At first, she would ask the harbourmaster if any ships were due from the Dutch coast. Then, as the days passed, she asked about every ship. Asking the officers, as they disembarked, if there were any passengers, if Tom was on board. Even if the ship had just come from Newcastle, she would ask. On Sundays, when ships rarely docked, she would still go to the pier; she did not attend church. There was no variety in her days.

One day, Joe's wife appeared on the dock with his family. There was a ship due from Campveere. The two women stood together with three of Joe's children, as they watched the ship emerge from the horizon, sail towards them, and, in agonisingly slow movements, find the dock. The gangway lowered and the mooring crew ran down. A pause and another appeared, tall and red-headed. It was Joe, not Tom. There was no Tom. Joe could not get to the family reception he had dreamed about. He was grabbed physically, arrested by Margaret. He did not fully understand her fervour but reassured her. Tom had not been on the *Reward*. He was alive on land. He was trying to catch this ship with Joe but had said not to worry if he was delayed.

Joe tried to explain calmly to Margaret that Tom would not have learned about the sinking until two or three weeks after it happened, and only then, if the letter Joe had sent had been delivered safely. 'He'll be on the next ship,' said Joe insisting that he get access to his wife and family.

Margaret waited a week, then another week. On the dock, come rain, hail or shine, day after day. When there were no ships due, she would walk out along the slippery, cobbled breakwater and gaze out over the estuary until someone came to take her home.

After a few more weeks, there was still no word from Tom and James Lockhart called for Joseph, who was still under his employment. He told Joe how grateful he was for his not being on the lost ship, – 'As am I, sir.' Joe acknowledged, – and for bringing back the porcelain which looked like it would sell well. Joe credited Tom for the decisions. James went on to explain about the current financial constraints. He offered him promotion with a rise in salary. James then said,

'I want you to go back to Delft, Joseph, and, if you can, find Tom, or at least what has happened to him. It will need to wait until spring. By now, there should have been a letter.'

'Gladly, sir,' said Joe, I do not need extra wages for that.'

Through the mild winter, there was still no word from Tom. Margaret's condition deteriorated and they confined her to the house. They tried in vain to make her see that there was no real point in behaving as she was. It had become embarrassing for the family. Even their close friends' sympathies were being stretched. She protested violently and they had the doctor come daily to administer laudanum. The boy was nearing ten years of age. He knew his father was missing presumed lost. James did not encourage any hopes in the boy by telling him of Joseph's survival. David, who looked like and mimicked his father in movement and action, was virtually ostracised.

The Lockhart family never fully recovered financially, socially nor in temperament from their loss. In his absence, blame was silently attached to Tom. David's home became a miserable and poorer place since his father went missing. His mother mostly stayed in her room with his grandmother in constant attendance. She avoided spending time with her son. His grandfather worked long hours to try to recover the money lost on the ship; there were problems with the ship's insurance – things David did not understand. Now, there were few visitors to the house, and those that came seemed to have business or some kind of financial grievance. Social outings and visits to the countryside had all but stopped. David spent much of his time reading books in his grandfather's library. He had lessons but even his tutor did not attend often. The most social contact he had was with their single remaining maid.

Six months on with no improvement in the family's circumstance, David was accepted as a *'faitherless bairn'* into *George Heriot's Hofpital,* in Edinburgh.

CHAPTER 5

Cupar, Fife, Scotland 1732

J ess and Cora were desperate to see Rosie the day
after her visit to Tarvit House. Over breakfast oats,
David had confirmed with his daughter the need to
keep her promise of secrecy in respect of her time with
Adeline. Rosie was ready for the onslaught of questions
from the two girls when they met at the Cross around
mid-day after chores were done. At first, she acted with
nonchalance, saying it was all a bit boring, that she just
had to sit while her father and Sir Peter discussed business which she was not party to. The girls knew her too
well and knew there must be more. Rosie released mor-
sels of her visit.

'Tell us what happened from the moment you arrived, even if it sounds boring!' insisted Jess, 'Tell us
what it was like.'

'Well, if you like then,' said Rosie.

'We do!'

Rosie said they were received in the hall and, while
her father was taken to see Sir Peter, she had sat in the
library for a while and marvelled at the books but was
too intimidated to take any down and she just read the
spines.

'But then...' she continued.

'Yes, yes!'

'A maid came and took me to the kitchen.'

'To work.'

'No,' she frowned, 'for food.'

'Oh, what did you get?'

And so, Rosie spun her largely truthful tale, carefully omitting the presence of her new French friend, making it as entertaining as she could. She told of the conversation with Mrs P. the cook, even though she had not actually said anything; it had all been Adeline. Then she told them about getting stuck in the privy. This story, they thought was hilarious. She mentioned that she was allowed to walk in the garden. The girls kept prompting. Rosie said she had climbed a tree and the footman came for her and caught her fully in his arms and carried her back into the house. The girls roared at this, then Jess said,

'I don't believe you.'

'It's true, I swear it.'

'Rosie Miller, you fibber, you would not climb a tree in your best dress in a strange garden, and get caught by a footman. I don't think so.'

Rosie just smiled.

'But it's a great story,' said Cora and they all laughed, going over the stories again, each one with greater embellishment.

Back at the schoolhouse, over family supper, her father asked how it had been with the girls, and she reported honestly on the afternoon's events. Halfway through, she realised that they did not know about the *Confession of the Privy* as the girls had termed it. It was too late to stop, and she continued. This made both her parents smile and look at each other in a strange way that she did not understand. She was glad to cheer them. Her mother had not been quite well recently. She looked pale and seemed unable to shake a dry cough. After supper when she had an hour at her books with her father, Rosie looked for guidance,

'Father, I tried not to tell a lie when I spoke to the girls, but I am afraid I might have. If they had asked me something directly, I would have lied to keep my promise to you.'

'Rose, I am sorry to have put you in that position, but it is an example of conflicts that happen in life and I am sure it will not be your last. Indeed, I had to examine my own motives in asking you.'

He thought some more.

'When you become an adult, which will be quite soon, you will learn to make what *you think* is the correct decision, and that should not necessarily be the one that benefits you most.'

'As a child I hope I will always be able to guide you and that you will come to me for advice regardless of the situation.'

'And mother?'

'Yes, of course, and your mother.'

'But how do you know what is right, papa?' She had not used Adeline's term for him before.

'It is always wise to listen to others and learn from what has gone before. This is why I devote my life to study and teaching and why I read so many *learn-ed* books.'

'Like the Bible.'

'Exactly, but not only the Bible, Rose. Man learns about God through the works of other men. St Augustine, for example.'

Rosie opened her mouth to speak.

'That's enough now, Rose, you were going to learn Latin verbs before bed.'

'One more, please father?' to his frown.

'I and the parish boys learn from you, father, but how can Jess and Cora learn?'

'Bed, Rose.'

'*Oui, papa,*' she skipped away.

When she had gone to bed, David reflected on having a mature conversation with his young daughter. To many it may have been trivial, but to him, and to Rosie it seemed, these were important and interesting issues to be discussed. He did feel disquiet; his daughter's last question had unsettled him.

The excitement of Rosie's visit diminished, and, for a couple of weeks, everyday life continued as normal for the girls and their families in the small town. As the minister droned on at church one Sunday, Jessie, sitting beside Rosie, noticed the repair in her dress and nudged Rosie, quizzically and repeatedly, in demand of an explanation. Rosie practised her enigmatic smile. Rosie arrived back one afternoon to find an envelope with a seal awaiting her father's attention. She knew not to appear overly interested and waited impatiently through the day, until supper to ask whether it was a second invitation to Tarvit.

David was working to finalise the structure of his proposed changes to the school and gave much thought to the address he was to give at the parish council meeting, which was now overdue. David would give priority to the inclusion of Latin and Greek, he would be at his most insistent on this point to the council. He would not be as strong on the inclusion of girls, yet, he was not entirely comfortable with his decision.

The message was from Sir Peter, as he expected, and he welcomed the further opportunity to test his arguments. He teased Rosie by not saying anything at all until the very end of supper. Rosie had been trying to be the angelic, dutiful daughter throughout, but ended up just being fidgety.

'I can't study with you tonight Rose, I need to prepare.'

'Father? Father!'

'Yes, Rose?'

Rosie stared pleadingly.

'Yes, Rose.'

'You mean–'

'Yes, Rose.'

'–and I...'

'Yes, Rose.'

At which point she excitedly ran around the table and kissed her father.

'Now, Rose, Latin verbs please.'

'*Oui, papa.*'

'And would you read for your mother tonight.'

'Yes, of course, father.'

Janett was not improving. David had consulted a pharmacist and a physician. There was no fever. It was not smallpox nor consumption, but the cough was worsening and there was a painful swelling in her abdomen. She was prescribed a herbal potion. The physician wanted to bleed her. Rosie was helping more around the house and spent the afternoons at home sitting with her, seeing the girls only occasionally. As Janett got weaker, Rosie lost her ebullience and prayed as hard as she could every night before bed, and throughout at the Sunday service.

'I won't come to the big house, father. I will stay with mother.'

'I don't think that necessary, your mother is unwell, but she is still up each day and managing to serve the house.'

Rosie thought that this was not quite true.

'Why don't you ask your mother what she would like you to do?' David said, knowing well what the answer would be.

This she did.

'Of course, you should go, Rose. I'm sure my cough will clear when the weather gets warmer. I want you to go and come back and tell me all about it.'

'Are you sure, mother?'

'I am perfectly sure.'

The message had said they would be collected by a carriage and gave a time in the late morning, three days before the council meeting. They were to attend for lunch.

On the day Rosie went to put on her repaired Sunday dress. She was just scolding herself for wishing for something prettier when her mother came in with a small parcel.

'For me, can I open it?'

Unwrapped, Rosie found a floral-patterned dress with embroidered collar and cuffs. Speechless, she looked up at her mother who just smiled. It fitted perfectly.

The carriage, a landau, arrived at eleven, and Rosie

and her father were taken to Tarvit House. The footman was standing by the open front door as they arrived, and he stepped out to help Rosie alight. A second carriage arrived behind them and several more people got out. The fire blazed in the reception hall and a maid took their coats.

Peter entered the hall to welcome them both. He moved to welcome the other party who, by their behaviour, seemed familiar with Peter and the house. Sir Peter's two sons and a minister, not their minister, joined from another room. An out-of-breath Adeline flew from the stairs, hesitated, then hugged Rosie first before moving to greet her father and the rest of the party more formally. A footman brought drinks in small crystal glasses and Rosie took one, even though she had no idea what it was. The other party were a man, a woman and two younger women. They were introduced but Rosie could not take anything in. Rosie watched Adeline as an example and followed her behaviour. Adeline sidled up to her and whispered.

'Hello, I'm so sorry that your mother is unwell and could not come.'

'We will have to eat with our fathers and the others, but we will get to play later.'

After some small talk as the party finished their drinks, a servant appeared and said that lunch is served, and they all went through to a dining room that Rosie had not seen on her earlier visit. It had a large table, a large dresser and long windows which overlooked a garden. A maid stood by the dresser which contained plates and bowls of food. Rosie was relieved when she was placed beside Adeline at the end of the table farthest from Sir Peter. The adults talked about all manner of matters, first the house itself, then their families and mutual friends, and lastly the church, the Queen and the government. Adeline listened in and was keen to contribute when she could spot a conversational gap. Rosie just listened, unless she was asked something directly, and then agreed with what was suggested.

They were served soup at the table, then Rosie got to choose as two maids brought platters of food around the table. She picked small portions, remembering her previous over consumption in the house, and avoided the wine. Lunch lasted a good hour and Rosie relaxed. Sir Peter said the three men had business to discuss and suggested the ladies withdrew to the music room. The three ladies, Mrs Anderson, her daughters, Catriona and Fiona, and the two girls went into an adjacent room which had shelves of books, paintings, large soft chairs and a small grand piano.

The younger Anderson ladies became frivolous and were vying to play the piano. The mother instructed them to stop and agree an order of play. Rosie sat on the edge of a huge soft chair, until Adeline pushed her hard right back into the cushions which made them laugh. Rosie thought the piano playing was wonderful, not at all like the turgid organ playing she heard in church. The lady then asked Adeline to play which she did quite well. Rosie admired her with a touch of envy. Rosie was asked if she played and she shook her head. The two girls played something light together and sang. It had a comical, repetitive chorus and they all joined in.

'You can sing, Rose?' asked the lady, to which Rosie nodded.

'See if the girls can find something for you.'

And a terrified Rosie went to the piano. Rosie said

she knew church hymns and some folk songs. She worried because she knew that any songs other than those of church were disapproved of, in the parish, but the church songs were dreary.

'I know some verses of *The Ballad of Tam Lin*.'

'Wonderful, I do not know it. Do you need the music?' asked Mrs Anderson.

Rosie shook her head and started quietly, stopped and started again, on key. Catriona at the piano quickly picked up the rhythm to help Rosie keep time. Rosie got bolder and it came out clearly. It was a risqué fairy tale that Rosie didn't really understand but it made them laugh as Rosie tried to express the moods of the verse.

I forbid you maidens all that wear gold in your hair
To travel to Carterhaugh, for young Tam Lin is there
None that go by Carterhaugh but they leave him a
pledge
Either their mantles of green or else their maidenhead
Janet tied her kirtle green a bit above her knee
And she's gone to Carterhaugh as fast as go can she
She'd not pulled a double rose, a rose but only two
When up then came young Tam Lin, says, Lady, pull
no more
And why come you to Carterhaugh without command
from me?
I'll come and go, young Janet said, and ask no leave of
thee
Janet tied her kirtle green a bit above her knee
And she's gone to her father as fast as go can she
Well, up then spoke her father dear and he spoke meek
and mild
Oh, and alas, Janet, he said, I think you go with child

*Well, if that be so, Janet said, myself shall bear the
blame
There's not a knight in all your hall shall get my baby's
name.*

When she sang all the verses she knew, she stopped,
and the others clapped enthusiastically.

'You both have done very well,' Mrs Anderson said,
'you both may leave us now if you wish and go to play
upstairs.'

Adeline went to kiss the lady and Rosie was beckoned to do the same. They burst into giggles. Closing
the door behind them, they ran upstairs.

'Will you teach me to play the piano please?' panted
Rosie.

'Yes, yes! Then you will be able to come more often...
and where *did* you learn that song!'

'Jess hears the travellers sing in the evenings at the
inn and she teaches me and Cora the words.'

In Sir Peter's study the two men sat comfortably by the
fire and listened to David's proposal to the council. Sir
Peter's guest was John Anderson, a family friend who
was a councillor from Kirkcaldy, twenty miles south of
Cupar. He sat on the schools' committee there. David
had written his proposal on two sheets of paper for the
men to study.

In brief, David's idea, he explained, was to teach a
four-hour morning class of English reading and writing plus some counting to all boys and girls, starting at
eight hours in morn. Then children who did not wish to
proceed to the grammar school would finish school at
mid-day, leaving to take up a trade, help in the home, or
do other work. In the afternoon, from two, those who

wished to attend grammar school would be given three hours of Latin grammar. There would be no teaching of Greek. Both sessions would be open to all suitable children, boys and girls. To him, this seemed a reasonable and viable arrangement. He thought releasing the less interested boys earlier in the day would be supported by the council. The three men discussed the fee structure and whether the general attainment would suffer. David admitted that there would be a reduction in standard because the time was less. The less able pupils, unsupervised, will not work as well.

Sir Peter considered the proposal carefully.

'David, I fully support your intentions. I feel, however, that your plans would not suit the town at this time.' He continued, 'The problem is that this is a compromise solution for two goals: the inclusion of girls, and the teaching of classics, and neither would be achieved satisfactorily. As you admit, the teaching of most of the ordinary boys would be detrimentally affected. And this would be exacerbated by the inclusion of girls, which, and many members agree, would distract the boys and may affect discipline.'

David acknowledged that this was a reasonable point.

'David, I do not want you to think I am not a supporter of your cause or indeed yourself,' adding, 'Despite our short acquaintance, I consider you a valuable friend and I hope you appreciate my plain speaking.'

'I am gladly in your debt, Sir Peter,' said a crest-fallen David.

'What do you think John?' said Sir Peter bringing in his friend.

'I'm afraid, David, that I agree with Peter's point.'

He continued, 'In Kirkcaldy, the burgh school teaches boys and girls, but they are segregated in two small classrooms. Although, it is a larger school, around forty pupils, most are boys. It is still too small for our growing needs. The teaching of each class is quite different. The girls learn sewing and music; they make stockings. The school has two doctors. They do not teach Latin at all; the master, unlike yourself, is not keen.'

Peter interjected. 'David, let us just think this through. I would not vote against your proposal, but I would abstain if I felt it was impracticable.'

Sir Peter rang the bell. David stood up thinking he was required to leave.

'Oh no, David, I was just ringing for the maid, please stay a little longer.'

David regained his seat. Two maids arrived with trays of port, glasses, cheese, cake, cups and a pot of coffee. David asked John about his girls.

'They were tutored at home. I have two boys also who are both at the university in Aberdeen. They stayed with my brother near Dundee, where they attended High School in Dundee for the classics.'

'I hope you don't mind me asking. I'm quite a young master as you know, and much of this is new to me.'

'Not at all, Peter invited me, I think, as he knew of my interest in the subject.'

'Did your girls show an interest in studying more widely or going on to college?'

'That's a sore point particularly for Fiona, our youngest. She has never accepted the limited social and educational limitations forced on her by her gender, Catriona is the more bookish and will happily spend a day or several in my library.'

'They both intend to travel to Europe next year, France and Italy.'

The three gentlemen relaxed and discussed the commercial and political benefits of education. Sir Peter and John opposed each other in a highly abstracted argument, trying to catch one another out. David took a back seat. He had not experienced such discussion since his student days and enjoyed witnessing the agility of these influential men jousting in debate. A knock and the footman entered to say it was five hours after noon.

'Gentlemen, we must join the ladies.'

Peter, John and David went through to the drawing room where the ladies had assembled. Adeline and Rosie, and Sir Peter's sons were summoned. The party sat and talked for a while. Port was served, and John understood the boys had avoided, 'singing for their supper'. Grudgingly the two young men stood up and stood by the fire. Catriona got up too and, pulling Fiona, offered, 'Oh, we'll help you then.'

Rosie could tell Fiona was hiding her willingness. The family had a routine and sang a four-part song with a funny chorus they could join. The ballad built up so that in the last verse they were all singing different parts at the same time. Rosie's mouth was agape. She had not heard such an entertainment, not even by the troubadours, who passed through the town from time-to-time and sang a song for a penny.

After the applause it was time to depart. You didn't just leave, Rosie learned, you had to go around everybody saying stuff and shaking hands or kissing. Mr. Peter, the elder Rigg son, leaned in and kissed Rosie on the cheek in fun as she rose from what she hoped was a curtsey. Her face went bright pink and she couldn't say anything at all in response to Catriona, who, next in the line, complimented her on her singing and said she hoped they would meet again.

Sir Peter and David quickly concluded their dialogue of the earlier meeting. It was dark when David and Rosie stepped into the carriage and headed for the schoolhouse. In the carriage Rosie asked,'What is the business with Sir Peter, father, can you tell me.'

'Not today, Rose, but I will tell you another day.'

'Does it trouble you?'

'Yes, a little, Sir Peter is very helpful.'

As they alighted, they saw only the firelight in the window. No candles were lit. They entered to find Janett lying on the floor.

'Mother!' Rosie cried.

'I'm sorry, I'm sorry, I can't get up.'

She had vomited.

David and Rosie now sobbing, helped her up.

'I'm fine,' she said, 'just weak.'

'We will get you to bed. I'll call the physician.'

'No, husband, I just need rest. I'm not going yet.'

They took her upstairs to bed. Rosie lit a candle; David helped Janett undress. David took Rosie out when Janett lay down more comfortably.

'Rosie, you must be strong. Your mother does not want to see you sobbing. She will rest easier if she sees you strong, believe me.'

'Yes father.'

Rosie swallowed her tears.

Her father, putting a hand on her shoulder, told her to lay a fire for the bedroom, bring a jug of water, and then heat some broth. She found that doing these things for her mother was steadying. David went in to be with Janett.

As Rosie put down the kindling Janett said she felt a little better and told Rosie not to worry. Later, downstairs, Rosie asked, 'Father, is mother going to die?'

'We are all going to die, Rose,' he barked, and she understood that it was not the time to ask such things. As she lay sleepless in her bed that night, Rosie shook with fear.

In the morning Rosie found her mother downstairs sitting by the fire. She looked brighter.

'Help me up Rose, we can make breakfast together.'

'I can do it mother.'

'No, let us do it together. I want to talk to you, Rose.'

Janett told Rosie that she would have to help with the management of the money for the house and the school, and they would sit down over the next few days and she would show her what needed to be done and how to do it. It was the same as running a business, she explained,

'Money comes in, money goes out…and we live on what's left.'

Letters had to be written and sent. Fees were collected from the pupils; the council was billed every quarter. Bills required payment, credit to be monitored, accounts kept properly, and taxes and a salary paid.

'Just in case anything happens to me.'

Rosie stifled a sob. She also had to look after the house money. Butchers and farm bills, coal, peat and more taxes. It all seemed quite complicated to Rosie who could add, subtract and multiply, but this was something different.

'I also want to talk to you about growing up.'

When she saw Rosie's anguished face she added, 'but there will be time for that.'

Starting on this new apprenticeship, Janett tired quickly and as Rosie did some exercises, she turned to find her mother asleep in the chair. She worked on as best she could and then went to tidy up and prepare lunch for them all. Janett roused a bit later and they did a little more.

The following days continued much in the same fashion. Some days Janett was better than others, and they found a little pleasure in their task. On other days, Janett could not rise from bed and Rosie comforted her as best she could. David taught and worked in the schoolroom and, with Rosie, read for Janett in the evenings if she was awake downstairs.

The day before the council meeting David spent the evening in the classroom preparing the papers he was to present. He was adhering to Sir Peter's guidance and would focus on a single issue. It was the one that was most important to him, the one that motivated him and that inspired him into the profession.

His aim was to achieve what he felt he was put on this small part of God's earth to do. He carefully wrote out his case for an additional three hours at the end of the current school day for the teaching of Latin, nouns, verbs and grammar. He wrote out eight copies which he hoped would persuade the committee.

Rosie had just cleared after breakfast. Her mother had managed some oats in bed. David was, as always, in the schoolroom. There was a firm knock at the front door. Rosie looked out the small street window and saw the rear of a fine black horse. She thought it might be the physician but when she opened the door, she found Mr Peter standing expectantly. Rosie even with the sobriety of her mother's condition could do nothing but blush silently.

'Hello, Rosie,' he said smiling, 'I have been sent to assist your father while he attends a council meeting.'

Rosie moved back allowing him to enter.

'Shall I tether my horse round the side of the house?'

Rosie nodded.

'How is your mother?' he said on his return.

'The physician says she is stable. She tires easily and some days she cannot rise.' Rosie was surprised that something coherent came out of her mouth.

'My family sends their regards and good wishes.'

'Thank you.'

'Now, your father?'

'He's in the school room,' pointing at the adjoining door, 'I am not permitted to knock.'

Mr Peter nodded and tapped on the door. The door opened promptly. He was clearly expected, and David invited him in. Rosie listened at the closed door for a while. An act that had become so much of a habit she had forgotten that it was sinful. She then understood that Mr Peter was to supervise the class for the morning. She left to attend to her mother.

After twenty minutes or so her father came upstairs to see them both. He was to address the council meeting and would be away for a few hours. Janett said she was fine and that they would go over some more bookwork for the accounts. They bade him good luck. David put on his Sunday suit, picked up his notes and headed for the meeting. He had time and so strolled from the schoolhouse through the marketplace toward the inn.

As he approached the Cross, he saw four girls talking idly on the steps. He smiled at Cora and Jessie as he approached. He knew the families of the others and nodded in their direction. As he passed, they were nudging each other, and it was Cora who broke ranks.

'Mr Miller, excuse me, sir, how is Mrs Miller?'

'She is not well but she is comfortable, thank you Cora.'

'She is in our prayers,' she said hesitatingly unsure of what to say.

David went to walk away but instead he went back to the group and greeted them all asking the girls about their own families.

'Can we visit please, sir?' said Jessie.

'Yes, just two of you, for a short while. One hour after noon would be fine. They will be glad of your company.'

'Mr Miller, we are sorry we went into the schoolroom,' Jess added, 'we won't do it again.'

'I didn't mind, Jess. I'm starting to think that is where all four of you should be, every afternoon.' David smiled at the thought. A spark was struck from a flint.

CHAPTER 6

Edinburgh, Scotland 1710

George Heriot's *Hofpital* was not an infirmary nor a school. Nor was it a workhouse, nor an orphanage. It was none, yet it was all these things. The charitable institution provided bed, board, work, pastoral care, religion and elementary schooling for sixty or so sons of Edinburgh merchants who, like David, found themselves bereft of income and a father.

The castle-like building stands to the south of the *Grafe Mercate*, overlooked by the backs of the houses on Castle Hill Street and the Castle itself. The *Hofpital* is an impressive, turreted, stone building enclosing a slabbed quadrangle. In 1710, it lay just within the burgh wall. The school's physical proximity to the College meant the convenient provision of excellent tutors and an enlightened range of teaching methods and texts. David had often looked over at the school from his house and envied the boys their outside activities and games. In the evenings, he could see the candlelit windows of the dormitories and imagined being on the inside.

David lived a solitary existence with his family, with no siblings and no cousins his own age. He was home tutored and thus had never been with a group of boys nor in a classroom environment. He had seen the *Hofpital* boys coming and going from the school, usually in small groups, and had longed to join them.

David was accepted into the school on the basis of his father's status of missing, presumed dead. He had to wait a few months until the start of the new term and went to join the school's entry class of ten-year olds.

On his first day, David left his house before seven hours wearing his Sunday suit and carrying a small bag. He walked up the Castle Hill Street and turned left to go down the narrow West Bow to the *Grafe Mercate*. Each subsequent floor of the tall buildings he passed, jutted out a few more feet over the street. The sky became a thin blue line between the gabled roofs of the upper floors. The cobbled street was damp and dark. In the early morning, he liked seeing the trading activities and the market bustle as he walked the streets: the clatter of horses' hooves, the clucking hens, the chatter of geese, the rattle of carts and the bellowing of the market traders. The sweet smells of fresh hay and bread baking masking, for once, the human and animal excretions. His walk then took him up the steep climb from the opposite side of the *Grafe Mercate*, across Heriot Bridge to the school gate. It was something which he had been keenly anticipating. He paused for a moment to look back and up at the castle walls which appeared at their most imposing from this viewpoint.

Then through the gate of the symmetric Jacobean grey stone palace. Four, wide castellated towers at each corner joined the high-roofed houses of the school. The impressive building was ornate yet elegant and, in its style, dominated every other Edinburgh building. Two

Doric columns on pedestals each side of the entrance supported a lintel under ornate stone carvings. David didn't stop to examine the friezes. Behind the door an arched pend took him into the quadrangle.

There was a new entry class of boys of his age and, for once in his life, he was not alone. He looked to pick out the other new boys; it wasn't very difficult. He joined them in looking nervously around. A master in the pend took each Foundationer's name and gave them a number. He instructed them to go into the quadrangle and stand still and silent on the flagstone which had their corresponding number. David's number was '33'. The quad had arched cloisters on three sides and the fourth side facing the entrance had a large double door centred in the high wall with mullioned, stained windows. This, as David would soon find out, was the chapel. The steep, slated roof held the dormer windows of the new boy's chambers. In each corner there was a convex, round wall with un-paned windows rising at an angle; these lit the stairwells to the upper floors.

David stood straight, still and silent. David thought those standing were mostly new boys. These boys were clothed in a range of styles, browns, blues, blacks and the odd pair of red trews. The garments of some boys looked well-worn and their shoes barely functional. When there was a little tittering and low chatter, it was sharply rebuked by an unseen master in the cloister. Then the older pupils came down from the dormitories. Uniformly clad in dark russet jackets over white shirts; all were well shod. They began to fill the numbered slabs in the square. David had estimated one hundred numbered stones in the square, just over seventy were filled when the school roll was complete.

The older boys were counted, one or two were called out for attention by a master, and the others were dismissed to classes. There were twelve new boys remaining. With David, they were then guided through the school by two men, one of the two, the schoolmaster, and the other, one of four assistants who were regents and addressed as *Doctor*. They went to a classroom, the dining room, their chambers, a wash room, the laundry, the chapel and then to a smaller room where they queued to be given a russet doublet and two pairs of breeches, three shirts, linen undergarments, hose, one pair of light brown shoes and a cloak and hat. This took a while as they were sized, and clothing found. Not that the garments they received seemed well matched to their dimensions. The boys stifled a little laughter. The master talked for some time giving instructions about the people and workings of the school. The boys were expected generally to be quiet. David and one or two of the other boys exchanged looks and smiles as if already in collusion.

These simple acts of bonding made David look forward to his new world. The timings of the school day were rung out by the chiming of the tower-bell, as if on a ship. David liked the size of the rooms, the view from the windows, the height of the ceilings, and amount of space in the school. The boys were then taken to their chambers to change into their uniform accompanied by the two older boys; one of whom did not seem at all pleasant.

The new boys' chambers on the second floor of the school had sixteen narrow beds, light, plastered walls and the boys looked up from their beds to dark roof timbers. The high windows lit the room and gave views over the rooftops of Edinburgh to the east, and over the quad to the west. The two older boys took beds near the end wall, opposite the door of the chambers, which had an unlit fireplace. They kept the two adjacent beds free. The master had said that they would be addressed by their numbers initially but, in time, they would get their names back.

When the morning bell rang at seven hours, they were to stand on their numbered slab. David wondered how they would know when to rise. Along with the two boys who had acknowledged him, David walked quickly up the room to find three beds together, about two thirds of the way up the east side. There was a door-less cupboard or a chair beside each bed and a chest at the foot. They were told to put their own items in the chest and their bags and trunks would be stored. One of the older boys said they could talk quietly as they changed into their uniforms. At last, they had a degree of freedom. David's new friends were Alan and Harry, '31', and, '43', they said in unison.

When the next bell rang, they were to attend in the refectory. The dining hall was a long high-ceilinged room with a large fireplace at each end. There were four doors: one in the long inner-side, one in each of the end walls, beside each fireplace, and one on the win-dowed outer-side leading to a staircase. Between the mullioned windows on the outer wall hung portraits of the founder and some of the governors. The room was light; the ceiling and chimney breasts were ornately plastered and painted. Twelve boys, now smartly clad, were instructed to sit at the centre of one of two long benches. Two maids brought out bowls of warm oats and a cup of milk for each of them on tin trays. David wasn't hungry enough to finish his oats and Harry will-ingly offered his assistance.

The boys were then taken, on the next bell, to the chapel where they were seated at the front. The older boys from the school then filed in followed by a few members of staff in gowns, and lastly, the minister. Psalms by the boys, interspersed with readings from some of the older scholars, were followed by a very long sermon which seemed to be directed at the new boys. The new boys remained seated at the end to be addressed by the Master of the school, Mr John Watson. He introduced them to their tutor who was referred to as Dr Hardie. He gave an abridgement of their school days to come. This was followed by a meal in the refec-tory and a short spell of free time within the quad. One of their older boys taught them some traditional *quad games*, which involved much combative exercise.

In the afternoon they began their lessons. Another older boy took them around the whole school build-ing, up and down every staircase, so they could find their way around. There were connecting doors on each floor; there were no corridors, and the boys' only per-mitted access to other rooms, was to go down the stairs across the quad and up another stair. There were six stairwells; four in each corner and two in the sides which did not contain the chapel nor the entrance. Scholars were not permitted to move between rooms along the same floor. He also gave valuable informa-tion informally and answered some questions until he thought they had asked enough and told the boys to keep their peace. The boys were chiefly concerned about food, free-time and discipline. At two hours after noon they attended their first class in Latin in a second-floor classroom on the north side where all their classes would take place. They were each given Simpson's *Dunbar Rudiments,* a popular Latin Grammar book. They spent the next two hours reciting and memorising Latin nouns from the text. At four they had an hour's break before supper followed by evening prayers in the chapel with the whole school. They were expected to study in their classroom till late after supper, and the tutor had already set them memory tasks for the next day which, he impressed, would be tested. The older boys supervised them at study.

In the evening, at the bell of nine, they were allowed upstairs to their chambers. There were bowls of water placed on a long table at the end of the dormitory opposite the fireplace; there was a privy chamber at the top of the stair well. The older boys would supervise for one week then two other boys would replace them. The boys had time to introduce themselves properly. Some were quiet and tearful, but most were untroubled. Alan, David and Harry talked about their backgrounds. One boy in the class, Daniel, was louder than most but was funny and brought a spark to the group. Another boy, Eduard, had an older brother at the school and quickly became valued for the mine of information he held.

At ten hours of evening, Dr Hardie came into the boys' chamber with a young servant girl. The boys were required to stand up straight by the end of their beds and call out their name and number in turn. The maid, Molly, Dr Hardie explained, took in the boys' washing, cleaned the chambers and privy, and would alter and repair their uniforms. The boys were to do as Molly asked, but on no account, 'No account!' he shouted, were they to give her personal instructions or demand anything from her. David noticed Molly disguise a shy smile to the two older boys standing behind Dr Hardie. Molly shared a room with the other servants on the ground floor. All candles were to be extinguished and checked at ten and the half hour.

The morning bell sounded the next day at six hours, all boys were to assemble on their numbered stones in the quad at six and the half and sent to their classroom for an assessment of their competency in their study and the learning of the previous day. At eight hours, there were morning prayers for all scholars in the chapel followed by breakfast in the refectory; usually oats, warm bread with cheese or butter, and a cup of milk. For the new boys, Latin classes, nouns and, later in the term, verbs would begin at ten hours. At noon, there were classes in writing.

The midday meal of meat, chicken or fish and eggs was served at one after noon. Afternoon classes in the rudiments of Latin grammar were from two to four hours followed by a class in either arithmetic or reading. The whole school assembled in the quad before supper at five hours after noon. Supper was a warm potage or stew and a cup of ale, even for the new boys. Evening study was from six to eight hours at evening.

Wednesday afternoons were free time and they were allowed to play ball games in the school grounds, work in a workroom or help in the physic garden. Sunday mornings were spent attending chapel and learning the catechism; the older boys were then permitted to leave school in the afternoons. All conversation between the boys and with their tutors during the school day was to be in Latin so the boys worked hard to gain enough language to make themselves understood. Their tutor was kind enough to make allowances in their first few weeks.

This routine became the boys' school life for their first term. The new boys were not allowed out of the school grounds. The older boys had a more varied day. After morning prayers, they were sent to the High School for classes which they shared with the High School pupils. The teaching of classics in the High School was more advanced. They made this return journey two or three times each day to learn Latin grammar, plays, verses and some Greek. In the later years the master struggled to ensure that, each day, all the scholars reached, attended lessons, and returned from the High School. Scholars were assessed for proficiency in all subjects by the schoolmaster once per month.

David found that he had been well prepared for the curriculum by his home tutor and did not have difficulty with the classes; he helped the others in the evening. Alan was very good, but Harry struggled. Daniel, the class clown, had moments of perfection and, to the exasperation of the tutor, longer periods of disgrace. David settled into the routine quicker than most of the others. The company of the other boys as they studied, the chatter at meal times and the domestic attentions of Molly made the days pass quickly.

The school was not a miserable place. Dr Hardie had a genuine enthusiasm for his subject and had invested in their progress. The boys could use the study time in the evenings for writing letters, reading books from the library or even playing card games, as long as they were performing well in class. David wrote to his mother every week and worried about the lack of a reply. He wrote once to his grandfather but received no reply. Eduard told stories of what the older boys got up to which made them look forward, with a degree of nervousness, to their later years, and Daniel kept them entertained with his harmless silliness. Eduard also knew how to gain benefits in the workings of the school. All the boys had a quite generous allowance which they could use to buy food of better quality from the cook by going to the kitchens at certain times in the week. There was usually a queue. You had to keep quiet about this, although everyone knew it went on. You could also pay Molly to buy and fetch things from the markets. A couple of boys in the class kept their own counsel and niggled, particularly Alan and Daniel, unnecessarily at times, but it is always thus and of no lasting consequence. As their proficiency in Latin improved, Dr Hardie would tell stories of great deeds, battles and murders which had them enthralled. In Greek he told tales of the Gods. Under their morning assessment, Daniel was capable of great errors, once saying he was going to eat the Colosseum for lunch. This even made Dr Hardie laugh, but earned Daniel extra supervised study. You never quite knew, with Daniel, whether he actually knew the correct answer. David was convinced he did. Daniel was the first new boy to be caned, not severely, when he picked the wrong moment to be funny.

Severe punishment was occasionally delivered to the older boys at the evening assembly in the quad, in front of the whole school. The schoolmaster or sometimes the steward, who was more strongly built, would cane one or more boys for a serious misdemeanour. This could be theft, or some such action done outside the school gates which affected the reputation of the school. The reputation of the school, David learned, was paramount. The older boys were only allowed to leave the school in uniform and thus were always under public scrutiny. Other offences deserved of corporal punishment were verbal abuse, staying out overnight, not attending classes or chapel, or bullying and fighting. There were few that could withstand ten strokes without a whimper. Once Eduard pointed out to them, the two square holes in stone slabs at the south east corner of the quadrangle. 'These,' he said, 'were for stocks and that last year the stocks were erected, and a senior boy was chained in them at morning assembly and left overnight. He had assaulted a young woman one evening outside the school.' Eduard also said that some of the tutors devised their own punishments, such as being kept in a locked room for hours without food or water, or walking around for a day without shoes, but this was not common. Mostly the new boys were merely rebuked for minor misdemeanours.

As the nights got longer, fires were lit, the chambers were illuminated by candles, and the quad and the pend by lanterns. Next to the kitchen the refectory was the warmest place and the boys lingered there after supper for as long as they could. As the end of the calendar year approached, the classes stopped and almost all the boys packed a case or trunk and left the school to visit their homes or those of relatives. Not all the scholars had lost a parent or were poor. Nearly a quarter of the boys, like Alan and Eduard, paid a good annual sum to attend the school. These boys were not local to Edinburgh and usually had family who now lived abroad.

David asked Molly for his small bag and he put two books in it with his old clothes and asked for permission to leave the school. This was not quite as easy as he thought as he had no written note from his guardian nor did anyone come to fetch him. As he was barely going a half mile, Dr Hardie sought to send one of the older boys with him to make sure he got home and that there was someone to receive him. A suitable boy could not be found so Dr Hardie asked the housekeeper if he could use Molly for the purpose. It was agreed. Molly was delighted to escape during her long working hours.

David found it strange leaving the school gate with Molly. They chatted as they walked along the flat path to the West Port rather than going down and over the bridge. The West Port was, unusually, busy with queues; soldiers were checking the carts entering the town. Molly asked about his family, but David did not have much to say except that he was not sure if he was expected. They then turned east and walked the length of the *Grafe Mercate*. It was midday. David enjoyed the familiarity of walking the streets he had not seen, heard nor smelled for three months. Molly dawdled. The tinker market was in the wide street, and Molly neglected David to look through the multitude of wares on the stalls. If David had wanted to escape there would have been no problem. He had no such desire to leave Molly's company; he was enjoying watching her pick up the scarves, blouses and rings and ask the dealer the price. Molly had her dark hair cut short; even under her headscarf and long drab clothes, David could sense she had a woman's figure. Something that Daniel could not stop rudely commenting on every time she left their chambers. David liked her round face, big eyes and her smiling nature most of all. She did not play a small part in making their ship a happy one.

David liked seeing the tinkers' horses in the marketplace and gave the smaller ones a rub on the nose as he passed. Molly paid particular attention to a necklace with blue stones. She enquired but it was two guineas and she had only a few shillings. No barter would make it affordable. She moved away to look at dresses and a smock. David drifted back to the stall with the necklace. He had money from his allowance and, without any sense other than instinct, he stood his ground with the stall-holder to gain the necklace for two pounds; a good proportion of his monthly allowance. He had the trader parcel up the necklace carefully and he put it in the pocket of his breeches. He caught up with Molly, who had not missed him, to find her putting fancy dresses up against herself. When she saw David, she turned to face him and wore a smile as she danced a jig for him. He bowed as if in a gavotte.

It was beginning to darken from cloud cover and David reluctantly suggested they continue. They went up the West Bow to Castle Hill Street. Arriving at the Lockhart's *Land*, they both walked up the narrow stone stairs to the door of David's family's rooms.

David pushed at the door, but it was barred from within; a couple of firm knocks brought a maid David did not recognise. He asked for his mother and the puzzled maid told them to wait where they stood and closed the door. Molly stayed with him more from curiosity than duty. The maid returned to let them in and asked them to wait in the hall. David looked around the familiar hall; he recognised his family's oak dresser and two chairs. As they waited David noticed that there was a large flat packing case sitting upright in the corner. He looked sideways at it to see it was addressed to his father at this address and had other writing in a language he could not identify. A youngish man came out and David asked for his grandfather.

'Ah,' said the man, 'he does not live here now. We have recently taken these rooms.'

'My mother?' said David.

'I'm afraid your family have moved out.'

'But the furniture?'

'Yes, we bought some of the larger pieces and there are still some of the furnishings to be collected.'

David stood silent and shivered.

'I'm sorry,' said the man, 'but if I cannot help further?'

The man gestured to the door.

As they turned to leave, it was Molly who said,

'If you please, sir, do you have an address?'

'You can wait, I will ask my wife.'

The man came back with a piece of paper with an address and said he thought it was south of the Canongate outside the wall.

'Ah, before you go, would you take these? They were found in the drawer of the large dresser we purchased.'

And he handed David a bundle of his own letters addressed to his mother. They were unopened.

David remained silent. Molly was unsure what to do, but decided she wanted to extend their excursion and continue to seek David's family. If there was no success by four bells, they would both return to the school.

They walked down the *Land Mercate*, past St Giles toward the Nether Bow. The High Street was full of hand barrows, makeshift stalls and trays of goods, as hawkers plied their trade. It seemed to David, you could buy the whole world here: candies, pears, apples, potatoes, salt, shoe ties, coal, sand, peat, combs, bonnets, pottery, glass, plates, tankards, and mirrors. There were knife-grinders, tailors, saddlers, candle makers, cobblers, pin and news-sheet sellers. He saw penny shows, fortune tellers, preachers, poets and balladeers. Men, tankards in hand, stood outside the overflowing inns. Inside the vennels, painted ladies pulled up their skirts for likely customers.

As David and Molly pushed and jostled their way through the throng to continue down the street. They stilled with the crowd at the familiar sound of horse hooves on the stone setts coming down at a trot from the castle; from the noise, there were many. A squadron of mounted cavalry headed down the Royal Mile. The crowds hurried to make way for the horses leaving them struggling for space, tightly confined by the close buildings. David had never seen such fine horses.

Forty or so smartly crimson-uniformed, mounted dragoons, straight-backed and towering over the crushed crowd, distracted him from his troubled thoughts. As the crowd parted, there was both cheering and jeering. 'Long live the Queen!' shouted one. 'Aye, the witch!' shouted another. Just as they passed someone from behind David and Molly threw a missile. Probably an apple from a nearby barrow. The rear dragoon moved his steed quickly forward up the side, crushing the crowd more. On reaching the front and the Captain, the troop was brought to a shuddering stop which quieted the crowd. After a pause, the Captain shouted an order and, to David's astonishment, the troop, as one man, unbuckled the leather handle-guards on their scabbards. You could have heard a button drop on the cobbles. The troop stayed, and the crowd were transfixed with a few moving away quietly, down a close. 'Long live Queen Anne,' another voice rose.

After a few long minutes, the dragoon returned to the rear, at walking pace, looking to the crowd as he did so. When he had resumed his position, the Captain again barked, and the troop walked their horses on. When they were well out of earshot a single cry of 'Long live King James,' was heard.

David and Molly waited for the crowd to thin and continued down the Nether Bow, following the dragoons through the port at the Head of the Canongate which, like the West Port, was well guarded. They turned right at the port to go down St. Mary's Wynd. David had lost his attentiveness and seemed largely unaware of where they were going.

Several highlanders, in the drab kilts of their clan and swords in their belts, were coming up the Wynd towards them. Molly pulled David into a close and waited for them to pass. A woman came down the stair to ask their business, and Molly enquired of the address they sought. The woman directed them to a *land* in a narrow lane off the Wynd. Asking again, they were shown to first floor rooms off a small external stair. For the second time that day, they walked up a stair and knocked at a door. Again, a maid, David did not know, answered the door; she asked them to stand in and wait in the small hall. The rugs and paintings were familiar to David, but this home did not seem welcoming nor prosperous. A far door opened and David's mother, looking thin and aged, paused, gasped for breath, then ran at him.

'Tom, Tom, Tom,' she screamed. I knew it, I knew you would come back.'

She grabbed him with such force David dropped his bundle of letters on the floor. They were now the same height, she squeezed him too tight and sobbed, wailing into his neck.

David froze.

His grandfather appeared in anxiety and limped as quickly as he could to get to his daughter.

'It's not Tom, Margaret, it is the boy. No, Margaret, it is not Tom. It's the boy,' he repeated.

But she held on desperately.

The grandfather, the maid and eventually Molly too, all acted to prise the sobbing mother off the stricken boy. It took some time to remove her into the back room, leaving David to stand alone. It was his grandfather who came out first.

'Why are you here boy?'

'It is a school break, sir,' he stammered, 'we are permitted home.'

'Don't be stupid, look what you've done to her. We can barely manage as it is.'

'But, sir...please.'

'No boy,' he shouted, as Molly reappeared.

'Sir, perhaps I can help...' David tried desperately to speak.

'No! Boy, you've seen how unwell your mother is.'

James Lockhart then addressed Molly. 'Are you from the School?'

'If it please you, sir,' said Molly.

'Will you take him back there?'

'Yes, sir.'

She pulled at David's sleeve to get him to move.

'Goodbye, sir,' he said without malice, as brightly as he could, 'I hope my mother's health improves.'

David and Molly made their way slowly and silently back to the town port and thence the school gates. Once inside Molly tried to jolly David.

'It's not so bad here over the holiday. The food is greatly improved,' and she took David directly to the kitchen.

David sat down in the kitchen and the cook gave him some broth which he could only toy with. Dr Hardie appeared and asked to see them both. They went into the master's room.

Molly recounted her slightly dramatised version of events with David silent and motionless except for nodding when his tutor looked at him for confirmation. Molly was concerned that she had *done right*. Dr Hardie told David he would join the other boys who were staying at the *Hofpital* during the holidays in one of the smaller chambers in the morning. Meantime he would be fed supper in the kitchen at six hours at evening and could read by the refectory fire until nine. David did as instructed and quietly thanked his tutor and Molly in one word.

Dr Hardie visited him later in his chamber and told him he could keep a candle lit if he wished. David said he was fine and thanked him again. David lay in his bed trying not to think of anything, but sleep wouldn't come. He kept going over events: his old home, his mother, the soldiers, the letters, Molly, his grandfather. It was all a mush. Around ten, he heard the door open but did not fully waken or look up. Molly found him quietly sobbing.

The first time Molly had ever tried to sleep on her

own in a bed was when she joined the *hofpital* fifteen months previously. She took so bad with it; she shared a bed with one of the other maids till she became accustomed. She still joined her friend on hard days and cold nights. In her family's two roomed accommodation there had been six children, a spinster aunt and her parents. Molly had always slept in a heap of older and younger siblings, brothers and sisters. It was natural for her to climb in with David and hold him from behind. He was a troubled child. Almost eleven years of age, David could not remember ever feeling the close warmth of another body in any shape or form let alone that of a young female. He smelled her fragrance; he sensed every part of her body that was in touch with his. He dared not move. He worried that any movement by him may not be correct and cause her to leave. 'Sleep now, child,' she whispered and kissed the back of his head. David felt a comfort he had never experienced. His tears still fell but they were different tears, and he lapsed into a dreamless sleep.

He was alone when he woke, suddenly from a deep sleep, at the sound of the morning bell. His arm had gone completely numb and it scared him as it took him a painful minute to revive it. He got up, washed and went downstairs, and he stood, firm and straight, on number '33', in the quad.

David remained at his place a good while. With neither scholar nor doctor around, he went to the chapel and sat quietly in his thoughts, his rumbling empty stomach louder than any other sound. The large chapel door creaked open before banging against its stop.

'Thirty-three, is it?'

'Yes, sir.'

'We've been looking all over, come quick, else you'll miss the *paist*...and don't call me sir. I'm not a master.'

David shot up to follow the boy and his stomach.

'What shall I call you s...?'

'I am Googe. Today, I am the senior scholar. And you are?'

'David.'

'No, boy, surnames or nicknames only.'

'Miller.'

'Oh dear, that will probably become Millie. Never mind.'

'Let's try Mills, come on Mills.'

And thus, for the next six years, he was Mills.

Across the quad in the dining hall, there were a dozen boys of all years at the end of one of the long refectory tables near the fireplace. They were finishing a meal of oats, bread, cheese and warm pork. David was salivating.

'Here he is,' barked Googe, 'This is Mills.'

Space was made for David to sit.

'Tell us, Mills,' said one boy, 'what is this we hear of a cavalry charge with swords drawn chasing Jacobites out of town?'

David already had an overly large slice of bread in his mouth and used the chewing time to think of a reply.

Molly had obviously told a highly embellished version of their mutual experience in the High Street. David looked up at the silence. All eyes were on him. In modest tone he gave an understated account of the events, leaving room for the boys' imagination. They seemed satisfied after asking for more detail. A boy asked why he was returned to the school. David swallowed hard and took a drink from his cup of milk to compose another response. How much had Molly said? He wondered. Unintentionally these pauses added to the interest and patience of the boys round the table. He opted for an attempt at humour, and made his family situation sound amusingly chaotic, a house in transition, rather than alluding to any illness or discomfort. He even threw in a few Latin nouns to aid his performance. A pause, then Googe said,

'Excellent Mills, and you, sir, shall be in our play. But I'm afraid the pitch of your voice will enjoin you to the fairer sex.'

There were fifteen scholars plus Dr Hardie, two other tutors and the schoolmaster staying in the school over the two-week break. David was the only new boy. The scholars were not instructed to study, although many did. They were expected to attend chapel twice a day and otherwise to occupy themselves usefully. Traditionally they put on a short classical play for entertainment after supper on Christmas day when the staff, the residential servants, the schoolmaster and a number invited guests feasted together in the refectory. Other activities involved helping in the gardens, writing out materials for the tutors, assisting in the workshops, such as the pottery and the wood shop which were hosted within the school buildings. Older boys were permitted to leave the school to do charity works. Some visited relatives. Some visited the inns, but until Christmas Day it was all hands to the play.

Unfortunately for David it was not a tale of warring Gods but a yarn of spurned love and unseemly revenge. David, with his thin elegance, pure skin and high voice, played the maid under aggressive pursuit in the romantic Roman drama. After a couple of days balking at his part and sensing Googe's quiet disappointment, he launched himself into the role and determined to be as *good a maiden* as he could muster. This was abetted by Molly whom Googe had surreptitiously recruited to coach David in the effeminate mannerisms of the wily wench. His practice reduced Molly to tearful hilarity on many occasions, at first due to his inarticulate ineptitude and then in response to his exaggerated exuberance. Molly was also given the duty of making the costumes which gave her a rare freedom in her duties. The carpenter made scenery and the boys without an acting part found out how to mix and make washes to add a colourful classical background.

The masters, rather than staying aloof, joined in with advice and ideas, correcting parts of Latin which were grammatically incorrect, mispronounced or misinterpreted. David began to enjoy himself. Once he became comfortable with the small group, he was confident enough to speak up and took instruction on poise and posture. He had previously sung solo in church when he was younger and was stimulated rather than incapacitated by the natural nervousness he felt when in front of an audience.

It was as if a switch had been set, and the moribund life he had previously led had served only as a period of incubation. Its boundaries, which formerly had been impenetrable, now possessed weaknesses and cracks that could be rent. In this school, with these people around him: the scholars, the masters, the maid, and his friends, he had found the means to burst out of his cocoon and break earth's mortal binding. He needed nothing else.

David was puzzled by the amount of time and energy,

not just from the scholars but the tutors and other staff, being spent on this insubstantial entertainment and re-marked so to Googe.

'Ah, Mills,' he said. 'It is the Governors. Thirty-two Governors oversee the school business, the teaching, the instruction, the money, the buildings, everything,' he paused, 'and most of them delight in attending our Christmas play. Some bring their families. The Master believes it is essential that they leave with a good re-port of what they encounter.'

David wished he hadn't asked.

The preparations continued; David remembering his lines; the continual script revisions and remembering them again: the stage instructions, entrances and exits, timings and positions. He was, however, at his most nervous when Molly had him strip to his linen under-garments to take the measure of him. On stage, he was to wear a tight-fitting dress. He squirmed and squealed red-faced as she tried to get an arm and a leg length. More lines, fewer lines, and then the fitting and the wig. Molly was amused but calm and purposeful. David was embarrassed, giggly, shy but inexplicably thrilled by this silly exercise. He ran away half-dressed at one point, despite Molly's protests, only to return calmer and apologise. As yet, no-one else had seen the dress nor him in it. He could not see himself as there was no mir-ror of any size. Molly and David had kept out of sight in the sewing room. Molly had David strike a pose and then went to get Googe. Googe arrived, smiled, and did not laugh or tease.

'Very good,' he said ponderously.

After a pause he continued,

'Molly, I think Mills needs some shape.'

'He is meant to appear a comely woman. Penelope has to entice one hundred suitors.'

'Can you do this?'

'If it please you, sir.' she said.

Molly got to work and, fortunately for David, rather than padding his undergarments, she sewed wool filling into the dress. Before the next inspection Molly applied some rose powder to David's cheeks and added a darkening around his eyes. She took her time with positioning and brushing his wig. As Googe entered, he looked at David then looked round the room and looked back.

'Good god,' he said.

'Sir?'

'Well Mills, you would earn a pretty penny in the High Street,' and he left.

The Pursuit of Penelope was a horrible corruption of The Odyssey in three acts. Googe and some of his year group had taken Greek in their final year and written this short variation of the story of Ulysses, played by Googe of course. Ulysses has left his wife, Penelope, to fight in the Greek war against Troy. In his absence, she must fight off the attentions of one hundred and eight suitors. Initially she rebuffs any approach and will not entertain any attention. Ulysses reappears every so often disguised as a beggar to check that she is being faithful and quickly dispatches anyone who has approached her. But the attentions of admirers are not entirely unwelcomed by the bored, lonely and abandoned wife. Over time, and unsurprisingly, the number and the attentions of her suitors diminishes, and Penelope is unhappy. She sees it as an insult to herself and her husband's status if she is not highly sought after. She thus goes to greater and greater lengths to attract male attention. On the last of Ulysses' disguised visits, in the final act of the play, he finds Penelope to be shockingly provocative in her attempt to maintain male attention. Ulysses reveals himself and walks toward her with his sword. The curtain falls.

The boys were up sharp for breakfast on Christmas Day. The cook needed them gone by seven so she could prepare the dinner. There was a short session of morning prayers before the boys began to ready themselves for the play and help with the rest of the days' preparations. When the visitors began arriving at eleven hours fore noon, twelve of the governors, including the chairman, assembled in the Council Room with the Master and the doctors for an official school meeting. The midday bells summoned all for the short walk to Greyfriars where they were joined by town council members, other merchants, their families and members of the general public for the Christmas Day Service. At three, the school bells summoned everyone to dinner and all visitors, staff and scholars assembled in the refectory for the celebratory meal.

The room was very warm and the smells almost overpowering. The masters and visitors sat at the high table nearest the fire and the kitchen. The scholars and senior staff were further down the room and the lower staff, including the maids, were nearest the stage which was already set up for the entertainment. Wine was served at the high table and joined by a meal of goose and venison. At the other tables, pork, chicken and eggs were served. Tureens of gravy, kale, turnips, oats and potatoes and jugs of ale were placed on the tables. The minister said grace and the scholars and staff waited for permission to start. The boys were allowed to drink ale and make more noise than usual, and there was a merry atmosphere. The high table was as relaxed as David had ever seen it. It was more than an hour before the Master rose, a little unsteadily, and banged his gavel for silence and attention. It took a while for the rippling quiet to move down the room. He announced the entertainment and left Dr Hardie to explain the arrangements for the governors' families and others newly arrived. The boys involved in the play left the hall.

Off-stage Molly fussed with David, making minor adjustments. She separated three strands from each side of the wig and made two braids that she then fixed round the back of his head. 'Perfect,' she said, giving him a peck as she wished him well. David left quickly to join his fellow thespians.

The staff in the refectory had to move to the end farthest from the stage, thereby allowing the children and visitors to sit at the front. The seating now overflowed with boys, girls, youths and maidens, parents, grandfathers and grandmothers. The staff were left to stand around the edges. This added to the festive atmosphere of excitement and anticipation.

On the small raised stage, Googe appeared tall and imperious as Ulysses the king, and spoke with authority in Greek. Penelope, and the rest of the cast, spoke in Latin and, for the first act, the play was presented as a serious tableau. By alluding thus, to a high standard of artistic endeavour, they hoped to impress the governors. The play was fully narrated throughout in English by a competent fourth year boy to allow the understanding and enjoyment of all present. Ulysses and Penelope spoke of their love and the pain of his leaving to war, the length of their separation and his return uncertain. As the first act closes, one of Ulysses' friends appears with a gift for Penelope.

In the second act, the one hundred and eight suitors were represented by ten boys. This was achieved by the boys quickly interchanging parts of their costumes on stage: a coloured sash, the addition of a sword or a flute or a limp, a variation in the length of their toga, a switch of wigs, and a hunched back. The boys ran on stage as a relay, wooing Penelope, getting caught by Ulysses, then being tragically skewered or sliced open. This brought farcical humour into the room and the pealing laughter of all present. Especially the younger children when a tall ginger-haired scholar made an exaggerated and increasingly pained performance of dying, each of the six times he was caught.

'*Ne quaestrum,*' he protested, '*Mors ultra.*'

Googe appeared to lose some of his haughty composure as he ran around in his beggar's robe to catch his impish targets. All was contrived to entertain, which it did.

The last short scene, which had no basis at all in Homer's epic, was staged only by Mills and Googe and they played it with gravitas. Penelope in a debauched state of undress, realises Ulysses, now in his Centurion's tunic, has returned and has recognised her. She is mortified. She falls at his feet.

'*Ego fidelis,*' she cries, '*te amo, te amo.*'

Ulysses releases his stiletto from its sheath, pulls her up close to him and looks deep into her eyes as he slowly punctures her heart. There was silence as she falls.

'*Quid denim foci.*'

'*Te amo.*'

He kissed her softly, and for far too long thought Mills, and he then took his own.

An audible gasp and a pause, the audience, fuelled with wine and ale, stood and broke into enthusiastic applause. Some cheered and laughed despite the tragic ending. Mills and Googe regained life and the rest of the cast joined them to stand and face the crowded clapping room. The schoolmaster and some of the governors went onto the stage and shook Dr Hardie's and Googe's hand, they didn't know what to do with Mills, so he curtsied in their hesitation and the audience laughed again.

'Is it actually a girl? She's very comely.' *Soto voce.*

'No, I'm told it's one of the younger boys.'

'A bonnie lad!'

'Indeed, I'd have him in my bed.'

'Egbert, I fear you have had too much wine.'

The master then ended the proceedings with a short prayer and, thanking all present, wishing a good and peaceful Christmas to all. They were not to speed away but stay to enjoy the ale, wine and any food which had managed to escape the boys' infinitely capacious stomachs. Molly found David and gave him a big hug before she was called back to join the other servants by the housekeeper. She was wearing a blue-stoned necklace.

The next day normal life resumed. The effect of that day, that whole pre-Christmas week, would not be so fleeting in the life of one eleven-year-old boy.

CHAPTER 7

Cupar, Fife, Scotland 1732

C upar parish council did not have a meeting room; there was no Town Hall in the burgh. The council held their full meetings in the church; smaller assemblies, on specific issues, were held in the house of one of the members. David was called to Captain Birrell's house in Bonnygate, where he was invited to present his case. He was received at the door by a servant, who asked him to sit in the hall. It was a low-ceilinged dark house. There was no fire and the hall was candlelit even though the sun was at its peak. David sat for a while before being invited into a large dining room with heavy furniture; it was smoky from a fire that needed rekindling.

The twelve members present sat on three sides of a long dining table. The councillors, including Sir Peter and the minister, greeted him warmly and asked him to sit facing them. David had his papers in his hand. He preferred not to sit at a table for the meeting. In his limited experience, he found round-the-table meetings tended to be badly managed; decisions were made in advance of the forum and the meetings perfunctory. David hesitated, moved forward, and then stepped back.

'Mr Miller,' said the chair, 'according to item seven in our extended agenda, we invite you to state your case in support of your submitted proposal for changes in the school curriculum.'

'Thank you, Chair, if it does not offend the panel, I would prefer to stand to make my case.'

The Chair looked at the others; enough of them nodded in response.

'By all means.'

David walked to the side and threw his papers on the fire which flared and briefly lit the room. The light from the brief flame highlighted the expressions of puzzlement and surprise on the councillors faces.

'Thank you, gentlemen. I crave your indulgence and ask for a little patience as I take a few moments of your time.'

'As I walked from the schoolhouse through the marketplace to attend you today, I saw four young girls on the steps of the Cross. I found I knew two of them well and am acquainted with the families of the others. I know that these four God-fearing girls have bright minds and a curiosity regarding their world. They are kind, generous, hard-working, faithful and well-meaning,' he paused.

'Now, one of these girls can add up your tally faster than Napier's Bones, yet she cannot write a receipt.'

'A second can estimate the yield of five acres of corn, she can tell you when to sew and when to reap, yet she cannot read a bill of fare.'

'The third, gentlemen, can sing a song sweeter than any blackbird; you hear her in the parish church every week, yet she cannot read any words.'

'The fourth would like to write an invoice in French for her father, yet she cannot do this even in Scots nor English.'

'These girls and many akin to them, help their family businesses here in Cupar which make profit and contribute to our economy and our community, our church and our charity. We know this. You know this.' David paused again for effect.'

'I also know how we celebrate the birth of a son and plan a succession of progressive tasks, growing their abilities, knowledge and experience so the boys can play an important role in the business that will profit them, and you, in your old age.'

'But for your daughters, it is all too easy to accept that their job is different, restricted to menial tasks and to solely assist in the home,' David said, pausing again.

'Now a gentleman may say, well they will soon marry and leave their family to start one of their own.'

'Sirs, I say this, these girls, the ones I saw today, are ten years of age. They will not likely marry until near the age of twenty-five.'

'Gentlemen, there are fifteen years of untapped resource sitting at your table, every evening, at your fireplace, in your homes.'

'What if these same girls, your girls, could read your orders, write your invoices, calculate your taxes, what if they could keep your accounting books? What if they could write down the yield of your crops and tell you which field for corn and which for oats? What if they could read and write your business letters and learn from the details in the news sheets?'

'A gentleman may say, we have only one schoolroom and one teacher. I say, yes sir, let us change this.'

'Another gentleman may say, I still don't agree with supporting this. And I say this, I can see, sir, *you* are without daughters.'

David took a moment to allow the members to assimilate his points.

'Gentlemen, my proposal is simply this. I will start the school day for the boys one hour earlier than present. The boys schooling will not change apart from this timing. At three hours after noon, the school will provide three hours of teaching for girls. From the extra fees I will employ an additional teaching assistant. The girls will study reading, writing, grammar and accounts.'

'Sirs, that is the sum of it. I thank you again for your time and patience.'

Sir Peter stood before David could respond to the Chair's invitation to be seated. The Chair had no choice,

'Sir Peter has the floor.'

'I support this proposal without reservation or qualification and, I offer this. I will provide the sum of three hundred Merks towards the building of a second schoolroom under two conditions: it must be completed within the next calendar year and, the council or others must agree to fund any additional requirement before building starts. Would this be agreeable to you, Mr. Miller?'

'Indeed, such a generous donation would be of great benefit to the school and the town,' David replied.

This pre-emptive announcement caused an extended murmur from the panel. David responded to a few questions of clarification and was asked to take his leave.

'Thank you, Mr. Miller. You will be informed of the

Council's decision at a later date.'

David shook hands with the Chair and Sir Peter and left. He hurried back to the schoolhouse, arriving at four just to catch the boys being dismissed for the day. Mr Peter Rigg was still in the class talking to two of the older boys.

'Good afternoon. Any concerns, Mr Rigg?' David enquired on entering the schoolroom.

'None at all, the boys completed the arithmetic exercise and copied out the text as you prescribed. These two boys were asking me about the High School in Edinburgh.'

'Off you go, boys, I'll see you tomorrow.'

David thanked Peter who said he had valued the experience though he thought is unlikely he would end up teaching. Peter said he had a message for Rose, from Adeline, if he could pass it on.

'Of course, please come through to our sitting room.'

David ushered Peter through the hall, and he entered the room to find the three girls looking at the door in silence.

'Hello, now you must be Coraline and you Jessica. Is that correct?'

'Sir,' said Jess.

'Pleased to meet you both.'

'Rose, I have a message from my wayward sister, you are welcome to come to the house at eleven on Saturday.'

Rosie nodded and thanked him.

'Goodbye, girls.'

'Goodbye, sir,' they echoed as a trio.

As he closed the door, the girls were aching to burst but were held silent as David then came in.

'Girls, thank you very much for coming. Please do come again.'

David stood by the door while the girls thanked him and Rosie and wished Mrs Miller better health.

The days passed and Janett spent less and less time downstairs. In her lucid moments, she spent time with Rosie, not dealing with the books, just talking about growing up and how to look forward and not back. Janett insisted that Rosie went to Tarvit house to learn the piano and read with Adeline in the library whenever she was welcome. That she was fortunate to have the opportunity.

'When you do these things, Rose, it pleases me greatly even in my infirmity.'

But she was in pain and took laudanum to alleviate the suffering. In her waking periods, she was often confused. Rosie noticed that her father had difficulty in dealing with Janett's illness. He did all that was required practically but seemed lost as to express any sentiment or make any consideration for the future. He looked pale and unwell and spent a lot of solitary time in the classroom. He did not always answer clearly when Rosie asked for advice. This was very much out of character.

One Saturday in the late afternoon after lunch, piano and reading at the big house, Sir Peter said he would take Rosie back himself as he wanted to call in on David. Sir Peter's gig drew up outside the schoolhouse and Sir Peter asked Rosie to check with her father that he would be received. Rosie found her father in the schoolroom and her mother asleep upstairs. Rose spoke to her father, and David tidied himself up as best he could and asked Rosie to show Sir Peter to the school-room.

'David, thank you for seeing me. I bring news.'

'You are always welcome, Sir Peter.'

'How is Mrs Miller?'

'Not improving, alas. I do not think that she has much time with us.'

'I am so sorry.'

'We must carry on as best we can. Pray Sir, do you bring welcome news?'

'I do. The council has supported your proposition. You may enrol girls at the start of the next session. There was only one dissenter'

'John Melville?' David smiled.

'I can only say it was a gentleman with no daughters, but there is more. The council also agreed to underwrite any additional cost for the extension to the school building. There is a signed authority, you can start making plans. David, I see this is clearly not the time. Do not concern yourself with any of this at present, you must attend to your family. When you are ready, let me know and we can discuss how we proceed.'

'Thank you, Sir Peter, again, I am most grateful.'

Rosie, sunken and sobbing at the schoolroom door, managed to get to the scullery before the two men came out. It was not anything she did not know, but the hearing of it, removed all her hope.

The following Thursday, at the time of year when the early morning sun shone directly through her parent's bedroom window, Rosie sat on her mother's bed. Supported by a pillow, Janett managed to sit up and Rosie brushed her hair. The light's path was made solid by gilding the dust in the musty air, flickering as if carrying a message from the heavens. Rosie read awhile as her mother settled back and closed her eyes. Janett's breathing deepened, then faltered, and started again.

In a gasp, her body lurched.

'Mother, mother!' Rosie shook her gently then ran downstairs, straight into the schoolroom. As he looked to the door, David knew, and made to come.

'You stay with the class, Rose.'

'No, father.'

Janett's body was laid out in the sitting room for a day before her burial. There were many visitors to the house and more turned out for the short graveside service of committal on that dry, autumnal morning.

As the girls remained quiet under the chestnut tree, a tall, slender girl, elegantly dressed completely in black, except for the single white flower pinned to her coat, came from within the graveside mourners towards them. She bore a quiet, sad smile. Rosie had her back to her but as she got closer Jessie noticed her approaching and touched Rosie's shoulder,

'Rosie,' as she gestured for Rosie to turn around and look.

Rosie looked up.

'Adeline.'

Adeline consoled Rosie and hugged her, kissing each cheek.

'*Tres difficile cherie,* please come next week, if you can. Your papa will be invited too.'

'Thank you.'

Adeline turned back to join her father.

'She talks funny.'

'Not now Cora,' responded Jessie sharply.

David was humbled by the kindness of friends and strangers. As a relatively new teacher, he did not fully appreciate the reach of his schoolmaster's voice into the minds and the families of his charges. Rosie had been fully tending the house for a good number of weeks now. At the moment, she had so many offerings of help and food, she had less to do than before. Rosie and her father felt indebted to their community for the support. David continued in the classroom and Rosie tried again to tackle the books. David remained quiet but each day appeared to gain a little more strength in mind and body. One evening over supper, Rosie confessed.

'Father, I have been looking at the accounts but there is so much I don't know. I did not understand enough of what mother told me.' She stifled a tear. 'It is not the arithmetic. It is that I don't know what sums to put in the different columns in the ledger. They must add to the same total on both pages, you see. Only I don't'

'Don't worry Rose. I think we both lack that knowledge. As a young girl, your mother worked in my father's office. She learned her skills there.'

'Rose, I do not want you to sacrifice your life to the school and our housekeeping. If I did that, while pressing to bring girls into my school for education, it would be a fine example of irony.'

'Ever the teacher, father.' For the first time that week they both managed a small smile.

'You know how hard I need to work. It would be a lonely life for you in the house.'

'I will do it father, I don't mind.'

'Your mother would not endorse that opinion.'

Rosie knew he was right.

David recognised his daughter was beyond her years, and he resolved to be more open with her.

'We do not bring in enough in fees to employ someone. I also hoped to pay for you to go to the grammar school in Perth.'

'Leave you, father. No, never.'

'It is not very far, and you would come home at weekends. But you do not have to worry. On my stipend we do not have enough for it.'

'Are we going to Tarvit on Saturday?'

'I have school matters to discuss with Sir Peter. I think we should.'

Rosie and David adjusted their lives to these sad days. Rosie became more sanguine as she adhered to her mother's parting advice. David regained his health but looked pensive and worried much of the time. Jessie and Cora became regular afternoon visitors. They chose not to spend so much time at their perch on the Mercate steps. She had to accept her friends' questioning about the Tarvit, and especially to satisfy their curiosity about Adeline. As Adeline had appeared at the funeral, Rosie was unsure as to the matter of keeping confidence and her promise to her father. She did not want to bother her father and decided to give some details to Jessie and Cora.

'My father has many school meetings at the house, so I go with him. Adeline has a French mother, and she spends time away in London and France. When I visit, she helps me with piano lessons, but she is not allowed outside the grounds.'

The girls were more easily placated than Rosie had expected. Jess was now interested, not so much in Adeline, but her two striking brothers. The tall young men were occasional visitors to town and were admired by girls much older than Rosie and her two friends. Rosie fed them titbits which made them frustrated and beg for more. The three were pleased that Mr. Peter now addressed them all by name and would stop to talk if he passed them in town.

The journey to Tarvit was becoming routine for Rosie but her visits were anything but. Sir Peter was very glad they both came and suggested that the four of them took a walk in the estate before returning for late lunch. It was a day of summer in the midst of late autumn. A soft wind came from the west. Cirrus clouds rose, in anticipation of the warm front. The leaves of ash and chestnut trees were turning. There were cottars in the fields with scythes gathering the harvest. Two men, two girls and two dogs walked down from the house to the brook, crossing it on stones - precariously as far as the girls were concerned - on to boggy moorland to the sound of a curlew. Then up the Hill of Tarvit taking in the fine views to the west over the Bow and Collessie. The landscape was of low, round-topped hills sprinkled with sheep surrounding a flat, partially cultivated plain. In the distance they could see steady smoke rising from cottage chimneys. A copse obscured their view of the small town. David and Sir Peter walked together, and the girls scampered with the dogs until they tired and plodded behind, chattering incessantly unless interrupted by some natural curiosity they had uncovered.

'This is a welcome respite, Sir Peter, Thank you.'

'Just call me Peter, David. We are friends now, I think.'

'I wanted to talk to you about the school. I see you are still burdened. If I can help in any way.'

'A man must bear his own burdens.'

They walked quietly for a bit and Peter tried another tack.

'I am very sorry that I did not have the pleasure of meeting Janett. You met at university?'

'Not really, originally at school, it's a long story.'

'I thought you went to a boys' school.'

'Ah yes, but for two months one heady summer it wasn't. We lost touch after school. It was during a university break we met again. I found her working as a bookkeeper in the trading business where my father had practiced as a merchant. The business, originally owned by my grandfather, who had run it into debt, was recovered. I worked there to earn some money during the long vacation.'

'We attended the same church in Edinburgh. At first, I thought, in character, we were opposites. She was quiet, pragmatic and suffered no nonsense. Yet after church one Sunday she told me, didn't ask, told me to walk out with her.'

David breathed in deeply and Peter put his hand on his shoulder to indicate he need not continue.'

She firmed the ground which allowed me to fly and she produced this beautiful child.'

They walked on in silence.

'Your speech to the council made quite a stir, it was not what I expected.'

'Nor I.'

'I thought a strong case for Latin was your ambition

143

and intent.'

'As did I. That went with the papers into the fire.'

'So why the sudden change, if I may ask?'

'It was as I said, I genuinely foresaw the prospects of those four girls. It became more important for me then, to try to change *their* lives than to chase my selfish ambitions.'

'Perhaps it was a bit more than that,' David continued, 'As I thought about the position I was taking - the girls' productivity being an asset - I realised that I should view the boys in the same way. And that a thorough knowledge of Latin and Greek may inspire myself, but on its own, it will not bring prosperity, at least in the short term, to small communities like ours. We need a balanced syllabus to suit the majority.'

'We should talk more of this, David?'

'But the speech itself, it was unprepared?'

'Yes, you think it was overly dramatic?'

'Not at all, it was well aimed and on target.'

'It just comes out like that sometimes. I have spent many hours on stage at school and at university.'

'Ah.'

'I have been Caesar, Brutus, Caius, Hero, Achilles, even Penelope.'

'What! With one hundred suitors.'

'All one hundred and eight.'

'Hah, I would have paid to see that.'

Peter had found the key.

As they were reaching the top David spotted a craggy outcrop of rocks. Later, on reflection, he could not account for his next radical action. Being outdoors talking with good friends, the exhilaration of the setting and the climb, the partial release from months of tensions, the shock of his wife's death, the talk of his school acting days - a fleeting image of Molly, a combination of any or all these. He leapt the few steep steps and scrabbled up the rock to reach the top of the crag. He stood tall and looked down to Peter and the girls and adopted what he still thought of as Googe's imperious posture. He swirled his cloak up and around his front to his shoulder and raised his eyes to the horizon. The sharp sun dipped under a cloud and embossed his face.

> *Fiat sic Caesari. Brutus ille nobilis*
> *(So let it be with Caesar. The noble Brutus)*
> *Vobis dixit Caesarem avidum esse;*
> *(hath told you Caesar was ambitious;)*
> *Quod si verum esset, grave esset crimen,*
> *(If it were so, it was a grievous fault,)*
> *Cuius poenas graviter persolvit.*
> *(and grievously hath Caesar answer'd it.)*
> *Hic Bruto ceterisque permittentibus,--*
> *(Here, under leave of Brutus and the rest,--)*
> *Qui enim vir honestus est;*
> *(For Brutus is an honorable man;)*
> *Sic honesti sunt hi viri omnes,--*
> *(so are they all, all honorable men,--*
> *Veni ut funere Caesaris contioner.*
> *(come I, to speak in Caesar's funeral.).*

He stopped with a wry smile. Adeline and Rose, their attention now on him, sat and clapped.

'More papa, more please!'

'Si vous plait,' echoed Adeline.

David continued.

> *Ille mihi erat amicus, mihi fidelis et aequus:*

Quem vero vocavit Brutus avidum;
Et Brutus vir honestus est.
Multos captivos Romam duxit,
Quorum redemptiones aerarium impleverunt:
Num videtur Caesar ob hoc avidus?
Cum pauperes ploraverunt, flevit Caesar;
Aviditatem materiae durioris oportet esse.
Brutus autem illum avidum esse dicit.
Et Brutus vir honestus est.

'That's all I can remember,' he said taking a small bow and climbing down to their brief applause.

'Is that French, father?'

'No, Rose.'

'Mark Anthony, I think.'

'Yes, at the funeral of Caesar.'

'The translation?'

'At school. That's why I can remember it.'

David rebuffed the girl's continued questioning, and they all began the descent.

'A well-deserved lunch, I think.'

The girls started to mimic the actions of David's performance to each other, making up the words. David and Peter walked down together.

'You sir, are not made for building schools, balancing books nor teaching trigonometry and trades.'

'It is my duty and my obligation to you.'

'You had the girls transfixed, yet they knew naught of what you speak.'

'You were born to do that,' continued Sir Peter pointing back up at the crag.

'A tragedian?'

'Hah. No, I am no judge of that.'

'You inspire the young, they are receptive in your

hands. You hold their attention with but a few words, you entice, entrance and excite them. You have the power to open young minds.'

'You praise me too highly, Peter.'

'Look to the stars David, not to the ground.'

As they returned to the house, Adeline complained of starvation.

'Hunger,' corrected Rosie with a frown.

'Your daughter is a good influence on mine.'

A carriage had arrived and was sitting outside the house.

'I have invited John Anderson to lunch with us again, I hope you don't mind.'

'Not at all, I enjoy the company of you both. You have known him for some time?'

'We go back many years and we share many interests. He is a first cousin of Isobel Oswald of Dunnikier. Their families became close after the death of her husband around fifteen years ago. They shared a passion for advancement and education in our communities.'

'Ah.'

'Isobel Oswald is sponsoring the new grammar school in Kirkcaldy. I think we, you and I that is, could benefit from their experience.'

'Indeed, that sounds most valuable.'

On entering the house, they were aided by a footman and a maid in the removal of boots and cloaks – an action, like many others, that reduced the hopping girls to giggles; having come in from the cold, their cheeks tingled in the heat of the fire in the hall. Both men smiled at their antics. Peter allowed the girls to go upstairs until the lunch bell was rung and asked David if he would mind waiting in the library while he sought out his friend, Anderson. David was glad of the opportunity to relax and look at the wealth of books Peter kept in the house. There were many religious texts, British and European history, military references, a series of Roman and Greek classics, but the dominant theme was one of travel and adventure in other countries; the names of some, David did not recognise. A servant brought warm wine and the apologetic message that Sir Peter would be a few minutes longer. Peter and John entered the room; their demeanour indicated that they had been in a serious discussion, which was curtailed on their arrival. John Anderson greeted David warmly, shaking his hand, and passed on his condolences. The three sat at the fire and John asked about David's ambitions for Cupar's parish school while they all took a glass of wine. David was relaxed in their company but was guarded in his response. The support of Peter as a friend and an ally on the council was immensely important to him, but he felt he had barely had time after Janett's passing to fully appraise his professional and family situation. There was so much to be done and without Janett's practical, and emotional, support he sensed it was not going to be easy for him to achieve what was expected. He valued the trust that Sir Peter, and now the council, had placed in him and did not want to disappoint. For the first time in his adult life, he felt the tremors of doubt in his own capability.

A footman entered to say that cook had prepared lunch and Peter instructed him to ring the bell for the others. David remarked that this reminded him of his own school days. The girls and the two Rigg boys joined them and David's comments led to some questioning about his schooldays. Rosie was envious of her father's

148

experiences of which she realised she knew little. Adeline said she was glad that it was something that she did not have to endure. The girls were curious though, about boarding in the school and staying with others in dormitory accommodation. David did not want to bring attention to his personal experiences and so told the tale of his school's dog.

The Heriot's Foundationer boys had a collie, they named Patch, he believed, which lived in the yards of *Heriot's Hofpital* and was looked after by the boys. The dog became quite well-known around Edinburgh and was made – by reason and means unknown to David - an honorary councillor of the town. This was all very amusing to the boys and, as it was commonly known and reported, the general public. That was until there was an important legal case which involved the Duke of Argyll. The Duke refused to take the *Test of Oath*: a test of allegiance to the crown, required of all public officials. The Duke's defence was that not all public officials had taken the oath; their legal precedent... Patch, the dog. The Duke's lawyers said the dog could not hold the office of councillor, unless it could take an oath. The boys, and indeed the Crown's lawyers tried in vain, using a variety of inventive ways using bones, biscuits and meat, to show that the dog had indeed agreed to uphold the law and obey the queen. Of course, it couldn't. Sadly, the dog ended up being tried for being *in breach of office*. The poor mutt was convicted of high treason and condemned to death by hanging. Fortunately, the Duke's fate was not so final. The case had gained so much public attention that the Crown decided not to further pursue the Duke in the matter. John, Peter and the boys, were entertained by David's tale; the girls were left bemused and unamused.

At the end of the convivial lunch, Sir Peter invited the girls and his sons to withdraw and said that he, David and John would join them shortly.

'Girls, perhaps you might prepare a small entertainment.'

The three men remained at the table. The butler brought port and cheese and David saw Peter give John a nod – *of permission?* – to open a conversation. David was puzzled rather than suspicious. These men had always been openly generous and supportive to him and his family.

'David, Peter has mentioned the new school we are building in Kirkcaldy'

'Yes, in passing.'

'I sit on the burgh council, but my cousin is the real driving force. The requirement is for a much larger building than the present school. Kirkcaldy will soon have three times the current cohort. The town is thriving with the growth in the linen industry.'

'Perhaps you would like to visit and see the plans?'

'That is kind John, but I don't quite see–'

'–and practically I'm confined to Cupar until the next school break.'

'Well to be clear, I would value your perspective on the plans. A fresh pair of eyes is warranted. There is more...Peter has related an impression of you to my cousin and she is keen to receive you.'

David looked to Sir Peter for his reaction.

'David, there is no obligation on you to do this– '

'Sir, it's just the timing. Normally I would be honoured and delighted.'

'Do take time, but if you could give it some consideration. Young Peter could mind the school for a day and Rosie, as you know, is always welcome here.'

At that they joined the girls. Adeline and Rosie had prepared a short piano recital and sang two hymns for the men's appreciation. The pieces were solemn and affecting in the circumstances.

It was early evening when David and Rosie climbed into the carriage to be conveyed back to the schoolhouse. It hit them hard when they realised, they were not going home to tell the tales of their day to Janett. Rosie could no longer hold it in and openly cried. David did his best to comfort her. Later that night, for the first time, he sat on his daughter's bed and read her a story as she drifted off to sleep. As, later still, he tried to find his own sleep, he could find little comfort in thinking of the days ahead.

CHAPTER 8

Campveere & Delft 1710

F ive months earlier, Joseph did not hesitate to accede to James Lockhart's request to return to Delft to find out what had happened to Tom. As the Lockhart family business struggled to clear its debt, Joe was working all hours to help his employer for a very small remuneration. His wages were drastically reduced; the promised rise, unfulfilled. Joe's own growing family were in want of new clothing and existed on basic provisions. Joe had raised the issue with James.

'We cannot leave it too long, sir.'

His willingness to go back was not entirely altruistic. The trade in the Delft porcelain he transported on his return voyage from Campveere had been brisk and he received several demands for the business to supply more. Tom's father-in-law's business could no longer raise funds to support a second voyage. Even if it had, Joe knew now that the effort would only serve to service a debt that was not his own. One of the porcelain buyers had approached Joe discreetly and offered to underwrite a second voyage if Joe would act on his behalf. Joe would be paid expenses plus a percentage of the margin. Joe had not mentioned this to James.

'Sir, I can work my passage if you will pay my wage to my family while I am absent. A small trade in linen would cover my lodgings and travel.'

James verbally agreed but agreed and disagreed much these days and was unaware of it the next day. Tom's father-in-law was often absent and rarely stayed in the office long enough to accomplish anything of purpose. Joseph bade him sign some papers to cover his request and began to make the arrangements.

And so, Joe departed again on, he hoped, a profitable venture sailing to Campveere, this time with his own junior clerk, Ruud, in search of Tom. It was May. He had found a larger ship than *The Reward* and sailed in a Dutch merchant convoy. The North Sea crossing was smooth and trouble-free, a contrast to his earlier journey, though he missed the stimulation of the lonely, rolling ship in the storm. Having not gone down with *The Reward,* he believed he possessed God's indemnity from a similar fate. His junior had a Dutch grandmother and a smattering of the language but had not previously ventured from Scotland.

Joe warmed to the sight of the dock at Veere, the sounds and smells sparking memories of his earlier visit. He wanted to trade the linen here in the port, then move on quickly to Delft to purchase porcelain and seek news of Tom. He found a room for them both in the lodgings where he and Tom had stayed before. They dropped their baggage and made for the nearby inn. Joe talked to some Scottish sailors in faint hope of gaining information. No-one remembered a well-spoken dark-haired Scotsman with a delicate cargo of paintings. The evening was entertaining, the food good, and they enjoyed the bier and music provided by locals and sailors.

Walking back to the lodging just after ten, Joe and Ruud came across three men standing around a woman arguing. They recognised her from the inn. They walked past but when Joe looked round, he saw the men physically assaulting the woman to her apparent distress.

'Hang on, Ruud.'

Joe was a large, strong, red-headed, and occasionally hot-headed, Scotsman. He walked up to the woman who looked at him directly showing her discomfort, and he pulled her to come with him, away from the men.

One of the men shouted at him and moved to take her back. As Joe pushed her toward Ruud who was standing back, the man took a swing at Joe and missed. Joe put his hands up open-palmed hoping to indicate he wanted no trouble. But the first man moved forward and took another swing. Joe threw a well-aimed punch which connected, and the man fell. The other two moved forward quickly and aggressively. Joe swung at the nearest one, but it was only a glancing blow. He pushed the third away forcefully and traded blows with the second. Ruud reached into his bag. The woman moved to join in, and Ruud pulled her back and went back to his bag. He gave the woman Joe's satchel and nodded at it. Joe was handling the two, but the felled man got up from the ground and picked up a metal bar, a discarded wagon lever. Joe did not reach for his dagger; he did not want to wound or escalate what he considered to be no more than a sailor's brawl. The man with the bar came quickly and hit Joe's leg from behind. Joe went to the ground, glad that it wasn't his head. But he was down now and all three started kicking and kicking hard. One stopped and looked to see the where the woman was.

'Run!' Ruud said to the woman, but she wouldn't go.

Ruud finished loading his pistol as the woman started loading Joe's gun. Ruud shouted a warning and fired the shot in the air. The other two men stopped and looked at him. The woman passed Joe's pistol and took the spent one from him to reload. He shouted aggressively at the men in Dutch and pointed the pistol, taking a military stance. The men looked at each other and backed away. He moved towards Joe who was still on the ground. The woman gave Ruud his gun back and ran to Joe.

Joe was conscious and saying he was alright. The woman seemed to be scolding him in Dutch. Ruud kept the gun up until the men were well out of sight. Joe was up on one good leg and leaning on the woman. His face was a mess and the leg that took the blow was weak, not broken he thought.

'We should go back to the inn,' said Ruud.

With the woman supporting Joe, Ruud put the guns away and the three made their way back. It was quieter now and Ruud ordered biers while the woman and Joe took a table at the back. Joe and Ruud sat with their back to the door, the woman faced it. No-one appeared to notice them. Joe and the woman did not have a common language, but they managed to establish their names. Grietje did manage to say in English, 'Thank you. Thank you,' placing her hand lightly on his good knee. She found a maid and brought back a tankard of water and started to clean Joe's face with a cloth from her pouch. She looked up as the inn door opened and grabbed them both, pulling.

'*Kijk niet.*'

'*Op deze manier.*'

'*Volgen.*'

They made their way up a number of steps to a back door.

'*Soldaten*'

'Soldiers,' said Ruud to the limping Joe.

Joe looked at Ruud for an explanation but he just shrugged. Both agreed they should follow.

'*Ik woon vlakbij.*'

'She lives somewhere close by.'

Ruud's latent Dutch was coming back to him. They went along the back street, up a narrow alley and into a close. Up one flight of stairs, Grietje opened the door to her room. Once inside, she pushed a heavy bolt to secure the door and lit two candles from the fire. It was a surprisingly large room. A large table by the tall single window was cluttered with pottery, paintings, paper, pens, ink, plus an untidy ensemble of the evidence of everyday living. Books and boxes were strewn on the floor. There was an unkempt bed in one corner. The fading fire included a cooking rack. There was a small table and two chairs, two other comfortable chairs and two stools. The small table had a vase with fresh, yellow flowers at its centre.

'*Zitten,*' and she escorted Joe to the armchair by the fire and put two logs on to revive the warmth.

'Sit,' said Ruud to Joe with a smile.

'Yes, I get it. Can you ask her why we had to leave?

'*Waarom zijn we weggelopen?*'

Grietje said she saw two soldiers and an official entering the bar. It was the pistols. Guns are not allowed within the town boundaries. The punishment is harsh. She thought that was what they were looking for.

'*Zijn we hier veilig?*'

'*Ja, de herbergier zal ons niet verraden.*'

Ruud explained to Joe that Grietje had acted to avoid any involvement with the officals and that they were safe in her room. Griet put a kettle of water on to heat and continued to clean Joe up. Ruud told her that they were traders from Scotland, selling linen, buying porcelain. Grietje finished attending to Joe and continued to talk but did not volunteer much about herself. When they looked over at Joe, he had fallen hard asleep.

'*Hij kan hier blijven. Je kunt gaan.*'

'*Zeg ik met hem.*'

So Ruud stayed with Joe and tried to sleep in the other armchair. Grietje made them both a dilute coffee then, turning her back, took her outer dress off and went to sleep under a blanket in her cot in the corner. Ruud slept quite well. He was aware of Grietje checking on Joe during the night.

Joe woke with a start and a shout, at first light, that woke them all up. Grietje went out for bread and returned promptly. She produced the warmed bread, made from a sweet dough, with coffee and cheese for their breakfast. Joe looked terrible and they both laughed at him. The blood had stopped but the bruises covered most of hs face. Grietje seemed knowledgeable as she checked him for broken bones. The three sat at the small table and talked in a mix of Dutch and English so they all could understand. She, once again, said how grateful she was for their intervention and they relived the experience for comic relief. Ruud asked Grietje,

'How did you load Joe's pistol so quickly?' mimicking the action.

'Joe's pistool?'

'After I had fired in the air.'

'Het spijt me, het is me niet gelukt, het is niet geladen.'

'She said she's sorry she did not manage, it was not loaded.'

There was a long pause before they laughed. Grietje said she would go out to make sure they were not being sought. After a while, she returned and said that the soldiers had been looking for the source of a shot, but there was no victim. The report was only half believed, so they did not pursue the matter much further. Nobody is looking for two unfamiliar Scotsmen.

'Apart from three sore robbers!' said Ruud.

'We must leave you and return to our lodgings.'

Griet nodded and helped them collect their things. As they bade her goodbye, she said she was a good cook and asked them to come to sup that same evening. They agreed, offering some payment.

'Nee, breng gewoon wat wijn.'

Joe still needed to rest. He was also very aware that the sight of him would cause interest and questions which he did not want to answer. He sent Ruud off to get a price for the linen and make arrangements for them to travel by *schuyt* to Delft the day after next. Staying away from the inns and coffee shops, then leaving the area seemed a good plan. As Ruud was leaving, Joe said,

'You did well last night, lad.' Ruud was only nineteen, 'I thank you.'

Ruud nodded in acknowledgment and replied, 'I'm glad you are not badly hurt. You did a good thing.'

Grietje was between thirty and forty years, it was hard

to tell. She was tall, slim and moved with poise. Ruud said she spoke with an educated accent and her clothes were worn but well made. She was clearly not the street girl they had first, ashamedly now, assumed her to be. They were but curious about her and hoped to find out more over supper.

Ruud received offers for their linen. They were not high, but he knew that the markets were low and that the purchase price of the pottery should also be low. Trawling the market, he found a carved, African, ebony walking stick and a black leather eye-patch for Joe so that he did not look so much like a losing boxer. Joe was glad to see him returned.

'Now I just look like a pirate.'

'Well, you'll fit in perfectly around here.'

They returned to Grietje's room in the evening. Joe's leg was stiff, and he felt the bruising on his face and body. Grietje had prepared a meal of pork, pickled herring, onions, cabbage and bread. Ruud had brought a flagon of wine and an open jug of bier. They found that Grietje knew some English and they managed conversation with only the odd misunderstanding. Joe asked about the paintings and pottery and Grietje said she was a painter, but there was little money in it these times, and she hand painted patterns for the porcelain houses. The grand families wanted individual patterns, often of their own houses or ships. She had a good reputation and did well enough out of it. She also painted commissioned portraits, but seascapes and landscapes were what she loved painting. Joe was very interested and asked about the porcelain and how long the patterning process took.

'So, if I brought etchings from Scotland, you could

put them on dinner plates and bowls?'

'*Ya*, just that.'

Grietje asked about their plans and Joe told the tale of his earlier visit, and the sunken ship and lost employer.

'You look him?'

'I will look, yes, when we have finished our business.'

Ruud asked why she thought the men had attacked her. Grietje said they may have mistaken her for a street girl, but it was odd that they were so forceful and violent. She reassured them that it was not common in Veere. She did not think the men were Dutch or Scots, probably visiting sailors from the east. They talked on about their families and life in Edinburgh and Joe said he needed to go to rest, but Ruud should stay for longer. It was only just after nine. Ruud looked at Grietje and she nodded. Joe reassured them that he would be fine going back on his own; it was a short walk. He fell on his bed without undressing and slept. Joe roused faintly when Ruud came back just as he heard the harbour bell chime five. As Joe fell back to sleep, Tom and Doortje appeared in his dreams.

They rose on six bells and boarded a sailing barge to Delft. It was a slow, coastal journey a full day and one-night stop. The early sun shone through a lightly clouded sky. The sea was calm and, as the day began and the air above the water became hazy. Only a soft wind, which occasionally lifted the single sail, stopped them from becoming becalmed. The schuyt, sensitive only to tidal movements, drifted. Joe and Ruud languished on jute sacks of wool in the soporific warmth of the midday sun, one body recovering from evil the other from love.

Later, the haze became a light fog. Joe was unaware of it until he opened his uncovered eye to the forlorn toll of a single bell. Joe looked to the master who told him it was the harbour bell at Brouwershaven. They had rounded the breakwater before you could see the quay. The *schuyt* nudged the high harbour wall as a port-hand tied the mooring ropes. The master and the mate started to unload sacks of grain onto the quay where a merchant was waiting to load them on to his cart. Joe kicked Ruud awake with his good leg to assist in the unloading. The merchant had a flagon of ale, which he passed around, and they took refreshment before setting off. The fog had not lifted, but the master said that the wind would rise around four and push it out to sea. The *schuyt* would arrive at Helvoetsluys before moonrise and they would moor there overnight. The next day was fresh and they made good speed for a barge. Maesland was sighted during the late afternoon and the *schuyt* found the canal entrance at Delfshaven as if it knew the way. At the end of the canal, Delft came into view, lit by the late evening sun. Its three distinctive towers, Nieuwe Kerck, Oude Kerck and der Stadhuis rose above the raspberry-red roof-tops guardedly cloaked by the madder town walls. A windmill marked the south-west corner of the wall's boundary.

They berthed outside the town wall at de Hooft, near St Jacob's Poort; Joe and Ruud paid and thanked the master. Joe agreed to send a message to the Master as to when they would return with, he hoped, a cargo of porcelain Delftware.

'You'll like it here, Ruud, not so many Scotsmen.'

They found convenient lodgings in Molstrat, a lane between the food and grain markets. Joe was reluctant to stay in the lodgings where he and Tom had previously been welcome. He and Ruud would complete their business before he tried to trace the movement and whereabouts of Tom. He felt sure that Doortje and her mother must know or would have heard something, but he wanted to tread carefully in what might be a sensitive matter. He was also concerned that his present appearance might cause fright on the door knock of an unannounced visit.

'Come, Ruud, let us leave our bags here and enjoy the evening air before enjoying a meaty supper.'

Ruud had been quiet since leaving Veere. Joe saw his mind was elsewhere and he was quite sure where that was. There were many people on the streets visiting the inns and coffee houses. The street traders were having a good day. Joe and Ruud walked round the churches and along the canal paths to reach the north wall. There they found open fields and a narrow waterway inside the wall which they took, in a circuitous route, to get back to the Grote Merckt at the front of der Stadhuis. They tried an inn with a good mix of young, old, male and female customers, but they were not welcomed, so they opted for one nearer de Kolk which hosted predominantly older males.

The following day was a business day. They were up early and breakfasted at a *Koffiehuis*; their lodging provided bed only. Joe told Ruud he needed him sharp and that he would lead the trading negotiations. Joe had brought porcelain samples from his Edinburgh sponsor with instructions to find bowls, dishes and jugs, of quality, in a similar style: thin, cobalt blue lines, Chinese decoration, in a translucent white glaze. A few had been broken in transit. Joe had relied on Tom's taste on his prior venture and did not have Tom's confidence nor experience in these matters. They spent the day viewing goods at the markets. Ruud passed on Grietje's comment that for a large order they would be best to deal directly with the potteries themselves. She gave a few recommendations. There were a few potteries in the town, but most were outside the walls. The next few days were spent travelling, reviewing the trade-offs between volume, quality, type, prices, style and decoration.

They hired a driver and cart to take them around. He was a quiet, old fellow, but after giving him a good tip on the first day, he became a font of useful information on the second, which they took at face value. Joe and Ruud got into the routine and Joe's language improved considerably. He asked about supplying his own artist and some of the factories they visited reduced the price significantly for this option. It took a further day to sit down and review the prices and the options for his budget. Joe set down a plan. Two thirds of the purchase would be of Delft blue porcelain of medium quality, mostly with Chinese decoration or scenes and the others with sea or pastoral scenes. These had to be robust enough to travel and use. The artwork had to be attractive but need not be the best. It would take a trained eye to spot the difference. The remaining third would be lower quality and in blue, red or grey-brown tones. Remembering Tom's approach, Joe would also purchase a few high-value items of the best quality and hope they could be transported whole.

The actual trade would be more difficult. Outside Campveere their Scots notes of bearer payment were not accepted. Joe realised how Janssen that been instrumental in the previous visit in arranging the finance for the transactions. Without him they would have to go back to the bank in Campveere to make arrangements. He was going to call on Janssen in any case to enquire about Tom, so he thought he would see if he would again assist in the trade. Joe sent a short note of enquiry to Janssen that evening, saying simply that Tom had not returned to Scotland and he wanted to trace his last movements in Delft. He did not mention the current business problem. At noon the next day, there was no response to the note from Janssen, so he decided to visit. Joe had hidden most of his bruised face by growing a beard, but it made him look more like a pirate than ever. He dressed as smartly as he could. He hadn't met Janssen previously, but he had met van Reit and mentioned this in his message.

Taking Ruud with him, the two men walked to Janssen's house and knocked on the door. A maid answered and closed the door. After five minutes or so, a young man came to the door and said that Janssen was not available. Ruud spoke in his best Dutch to explain, but the young man cut him off with an unconvincing apology that he could not help and closed the door. That evening, while having a bier after supper, Joe told Ruud to go back to Veere and raise a letter of credit or exchange Scots for Dutch notes from the Scottish Bank. He should travel there by horse for speed, but if he was to return with notes he must sail as it would be more secure. Joe would use the time to try to find out more about Tom. Ruud brightened considerably.

'Ruud, it may not have meant anything.'

'Pardon?'

'To her, I mean. 'I'm saying that the women are different here. They have more freedom. You must not think that you will be welcomed in the same way.'

'But...'

'Just think on what I say. By all means visit, but do not expect. If you get my meaning,' advised Joe.

'How do you know what I...'

'I know when a dog gets the scent,' Joe continued, 'in the future I may need her artistic skills.'

'Oh, why, what have you in mind?'

'Let us complete our trade first. I will tell you more when we embark for Scotland. And we will embark for Scotland, the two of us together no matter what - else your grandmother will surely kill me!'

It was not as straightforward a journey as Joe had hoped. He could not obtain a horse for Ruud without the surety. He saw now, that Tom had arranged matters on the earlier visit more carefully than he had understood; he wished he had paid more attention to the practical details. He had also been in a job for years where he had not made any key decisions. He had kept the books and followed orders. He knew Tom well, however, and had learned to think calmly through difficult situations. Further enquiry found that they could obtain a horse for the trip, provided Ruud was escorted. The escort would then return with the horse, with or without Ruud. The other option was the mail carriage, which was not any quicker than the *schuyt*. The Stable accepted the Scottish money. Transactions within Veere were common enough for them to know they would be honoured. Joe could cover this expense with the funds he had with him.

Ruud set off with the horse and an amiable escort. It did mean he would return quickly. Joe supped alone that night and became concerned about the cost. The arrangement with his sponsor, Edward James Clerk, was that reasonable expenses would be covered, but would that take account of errors he had made. He was offered a percentage of the profit, twenty five percent, what was the estimated profit? He had no idea. How would he know the market price? He did not even know where Clerk intended to sell the goods. The money he got for the linen was lower than he hoped. That profit was to cover his wage and passed on to his family during his absence. He did have a good sum to purchase the porcelain and his sponsor would honour their agreement. Joe had no worry on that score. Clerk, a burgess of the town, was an honourable man, so are they all, honourable men.

As Ruud was away, Joe had time to enquire about Tom. He had been so engrossed with the business, and distracted by the assault, that he had all but forgotten his reason for coming, not just for Tom's family but for his own sake. Joe rose to go to the *postkantoor* to send a letter to Ruud in Veere, care of the *Conciergerie*. He had arranged with Ruud that they both do this every day. A reply using the fastest message service should take no more than two days.

He took breakfast at the *koffiehuis* and went carefully though the figures, using estimates, to reassure himself and get a good measure of the finances. Joe decided to start his quest for Tom by approaching Janssen again. Rather than knock at the door he waited near the house in hope that he would appear. An elderly gentleman would normally take a walk after breakfast on a fine day. Nearly two hours passed before the door opened. An old man with a cane, well-dressed, upright, not crouched, came down the steps walked the path in a direction away from Joe. The street was otherwise empty. Joe limped as quickly as he could to catch him.

'*Pardon Meneer.*'

Janssen turned to look at him.

'*Ga weg, ga weg!*'

'*Meneer Janssen, Ik vraag om wat tijd.*' Joe had rehearsed the words.

'Away, I said!' Janssen had seen through his accent.

As Joe kept approaching, Janssen pulled a long dagger from his cane.

'I warn you, sir, you will not be the first.'

Joe stopped and put up his hands to indicate no threat.

'I am sorry, sir, I mean no harm.' Joe withdrew.

He went to an inn and sat at an outside table with a small bier. *Not a good start, Joe,* he thought. He decided to go to the previous lodgings, but first the barber and a shave. The only other option was to try to find the house on the polder where they had stayed that first night. He did not know where it was nor could he remember their host's name. He thought he would recognise the house and knew roughly where it was, but would the reception be any different from this morning?

Walking by the Oude Kerck toward their previous lodging triggered memories of his prior stay there, fond memories of Tom and Doortje. Another house, another tentative door knock. He took off his eye patch before the door opened. A maid he did not recognise answered. Joe asked for Doortje in English. The maid ushered him in to wait in the hall and went toward the kitchen. Doortje's mother appeared and was brusque with him.

'Sir, we have no accommodation.'

'Ma'am, it is Joe, I apologise for my appearance, an accident. I have lodged with you. I was here with Tom Miller.'

'Sir, I have many guests. I have no rooms.'

'I wish only to ask about Doortje.'

'She is no longer here.' She turned, asking the maid to show Joe out. She watched him go to the door. Joe faked a stumble at the door, dropping his stick and pretended to struggle to rise. He allowed the maid to assist.

'Where is Doortje?' he whispered to the maid offering the largest Dutch note he could pull out of his wallet. She grasped for it, looking around. Joe held it back, 'Where?'

'Monster' she said softly.

Joe was shocked and kept the note. The maid's face dropped.

'Doortje at grandmother house, Monster.'

Joe gave her a smaller note and quickly left. He felt defeated. Did he deserve this abuse? He had no chance of finding out about Tom if no one would engage with him. He tried to remember more about Doortje. Was there anyone else he could talk to? He was running out of options. He would sup in an inn nearby tonight and ask or bribe the staff or any willing locals. He went to the church in the late afternoon. A boys' choir was practising. Sitting for a good hour, his balance restored, he went to check the post and found a note from Ruud. The message said that Ruud had arrived safely and did not think there would be a problem with the money. He hoped to get back to Delft, on a small sailing boat, later the next day. Joe's spirits lifted. He wrote a longer note to Janssen with an apology for accosting him in the street and a fuller explanation of his mission to find out about Tom for his family's sake. One last try, he thought, as he gave the message to the boy to deliver. He found a small inn at the corner of Papenstraat and Choorstraat which served a good pie. Neither the staff nor the locals would enter into a dialogue. He offered the serving wench some money, but she was not local. An Englishman, of similar age to him, approached his table.

'We are the only two British here tonight, I think.'

'Indeed, sir.'

'May I sit?'

'Please do.'

'Scottish?'

'Edinburgh, and you?'

'London.'

'Trading, in porcelain perhaps?'

Joe nodded, 'and you?'

'I'm a water engineer, canals and harbours mainly.' The man paused. 'The Dutch are well ahead of us in their designs and structures. I am here to learn and recruit if I can.'

'William, but Henry,' and he offered his hand.

'Joseph, but Joe.'

The two men quickly continued the talk. Henry was confident and well spoken. Joe suspected he was of landed heritage. He had been to the Low Countries twice before. Most of his business was in Rotterdam and Amsterdam, but he always included a visit to Delft particularly to look at paintings. Joe reserved his conversation to his porcelain trading initially. Henry was very interested in the Scottish Staple at Campveere.

'I do see the opportunities you have for good trade therein.' He was not in trade, but he did offer assistance, if Joe required any, on the completion of his transaction.

Joe asked Henry 'What do you think of the demand for blue porcelain is in the London market?'

'I think that you have hit a good seam there, Joe. Oriental designs and patterns are the fashion, I believe, but do not trust my word, it is only an engineer's opinion.'

Joe then spotted a bottle of whisky on a shelf behind the bar. Henry admitted, on occasion, he enjoyed a *wee dram*. Joe, glad of the company, saw no harm in sharing the tale of his earlier visit with Tom and ended by telling of his morning's experience.

'She said what?'

'Monster.'

Henry smiled to Joe's frown. 'Pray, tell me exactly what you asked and what she replied.'

Joe did.

Henry could not stop laughing to talk.

Joe was unnerved by this response. 'What is it, sir, what?'

'*Monster* is a small village on the west coast,' trying to suppress his smile.

'No, you tease me, sir.'

'No sir, I assure you.'

'More whisky, I think,'

'*Meisje, de fles!*'

They sat until they were the last two customers in the house. The Honourable William 'Henry' Egerton offered Joe his card. Joe offered him his full name and the Edinburgh business address which, taking out a small silver pen case with its own small bottle of ink, Henry wrote down in a well-used notebook before they parted. They agreed to meet again before either left. Henry was keen to know if Joe would find out what had happened to his colleague.

Joe had never talked at length to a member of the gentry before. They were referred to in reverential terms by the merchants. His conversations with Edward Clerk were business-like and perfunctory, as master to servant. And yet here was one, happy to sit in the inn and talk openly and respectfully to Joe. It might have been the drink, but Henry behaved like an ordinary, agreeable man.

Joe slept late the next morning, more at ease than he had been for a while, then *koffiehuis* and *posthuis,* his new routine. A message from Ruud confirmed his expected return later that day. Joe hired a cart with driver and took the two-hour journey to Monster. As they neared the village, the fields were marsh not meadow, more water than land. The coast was not a single line marking the end of *terra* and the beginning of *aqua,* the land just got lower and lower until it became sea. There was clearly a living from it, each raised bit of land supported a house or hamlet, most with roped poles with hanging nets.

Monster was not much more than a village. It was based on the site of an old monastery; there had been no Leviathan. Surrounded by marshland and the sea, there were three raised houses, each with two floors on top of an animal shelter, an old stone church, and a number of smaller cottages. Next to the sea there were two workshops, a number of sheds and several upturned boats raised on the breakwater. A few boats were moored, others anchored in a bay. The detritus of the fisherman and his trade lay haphazardly in disorderly bundles. It was a calm place, not a hive of industry. Joe had the cart stop at the harbour. The only sounds were the wash of sea, the haunting cry of the curlew and faint voices of children. He saw that one of the nearby cottages was an inn, there were men, with the timeless faces of lives spent at sea, drinking on a bench outside. Any movement he made was observed. He told the driver to take refreshment if he wished.

Joe spotted several children playing in the street by the larger houses and he walked toward them. He was keen to avoid approaching another stranger in the street or any intrusive questions from proprietorial locals. '*Hei, Doortje huis?*' he asked the tallest girl. She turned and pointed to the house at the end of the three raised buildings. He slowed his walk, there was no going back. Joe had shed his cane, but the leg still ached. The first-floor, house door was accessed by a wooden stair from the track. He tapped gently on the door and waited.

'Hello, god...Joe, oh!' Doortje put her hand to her mouth, 'What has happened to you?'

The softness of her voice, the touch of her hand on his cheek. No barriers, tension, aggression or fear, just the welcoming voice of a friend. Joe was aware of his eyes filling. He stumbled and found it difficult to find the right words.

'Come in, Joe, come in. It's so good to see you. I don't have much to offer. Some bread and herring, a cup of ale.'

Joe nodded as he accepted the seat offered at the kitchen table. 'It was difficult to find you, I'm glad to find you well.'

Before she could respond, Joe said firmly, 'Doortje, have you heard anything from Tom? Do you know what happened to him?'

Doortje's demeanour changed.

'Joe, no. He has not written,' anxious now, 'Please tell me, what has happened?'

'He did not arrive back in Scotland.'

'What, when? I mean, from here in November?'

'Yes, I haven't seen him since I left here.'

'*O mijn God.*'

Doortje started to ask questions, but Joe had no answers. Joe apologised for being sharp and told her of his difficulties. Doortje sat silently for a moment, then told of her grandmother and that she stayed here to look after her. 'You adapt to the quiet life,' she said.

It was cooling as the sea air moved inland. Doortje took Joe through to a pleasant sitting room with a view through two large windows to the sea. She lit the fire and made some coffee. Joe sat in a leather armchair. There were books in English and another language in a small bookcase. A few small paintings of boats and seascapes hung on the wall. There was a table with paper and pens plus the tools of needlework.

He looked up when she brought the coffee in, she was beautiful; she looked radiant. Their talk was subdued. Doortje brought up Tom's family. 'How is the boy... and his wife?' Joe did not want to say too much. Doortje was concerned as to their welfare. Joe assured her that the boy was doing well - starting a boarding school in August - but the wife was suffering in Tom's absence. Doortje closed the windows and the smells of the sea gave way to the scent of the house. The sun was getting low, Joe had to return. The driver said four at the latest and it was four plus a quarter. Doortje said he was welcome to return and made him promise to write to her especially if he heard any more about Tom.

'Can you suggest where I can ask?'

'I need to think.'

'Do you ever get to Delft?'

'Yes, my mother comes sometimes.'

'Can you approach Janssen?'

'I will try. Remember, I am only a maid.'

'If you could just get him to read my letter.'

'The driver!'

'What?'

'Have you spoken to the cart driver?'

'Of course,' with some exasperation, 'No, I haven't, I had forgotten his name.'

'Henrik, I think, he worked from the harbour at Veere.'

Joe got up to leave.

'Doortje, thank you.'

She kissed him on the cheek, 'Write to me.'

He limped to find his driver.

He sat silent in the cart. The meeting with Doortje and their conversation was going round and round in his head. He could not help feeling there was something odd, but his going over and over it revealed nothing. The sandy roads were quiet and smooth. Flocks of small water birds chirped and squeaked in protest as, disturbed by the cart, they rose as one, from the reeds in the marshland, only to descend when it passed.

Joe found a light sleep. He had a nonsensical dream about Tom. When he woke, it was with a jolt.

It was the scent, the smell, the smell. When Doortje

closed the windows, he took in the house smell. It was a long-time familiar smell: leather, tobacco, damp wool, and he knew now, what memory it stirred. There was a breath of it when he sat down in that armchair. It was unmistakeable. The old chair and the room smelt of Tom.

CHAPTER 9

Cupar, Fife, Scotland 1732

The weeks following Janett's death found a new normality for David and Rosie in the schoolhouse. David gave up the time he reserved for letter writing and personal study to prepare for the changes in the school day. He taught his classes; Rosie kept the house and prepared their meals. They sat together in the evenings and dealt with school administration. He had taken on too many charity pupils, and many of the paying parents were in arrears. His stipend was short. The council were not fulfilling their obligation as they had not received the due subsidy from the heritors. Some pupils paid in peat, potatoes or a chicken. Additionally, there were the demands of building the new classroom.

Peter had placed a limit of a year on his donation; a deadline which began to look very short. David needed to find the time to talk to the builder and discuss costs. He spent an hour with his daughter each day – despite all the other demands, he made this sacrosanct. He went to bed late and exhausted every night. His teaching, health and his pupils suffered under these new circumstances.

As time passed, David and Rosie got more efficient with their time. David allowed Rosie to visit Adeline for piano practice most Saturdays, and she saw Cora and Jess for an hour or two after church on Sundays. Friends were generous in inviting them for meals; they gratefully accepted, but the time taken to eat, ate into their time. They looked forward to the regular invitations from Jessie's father. He fed the girls at the inn and included David in the invitation to join him at their family table. David's fear however was debt. He had no reserve. Rosie sensed his anxiety and during supper one evening she spoke.

'Father, I could teach in the school?'

'No, Rose, you have the knowledge and are clever, but you know nothing of running a class.'

'There is only one boy older than me, Ben, he could help.'

'No, Rose.'

'Is the reason only that I have not been in a class.'

'Yes,' he hesitated, 'I know you helped Cora and Jessie but a real class, a class of boys, is not the same thing.'

'Father, I have a question and a confession.'

'Yes?'

'How do you think I learn things?'

'You read books, and I thought your mother helped, I felt the sin of pride for you.'

'Father, I sit outside your classroom door, day-after-day. I have done so for years.'

'I do the writing, the reading and the counting.'

David tried to compose his response.

'I get away before you open the door.'

'But how did you avoid your mother catching you?'

'I didn't, she knew.'

'She knew!'

'I can tell you all your pupils' names and what they are working on at the moment.'

David was taken aback. He did not think Janett would have kept anything from him. He then felt a waft of love for them both.

'Let me think about it. It would help me work on the plans for the new classroom.'

'No, we can try it...father, we can try it.'

'Rose.'

'Yes, father.'

'Thank you.'

David did not tell Rosie that he was concerned about the parish's reaction. If it was raised, he would argue that they had just approved the admission of girls as pupils and female schoolteachers were not uncommon. They could be an objectionable and obstinate committee when they did not approve of something.

One Saturday around a month after David's last visit to Tarvit house, Rosie returned saying that Adeline had asked her to stay with her overnight in two weeks' time to attend a house party. She would be returned in time for church the following day. Then, with timing that could not be coincidental, a liveried messenger on horseback delivered a letter with an impressive seal for David. He did not recognise the elegant hand of the address.

Dear Mr Miller,

I am aware we have never met, but I have heard much of you from my first cousin, John Anderson, and, indeed, you are very well regarded in Edinburgh and St Andrews. I understand that you have

*heard of our planning for a new school in Kirkcaldy.
I am currently in discussion with our incumbent
schoolmaster and the council about the curriculum
and means of assessment for each of the classrooms. There are contrasting opinions on content and
method.*

*Given your experience in this area, I would greatly
value an independent opinion on the issues of contention and invite you to visit Dunnikier on Saturday
next. I assure you that this would be a discreet council and, other than Peter Riggs and John, no-one shall
know of this.*

*As you have to travel a fair distance, you will
require an overnight stay, and John has generously
agreed to accommodate you.*

*I hope you find no offence in this request and,
should you accede, I look forward to our meeting.*

Yours, in sincerity,
Isobel Oswald

David felt out of his depth. These were able, clever
and powerful people. He was being manipulated. He
was troubled; but were they being unkind? Were their
intentions honourable or self-serving? If self-serving
for a good – the education of the children in the community – was that still a sin? So many questions. Was
there any ill that could come of it? If so, he could not
see it. It was beyond his world and his experience.

Sir Peter and Isobel Oswald gave so much to their
communities. It did not seem to be for self-gratifica-
tion, at least not in Sir Peter's case, as far as he could
tell. If he said no, and stepped away, where would that
leave him? In a small school, in a small town, and in
debt. Was he being pulled into local politics? Isobel

had promised discretion. Too much thought, too much consideration. Was he curious and interested, did he want to go to help? Yes, of course, he did. Oh, how he missed Janett, every day.

David talked to Peter after church the next Sunday, more in regard of Rose's invitation than his own. It was Adeline's fourteenth birthday. Her mother, along with Adeline's older stepsister and two French cousins, were due arrive by sea at St Monans on Tuesday. They would stay for a few weeks before returning to London, initially, then France. John's girls, whom Rosie had met, would also attend.

'As you can imagine, I am staying clear. We will have a family gathering after church on the Sunday'

'I am not invited to Dunnikier, nor is John, but I will be at John's when you stay overnight. We should be able to sup together and can travel together to the Sunday service, if you have no objection.'

'That will be most convenient, thank you.'

'David, can I also add that the meeting at Dunnikier is your business and not mine. I know John has an interest in the school, but you are not obliged to me in any way.'

'Thank you, Peter, that does help.'

'If ever there is anything you wish to discuss, I am available as a friend and confidant.'

David told Rosie she was free to attend Adeline's party, and of his intended trip to Dunnikier. Rosie's face lit up, as much for her father as for her own pleasure.

Later, while tidying that evening, Rosie asked,

'Father, what will you wear?'

'When.'

'For Dunnikier.'

'My Sunday suit.'

'Father it has holes in both elbows. It's threadbare.'

'I'm sorry, Rose, I know, but it is all I have.'

'Can we not afford a new one?'

'Money is short, Rose, I cannot justify the expense.'

'Oh father, you cannot wear it there,' slipped from Rosie's mouth.

'Rose, we are only poor compared to the landed and the gentry; we are rich compared to many others. I have a respected position. I have no embarrassment in regard of our circumstances.' David said firmly.

'Sir Peter accepts me as such, and so must Mrs Isobel Oswald.'

The next day while David was in the schoolroom, Rosie raked through all her mother's letters and belongings in vain hope of finding some hidden savings. She did come across a letter about her own silk dress which she did not understand. It sparked an idea. She went to find her dress and hurried down Bonnygate, to the tailor's shop.

'Hello, Rose, what can we do for you?' said the tailor.

'Mr Reid, please Sir, do you take clothing in exchange for cloth?'

'We can. What is it you have in mind?'

'It is this. Sir, is it of any value?'

The tailor looked at the dress,

'This is very fine lacework, Rose.' He called his wife.

'Hello, Rose, this is French silk, it is rare here, and very fine, is it yours?'

'Yes, Mrs Reid, it was a present.'

Mrs Reid was a seamstress.

'We would take this, but what do you ask in exchange?'

'I would like cloth for a suit for my father.'

Mrs Reid nodded at her husband who was considering the matter.

'Rose, I can make you a suit for your father for this, but won't you need this dress?'

'I can make do.'

'This is a fine dress,' Mrs Reid interrupted, 'Mr Reid will make your father a suit and I will make a simple linen dress for you. That would be a fair exchange. Now, are you sure? Should you ask your father?'

'No, it's a gift for him.'

'Let me show how to measure, and you can come back tomorrow with the sizes.'

The next day Rosie arrived early at the tailor's house. Mrs Reid chatted as she took her through to the back room to check the list of measurements Rosie had obtained from an old suit of her father's.

'These seem about right. I shall make the jacket double breasted with high shoulders and a longer fit, and the breeks high-waisted and a little tighter, as I think he has recently lost weight. Now let us look at some dress material for you.'

'There is a light, warm cream or a royal blue which would suit you. What do you think, Rose?'

'I like the blue. Mrs Reid, I have no money.'

'That was an expensive dress you brought in, Rose. We can sell it on for a good profit.'

Rosie was not sure if she believed Mrs Reid.

'Our three boys went through the school. Years ago, the eldest got a charity place and the younger two in your father's time.'

'They found it hard, but they have the benefit now.'

'Are they still in Cupar?'

'No, they have their own linen trade in Edinburgh.

Doing well by all accounts. We don't see them, but they write. I have two grandchildren.'

'I always wanted a daughter,' she said softly, more to herself than Rosie.

On the Saturday, it was a High Day - there was no school and many from the county came to buy and sell in the town market. David went early to fetch his horse from the stables. He was to go to John's house first. There, he would be collected by carriage at one hour after noon. He had packed his old suit and his linens in a saddle bag that lay on his bed. Later, Rosie sneaked in and swapped the old suit for the new one. Easier than she could have wished. She also worked the wax into his shoes which made her sadly recall the working of Titch's boots. As he put his bags on the horse to go and bid Rosie goodbye, Rosie said,

'Father, can we presume that mother is watching over us?'

David paused, then smiled,

'I hope we can make that presumption.'

David set off on his mare at dawn, down Crossgate through Millgate, taking a left to head past Rosemount Cottage to the south toll. He travelled so rarely he had forgotten about the new toll road and dug in his pouch to find the only shilling he had brought. The toll keeper recognised him and smiled as he waved him through without charge. The newly metalled road made easy going and he got to John's house, outside Kirkcaldy, in under four hours.

It was a fine house, a square, Scots tower with what looked like a recent addition to the front, not as stately or as large as Tarvit. It sat near woods, overlooking the river. A servant opened the door and called for a boy to come to stable the horse. John received him warmly and he was shown to a room to change from his travelling clothes. A jug of warm water and a bowl were brought by a maid who also put a log on the fire.

David stripped to clean himself before opening his saddle bag. He pulled out the suit, thinking it had been freshly laundered and pressed. Laying it on the bed he saw that it was not his suit. He sat down on a chair and looked at it, bewildered. He got up, looked again, smelt it, it was a new suit of clothes, *jaiket, weskit and breeks*. Rosie, what had she done? He was reluctant, but there was no other option than to put these clothes on. His travelling clothes were wet and covered in mud. He was almost disappointed to find it fitted beautifully, yet there had been no fitting. He was more worried than pleased. How had she done this, good money ill-spent? Credit? Charity? And why? The pressed shirt and the shiny boots were his alright; she'd done a good job there. He must leave the matter until he returned and put his mind to his purpose. A knock at the door and a servant looked in.

'It is midday, sir. Mr Anderson would like to know if you require to rest or would you take some broth with him before the carriage at one?'

'Broth would suit very well. I shall come down presently.'

'Very smart, David.'

'Yes John, thank you. It is not my doing, and the doing of it has me at a loss.'

'Your daughter?'

David nodded affirmatively in puzzled expression.

'She is an exceptional girl.'

'And sometimes that worries me,' David replied.

The Oswald carriage arrived at one. David settled himself for the short journey and the meeting, hoping it would be of interest. John's parting advice was that Isobel Oswald was pleasant, challenging, did not mince words and neither should he.

Dunnikier was a tall L-shaped tower house, sitting impassively high at the top of a cliff overlooking the Forth estuary. It sat just outside Kirkcaldy near the hamlet of Pathheid. Renovations and building work were in progress. The entrance was at the bottom of the round tower at the join of the two orthogonal wings. David was welcomed by a footman and taken up the circular stair to a long, dark-panelled, low-ceilinged dining room on the first floor. Isobel Oswald was standing by a candlelit oak dining table looking at documents as he was ushered in.

'Mr Miller, thank you very much for coming, I hope it hasn't inconvenienced you.'

Mrs Oswald offered her hand.

'Not at all.'

'I was just looking at the physical plans for the new school although the building work has started. Would you care to see them?'

'I am interested, of course.'

They looked at the plans and discussed the options regarding room sizes, the janitor's house, grounds, whether a hall was required. David confessed he was no expert.

'I believe you are more expert than the many advisors I have in this burgh. The important question I have for you: is there anything missing?'

'Is there a church nearby which will take the whole school?'

'Yes.'

'Does the burgh have a library?'

'No.'

'Then a library is missing.'

'Thank you, sir. You have already earned your lunch.'

Mrs Oswald rang the bell and had a footman clear away the papers and a maid prepared the table for food.

'Let us sit by the fire and discuss more difficult issues.'

'Mr Miller, I know you stay in regular contact with the Universities of Edinburgh and St Andrews and attended two good schools yourself, George Heriot's and The High School. I hope you will forgive my enquiries of you, but I would value your opinion on what will be taught. We currently have one traditional master and one assistant. We, as you have seen, are building a two or three-room school for a growing and thriving industrial burgh. My question for debate is, what do we teach?'

'Before you respond, let me say that, at present, our one master is devoted to the teaching of Scots, English, writing and reading the Bible. He does a little Latin for the older boys.'

'Shall we sit at the table?'

A butler offered some wine and two maids brought warm meats and vegetables which they placed on a side table before serving David and his hostess.

'Mrs Oswald, I do not criticise what you already have. I only have an opinion, there is no right nor wrong.'

'Of course.'

'The three rooms are a luxury. There are some good high schools with less.'

'We have a population approaching five thousand. The next ten years may bring nearly one hundred pupils.'

'All pupils aged up to ten years should study writing, English grammar, arithmetic and a good range of reading. If a habit of reading is instilled, then the battle is won.'

'From the age of ten upwards the boys will bifurcate. One stream should undertake learning appropriate for apprentices: accounting, measurement, mechanics, drawing, perhaps even some craft, until the age of fourteen then they will leave for employment. The other stream will undertake learning for university, the ministry, the military or politics: Latin nouns, verbs, grammar and translation of classical texts, until the age of achievement, usually between sixteen and eighteen. My estimate of the division, no more than one fifth will rise to classical education. You will need a good master and one regent for the apprentice cohort.'

'There is a certainty in your presentation,' responded Mrs Oswald.

'It is only my view. I do firmly believe that it is in the schools and the churches that society is formed, from the lectern and the pulpit.'

'You do not see conflict there.'

'Very much, but each should present differing, yet acceptable, views and moderate the extremes of the other.

David and Mrs Oswald talked on amicably over lunch and although Isobel was matter-of-fact in her discourse, David was aware she was enjoying the discussion. It was not all sacrifice for the benefit of her school.

'I ordered a carriage for five hours at evening for you

to arrive at John's by seven. He was keen to entertain you for supper.'

'Is there anything else I can help with?' said David.

'I think we have covered the important areas. Are you aware of any omission?'

'You realise, I think, that I could talk for many hours on this topic; it is often to my pleasure and all else's pain. I apologise if my approach is overly impassioned.'

'It is welcome here.'

'Build a good house for the janitor. It may seem trivial, but his position maintains the ethos of time-keeping and discipline within the school. The master should delegate these minor matters to him. If he is too meek, the boys' teaching will suffer; too hard and their lives will suffer. You want to attract a good man.'

A knock on the door brought word of the carriage.

'Mr Miller, we will meet again. I look forward to it.'

'I hope so. Thank you, Mrs Oswald, for your hospitality.'

As David rose to leave, Mrs Oswald, in what seemed an afterthought, added,

'Mr Miller – you are bound to Cupar aren't you?'

'I am indebted there, yes,' he replied after a hesitation.

Caught unawares, he knew his answer was not clear and offered his hand before taking his cloak from the maid. He was unsettled by the content and the timing of Mrs Oswald's loaded question.

The carriage did not leave immediately; he was unsure why. As he sat, he realised he was becoming used to this life of country houses, servants, good fare and wine and stimulating conversation. Was he becoming a man of influence of was he a pawn in some larger game? He did not know. He would take the matters as they were presented to him and hope he was serving some greater good. A maid appeared from the house and went to the coachman. The coach then departed.

On arriving at the Anderson's, a footman received David, took his cloak and shepherded him into a small library where John and Peter were enjoying what was not their first glass of wine.

'David, welcome. Do you feel you have had a tooth extracted?'

'A glass of wine I think!' John continued.

'Thank you, it was to a degree, intense yes, but not painful. And I think I am still whole.'

'Good to see you, David,' said Peter.

'And you, sir.'

David fully appreciated the degree of his earlier tension only when he relaxed in this company. A few glasses of wine were drunk over a meal of well-hung venison. The talk was of politics, wine and university tales. They did not enquire about his visit to Dunnikier. Peter prompted David for an example of Roman oratory, but he declined offering instead his school tale of playing Penelope which made John fall back in his chair to the hilarity of the other two and the immediate concern of the attending servant. He was fine. As it got colder and the candles began to flicker, John himself fetched some whisky while Peter stoked the fire.

It was John who said,

'Are you well, David? Difficult times, we understand that.'

'I have challenges, with God's grace I will rise to them.'

'If there is anything we can do?'

'You both have done so much. I value your counsel – '
he opened his arms, ' – more than you may appreciate.'

Twenty miles further north, at the birthday party in
Tarvit, the girls spent time readying in their rooms.
This involved a lot of merriment and running back and
forth. The material of Rosie's linen dress had been finished with a sheen. Mrs Reid had crafted it with a high
waist, a sash, a large bow at the back, puffed sleeves
and quite a low-cut bodice. Adeline offered Rosie the
choice of her wardrobe, but Rosie was very happy with
her new blue gown. Encouraged by Adeline, she applied
powder and put a little rouge on her cheeks. Adeline
then put a jewelled pendant on a chain round Rosie's
neck which she liked. The bell summoned the guests
downstairs. There were ten in all. Rosie shyly stood,
half-hidden, behind Adeline. She was glad Carolina and
Fiona Anderson were there. A maid served drinks in
thin-stalked glasses from a silver tray. Rosie wondered
if it was wine. It was creamy-pale in colour with bub-
bles in it. Adeline took two glasses and gave Rosie one.
Three women came over to speak to them.

'Rosie, this is my mother, Cecile, her companion, Estelle, and my grandmother, my father's mother, whom
we call Nan.'

'*Boujour Rose*, I am so happy to meet. Adelle has, eh,
tell, told me so much of you,' said Adeline's mother.

'Pleased to meet you,' Rosie said, shaking her, then
her companion's hands.

'You play the piano?'

'Not very well. Adeline is very good.'

'Perhaps was shall hear later,' and they moved away.

Adeline took her to meet her stepsister and her cousins.

They then stood beside John's daughters who were equally glad to have a familiar person to talk to. Cecile tapped her glass with a spoon to draw the room's attention.

'Welcome all, to this small celebration to *ma belle* Adele.'

She raised her glass to sip and everyone followed her action. Rosie giggled as the bubble hit her nose then fizzed on her tongue. It was sweet tasting and pleasant.

'What is it?' she whispered to Adeline, but Cecile overheard.

'*C'est du champagne, ma petite*, from France. Your first?'

Rosie nodded and they all raised their glasses again and she took another sip.

They were formally seated by Cecile. Adeline next to her stepsister, with Rosie next, then John's younger daughter, Fiona, Cecile and her companion were on the other side of Adeline. Rosie was worried about having to make conversation, but she need not have. Every one of the guests was keen to talk and there were all sorts of funny stories about their long journey and the differences between France and Scotland. John's girls told tales of their time in Edinburgh and London. Rosie was happy to listen and to answer any questions. She felt very unworldly compared to the others.

Adeline's stepsister was seventeen and knew little English. She was keen to practise with Rosie, asking about her life in the town. She then had to help Rosie understand the food. The meat dishes were heavily sauced. They were delicious and Rosie tried not to eat too much. The oddest thing was that the meal went on for such a long time. Just as you thought it was over, more food came out. John's daughter told her she did not have to eat everything.

At the end, sweets were served, and Cecile gave a small speech wishing Adeline '*Bon Anniversaire.*' It was well after ten when they withdrew to the drawing room. The four girls rushed to the piano, keen to play. Cecile called for order.

'We shall have some classical music first, girls, followed by a poem or a recital, then we shall play games. We can have some silly pieces after that.'

Rose had prepared two pieces and sang when invited. There were party games with the girls having turns at being blindfolded, and a funny game about trying to guess a card on your forehead. During a lull, while they arranged the next game, Adeline's Nan came over to Rosie and said that she was very sorry to hear about her mother, and that if she felt low at any time to come and talk to her. Rosie thanked her for her concern and said she would.

When they were exhausted, they flopped on the furniture and in various pairs played and sang on the piano. The Anderson girls played a gavotte and Adeline's cousins started to dance together. Adeline and Rosie tried to mimic the dance to the amusement of the others. John's girls insisted on a repeat of Rosie's *Tam-Lin* to which one of them played an accompaniment on the piano. They laughed and responded with enthusiastic applause.

'And we thought she was a quiet one,' said Estelle.

When they began to flag, a maid came in with a tray

with glasses of a warm dark-red drink. It was syrupy. Rosie looked at the clock, it must have been broken because it showed two hours and the half. They began to retire, starting with Cecile and Estelle. Nan stayed and prompted the others to follow. Rose went up with Adeline. They were feeling giggly tired. Rosie was not sure where she was going to sleep but as they both readied themselves for bed, Adeline made it clear that Rosie was to join her. Nan came in and kissed them both.

'Are you able to sleep, Rose?'

'Yes, I'm fine thank you.'

'I'm just next door.'

'Thank you, ma'am.'

She blew out the candles and left them the glow of the fire, bidding them goodnight. Rosie turned away from Adeline and thought she might sob, but Adeline moved over and put her arms around her gently pulling her close. Rosie had always had a cot to herself; this was a new, strange but comforting feeling. They both fell quickly to sleep.

Rosie was exhausted when the carriage arrived the next day with her father and Sir Peter to collect them for church. The time was tight, so David did not alight, and Rosie was guided to his carriage. Two other carriages were brought around for John's and Peter's families. Rosie had forgotten about the suit and so, almost, had David. She didn't remark on it and understood that words would be said later. She was wearing her normal, white Sunday frock, the new dress was in her case. Adeline rushed to her window to thank her and expressed a tired excitement about their next meeting. As the carriage moved off, Rosie said,

'Are you well, father?'

David wondered why this was becoming such a common enquiry.

'I am.'

'Did the meeting go well?'

'Yes, Rose.'

And they sat in silence for the rest of the journey. Rose wanted, of course, to tell her mother all about it, and she hoped she could find time after church to attend her grave on her own. She had had a thrilling time.

The church was full; there was some rearranging of seating to accommodate the extra numbers. Sir Peter gave the sermon. It was a cold but bright day with no wind. The congregation dallied a good while after, to catch up on the week's news and gossip. Rosie met with the girls but did not think it best to say much about the party. Jess was growing taller and was predominantly interested in her appearance, and boys. The increasing demand for Cora's labour on the farm gave her little time to meet with them in town.

Later, Peter caught David outside.

'An inspiring reading. Thank you, David.'

'How *was* your meeting with Isobel Oswald?'

'Forthright and determined, she has a drive to get things done that I envy.'

'Yes, and she has the power.'

'Her genuine concern for the town's new school impressed me.'

'She has six male grandchildren of ages eight to eighteen. She wishes to have them well-schooled.'

'She could do that privately?'

'She would rather see benefit to the town.

'That is to her credit.'

'Her husband, God rest his soul, was a well-respected

Provost and Member of Parliament who was influential in obtaining the investment to grow trade and thus prosperity in this small town.'

'It is a much grander scheme than our small enterprise.'

'Quite a challenge.'

'Yes, not one I envy. I think I have enough to do here.'

'Really?'

David left the conversation with his daughter until supper time.

'Rose.'

'Yes, father.'

'The suit.'

'Yes, father.'

'You left me with no choice but to wear it. We do not accept charity.'

'It was not charity, father.'

'You spent our money?'

'No, father.'

'Then tell me where it came from.'

'No, father, I won't,' wiping her eye.

'Pardon.'

'I won't tell you. It's a suit for you, you needed a new suit.'

'Rose, if you won't tell, you will not sup with me.'

Rosie got up sobbing and left the table.

'Rose, you must...'

At the doorway she turned and said,

'If mother had put that suit in your bag, how would you have reacted?'

David was silenced. He got up and pushed past her to go to work in the schoolroom. He sat at his desk and realised his daughter had made a valid point. He accepted that if Janett had done such a thing, he would have known she had obtained the suit honourably. He would not have even thought to question her. Just because he did not know what Rose had done, he had assumed she had done something wrong. Why, due to her youth perhaps, but she had never given any reason for him, her own father, not to trust her. He was not in the right.

Later he went up to her, she was sleeping. He saw the darkness of a damp patch on her pillow but did not wake her. At breakfast he came down while Rose was at the stove. She had cleared away the unfinished supper. He sat at the breakfast table.

'Rose.'

She turned.

'Thank you for the suit of clothes. You were right, I did need a new one.'

Then he added, 'It was admired by Sir Peter and John Anderson, it fitted very well.'

Rose walked over and put her arms around him burying her face in his neck.

'Enough, Rose,' he said.

A week later a messenger brought a sealed letter for David. It was not from Sir Peter nor John Anderson. He read the first page. It was an offer to him of employment as the schoolmaster in the Royal Burgh of Kirkcaldy. As David read it, he was not entirely surprised. The letter was from the Kirkcaldy Burgh Council. The interview had already taken place. Of course, he would not consider it. His present burden was enough for him.

He could not leave his home with the good people of Cupar whose friendship and support had been of great help to himself and Rose, especially since Janett passed. He knew every family through their children. He could not let Sir Peter and his school down. Rose's town friends and Adeline provided a comfort he could not replace. The girls, there was no mention of girls in the Kirkcaldy school. He laid the letter to one side.

Saturday came and Rosie returned from Tarvit with a note inviting David to lunch after church the following day. There was no mention of Rosie, but she insisted on coming too. Instead of using the cart, David put her on a small pony, and they went together on horseback. Rosie was not accomplished and trotted along at a grump. Peter asked and David acknowledged he had been contacted by the Kirkcaldy council. Peter was surprised when David said he had already written to refuse the offer.

David explained his thoughts, which included a degree of loyalty to Sir Peter, and concerns about the additional workload.

'David, do not let my contribution burden you. That was not my intent. An extension to the Cupar School is necessary, whether you are master or no.'

'You would have me move?'

'I would support it for your sake.'

'You feel I would benefit?'

'Did you read the terms?'

Embarrassed, David confessed he had not fully read the offer. There had been three or four pages of small, tightly written copy. He was too tired when he opened the envelope and had dismissed the offer out of hand.

'On your return, may I suggest you do so?'

'Of course, but I am unlikely to change my reply.'

'Just read it, David.' he said, with a firmness that David conceded was due.

Adeline's mother and the other visitors joined them for lunch and the animated talk was mostly of Adeline's party. David found Cecile to be younger than he expected. There was so much going on that he found himself a bit of a bystander. Some of the tales from the party involved Rosie. He was constantly surprised and more than a little disturbed by her behaviour these recent days. He no longer had any counsel nor measure of this matter. Indeed, his experience of girls, and women in general, was severely limited. Peter shook his hand warmly as David and Rose left early to ride back while there was still daylight.

The schoolhouse was cold when they returned from leaving their horses at the stables. Rosie lit the fire and David said he would do some work in the schoolroom. Rosie noticed that, unusually, her father had left the hall door to the classroom ajar. She knocked quietly and entered.

'Are you well, father?'

'Quiet, Rose, I have much to think about.'

'Rose.'

'Yes.'

'When there is no school and I am at my desk, you do not need my permission to knock and come in if there is something you need from me.'

'Oh, thank you father.'

'Not idle conversation mind.'

'Of course not, father.'

'You have a letter?'

Rosie's mouth moved; David heard Janett's voice. He paused and said,

'Yes, Rose, it is an offer of another position.'

'Father?'

'I cannot read the small print of these sheets by candle and I have no glass. Can you read them to me slowly and I will take notes?'

'Shall I light a fire?'

'We will go to the parlour where it is already lit, I can write at the table there.'

'I have made no decision, Rose. We need to read and understand this letter first. Then we can discuss it.'

'You and Sir Peter, you mean.'

'No, Rose, you and I.'

As Rosie read and David took note, he realised why Sir Peter was keen for him to understand the offer. It was a Burgh Grammar School not a Parish School. It would not come bound with the duties of Precentor, no sermons to write, no Sunday oration. There would be so much involved in launching the new school. He would be making decisions regarding class sizes, syllabuses and timetable. He would employ the doctor, a janitor and a bookkeeper/librarian. There was a bigger house for the master, and he would be able to afford a housemaid. He would be paid one third of his wage on acceptance, while still in Cupar, to prepare for the start on teaching next August. That was months hence.

The most important difference was that the new master's wage was paid by the burgh and did not depend on chasing parents for fees or reminding the council of their dues. The stipend itself was nearly three times what he currently received Rosie said only the written words as she read the text, but she looked at him when she read that part. He asked her to read it again. She said there was no error. Yes, there was a lot to do and still much to discus, but it was an exceptional opportunity. It took a while to go through the rest of the three pages, much of which was detail.

'I need to sleep on this, Rose. We can think first and talk tomorrow.'

'Would you like some broth before bed, father?'

'Yes, Rose, thank you.'

Rosie was up early the next day; she prepared porridge and went quickly to the dairy for fresh cream, returning as David came downstairs.

David struggled in indecision through the night. The offer he had was very good. He felt easier about the new post, perhaps naively, than the problems that Cupar presented. Oh, to be rid of these financial worries. Yet it would mean taking Rose away from all that she held dear. He would talk with her, as promised, that evening and gauge her feelings. He would put it out of his mind and stick to his original decision. They would pull through.

'We have some honeycomb still; would you like some this morning.'

'Yes, that would be a treat.'

'Father. I want you to take that position. I want us to go to Kirkcaldy.'

'You don't feel we would be leaving your mother behind.'

'No, she will come with us. We can leave the pain behind.'

'We can talk this evening.'

'Of course, but I will not change my view.'

'Then I will write the letter.'

Having woken every hour throughout the night, waking in the fog of indecision, David now felt that the right decision had been made, even if he had not made it. He rose early to write to the council accepting the offer and apologising for his first response. He asked Rose to take his response to the inn and pay for a messenger to take it directly. He wrote a second message to Sir Peter.

CHAPTER 10

Delft, Zeeland 1710

J oe tried to stop his mind drifting back to his visit
to the house in Monster and the anomalies between
Doortje's conversation and his instinctive sense
of her appearance and behaviour, and that of the house
itself. He had to concentrate on the trade, the finances
and getting aboard a ship to Leith or Culross with Ruud
and the cargo.

The cart sat outside the lodgings while Joe went to
check if Ruud had returned from Veere. He had not, so
Joe continued to the de Kolk basin, at the end of the
canal, in anticipation of his arrival. The sun had gone
down but the sky to the north was still light. A small
sailing boat came slowly down the Delfshavensche
Schie into de Kolk. Joe stood on the quay at Schiedmse
Poort and watched it tie up. He recognised Ruud immediately as he helped a woman disembark. Ruud handed
her two bags then followed her ashore. Joe was expecting one person; there were two.

'Joe, I have brought the Dutch notes. They are well
concealed. Grietje has come to help with the selection
of porcelain.'

'*Hallo, Grietje, Dank je.* Let us leave the bags at the lodgings and find somewhere to sup.'

As they walked, Ruud told Joe that he had spoken to Grietje about the porcelain and found she had a good knowledge of Delftware. '

She worked as a porcelain artist for many years. She has worked for *de Porceleyne Fles,* the royal house. She offered to help to view and price the prospective purchases. I suggested she returned with me.'

'I cannot pay her Ruud; we are short of funds.'

'She asks for no payment; she feels indebted to us.'

'In that case, I welcome her advice. Ruud, I'm glad to see you returned.'

They went to the Mechelen Inn where Joe had enjoyed the food and company the previous night. Joe saving his tale until they were sitting round the table. Grietje chose a good wine; fish and cabbage were served and wordlessly consumed. It was getting late, Joe said he was ready to retire.

'I do not know where you two will sleep, but I am not giving up my half of the bed!'

'Joseph, Joe!' a voice, and Joe turned.

'Ruud, Grietje this is the gentleman I told you about.'

Henry had been out at a dinner and had been drinking wine.

'I was passing, thought you might be here. *De Keeper, whisky, vier glazen!*'

Henry was very interested in Grietje and her porcelain knowledge. Grietje explained for their benefit. The conversation kept switching between Dutch and English even in mid-sentence. This caused amusement. Henry had a good grasp of both languages and teased the others by deliberately using the wrong word.

Grietje went through the different qualities of ceramic. The highest was fine grained, pure white, almost translucent. It was strong, but its thinness made it delicate; it needed to be wrapped and transported very carefully. It was decorative and often put on display. The glaze had to fully cover the plate and the cobalt blue should also be even and deep in tone. Well-drawn, detailed artwork on a fine plate was the best. It is rare and expensive. 'A dropped case would severely diminish your profit.' Henry interjected.

Joe, Ruud and Grietje agreed they would visit three designated potteries in the morning. Each one produced a different grade of Delftware. Grietje was familiar with two of the factories. Henry held a frown, and they all looked at him quizzically.

'May I join you, please?'

'Of course, Henry, most welcome,' said Joe.

'Grand, we can travel in my landau,' Joe and Ruud did not know the word, 'I will collect you from this inn at ten.'

Joe rose to leave, apologising for his early departure and went back to the lodgings. The others stayed, so engaged in conversation they barely noticed him go. He was almost asleep when he heard the door opening. There was light laughter; he was assured it was Ruud and Grietje.

He woke early as a beam of sunlight came through the window and hit the opposite wall prematurely lighting the whole room. Turning in the bed he found Grietje next to him and looking past her saw Ruud snoring under their cloaks on the floor. He smiled at the odd arrangement and hoped this day would be usefully spent. He would agree the purchases by the end of the day and sign bills of sale today or tomorrow at the latest. Time was passing, he needed to return to Scotland, his wife his family, his sponsor and James Lockhart.

Grietje disturbed sleepily.

'I am going to the coffee house to look at the figures. Remember we are meeting Henry at ten,' Joe whispered.

Grietje, murmured and closed her eyes tight as the sun moved its piercing rays onto her face. Stretching, she asked, 'What time is?'

'It is nearly seven hours.'

At eight of the clock, Grietje and Ruud joined Joe in the *koffiehuis*, Grietje bright eyed, Ruud half asleep. Joe wondered if he should be angry with Ruud and manage him with more authority, but he could see no reason and enjoyed his youthful moodiness. The three went back to the room to dress as smartly as they could. Grietje helped Joe tidy himself up. They divided the Dutch notes between them, hiding it discreetly on their person. Joe found he trusted Grietje. On the quarter, they walked to meet Henry.

The open carriage was already by the inn when they arrived. There were two footmen. One stepped down to open the door; Joe sat opposite Henry and Grietje sat beside him. They had agreed the order of the visits and Grietje directed the driver at Henry's request. Henry had the driver stop by a series of canal locks. He pointed out to them, in detail, the pumping mill, the challenges of water control and the difficulties of the engineering. Joe appreciated his excitement for the industry. 'There is a future in this industry, Joe.'

They went to the first pottery at de Wit, a good quality factory. This was where Joe thought they would place the largest purchase for the medium market. Henry was at ease. Joe noted the difference in the manner of their reception compared to when it was just himself and Ruud. The looked at their volume products: pots, vases, plates and cups. The pottery salesman offered examples, but Grietje insisted in looking at the ones on the factory floor. Henry was interested in the process, so they took a tour. 'The secret is in the clay mix and the glaze,' they were told, 'Your potteries in Stafford and Liverpool cannot match this.' There was a long bench with chairs on one side where more than a dozen artists sat working. Grietje knew one of them who looked at her in surprise, but then kept her head down.

They then went to sit in a comfortable office to discuss terms. The trader tried to isolate Joe for the discussion, but Henry intervened and asked for the factory owner to attend. Joe had his list and prices from the previous visit. Grietje asked to look at it and she had a rapid conversation in Dutch with Henry.

'Do you trust me to negotiate, Joe?' said Henry.

'If you can agree a better offer...by all means.'

They all stood to greet the owner. Henry led the charge. The language was too quick for Joe to follow all of it. The owner frowned and appeared to turn down Henry's initial suggestion.

Henry turned to Joe. 'You will come back for a larger load, within three months?'

'That is my intention,' said Joe, cottoning on.

'And this is a trial batch for the London market?'

'Yes, to sell this summer.'

Henry the turned to Grietje, 'What do you think of the quality?'

'The ceramic is good, slight shading on some pieces, the artwork is fair but, em...*onbelangrijk*.'

Henry spoke again to the owner and who paused before nodding in agreement.

The owner rose, shook Henry's hand, nodded to the others and left. Henry told Joe the price. It was nearly half the earlier estimate.

'You will need to sign today.'

Boyed by this, Joe committed without hesitation, and they travelled quickly to the next pottery; the one at their cheapest end.

There was less money involved there. They wanted a large quantity of robust and attractive goods, but wares aimed at the street markets. The artwork could be quickly produced and crude. Henry did not push hard; the salesman was not overstating on quality or price. The price came down a little and Joe agreed. As with the previous pottery the goods had to be packaged carefully and delivered to the harbour at de Kolk by four in the afternoon, the next day. As they pulled the money out of shoes, stocking, breeks and shirts, much to the amusement of Henry, Joe looked at Grietje.

'I only go into my undergarments for Royal Porcelain' she replied.

'Lunch!' cried Henry in delight.

It was another windless, timeless, summer afternoon. The cloud offered intermittent shade. Henry instructed the driver to stop by the river. They got out on a grassy bank with a view to the west by a windmill. There was no inn. The footman brought two large baskets and two rugs and a small folding table from the rear of the carriage. There were pies and meats, cheese, water and, of course, wine. Joe looked to Ruud as Grietje helped and Henry directed the footman in organising the picnic fare.

'Does all this make you angry or envious, Ruud?'

'No sir, it makes me want to work hard to do better.'

They all sat and drank to the success of the day.

'One more to go, a Royal visit,' said Henry.

Henry brought an energy and enthusiasm to life that Joe, in his adult life, had rarely seen. He saw glimpses of it within Tom, but knew he kept it hidden. They lay back on the sunny bank and rested after they had eaten. Grietje was vexed to find cover to relieve herself. Ruud, typically, dozed off.

'Joe, I have to ask you, what happened?' said Henry pointing to his eye.

'An accident,' replied Joe.

'It was not! These two men saved my life,' said Grietje arriving back and overhearing.

'Hardly that,' said Joe.

'I tell tale,' Grietje insisted, and she did…

'So the pistol was not loaded!' said Henry.

'No, I was shaking; I could not do it.'

'I hesitate to laugh, that was very serious, but well done. Joe, Ruud, I salute you. I am proud to have you both as fellow countrymen.' Henry got up and Joe kicked Ruud awake.

'There was no motive?'

'They were men,' said Grietje.

It was not the time to discuss this; Henry well understood Grietje's bitterness. The footmen who had stood a short distance away came and cleared the baskets, table and rugs. Joe walked with Grietje to the windmill.

'Grietje, I need to take Ruud back with me. We will

come back.'

'That is best for us all I think,' she replied, 'I hope you will write and let me know when you return.'

'I will, I have more business to do here and I have plans for you, if you are interested.'

'I am, of course.'

They mounted the carriage and headed for *de Porceleyne Fles*. As they travelled, Joe had a closer look at the receipts. The first receipt was for a larger amount than they had paid. It was the value of the original estimate. He queried this with Henry.

'Ah yes, I had asked around before we re-met. The Delft potteries have a restrictive trade organisation. They do not compete nor undersell each other, particularly to foreign trade. But trade has been declining recently so they do undersell in practice, but there will not be a written record.' Henry continued. 'Your receipt with the items of sale would be evidence of a break in their agreement. This would lead to a penalty or restrictions in the supply of powder or glaze. It is a powerful organisation. The customs men will report to the organisation if they suspect a dubious trade.'

'I see.'

'You will have to pay tax at the higher amount.'

'We did not pay tax last time as we left from Veere.'

'I think that was lucky. The tax-free status of the Staple is only for goods bought in Campveere.'

'I would allow for the tax just in case; you may need to pay. When the goods pass into the town the crates will be marked.'

'Before, they just transferred the crates directly from the *schuyt* to the ship.'

'Maybe the customs officer was having lunch,'

laughed Henry.

The last pottery of the visits was a more refined establishment. They were served coffee in a wood paneled room furnished with a long table, chairs and glass-fronted display cases and showing a range of fine pieces. Grietje was not as suspicious regarding the quality as she had been at the other potteries. She took a plate and showed Joe and Henry the smoothness and the glaze and pointed out the consistency, hue and the detail of the decoration. She then held it high on one finger, as if a plate spinner at the fair, and bade them be quiet as she hit the plate edge with the fingernail of her other hand. The plate rang as the chime of a small clock. She held the plate up to the light and borrowed a glass to look more closely. She then hit the plate quite firmly on the corner of the table. It did not break. 'Royal Delft,' she said with a degree of pride. Henry negotiated a small discount with the promise of a following order and new markets. The trader knew the value of his product. Joe bought more than he had intended using the money saved on the second purchase. Henry urged him to invest in small plates, cups and saucers.

'Now we need the money,' said Joe looking at Grietje. She widened her as eyes as they all looked at her.

'Oh, sorry. Gentlemen, turn your backs, please.'

She looked at Joe with an elfin smile, unseen by the others, as she handed him the notes still warm from their concealment. Grietje was concerned about the packaging of the goods, and they were taken to where the Delftware was boxed for shipping. A foreman who knew Grietje came across and greeted them all.

'We even ship to China,' he said.

Their day was done. The sun was meeting the horizon as they boarded the carriage to return to Delft.

'It is my last evening in Delft tonight. I insist you join me for dinner,' said Henry. 'Grietje can you suggest somewhere suitable. Spare no expense!'

Henry was ebullient. Grietje knew of a small hostelry used by the owners of *de Porceleyne Fles* with a private dining room and a reputation for good food.

'That is excellent, I shall arrange it. Shall we all meet at eight?'

They filled their glasses and their stomachs in the small dark candle-lit room on the first floor on a house by the river Oude. Grietje, when questioned, talked more of her artwork and work at the pottery. Henry had a wealth of amusing stories and Joe, for Henry, retold of his recent visit to Doortje's house and, having had nearly a bottle of good wine, probably said too much about the puzzle of Tom's disappearance. He told them that he did not have time on this visit to pursue his enquiry, but he will try to find the driver when they returned to Veere.

Henry was leaving for Rotterdam the next day at midday, but he arranged to meet Joe at the coffee house at eight in the morning to talk about business. He made a great show of his farewell to Ruud and Grietje, thanked them for their companionship and made them vow to return to meet with him again. Joe, Ruud and Grietje walked back to the lodgings together, Grietje in the middle, linked her arms with them both. There was a moment of awkward hesitation due to the sleeping arrangements, but the three follow the precedent of the previous night. Joe was aware in the night of having an arm loosely draped over him. He made no responding movement and was up an out in the morning before

Grietje and Ruud wakened.

Henry was sitting with a coffee and a plate of French bread and honey. He rose to welcome Joe.

'I wanted to talk without the others, nothing mysterious, just an opportunity perhaps to arrange some more trade. I know we had talked openly, but I wanted ensure I understood your position before I suggest something.'

'I welcome the discussion, but I have one question, if I may ask it first?'

'Please do.'

'Henry, you have been generous, open and supportive to two low ranked Scotsmen with an unusual Dutch girl in tow. I am extremely grateful. I would have not done near as well without you. But I must ask why, sir, what is your profit?'

'Ah, Joe, you are a serious man. I appreciate that and understand the need for your query. Time only permits a short explanation. I am the fourth, and not the last, son of a landed family. The first inherits everything, my brothers and I take other paths. One is a man of the cloth, one a soldier, another a member of parliament. My father has an interest in land, mines and transport. I do not have his mathematics, but I follow his path. It is for him I discover, and to him I report. During these travels particularly to Europe, I find it a hugely interesting and stimulating place. It is not Britain. I have enjoyed meeting a wide range of people.'

He gestured at the coffee house. 'The alternative life for me would be hunting, shooting, gambling in company I take care to avoid, then getting married to some English frump who failed to catch a first son.'

Joe's coffee arrived.

'Let me ask you something, Joe. You spend most of your time in Edinburgh at a desk and going home late to your family?'

Joe nodded.

'How has this past week affected the thoughts to your future?'

'If I had a choice, this is how I would live my life. I'm duty bound to go back. I miss my wife and children, but it is hard to leave here, to leave this life. I see there are opportunities open to me here not at home. My drive to profit, in part, is so I may return.'

'Exactly, you see we are not much different. Now may I continue?'

'Of course.'

'I want to ask about your business. You are not a merchant you act on behalf of someone else.'

'Yes.'

'May I ask who.'

'Edward James Clerk. He is a son of a landowner and well-known in Edinburgh. He bought much of my earlier shipment and sold it on, I assume. Now, I think of it, your family position is similar to his.'

'He sponsored this one trip, no other obligation?'

'Yes, none'

'The purchased goods and the receipts go to him and he pays you.'

'Yes, a percentage of the profit.'

'And then what do you hope to do?'

'Ideally, I would like to use the profit to establish a small company and become a burgess, trading for myself. It is difficult in Edinburgh. So much depends on who you are. Credit is hard to obtain'

'Well, let me offer something. I believe you have it

in you to succeed in this. This is low tax route to buy goods such as the porcelain we saw yesterday. It will sell well...in England. And there are no tariffs between Scotland and England. The timing is good, you now know the process and you have quality merchantise. I am not being generous here. I desire to profit as much as the next man. But I would structure it differently. I want you to setup your own business as you say. I would take a stake but not more than fifty percent and I would want us to grow the business, not taking too much out until it is established. I put this to you to consider. I'm perfectly serious and providing this trade goes well I can offer you a substantial sum. Will you give it some thought when you return?'

'I will sir, I am honoured and I thank you.'

'No need for gratitude, Joe, we are presently friends and I hope we both may prosper.'

'Now I must leave you, I wish you a safe voyage. Oh, there was one other thing, two actually.'

'Yes?'

'You mentioned the receipts?'

'Yes.'

'You will give these to Mr Clerk's accountant?'

'Yes.'

'And leave yourself with an excess of funds?'

'No, I would report the circumstance.'

'Then you would give him false receipts?'

'Oh, I hadn't thought...'

'And pay the extra tax yourself?'

Joe went quiet and thought for a few minutes.

'Can I offer you some commission? You have earned it.'

'No, not at all. I would not accept. I only mention

this to give you time to consider. If the business was your own it would be easier to deal with.'

'Thank you, Henry. The second thing?'

'Ah, yes, as I say I have no need for reward, but, and I hope you don't mind me mentioning it, perhaps Grietje?'

'Yes, of course. I also have it in mind to involve her in our future business. She cannot have Ruud though, not yet anyway, I need him.'

Henry smiled. 'Excellent, now, sir, I must leave. May the fates stay with you.' At that Henry was gone.

Joe wondered if he would ever see him again.

Joe walked back to the lodging and found Grietje in the room tidying.

'Ruud has gone to arrange a boat.'

'Good, I will go to find him.'

'I will come too,' and they left.

'Before we leave, I have something for you.' Joe went to his bag and counted out Dutch notes; quickly calculating the conversion to make sure he was not being over generous nor insulting.

'Grietje, you have worked for me these past three days. I must pay you.'

'I said, that not necessary.'

'I, we, have all profited from your expertise and hope to do so again. You must accept it.'

'For business, I accept. Thank you.' She did not look or count the amount. 'It will allow me paint.'

When they got to the harbour it was just after midday. The largest of the loads had already been delivered. Grietje went to the crate and checked a few items. Ruud was in conversation with the *schuyt* owner. They agreed to load the barge with it. He understood it was pottery and was used to handling these crates with care. He would wait until five for the remaining crates, but he would have to leave then, hoping to sail for three hours before anchoring for the night. He was fine about taking the passengers, but stressed there was no covered accommodation, just the deck and a wheelhouse. He pointed to a small, sleek sailing yacht and looked up at the sky.

'That one is leaving at one. It takes the mail. Today, it will get you to Veere by nightfall.'

Joe saw advantage it one of them going to Veere early, to arrange for the transfer or their cargo to the ship as soon as possible. He did not want the load sitting around for longer than was necessary. It was also easier and cheaper, he had learned, for ships to load directly from a barge. Joe asked Ruud if he needed anything to travel, they could bring his things later. He was fine.

'Find us a fast ship to Leith!' Joe gave him money and they went to find the captain of the small yacht. Ruud smiled as he leapt on board, 'This might be fun.' His face dropped when he signalled Grietje to join him and she shook her head.

'I need help here, and I collect things, we will follow on *schuyt.*'

Joe was a bit surprised too but would value her help. 'Grietje, I will manage. It is fine to go. It is your decision.'

'Which I make!'

The yacht left a few minutes later. Joe and Grietje watched it. Joe thought it was skilled the way they could raise the sail, even in the narrow waterway, and move quickly down the calm water. The barges were towed to Delfshaven by horses and were much slower.

Ruud turned and waved as the yacht disappeared from view.

'I have not eaten,' said Grietje.

'In that case let us eat a good lunch. If we sail at four, it may need to satisfy us for a while.' Joe was aware that Grietje now appeared to understand most of the conversation as long as he did not speak quickly. She spoke it well enough for basic conversation. 'We can then pack up our belongings and go to wait at the harbour for the other crates.'

'We go to the Market Square. It will be lively, *van daag*.'

They sat outside a coffee house not talking much, watching the stall traders and the hawkers. There were performers, musicians and jugglers with shows for children and adults, street artists and pamphleteers.

'The Town Hall is an impressive building.'

'You have such in Edinburgh.'

'No, our grandest building is a school.'

'No *kerk*.'

'Yes, large, old and squat, and not ornate.'

'I don't understand,' and Joe tried unsuccessfully to use his hands to explain.

'Flat and plain. In Scotland the grand cathedrals were razed after the reformation. I believe there are great churches in England, but I have never seen them.'

'Raised...lifted, *Opgeheven*?'

'Hah, sorry, raised can mean lifted or flattened.'

'I will never understand English.'

'You English is very good.'

'You can see from eye?-'

'Yes, it is not sore now.'

'-and leg.'

'Getting better.'

'You look better, do you need still stick?'

'No, but I have become used to it.'

'*Goede!*'

They paid and left the square to walk to the room where they collected their things, thanked and paid the landlady, and walked to the pier. The crates from *de Porceleyne Fles* had arrived. Grietje opened the crates carefully and inspected their contents. Repackaging them carefully when she had finished.

'I do not expect problem. It is good to check.'

Joe agreed and put their bags on the barge. They walked round the small dock looking at the seabirds and sailboats, then sat where they had a clear view of the barge. They strolled back to the barge at four hours after noon, to find the last crates had still not arrived. The barges had windows-in-time to travel down the *Schie,* so they did not meet another coming in the opposite direction. The captain said, 'Five at the latest.' The last crates were about ten percent of the total value of the shipment. He would need to pay more for the *schuyt* to wait and for another day's expenses. Grietje readily agreed to dispatch them later if they were left behind but that would add a further sailing cost.

Joe thought of his old life of just doing what he was told. They would go at five, he told the captain. With Grietje, he boarded the barge made a comfortable seat out of their baggage and oilskins. Grietje went to find some food to take with them.

'We will make good time but it will be cool tonight,' said the captain. 'Have you arranged the shipping?'

'My clerk has gone early to do that.'

'There will be ships in Veere for you.'

As the harbour clock reached the quarter. The barge ropes were attached to two harnessed horses when a large wheeled cart arrived at the pier with four crates. They were quickly loaded. Joe tipped the stevedores and the *schuyt* departed. There air was still and warm.

Grietje spoke first.

'What is business you talk, will you come back?'

'I don't know if I can tell you. You will push me overboard and make your own fortune.'

'Joe, you made joke!'

'It is the designs. The Chinese and Dutch patterns are in fashion now, according to my sponsor and Henry. I think there will be demand for other scenes. Scotland, London, castles and palaces. I just need someone to draw them for me. Can you think of anyone?'

Grietje looked at him.

'I also think the patterned ceramic tiles, we have seen here, would sell. I have never seen any in Edinburgh. I should have bought some samples.'

'You get some in Veere perhaps.'

'If we have time. The profit on this has to be enough to fund the next. I will not get credit as I am not an established merchant. I'm not sure that it will be enough.'

'You will come back?' She asked again.

They rested and talked little as the barge released the horses and hoisted its sails before passing though Delfshaven. There was a light breeze, the three raised sails caught it and the *schuyt* picked up speed heading for open water. As the light faded, the air cooled, and Grietje move closer to Joe and they covered themselves. The mate and the boy adjusted the sails to get the best from the evening breeze. The captain came out of the wheelhouse with two hot tankards.

'The wind has dropped; we will put to port until dawn.'

Each time Grietje looked to the sky she saw a thousand more stars. Soundless, shadowed birds swooped around them. The nearby splash of a large fish was amplified in the silence of everything else. The dark line of the coast, a hard black, sat gently, rising and falling, in the distance. The glow of a lamp or a fire, the only yellow light to be seen from the shore. Then the sound of the harbour bell, and the mate changed the rigging as the boat tacked towards its source. They berthed at a narrow pier. There was no one ashore and the boy completed a skilled jump onto a narrow step; he climbed the pier wall to receive the mooring rope.

'There is no inn, but anyone the harbour cottages will take you in. We will leave in the morning at five hours and the half,' said the captain.

Joe looked to his fob watch; it was still before ten. They knocked on the door of a cottage where they could see a fire in the grate.

'*Heb je een kamer?*' enquired Grietje.

The woman gestured them inside. The low-ceilinged house smelt of sweet-smoke and fish.

'*Ik heb een kinder bed in een doos en een stoel in een vuur.*' she pointed, '*Een stuiver.*'

'She has a small box bed and a chair by the fire,' repeated Grietje to Joe.

'That will do.'

'*Ontbijt een stuiver,*' offered the woman.

'With breakfast two silvers - coins.'

'At five hours, the morning?'

This was agreed. Joe gave the woman two coins and she disappeared into the back of the house. Joe felt they had just taken the chair she had been sitting in, and her bed too, but did not ask.

'You have the bed, I'll sit by the fire.'

'But your leg?'

'I'll be fine.'

'You are a good man, Joseph Grieve.'

'If the mind can be a sin without the body, I am not.'

'You will come back here, Joe. I am not done with you.'

At dawn, the light crept in, both were woken from a deep sleep by a knock on the inside door.

'*Ontbijt*'

The woman brought in a wooden chair and put it to join the other at the small table which was placed by the window. She added a log to the fire. She brought oats with cream followed by freshly smoked fish and eggs. Joe and Grietje looked at each other. Such a meal was not what they were expecting. The coffee was not good but it was coffee. Joe was chasing the last piece of fish round his tin plate when he looked through the window to see the mate and the boy readying the boat. They thanked the woman and left. Setting off quickly, the captain told them they should reach Veere before nightfall. Joe remarked on the time. 'It is a fair wind and a calm sea,' said the captain.

The day dragged despite the boat's speed. They were keen to arrive. Joe and Grietje slept a little more, talked a little, Joe telling Grietje more of the story of his visit with Tom. They watched the small islands pass, looked for life on the coastline, and wondered at a pod of playfull porpoises which sported on the boat's bow-wave.

There was not much activity from the crew, the yacht piloted itself. Grietje had brought bread, cheese and wine which they did not take until late afternoon. As the sun sunk below the horizon, the captain pointed to the shore.

'Walscheren, the Veere inlet.'

It was taking effort to slow the boat down. The captain tacked it hard to port and lightly back to starboard, several times on one sail, to reduce the speed. As they approached Veere harbour, Grietje spotted Ruud on the harbour wall, waving in recognition and relief. Among the few ships and many bobbing barges, an ornately decorated large ship which looked like a foreign Navy ship, a frigate, was anchored near the harbour entrance. They found room to dock and Joe told the captain to hold the load until he saw if a ship was available for them. Ruud was at the top to the ladder smiling and pulled him up from the last rung.

'Do we have a ship, Ruud.'

'Yes, Sir,' and he pointed to the Navy ship.

'The marines?'

'No, it is now converted to a merchantman. It leaves tomorrow at ten. Bound for Dundee, but will put in at Leith if you agree a price.'

'How do I get to it? How do we load?'

'They have a hoist on board. I spoke to the captain, he was agreeable.'

'We can row across now.' Ruud pointing to a rowing boat tied farther down the quay.

Grietje had joined them along with the captain of the barge. The three started towards the rowing boat.

''Grietje, you stay here.' commanded Joe.

'*Nee!*' She replied and followed them onto the small

boat. Ruud took the oars, the capatin untied and they set off. The captain laughed, took the oars, and they set off again, in the rigth direction. Close up, the ship was even more impressive, despite being worn and in need of paint. The bow piece was a large naked maiden surrounded by cherubs, with enough anatomical detail to interest Ruud. The rear of the frigate had two layers of low mullioned windows surrounded by elaboratly painted wood carvings, both religious and grotesque. As they neared the ship's rope ladder there was a shout and the barge captain replied. Joe with difficulty went up first then Greijte, Ruud and the barge captain. The *Grace of God* was the largest ship Joe had been onboard. It smelled of the farmyard not the sea. They remarked on this to the hand who was escorting them to the captain's quarters.

'We have delivered a load of livestock. We were glad the seas were smooth.'

The captains quarters was like a Tudor drawing room. Rich redded wood panels and furnishings. The signs of wear only added to its allure. Signs of carelessness or battle, who knew. The darkess with in the room contrasted with the startingly bright view over the top of the town through the long window. They were high up, as if on a mountain, in a land where there were none. They could see forever. It was a scene of which, if mounted, one would never tire; it demanded to be painted. The captain facing the door, his back to the window arose from his desk. In sillouete, he was hard to see clearly but he was younger than Joe expected. They all shook hands; he was particularly pleased to meet Greijte, and he invited them to sit at a table with a chart on it. The captain explained that their normal route was to Africa and the West Indies. The ship was fitted for human cargo. The new owner's preferred tobacco and he was a fresh captain, ex Navy, for the merchantman. He was recruiting and training a young crew before heading across the Atlantic next month. He had plenty of room for more cargo. He asked about the load and Joe stressed its fragility.

'It is worth nothing if dropped.'

'The crew lifted over twenty cows in the net and no broken legs. I will make sure they take care. You can load before eight tonight or early in the morning. We sail in the morning at ten hours. You can oversee. You will find my first mate is experienced, a good man.'

The captain offered a price saying it will be a fast trip. Joe replied that he would have counsel with this clerk and give an answer within the hour.

'The mate will give you a tour if you wish. I have one question. Is the lady travelling?'

Grietje's eyes lit up.

'No', said Joe, and then looking Geitje's expression, added, 'not this time.'

'Ah, as well, some of the crew are still nervous about women at sea. You may use the wardroom below if you wish to sit.'

'Let us do that first,' he said to the others.

As they sat in a room smaller but similar to the captain's quarters. Ruud said, 'Joe there was a letter for you at the *Conciergerie*. and handed Joe the envelope. It was not a sealed letter, he recognised his wife's handwriting. Joe excused himself to read it.

Dearest Joseph,

Do not overly worry we are all fine but if you you receive this and I so hope you do would

*you please hurry home soonest or pray send
some money. We have received not a penny from
the company. I went to the office many a time
but there was no attendance, no clerk, nothing.
Anon, I went with the children to the Lockhart's
rooms. Mr Lockhart was there after five knocks
and asked us to the hall but it took sometime
to make him understand if ever he did. After
some time he promised to dispatch some money
to us but nothing came. We are not destitute
nor starving with grateful thanks to our Godly
friends and neighbours and our kind landlord
has allowed the rent though I fear he is running an interest. I have managed to earn a little
by sewing and cleaning but it is not much. This
children cannot attend school. I would need to
ask the church which I know you would disdain.
All would be mended if you could send ten or
even five pounds. I am so sorry to worry you. I
hope this finds you well. I long to see you.*

Your only love,
Mary

He went white, Grietje noticed immediately.

'Joe?'

'We will sail on this ship. Captain can you bring up
your barge presently to load. I will pay for your service
to help with the loading. Ruud will do what you need.'

'Yes, sir. Can I suggest a tip for the winch man, just to
keep his attention.'

There was no point in replying to the letter. The ship
would return quicker than any mail.

'Grietje we will ashore. I need to attend the harbour
office.'

They left the mess to arrange the loading, with the first officer, then take the small boat back to the barge. Leaving Ruud and the captain, Joe and Grietje heading to find the harbour master and attend the *Conciergerie*. to see what papers and payment were required.

'Joe, you are shaking, what is it.'

He could not speak though anger and so handed Greijte the letter. She struggled to read but got the sense of it. She let it sit awhile before she said.

'The date is four days past, another four to get there. That is not long. It will be mended,' she paused. 'I'm sorry Joe, it will be fixed,' and added, 'Anger will not fix it. Save that for later.'

He looked at her and realised she was right.

Calmer, he walked with her to the harbour buildings. There was not much to do. An inattentive offical directed them to a logbook to record the ship and the load. There was another letter addressed to Joseph Greive which was sealed and he tore it open. It was a short note from Henry. At another time he would have smiled. At last he could speak,

'Its fourteen hours to sail, I wish it were sooner.'

'We could watch the loading. Is there anything else.'

Joe had to think hard.

'I don't think. Oh, I was going to try to find the coachman.'

'I am not now well disposed to aiding the Lockharts.'

'Was it only for them?'

'Let us go out to the ship again, on the barge. We will eat tonight near the harbour we may find some local seamen and ask of Henrik then.'

The loading went well. The barge captain and Grietje got their tour of the ship while Joe and Ruud were shown their berth.

The lowest deck was last on their visit and it was the one which lasted in their minds. It stank not of animals. The black stench was of illness and death; its origin was human. The deck and had no air, no open ports. On each side, two layers of narrow beds, one above the other, each bed with two chains and clasps. Grietje tried to count but lost the number as she retched. A slurry channel ran along the centre and then off to a sealed opening at the side. None of them spoke and they were glad to get to back to the top deck. Retuning to the mess deck to meet the others Geitje was first to speak

'It is a short distance from hell to heaven.'

They left the ship on the barge together. Joe paid the captain well and thanked him for his service. The ate a solemn meal at the Scottish Inn at the harbour. They were all quiet in empathy with Joe and also because of the iminent parting. Grietje kept Ruud bright by telling him he can come back to Veere on Joe's business and that she may even travel to Edinburgh. Ruud asked if she would wait for him,

'No, Ruud, happy your return. I will not spend life waiting, I done much of that.'

At that, she went and spoke to a few locals at standing at the bar. Joe asked,

'Ruud, you have everything?'

'Yes, sir.'

'We will embark soon and spend the night on board.'

'May I not...'

'No Ruud, we will say our goodbyes here. I will walk Grietje back to her lodgings.'

Deflated, Ruud accepted Joe's authority. He allowed Ruud some time outside with Grietje before sending him back inside to wait on his return. He walked with Grietje in silence,

'I asked about Henrik. One man remembered a driver by that name. He said he thought he drowned in the flood six months past. He left a wife. She lives in a cottage, *Zeezicht* at the end of the breakwater.'

'Thank you Grietje. Not just for that. I'm too set to return. I will miss..., I will see you again.'

At the stairway to her rooms, she stood to kiss him, said nothing, turned and hurried up the stair. Joe turned, so full of thought, he lost his way back in the narrow alleys leading from her rooms to the harbour. He turned and went along a narrow alley he did not know. A man was coming toward him, walking in the direction of Grietje's rooms.

In an instant he knew who it was. There was no doubt in his mind. He stopped thinking. He fell back into a recessed doorway. Since an event in his youth, Joe vowed to fear no man, and turned to walk towards him. The man, oblivious to Joe's approach, did not look up. Joe moved to the left. As he passed, Joe caught him with a hard right hook to the unguarded jaw, the rising blow twisting his head. The man's body jerked and he was out before he hit the ground. Joe stood over him. He thought about using his stick. Instead he stamped down hard, once, twice, on his victim's left knee; he heard it crack, and once more between his legs.

'This is your world. It is not mine.'

Joe spat on his assailant's vacant face, 'Bastaard.'

CHAPTER 11

Edinburgh, Scotland 1711

Teaching in Epiphany term started before the turn of the calendar year. The boys who had left over the winter break returned to Heriot's and provided entertainment with their tales of families, travel and festive food. David and the others, who had remained, kept a collegiate relationship which lasted a few weeks, then dissipated into the term-time routine. David was glad to have Alan, Harry, Daniel and Eduard back. David noticed that Googe kept an eye out for him and, he thought, protected him from the inevitable bullying that many of the juniors suffered in the claustrophobic regime of a boys' boarding school. They had tea together in Googe's room most Sunday afternoons, sometimes just David and Googe, but more often with one or two others. Googe told David that there would be a school summer theatre conducted in the grounds. One performance for all the boys, parents and guests at the start of June, and then more for the public for the few days following. That event took place after Founder's Day and David was forewarned that he would be given an important part; yet the play was not decided. There were also concerts in the summer term at which he would likely be expected to sing.

January, February, March passed in batches of rain, wind, hail, wind, snow, wind, with the occasional flash of low, dazzling sunshine, and wind. There were very cold nights, when it was common, on waking, to find another boy in bed with you. David's wakeful thoughts were always of Molly.

He learned that, in the coming year, you had to fag for one or more of the older boys. This meant you were at their beck and call, having to respond immediately and on demand to any service, any task. At tea one Sunday with Googe, David gained some sage advice. Googe warned him to find a reasonable boy whom he got on with, and who was currently in year four. That would mean he would fag for the same chap for two years.

'And take care he is not a fellow who is overly fond of malicious beatings nor is interested in your arse. Try to give a good impression of yourself and be of useful service. The ability to obtain beer, tobacco, extra food and trifles from the markets are good skills in this regard and may save you from an unsavoury time.' Fagging was only a burden after supper and occasionally before morning prayers.

In the second year, all but a few boys would attend the High School for their lessons. If the tall tales were to be believed, there were many adventures that could be had on the walks between the *hofpital* and the High School. They would also be permitted out on Sunday afternoons, providing their record was clean and there were no other demands on them. There was a summer term before that, however, and, although it was not yet Easter, the other boys were talking of their summer plans.

The Christmas break had been well spent in school, but David did not welcome the idea of spending the whole summer in the confines of Heriot's. He was interested in finding out if his mother had recovered, with no expectation of going back to reside there. He was not sure how to approach this and would try to talk to Molly when the opportunity arose.

The days warmed. David found himself in church more often. His high pitch voice at a good volume was in demand and he sang in Lady Yester's, Greyfriars, Canongate and St Giles during the Easter services. It kept him busy and he was allowed to walk there and return for practice and rehearsals with the other choristers. David had no academic problems with the studies in his first year and spent much time in the school library reading anything that he could find. As summer approached, he tried to teach himself Latin in order to read some of the classic texts and poems. If he did get stuck in school for the summer, that, at least, would occupy him. Meanwhile, the term-time daily habits of the boys were those of a monk: worship, study, eat, study, worship and eat. There were short bursts of frenetic activity in quad before the morning bell and in the dorms after supper, before lights out.

Shortly after the Easter festival, when the cherry was starting to bloom, the crocuses were up and the daffodils were opening, a cold snap hit the town. A freezing north wind held sleety snow which fell, covering the town and the school overnight. Daniel, who had had a restless night, awoke with spots and lumps over his face and body. The boys laughed at him and Daniel found it funny too when a boy brought a glass. David fetched Molly and saw a hint of fear on her face when she looked at Daniel. He was sitting on the bed and she just shouted at the boys to go to their beds and wait. They had not seen Molly react in such a way before. Her face was white, not red with anger. 'Come,' she said softly to Daniel and he did, looking back at the others who had stopped their jokes. Molly took Daniel directly to one of the rooms reserved for boys who were taken ill.

As the boys resumed their dressing, the Master arrived in the dormitory. He told the boys that they would have to stay in the dormitory for a few days, leaving only for privy. Meals would be brought to them. Molly would stay in the adjoining room; she would eat with them. He explained it was for fear of contagion. Should any other boy have a high temperature, pains or spots, he must tell Molly immediately, day or night. The boys' first reaction when the Master and Molly left, was one of annoyance. Stuck in the dorm, for how many days? Eduard could not offer any insight except that contagion meant that it was something they might catch. Nervously, the boys got dressed. Poor Harry, who slept next to Daniel, was kept at a distance by the rest. When Molly came back, the boys were made to go to the washroom and stay there until called back. It was cramped with them all inside, some tried to hold their breath. Without Daniel there was no one to break their fear with a silly remark. Molly came to summon them, and when they returned to the dorm there were two long tables and four benches set out down the middle of the dorm between the two rows of beds. There was also a box of textbooks, the boys' own psalters, paper, quill pens, a knife and ink.

'For how... how long, Molly?' asked Eduard, as the

implications of the situation were sinking in.

'As long as it takes.' A typical Molly reply.

Breakfast was delivered to the anteroom and Molly went to fetch it. The boys relaxed a bit on the arrival of the food and the novelty. It was a richer breakfast than the usual serving, eggs and ham being the treat. Molly was not going to do all the work and co-opted David and Eduard into bringing the plates, tankards, knives, and spoons, then setting them out. The boys sat to eat, quite sombrely; their clown was missed.

'Where is my tankard?'

'Shut up, Donald!'

'Molly, will Daniel be all well?'

'It takes time, we will all say a prayer for him to-night.'

As Molly sat to eat with them, David realised she was also stuck. He struggled to come up with the word, forty days, *quaranta*, he thought. Two other boys cleared away after breakfast. Molly made them all sit and say a small prayer. It was all she knew. She told them to look to their books but had no idea what was required. David went to the box and found a note on the top. He stood up and went to Molly, he explained that they were to sit silently and copy text. Molly could silence the boys and she did. She instructed David to tell the boys what was required. David did not like the prospect of copying for how long, forty days; he set some arithmetic instead. He kept the sheet to himself. He had them write down the questions he made up. He hadn't done them himself yet, but he knew he could. To his surprise the boys did exactly as he asked. The morning passed.

Communication with the rest of the staff was by

notes delivered with the meals and Molly's replies went with the collected pots. They were aware of more commotion in the quad than usual and tried to peek out when they heard a horse or a barrow arrive. Lunch was delivered, served and cleared as with breakfast. In the afternoon, as David was conjuring up another lesson, there was a rap on the door. Molly instructed them to sit as she attended. A young man whom they had never seen before came in to take the lesson. They had to remain seated at all times. They would stand only to offer an answer. He stayed for two hours only. Molly cleaned and took washing as much as she could, otherwise she just sat watching the boys work.

On the first night, the tiredness and the memory of the day made them worry. Molly attended phantom spots and aches and pains throughout the night. In the morning there were no clear symptoms. The next day echoed the first. They added psalms to the morning and evening prayers. There was no point to enquire of Daniel, Molly would not know.

On the third morning, Eduard and one of the other boys had spots and were removed as immediately as Daniel. The tension recurred; they were not immune.

'How long?' they asked again. Molly confessed she did not know and tried to hide her signs of strain. And so, it went on for several days. The young tutor came some days and not others. The boys insisted David kept them in lessons. Molly, bored, suggested a play or some singing be prepared. They jumped at that. There were no more casualties. It was lessons in the morning and theatrical preparations in the afternoon.

They lost count of the days. The one benefit was that the food was of good quality and varied from day to day. Someone, whether it was the cook or the Master, cared for their circumstance. They were not forgotten. There was comfort in that. One day, a commotion in the quad, a bustle of visitors, the noise of a cart and a carriage, they could see best from the window in the anteroom. David thought he recognised some of the governors from the Christmas event. From the cart, a long, thin wooden box was delivered. David said nothing to the boys but told Molly.

A weekend came, noted only because a young minister, again one that they did not know, arrived and gave a short and gloomy sermon while the boys sat on their benches; then another weekend, then another. No more of the boys became afflicted. There were tears and tantrums at times and David went to the anteroom once and found Molly sobbing. Of all things, the play kept them going. David had asked Molly to request books and they came the next day. Arithmetic became more competitive and they kept scores. Every boy knew the Catechism by heart. David got better books to read and they took turns at reading in the evenings. Some boys made up stories to recite in the evenings. Others, including David, sang after supper. But rehearsing the play brought lightness to the monotony. They asked for clothes but that was refused. They asked for a needle and thread and Molly got to work. Her mood changed with this industry. On a Tuesday garments were shaped, lines remembered, entrances, exits and cues, learned; at last, the play was ready. They had no audience. 'We shall play for ourselves,' said one boy, 'and for Molly!' said another. There was no knock, the door burst open,

'Ahoy, you curs, I have come to rescue you!' and Daniel stood in his finest form.

The boys were not sure how to react. Was it a tease? Daniel was smiling and nodding. Some cheered; others clapped. They did not rush to shake his hand. The physician, coming in behind him, was expressionless. Molly went quickly to him. David watched. In answer to her first question, the physician nodded; a second and he slowly shook his head. Molly went straight out and down the stairs. The Master came in.

'Boys, the physician will examine you just to make sure, but we expect that your incarceration will end today. Line up down the centre, remove your shirts, breeks and hose. Well done all of you,' and he left.

The relief expressed itself in smiles, nudges, punches and giggles. Daniel had to be brought to order more than once. As the physician neared the end the line of boys, releasing each one with an affirmative nod, Molly reappeared at the dormitory door. She walked to David,

'It was Eduard, dearest, Eduard,' she said softly.

He turned to the room, 'Boys, boys!'

He looked to Molly, but she shook her head.

'Eduard was not saved,' said David calmly. The boys' initial silence changed to whispers of gentle oath and expressions of regret. Eduard's older brother had also succumbed. They heard later that Eduard had been infected by him. They had neither parent; their family lawyer had put them forward for the school. They had no relative to attend the memorial service which the school hosted in the following week. The school eventually received a substantial bequest in their name and a statue was commissioned for the grounds.

That last day of their confine, however, a bond

formed within the group of thirteen eleven-year-old schoolboys and David had learned what he was to become.

In late May, Edinburgh got a scent of summer. There were outdoor lessons, concerts, plays and games to be performed in the lead up to June Day, the religious, festive and floral tribute to the institution's founder. The marble bust of George Heriot in the quad, and the pillars themselves, were decked in flower garlands. On singing soprano for his fourth day in a row, David's top note was missing. His throat sore, his glands swollen, he begged off the next performance, but the Master insisted. He got through it by changing key. The music tutor noticed. He overheard him having a conversation with the master after the performance.

'Other than castration, Master, there is nothing I can do.'

'I suppose we must give in to God's grace. Is there another boy?'

'Not quite of that standard but, yes, I can fill the place.'

David was excused choral singing for the rest of the term and desperately hoped he may play a male in Googe's epic swansong. It was not to be.

'We can drop the singing, Mills, but you are by far the comeliest wench we have in school. Especially when Molly gets her hands on you.'

David was ambivalent, unsure whether that was compensation enough.

To Googe's disappointment, the Master ruled that a

two-hour Greek tragedy may be noble, but it was not well suited to the occasion. 'And we must involve more of the boys. Every boy with an attending parent must be seen. Those with the biggest purses would be given the biggest parts.'

Three pieces were agreed. A Greek tragedy, a noble Roman deed, and a Shakespearian farce; the half hour each. David thought he might be omitted completely under these criteria.

He was cast as a goddess in the first and the fairie queen in the last. June Day was upon the school. The boys and a good number of representatives of the town itself gathered in the quadrangle at eight in the morning

> Upone the first Monnonday of Junii everie year sal be keipt a solemne commemoratioune and thankisgiving unto God in this forme which followeth. In the morning about eight of the clock of that day the Lord Provost and all the Ministeris and Ordinarie Coucell of the Ceittie of Edinburgh sall assemble thameselffis in the Committee Chamber of the said Hofpitall and with all the Scholleris and Offcieris of the said Hofpitall going before them two and two to Gray Frier Church where they shall heare a sermon preached by the Ministeris of the said Ceitte.

After the ceremonious beginning, the day became a celebration of the school and the summer with food, music and theatre, all hosted within the *Hofpital* grounds. The end of June Day brought the school year to a close. Following academic exhaustion for the boys and the staff, the day had been a culmination of a growing energy, enterprise, excitement and good humour. The change in mood mirrored the weather. David had been so involved in rehearsals and preparations, he had little mind to consider anything but the tasks in hand.

The days following June Day, the Tuesday and Wednesday, involved clearing up, packing and farewells for most of the boys and, when Friday came, the school had gone dreadfully quiet. David found only four boys from the whole school who were residing during the summer. None from his year. Not all boys had families, but most had someone. Others, he knew, were invited to join with their friend and stay elsewhere for the summer break. David was aware he had not discussed his situation with his friends. In fact, he avoided these conversations because he knew he had no plans over the summer and did not wish discomfort nor place his friends under any obligation. He was now regretting this. The Christmas break had been short, active and stimulating. These next twelve weeks did not present such prospects. Google had caught him on Tuesday, hugged him and ruffled his hair. He congratulated David on his performances and thanked him for his help. He then wished him well. David did not realise that that had been goodbye. Saying farewell to his bonded baker's dozen had been so hectic that it took the few days to register. He went to find Molly on the pretext of going to thank her.

One advantage was that the school was so quiet you could wander around with impunity. He knocked on the door he knew to be the maids' room. Only Molly was there sorting some clothes on a bed.

'You shouldn't be here, David.'

'I just came to talk. Are you also leaving?'

'Yes, on Saturday. There will be a new maid to look after the summer boys.'

'I wanted to try to see my mother again, how she is.'

'Oh, David, I don't know if that is wise.'

'I'd hoped you might be able to come.'

'I leave tomorrow. There is not time. Come here.'

Molly pulled David close. She squeezed him into her bosom, held him for a moment, released him and gave him a kiss on his head.

'Take care of yourself, mind.'

David nodded then left and went to look for a Doctor to see if he was permitted to leave the school. He went up to the masters' study room which also acted as a library. No answer to his knock, he pushed at the door, unlocked, he went in. It had that quiet calm atmosphere, only found in cathedrals and libraries, and perhaps natural caves and woodlands. He walked round looking at the books, finding one he could not resist, in English, the history of Anglo-Saxon kings. He sat down to read. The leather chair was comfortable, he dozed off.

'What are you doing here, boy?'

'Sorry Sir, I was just looking...'

'Oh, it doesn't matter. You'd better leave though. What is that book?'

David showed it to the master whom he did not know.

'You can borrow it. Mind bring it back. What is your name?'

'Miller, sir, David Miller.'

'Ah, yes of course. I'm Brown, I am attending over the summer.'

'Sir, thank you sir.'

Cook was still cooking. There was a library, he could borrow books. Now, if he could be let out for a walk, it might not be the active school life he had become used to, but it was a life he recognised and found tolerable.

On the Saturday morning, after prayers and breakfast, the boys, five of them now, were not given any study nor duties. David went into the grounds at first, then he left, unhindered through the school gate. He did not know what the other boys did, he had not found much conversation in any of them so far. He would try harder. He walked through the Greyfriars' churchyard and turned right to go through the Bristow port in the town wall.

It was a sunny day; at first, he walked further south. There was a meadowland, common grazing, not far from the school. Boggy in winter but pleasant pasture in high season; a few sheep and fewer cows grazed. The good number of people crossed it on foot, horseback and with hand carts and barrows, heading towards the town. The sun in the west illuminated craggy hills to the east; its heather coat in bloom. He could just see some sheep dotted on the lower slopes and two or three people at the very top of the crag. He turned east and walked toward cottages which lined the main road south. He did not know this route, but you could see Heriot's and the castle for miles, he would not get lost. It did not seem a day to be troubled by beggars and vagrants.

David crossed the fields and two roads: the Back Row and the Pleasance, both busy, and headed for the

Royal House which he knew was at the bottom of the High Street. He found a quiet, but well-trodden path just under the Crags which took him to the rear of the Canongate near the foot of St Mary's Wynd. The sunlight barely penetrated these densely packed closes, only occasionally finding the narrow gaps between the buildings. There were many people outside the *lands*, sitting in shade, nursing, sewing, and talking. Unshod children ran and played with sticks and balls of paper. Men stood on the corners in smoking groups. He realised his route had been unmindedly intended. He arrived at the bottom of the close of his grandfather's house.

There was no lower rung on this ladder. If he was chased away, then he had lost nothing. He was worried that he might upset his mother, if she were there, but then, at least, he would know. He passed several *lands* to find the one he recognised and asked a woman who was sitting on a chair, sewing, at the foot of the stair.

'Excuse me, Ma'am, I'm looking for Mrs Lockhart?'

It's the richt stair but yee'l no fin' 'er.'

'Mr Lockhart?'

'*Very seldom, you cuid chap and see.'*

He went up and *chapped*. There was no answer, so he sat down and waited at the door, knocking again every so often. Nothing. He went back down the stair.

'*Wha are ye'? Eh'l tell 'im ye caud?'*

'I'm his grandson.'

David, to his own surprise, was not downhearted. It was a bright warm day. He was enjoying this freedom. He went up to the High Street and walked slowly up it, looking at every tray, stall and hawker, sometimes going down a close to see what lay hidden. There were soldiers, tall in red coats, with thin swords in their scabbards, usually in twos, relaxed, their top buttons undone. There were Jacobites, in threes and fours, identifiable by their long plaid cloaks, broaches and bonnets. They were not armed. There was none of the tension of his last walk down the High Street with Molly. He had a shilling plus a few pennies and bought a shiny stone, small knife and a pie. Why was he always hungry?

Tossing a penny to the jugglers, he moved on to find a young girl with dark skin in a flowing skirt, dancing and singing to the accompaniment of finger bells and a man playing a mandolin. He stood and watched for a while. She got tuppence from him and a few more from the soldiers. He went into St Giles and said a prayer. It was not his church nor even his faith. It was still his god.

Coming out, he bought a newssheet for a penny and listened to a preacher standing on a box outside. *We are all guilty and will suffer*, David did not feel like that today. Nearing the Lawn Mercate, the street got busier. He found a bookseller he did not recall seeing before. He went in but was chased out. He got shouted at by some older boys – he was in his school russet – but he made his way quickly and they did not give chase.

He arrived at his family's old rooms. Driven by habit rather than reason, he went up the stair. A knock this time brought a quick reply. It was a woman who did not appear to mind the interruption. He excused himself and explained that he was trying to contact his family and wondered if they had a forwarding address. The woman was sympathetic but said she couldn't help. Oddly, he thought, he could see the crate he noticed on his last visit; it was still sitting in the hall. He pointed to the package. She said they had been trying to get it dealt with and had been in contact through the lawyers.

'There is a sending address on it,' she said, 'You can look.'

She allowed him a pen and paper to copy down the label.

'Would you give me the name of your lawyers, so that I could help you with this?'

She went to find it.

'If you call again, David, best be in the mornings when my husband is out. He is not patient on this issue. I am afraid your family owes us some money and he will not release the package until it is paid.'

'Take care, lad, it's a sorry mess.'

David made his way back to the West Port and thence to the school; he walked past the Porter's house.

'Yea have to sign the book!'

He went to the book and saw that other boys had signed the book to go out. Three of the boys had put St Giles as their destination, he had not seen any on his visit there. He signed himself out and in. He had actually attended the High Kirk. Heading up to his dormitory, where he now had sole occupancy, his things were gone. The rows of beds lay naked of cloth, void of occupancy. 'Another plot,' he said out loud, an easier one to solve, I hope, and he set off to find his new ward.

So it was, for the next few weeks. The new master, Brown, gave them some tasks which he completed in the morning. A midday meal, then he ventured out exploring the town or walking through the meadows or along the river he had found to the west. The other boys were older and did not disclose much of their days. A funny tale was sometimes told over supper. David realised this type of summer was not new to them. Like him, they had no family, nor did they seek comfort, they had little experience nor want of it. Some days the boys arranged to play a field game in the grounds. David was invited to join, hitting a small ball with a long-handled club. Despite his paucity of skill, it became an absorbing habit. On wet or damp days, he went to explore every nook and cranny of the school; there was a lot of it. He found a small room on the ground floor, where the hitting balls were made from leather and feathers. There was no one in it. Next to that, a larger room, empty but for a few benches, which was of no interest until three carts arrived with crates and large, oddly shaped packages. He stood by and watched as the carts were unloaded by several men. When the empty carts left, two men, one older and one younger, remained. They started to unpack and carry things into the large room.

'May I help, sir?'

'We are fine, boy.'

'I will take care and do as you bid.'

'Alright, there is no money in it, mind.'

'May I ask questions, sir?'

'Aye, if ye must.'

David spent that morning lifting, moving, unpacking and sorting. When he and the men were done there was an organised assortment of shaped and dressed, large wooden pieces placed in the middle of the room. In floor space beside these pieces, all else was put to the side. David had enjoyed the labour.

'Now, lad, the Steward said we will be fed.'

'I can show you where, sir.'

'Lead on, we shall go now and assemble it after.'

'Pray, sir, what is it?'

'It's a printing press, lad. You have done well. You can come back to watch if you care.'

David took them to the refectory where he sat with them to eat. He didn't really know what a printing press was, so did not ask any more. It looked interesting though. David went back with them and watched the two men assemble a large contraption out of the parts. There was quite a lot of adjustment, hammering mostly, needed to make the pieces fit and they had to rake through boxes to find parts that had been missed. The parts had terms he had not heard before, platen, head, tenon, till, collar, chase, carriage, coffin and gallows, morbidly. David stood and handed them tools when they asked, learning the names as he went along.

'Tell you what, lad, you can sort the type into cases. That would help us.'

'Do you know your alphabet?'

'Yes, sir.'

The older man found the boxes of many metal letters of differing sizes and eight wooden trays. He asked David to sort each size of letter, in alphabetical order, into a case. The case was a tray of many small boxes.

'Start with an A top left, and work left to right. Small letters in one case, capitals in the other. Got it?'

'I think so, sir.'

'And mind the letters are the wrong way round.'

As David set to task, it dawned on him that the machine was for making newssheets, leaflets and books. He couldn't quite see how it worked yet, but he was fascinated. The metal letters were tiny. By the window he spotted bottles of ink, then he had it.

You put ink on the wrong-way-round letter, pressed on a paper and you get a printed letter. It seemed obvious once he realised.

'Sir, how do I tell p, d, q and b?' David was starting on the small letters.

'Leave those for last, then I'll show you.'

David was absorbed. It was time consuming, there were sixty-four cases. 'Four *points*, four *fonts*,' said the older man, McDonald he was called. There was an upper case and a lower case. He started with one font and finished two points, four cases, but was then called to prayers.

'Can I come back tomorrow, sir?'

'Aye, lad, and here's a shilling for your work.'

'Thank you, sir.'

After morning prayers, David pleaded with Brown, who was eminently reasonable for a master, to be excused his study in order that he may return to McDonald and his machine. Brown was also interested and said he would come by later to see it. As David sorted the type, the printing press grew.

By late afternoon, there were no parts left in the middle of the room. The machine was taller than a man. An upright, rectangular frame over a raised bed. The sturdy frame held a weight and a flat wooden block, the platen, which could be screwed down vertically to press on the bed. The raised bed held a tray called the coffin which would hold the type trays, galleys, with letters. There was one galley for each page.

'Is it done, sir?'

'We need *tae* adjust it.'

This took some time. David sorted. McDonald gave David a set of long shallow trays, composing sticks, and a larger one, the galley, with no divisions. He asked him to fill the small ones with letters, then fit them together in the galley. McDonald said they did not need to be in any order. David, being David, tried to write part of the catechism, getting a few lines wrong until he realised the lines of type had to be backwards too.

The lad, Jack, he was, went to a bench with the ink. He mixed the ink, it smelled, and worked it onto a flat plate using leather pads with wooden handles. He picked a few sheets of paper from one of the unopened boxes. McDonald kept fiddling with the press. The midday meal interrupted them. David was partway through his task. Brown joined them to eat, enquiring about the press. It was not the school's press; the printer was just renting the room. He would print for the school in lieu of rent. Brown asked to visit later in the day. After the meal, which David finished in five minutes and fidgeted impatiently for another forty, they returned to the printing room.

'Right, we'll try it, Jack.'

McDonald clamped a sheet of paper on the end of the frame – that part folded over – and slid it along the bed to sit under the platen. He then turned the large, vertical screw to move the platen down. He took a good look around the parts, lifted the platen, adjusted, and lowered it again. He did this several times, giving David enough time to finish putting his type in the small trays. Jack showed him how to fit the composing sticks into the galley.

'Right, lad.' McDonald said to no one specific. He took the galley and fixing it on the bed, went through the same routine of adjustment, twice through.

'You can ink up now.'

Jack took the galley and, using the leather pads, put ink on the type surface.

'Not too much now.'

David saw it akin to a pious ceremony.

The galley was clamped back on the press, and finally the platen which held the paper was forced down by turning the handle of the screw, pressing the paper onto the bed which held the trays of inked blocks of type. In a beat, the platen was lifted and the frame, with the paper on it, slid out.

McDonald lifted the paper. He looked at it closely, muttering. He picked up a glass and looked again, then returned to his task of adjusting the press. McDonald discarded the sheet and repeated the operation. When David got the opportunity, he snatched up the sheet of the printed paper and saw the printed lines of his text. He looked on it amazed. It was his writing, in print, on a sheet of paper. It looked fine to him. Then the realisation; you could make scores of these, all the same, very quickly. He knew what he wanted to be now. He wanted to be a printer.

David spent the following days there, forgoing walks and sunshine. Brown summoned him back to study in the mornings, but he still had the afternoons. Other printing staff arrived to take over the tasks David had learned. Two men set the type, compositors, a woman who collected the printed paper, dried it, cut and collated the sheets; she was the finisher. Jack did most of the printing overseen by McDonald. There were artists who cut illustrations in wood blocks. A smartly dressed man brought in hand-written work and kept the books, and a boy of his own age moved boxes and parcels. It was a busy enterprise, carts came with supplies and left with printed sheets, many larger than the one David produced. They tolerated David's presence and allowed him to print his own newssheet for the school. He supplied the paper and, under supervision, typeset it himself. He learned how to use the press. As it got busier, he felt redundant and returned to the routine of visiting the library and going on exploratory walks. Still, he usually called in to talk to McDonald and Jack at the end of each day and liked reading the day's printed sheets.

As the summer moved into July, David's thoughts turned again to his family. He spoke to Mr Brown about it, could he approach the lawyers perhaps? Brown expressed sympathy but could offer no advice other than to wait until he reached the age of maturity. He could write, of course, but he had tried that.

In the printing room, he spotted a notice in a newssheet regarding a planned public recital in the Lady Yester's Kirk, on the Canon Gait. They were still recruiting singers. David had lost his top-end, but he could still sing, so he asked Brown if he may attend. The rehearsals took place in the afternoons, the actual recital would take place on a Saturday. Thus, he was occupied again.

One Monday morning in July, following prayers and breakfast, David and the other boys were heading across the quad to go to the study room when they stopped dead. There was a group of eight girls, lined up in twos, accompanied by three women. The girls were poised and smartly dressed in brown cloaks and hats. Each carried a small valise. They were looking up and around the quad. One boy tucked in his shirt, David and the others just gawped.

'All right, boys, continue to your study.' The master's voice.

The boys gossiped for a good half hour before Brown arrived. He was quite stern with them. Brooking no questions, he made them sit together at the table farthest from the window. They were set to recite Latin verbs.

'Please, sir,' a boy called Robert wailed.

Brown might have been about to answer, but there was a knock at the door. Eight girls came in, in cloaks and hats, and were invited to sit. The girls sat at two tables facing the front. One of the women came in and sat at the back. David thought the girls looked older than him; they were certainly more composed.

'Boys, these young ladies are from the *Trades Maiden's Hofpital*. They are in the same position as yourself, with no guardian or family to care for them during the summer due to circumstance. They will join you in study and some other activities. There will be careful supervision at all times and your freedom will be more restricted. All pupils will suffer new rules and restrictions. This is Miss Jamieson,' she stood, 'she is a schoolmistress and she will give some lessons. Boys, you will act for her as you would for me. Now, boys, you will each stand and give your name.'

The girls were then instructed to remove their hats and cloaks and introduce themselves. There was no further interaction. They sat at separate tables during meals, different pews in chapel or the kirk. They were quieter and cleverer in class. They were given a dormitory well away from the boys and were not seen after the evening meal. In an occasional unguarded moment, they could be caught in a giggle or a shriek. David thought there wasn't any point in eight girls knowing his name; there was no chance to interact.

The boys were instructed to stop staring at the girls. Thus, the staring became more discreet. Brown said David was still permitted to go to the choir rehearsals. When he tried to leave at the next opportunity, he was stopped by the gateman and told he needed a master's permission. Miss Jamieson arrived with three girls in tow, as he tried to debate the issue.

'What is the problem here?'

'David explained to Miss Jamieson what he was about.'

'Well that is good fortune, for that is where we are heading. You may come with us. And you will return with us.'

David looked up at the girls but there was no acknowledgement of his presence, no glance in his direction. The church was not far from the school. Miss Jamieson led two of the girls, the third walking at the rear trying to stay joined, and David waddled sheepishly behind her. It was not at all far, next to the High School, and Miss Jamieson instructed David firmly to await them at the end of the rehearsal. The girls had their own choir. David enjoyed singing in the boys' choir. He had no special role and he was getting to know the others. He noticed the three girls from the *Hofpital* sitting in the rear pews awaiting their practice. Their heads down in silent chatter, barely looking up. He stayed as instructed and watched the girls sing. They each wore a white dress with a narrow waist and a frilled collar. The singing impressed him; it was light and melodic compared to the dirges he was most times required to sing. On the third such outing, the walking formation always the same, the rear girl lagged a little more than usual and David neared her. She turned, expecting him to catch up which he did.

'You are David?'

'Yes, miss.'

'Don't call me miss, my name is Janett,' she laughed.

The other girls turned out of curiosity. This pleased Janett.

'You sing very well.'

'Thank you, miss,' was all David could muster. And that was it for conversation, but they walked together then, and on the two other remaining journeys before the concert date. The Saturday performance was a bigger day than David had expected. All the boys and girls in the school were instructed to attend. The singers set off early. Janett asked him if he was nervous and he said he was not. He told her that he used to sing soprano and did not worry about being in a choir. He found she was nearly two years older than him. They talked about their school lives and friends. They talked about the classes, the food, the dorms and the teachers. David was surprised to find Janett had classes in the bible, writing, music, poetry, dance, embroidery, and the making of lace and stockings. She did not envy the boys their repetitive memorising of ancient languages. David said he thought the girls' tutors seemed strict. Janett said they were kind but very protective of the girls. David confessed that the boys were very, very fierce, which made her laugh aloud causing one of the other girls turn and stare.

'I think my reputation is ruined already,' Janett said,

which David did not understand.

The kirk was full, the performances pleasant and accomplished. It was a sunny day in the middle of August. After the event, refreshments were served and the musicians, singers and the audience mingled in the church grounds.

'It *is* David isn't it, young David Miller?'

David turned to find a tall man and a lady. The man wore a dark Sunday suit and had short, unkempt, red hair. The lady wore a pretty dress. He looked familiar.

'Sir.' David went white.

'It's Joe, David, Joseph Grieve. I worked in your father's office. This is Mary my wife.'

As he now recognised him, David started to cry, he could not help nor stop it.

'Sir, sorry sir, I can't, sorry sir, sorry...,' and made to move away.

Mary went after him. 'It is alright, David, we did not mean to fright you. We mean no harm. Come aside and talk.'

David allowed himself to be led to a quieter part of the garden. Mary gave him a few minutes to compose himself.

'It was just a shock, Ma'am. I have no contact with my family. I do not know what happened to my mother, her family or my father really.'

'Are you fine now?'

'Yes, ma'am it was just a surprise,' he sniffed, 'I am very pleased to meet you.'

She waved Joe to come over. Janett had been watching and alerted Miss Jamieson, who also came over.

'I'm Miss Jamieson from the school. Is the boy unwell? Do you know him?'

'I'm Joseph Grieve miss, at your service. I know the boy and his family. I fear we have given him a fright.'

'Sorry, Miss.' David apologised.

'You'd better come back with us, David.'

'Miss, may I talk a minute with Mr Grieve.'

'A few moments only.' She did not withdraw.

'Perhaps, sir, it would be better if you attended David at the *hofpital*. I do not know the situation.'

'Of course, I apologise for any upset. It was not intended.'

'Please come, Sir. I would like to talk about my father. You know the school?' said David

'I do, David. I will come to see you. I promise you that.'

'Please do, sir.'

At that, Joe thought it best to leave. Mary put her arm round David and, with a squeeze, whispered for him not to worry, they would come to see him soon.

'Mr Brown is the master.'

'Goodbye, David.'

'Goodbye, sir.'

Janett took David by the arm, smiled at Mary, and pulled him away.

'Poor lad,' said Mary, 'he's not much older than our John. You *will* go and see him, Joe.'

'Of course, dear. He must feel like the forgotten child.'

'He *is* the forgotten child.'

In concern, Janett asked David on their walk back to the school what had happened. David told her that Joseph, Mr Grieve, had been with his father when he was lost, and he had assumed that Joseph had been lost too. He found it easy to talk to Janett.

'So, it was as a ghost I saw him.'

'A ghost!'

'Yes, as a ghost. It is not funny, Janett.'

'I know, I know, I'm sorry.'

'It is *not* funny.'

'I know, I know. You went to church and saw a ghost...not funny.'

David laughed.

Joe wrote to Mr Brown at the school, explaining the situation and asking to visit David the following Sunday. Mary rewrote it in a manner that was less business-like, adding that Lady Yester's was their own church and signed it herself. Joe agreed this was better. Letters were exchanged and a visit was arranged for the following Sunday.

David was pleased when Mr Brown told him about it and looked forward to their visit. Joe and Mary arrived with their minister, and Mr Brown, Miss Jamieson and David received them in the Council Room. It was not a relaxed meeting. Firstly, Joe explained to David and the others how he and David's father had become separated in Delft, and why he had returned on his own. He had fully expected Mr Millar to follow. Joe went on to say he had since returned to Delft and Campveere to seek news of him, without success.

He explained that when Tom was last seen, the weather had been violent, a dam had been breached and there was much flooding. David asked about his grandfather. I'm afraid I have not had contact with him, only his lawyers. It has not been easy. There have been problems with the business which I am currently try-ing to resolve. David thanked Joseph as a maid brought in a tray. Mr Brown, Miss Jamieson, the Grieves and the

Minister talked on general matters for a while as they were served tea and cake. David sat with them, refusing any sustenance. It was Mary who brought the subject back to David and his family.

'Perhaps Joseph and I could walk in the grounds with David for a while to have some confidence. He is without family and we are happy to support the boy as much as we are able.'

The others looked at each other and nodded their heads.

'Joseph, will you sit for a while, then come to join us.' Mary was a mother of four. 'Will you come, David?'

His speed in rising showing his keenness to leave the room.

Mary asked David if he enjoyed the school.

'I do very much, ma'am.'

'I am sorry your family has fared so badly. Does your mind dwell on them?'

'Not very often, I keep busy, but I think of my father from time to time. I had a solitary life at home, and I do not miss that. At the school, I have many friends and there is much to engage me.'

'Would you return to your grandparents if that were possible?'

'No, I would not want to do that. I would like to see them, but I would choose to stay here. I wish my mother well, but I want to continue at the *hofpital* if I can. I would like it best if my father returned.'

'Mr Grieve is over there, would you like to talk more with him?'

'Very much, ma'am.'

It was not an address Mary was used to.

'David is content here, Joe.' Joe joined them as they

walked, looking at the herbs and flowers in the Physic Garden.

'If you have any questions about your father, I will try to answer,' said Joe.

'I would like to hear more of the travel to, Delft was it, and I would like news of my mother. I know she was unwell.'

'I am trying to contact your grandfather, as I said, there is business to conclude. When I do so, I will enquire on your behalf.' Joe hid the fury he retained from the Lockhart's neglect of his family during his last journey.

'Thank you, sir, thank you very much.' Their kindness and the talk of his father put David on the verge of crying again.

Mary interjected. 'I'm not sure there is time today, I see the others are coming over, but would you care to visit us when you have free time.'

David was delighted at the offer, 'I would be very pleased to do so. Sir, there is something. I visited our old rooms in the Lawn Market recently and there is a large crate there with foreign writing. It was addressed to my father.'

'Are you sure, David?'

'Yes, I have seen it twice. I examined it. It was still there last month. The lady of the house said there was a payment due on it.'

'That does not surprise me.'

'I'm sorry if it is bad news, sir.'

'Not at all, you were right to tell me. How curious.'

At that the others arrived, and they walked back to the school together. Mary walked back to the others with David.

She whispered, 'And who was that young girl, David Miller?'

David turned pink as she nudged him and laughed. He liked Mary; although much older there was something comforting about her that reminded him of Molly.

As August neared its colourful chapter, boys started returning in ones, twos and threes. Janett and David had managed a few exchanges in the classroom and the garden. The girls returned to their own school and Janett promised to write. David's visits to the Grieves became a regular Sunday occurrence. He enjoyed feeling part of their larger family life. Joseph was often away on business; Mary would explain his absences. When he was there, David valued hearing about trading and his travels to other countries. The Master, the Doctors, Regents and maids returned to the *hofpital* and the quiet comfort of daily habit enveloped the school. There was a surprise for David when, one morning, he ran late down the spiral staircase, buttoning his jacket as he descended from the dorm, to take his position standing straight and firm on stone number '33', a group of fresh young faces shyly entered the through the pend.

CHAPTER 12

Kirkcaldy, Fife, Scotland 1733

The winter was mild compared to the previous year. David and Rosie found their way through it. Rosie had low spells of sadness. They seemed to happen quite regularly. She was leaving the only home she had known and she knew she would miss the familiar town, her friends and their families. It only lasted a day or two before she felt her inspiration rise. 'Remember what mother said,' was her mantra. Many of the women in the town who knew her, were very kind, in passing, and understood why Rosie and her father might benefit from leaving. 'Best thing,' they would say, and, 'God bless.' And truly, she did look forward to the prospect of the new.

The pace of David's and Rosie's life had picked up as soon as his acceptance of the new post was acknowledged by the burgh council. The consequence for Rosie was that she now saw less of her father and she also worried about him less. He was occupied, inspired and not as fretful. A local maid was employed to mind Rosie, clean, and provide meals. At least one day a week, David was kept away in Kirkcaldy with, what seemed to be, endless planning meetings. The daily would stay over to look after Rosie or Rosie would sleep at the inn with Jess, which is what she preferred. David returned to take classes three or four times a week, otherwise he was at his desk at his books or writing letters. He had found a student from St Andrews to teach the older boys and Rosie helped the younger ones with reading and writing. He found a bookkeeper to maintain the books; the additional income only just covered the increased expenditure. Their busyness dulled the daily pain of loss. David had given Rosie a Latin textbook and told her to learn the nouns and verbs such that she could form sentences in the past, perfect and future tense. He let her read them out as he worked in the evenings, correcting her wayward pronunciation. She didn't question this task; it was clear to her, her father had some purpose in mind.

David would find time at breakfast to tell her about the progress with the school and their new house. Rosie was desperate to see the place, but David travelled on a good horse, the journey taking around half a day. A carriage would take at least twice that, he explained, there wasn't the time. Once the house was near ready, he promised they would go to Kirkcaldy by carriage. Rosie could comfortably sit on a horse and have it walk, but she was not a horsewoman like Cora or Adeline, who could safely control a horse at speed. She resolved to remedy this.

Both Jessie, who visited regularly, and Cora when she could, got caught up in Rosie's excitement for her forthcoming move. Reassured by Rosie's promises of weekly letters and frequent visits, they supported her plans when they were together. Cora and her brother Sam found a mare for Rosie to ride while they worked nearby. Rosie had first arrived at the farm in her usual dress and was promptly re-dressed by Cora using her own clothes.

'I look like you.'

'You look like a boy.'

'Exactly!'

She sat on the horse like a man, Sam giving instructions on how to sit forward and grip with your knees.

'*Trie ti move wie the beast nae against it. She'll follae yer movin' aince she gits used ti ye.*'

The cantering was easy when you were in rhythm with your horse, 'Bet', she was called. But, if you were going down as she was rising, it was hard to stay on. The ground was neither fair nor flat enough for a gallop, so they tried a few low jumps. Rosie a few times finding the hardness of the ground in a fall. She knew her father would be furious, but she persisted until she found herself confident. Sam took her out on the metalled road a few times and said she was fine to go herself, if she wanted. She asked about borrowing the horse, saying the horse liked her.

'I think she likes the apples you bring,' remarked Cora.

Sam said that *faither* would want some payment.

'Of course, I will ask my father.'

There was the problem. She would have to choose her moment very carefully.

Adeline was no longer at Tarvit, she had gone back with her mother and her half-siblings to London, Rosie thought. She hoped her friend would return soon. She worked on her Latin verbs and hoped her father would be sufficiently impressed to consider letting her ride with him to Kirkcaldy. His mind was on other things and she could not fully engage him, so she took the opportunity to mention she had been getting riding lessons from Cora's brother.

'Very good, sweet,' he said without hearing a word. It was a phrase of his she knew her mother had heard many times, and she smiled at the thought. The weather through February and March was wet, windy and not suited to travel by horse. In early April, the school was closed for Easter and her father announced that she could come with him to Kirkcaldy.

Travelling on a Thursday, they would return the following Tuesday. They would stay at the Oswald's. Her expression was one of concern.

'Are you not pleased, Rose? I thought you were keen to come with me.'

'Father, I'll need some clothes.' She had been growing... her legs! An inch a day, she thought.

'Oh, Rose. I don't know what...'

'If I could please buy some material, I can sew. I think Mrs Reid would help.'

'Of course, of course. Please do that.'

'Rose, I believe there is a celebration on the Saturday evening. I am not sure whether you will attend, but it may be wise to bring your best dress.'

'Thank you, father. Will it be like Adeline's?'

'I expect so.'

'I will need to lengthen it. But I won't know anyone.'

'Rose, you will be with me.'

It was the way her father said it that made Rosie catch a glimpse of a future self. Was it possible that on this visit she was not with her father as a child? That if her dear mother had been spared, it would be she that attended, not Rosie. It was her duty to attend with her father, one that she was pleased to honour. She must not think of herself now, but act for his benefit. Rosie resolved to do her best and thought again of her mother.

It was a spring morning that promised summer. Rosie was up early, dressed in her travelling clothes. She had packed a small case. He was not expect her to ride and brought a single horse and jig from the stable, Rosie gave the horse some attention with fresh grass. She was more confident and familiar with horses now, receptive to their character and behaviour. It felt to Rosie that they were leaving Cupar forever, at that moment, and she had to be reminded they would not move properly for a few months.

'Unless the new schoolmaster for Cupar arrives early,' said her father.

The farthest Rosie had ever been from her home was along the Eden river for about six miles or up the hill at the back of Tarvit. Her mind had been on the people and the practicalities, she had not thought about the excitement of the journey. She started talking without expecting to be heard, and, as they went further, she became unusually quiet; she was happy to look at sights new to her. A trip in the cart with her father was not common. She liked going through the villages she knew the names of and had pictured but never seen. People stopped their business to look and often waved. Around two hours into their journey the road took them up an incline to the top a dip between hills to the south, and she saw it.

'Father, father, what is it? Can we stop please?'

They were not traveling fast, and her father pulled to a halt.

'What is what, Rose?'

She pointed.

'We cannot see the town yet,' said David

'That, father,' said Rosie, pointing, 'the grey between the land and the sky.'

And David realised, his daughter had never seen the sea.

'Oh, of course. I can see a ship, I think!'

'Look carefully, you can see land on the other side.'

'Are we going there? Is it France?

'No, Kirkcaldy is at the water's edge on this side.'

Rosie was happy with this and David hoped she would never lose her child-like sense of wonder. He knew he would never lose Janett; she was within the girl sitting next to him. They stopped at a small inn near Markinche, to rest the horse and restore themselves.

'Is it much farther?'

'We are just over halfway. It is not a sea, it is the mouth of a river that flows into the North Sea.'

They got more and more glimpses of the mouth of the river as they approached the town; it kept Rosie transfixed. As they got nearer still, it disappeared from view. Then, as they cleared a wood, the dark water was there, filling the horizon. Rosie gasped.

'Can we please stop again, father?'

'No, we are almost there. You will likely have the view from our room.'

Rosie was desperate to go to the water's edge, but she contained her ambition lest any insistence should place it in jeopardy.

They arrived at Dunnikier House in time for tea in the afternoon. A servant welcomed Mr Miller by name and went to the cart to collect their bags. Another moved the buggy to the side of the house, uncoupled the horse and took it to a small, enclosed pasture beside the stables. The servant said he would show them to their room and asked if they would join Mrs Oswald in the drawing room at four hours after noon. David had visited several times before and was well used to the house and its routine.

They were shown to a sizeable bedroom on the third floor. The room had two chairs, a table, a large bed and four windows. Two had views to the south, over the estuary. The other two, on the adjacent walls, mirrored each other, facing east and west. The fire was lit. There was an anteroom with a table, wash bowl with towels and wooden box for the bucket. Rosie ran to the window and exclaimed at the drama of the view. It was not just the sea that excited her, she had never been on the third floor of a building.

David did not think that Rosie would have met anyone quite like Mrs Oswald before. He told Rosie that Mrs Oswald could be quite forthright in manner, but Rosie should not shrink from replying should she be called upon. He said that Mrs Oswald was a very kind woman and generous to the community.

'She demands high standards. In defiance of her age, she is very sharp witted!'

Again, Rosie thought that her father was talking to her as an adult, with unguarded words.

A bell was rung, and they assumed it was for tea and they made their way down the spiralled staircase.

A servant opened the door to the drawing room for them. This room was in the other wing on the floor below their room. It was bright with four windows which all faced south. There were three women and two men standing in the room. David introduced his daughter to Mrs Oswald who was seated in a comfortable chair by the fire.

'Rose, I am pleased to meet you at last.'

Rosie curtsied and took her offered hand.

Mrs Oswald held on to her hand and spoke quietly just to her.

'Rose, I am very sorry for the recent loss of your mother. A girl of your age is in need of a mother, but I am sure you will persevere. I lost my beloved husband eight years ago. There is not yet a day gone by without me speaking to him and gaining from his advice. He is my strength.'

Rosie looked up to her eyes, 'Thank you ma'am, you are very kind.'

'Not at all. This will be a busy few days, not a bad thing, I think. I hope we will be able to talk *a deux* in the days to come.'

'Thank you, ma'am,' and Rosie withdrew and found there was no barrier in age between herself and Mrs Oswald.

Reacting to a noise from the stairwell and speaking up now, Mrs Oswald announced, 'Oh, I almost forgot, we have a number of boys with us, but I have managed to find one other girl, who will arrive presently.'

At that a bundle of boys tumbled into the room, brushed down their doublets and lined up, tallest first, to greet Mrs Oswald.

One of the men said 'Boys,' very sternly.

'I have to meet them in order, so I may remember their names.'

The party laughed and Rosie thought that this might not be as sombre a visit as she had envisaged. Rosie watched carefully to try and catch their names: James, John, Mathew, Thomas, Henry and William. They were Mrs Oswald's grandchildren. John and James, or Jamie as he was called, looked older than herself, Mathew and Thomas about the same age, Henry and William were nearer six or seven years of age. Another family was shown into the room: two adults, the Ramsays, with a girl Rosie's age, and a boy at ages with the younger Oswalds. Refreshment, introductions and greetings took a long time. The other adults were, the minister, the parents of all the boys, and Mrs Oswald's children. Rosie could not remember all the adults' names and decided to call everyone Sir or Ma'am, though she wondered if she could get away with calling everyone Mr or Mrs Oswald. The minister was kind, but austere. The bell rang at six and the gathering broke up. Dinner was to be served at eight and that meant they would convene again from seven. Rosie went back to the room and her father came in a short while later. She was desperate to get outside, but her father bade her to be patient.

The evening meal was quiet and convivial. Rosie put on one of her new dresses which was a very pale yellow. The adults were at one end of the long table and the older children at the other. Rosie sat between her father and Jean. Jean seemed more uncertain at the table than Rosie and Rosie led most of the conversation, asking about the town and the school. Jean did not ask many questions in return. She said she played the piano and that gave them something to talk about. Rosie was glad the dinner was not a feast, and here the adults were rationed to one small glass of wine. At the end of the meal, Mrs Oswald, sitting at the head of the table, said she would not withdraw with the ladies but would look forward to a good walk in the morning, should the weather permit. Jean was going straight to bed and Rosie did the same. Rosie was asleep when her father came in, she was barely disturbed.

The house bell was rung at eight and breakfast would be served until ten. David said that they would join the walk at ten; everyone was expected to go. Rosie put on her other day-dress, a dark reddy-brown. She was glad she had not eaten much at the dinner as breakfast was feast of eggs, ham, fish and bread. She pointed to what she wanted on the serving dresser and a maid filled her plate and brought it to her place at the table. Many of the adults just helped themselves, returning several times. She tried some coffee under her father's frown and didn't like it.

It was the brightest day; the morning chill felt only in the shadow of the house. The southern aspect over the estuary meant they were kept in full sun. A light wind swirled in different directions. The air was never fresher; the view across the water was breathless. There was, new to Rosie, a pervasive smell. 'The sea,' her father said.

They assembled outside the house with the others, in cloaks, boots, hats and gloves. There were many, more than yesterday she thought. Hounds were brought from the stables. The eldest Oswald grandson, James said he would exercise a horse that was recovering from being lame. Accompanied by another elderly lady, Mrs Oswald, aided by a stick, set off at a good pace.

They headed east along the cliff top. Disappointingly, for Rosie, not down to the water, but she spied a stone tower ahead, on the edge of the cliff, which piqued her interest. You could see all manner of craft and ships in the estuary: many small boats near the shore, coming and going, and one large one further out with Canon ports, which her father said was a navy ship, a 'man o' war'. Rosie saw some of the other women link arms with the men as they walked together. Rosie did the same.

'You are getting taller every day.'

'It is a beautiful day, father.'

'I wish...'

'I know, Rose,' and he squeezed her arm under his.

They walked down through a village called Dysart which had a harbour with small fishing boats, stepping on stones over a brook, through woods then up again to a cliff top, regaining the view of the sea. Rosie looked over her right shoulder to the west and in the far distance, at the other side of the estuary, she saw a layer of land, then one of cloud, then the peaks of crags and hills. There was smoke rising from the land beside the crag.

'Can you see, what is there, father?' She pointed.

'I think that will be Edinburgh, where I went to school.'

Of the group, the boys were way ahead with the dogs running, chasing, falling, crying, and shouting. They seemed to be in a perpetual battle of attrition, fencing with sticks, throwing sods at each other and feigning a bloody death scene in jerking agony. The smaller boys always coming off worse, but none would return to their parents' care.

'Rose, our lives will not be quite like this when we move here.'

'Oh.'

'Our days will be pleasant, I hope, like in Cupar. It is a more prosperous town and we will have a bit more time and money for our own pursuits.'

'And we will have the sea!' added Rosie.

'What I mean is that we are included here, today, and welcome at Tarvit because Sir Peter and Mrs Oswald are kind people who believe in betterment and are thus interested in providing education and improving the prospects of their own children and those of the town. I...we are invited because that is my employ. This is not really our world.'

Rosie thought for a moment. 'I think I understand, father.'

David continued, 'A teacher is like a minister or a physician. He holds an important place in the community, but it does not have a high social status.'

'Does that mean I should not be friends with the others?'

'No, not at all. You should enjoy these days as much as you wish. But can you imagine us trying to host a weekend party like this for twenty people in our cottage in Cupar?'

'With Mrs B. doing the catering!' Rosie laughed, 'We could sit them in the schoolroom in rows at the small desks.' Rosie's mind was overactive. 'I could make pie. They shalt have pie and cabbage! And you, dear father, shall recite Latin verse from the lectern until all the pie is finished.' At that she unlatched and ran off to catch up with Jean, before she was reprimanded.

One of the Oswald boys, John, caught up with David

and asked if he would care to join his grandmother.

'Gladly, John.'

'Your daughter is a lively girl.'

'Yes, too lively for me sometimes.'

Mrs Oswald wanted to talk about school business, and she agreed with David to spend time the next day with some of the others to go over the practical and educational aspects. David wondered if she was trying to influence him, but if she was, he hadn't felt pressurised.

Rosie was getting a bit more out of Jean, she seemed glad when Rosie caught her, and they prised themselves away from the adults by walking at a greater pace. Jean didn't go to a school either, her parents hired private tutors. She was taught reading and writing, music and dance. A lady came to teach her piano, and all things ladylike. Rosie had no idea what that meant. Rosie told her that she had never seen the sea and that she thought Edinburgh was Paris. Rosie was rewarded when Jean laughed.

The path then took them down into a long wood. It would have been absolutely quiet if not for the shrieking of the wolf pack of younger children. Then there was silence, just the birds, and wind whistling through the swirling treetops. The boys had disappeared. You could just hear the dogs barking in the distance and the odd giggle, the source unseen but nearby. None of the parents seemed concerned.

Rosie noticed a boy about her age who did not join with the others. He arrived outside the house at the assembly in the morning with his mother. On the walk, he engaged John in, what seemed, quite an intense conversation, or else he wandered off on his own, looking at things on the ground or up in the distance. Once, he strayed too near the cliff edge and his mother shouted him back. He was tall and ungainly, awkward in movement. He ran for no apparent reason at times and responded easily, when addressed. 'Come and join my Jacobites, Smithy,' shouted one of the boys, wielding a wooden sword. He just smiled and shook his head. Later, Rosie thought she saw him talking quietly, even though there was no one around.

A carriage came by with two footmen who stopped for a moment to talk to Mrs Oswald. The group walked on. Out of the wood they walked on and up again, climbing an escarpment in the direction of the screeching cry of soaring gulls.

A familiar, deeper beat came from the other direction, behind them, away from the sea. Rosie looked north to find the source of it. Hooves, horses at speed two, maybe three. The land was rising but flat, the pasture was firm and shorn, presumably by the grazing sheep. She saw the horses, three at a canter. The riders were looking up and moving toward the group. The noise got louder; the beat quickened. Two moved ahead. They were big horses, two young men it seemed. The horses' forelegs stretching out from the rear quarters then back together before stretching again. Their necks bobbing low in rhythm with the sound. Each rider leaning forward, lowering their torso to the horse's neck. You could see the two urging the steeds forward. At full gallop, an impressive sight. Sheep scattered, grouse rose and fled squawking from the grass, a hare, two, zig-zagged in escape. The horses charged on, with an urgency as if they were pledged to enjoin the boys' battle and save the day. They changed course slightly to avoid rocks, one gaining a lead. Rosie saw the fence, partly broken, no gap through. Had they seen it? There was no drop in pace. The front horse slowed and the second caught it as they closed on the fence. From quite far back, the rider of the catching steed pushed on and the horse took off. There was a gasp from the onlookers then silence as they watched the horse leap: the fore legs rising high and stretching out…the beast cleared the hurdle the rear legs meeting the fore as they landed on firm ground, still in full gallop. An audible exhaling of breath as the riders and horses neared the party, slowing to a trot to greet them.

The adults behind Rosie and Jean had all stopped and turned to watch the horses approach from the rear. Rosie saw it had not been a man leading, but a lady riding side-saddle. Oh, to ride like that, how did she stay on? thought Rosie. The young man caught up and pushed her, laughing. The horses panting, wide eyed, whinnying, foaming at the mouth, restless, their smooth-muscled limbs wet with sweat, took a bit of calming down. They appeared keen to keep going and nuzzled their heads together as if the race had been something amongst themselves and nothing to do with their masters. As the third, older, rider reached the group, the male riders dismounted; the older apparently rebuking the younger. Two of the party's hounds followed their instincts and arrived back to find the source of the new scent and the commotion. The group walked on, Rosie and Jean still walking ahead, looking for the blooded boys. Rosie heard hooves walking again, coming up slowly from behind her. She moved to turn around.

'Bonjour, Mademoiselle Rose.'

CHAPTER 13

Edinburgh, Scotland 1711

J oseph sat at his desk poring over the accounting books, trying to concentrate, but his mind kept drifting. Drifting to Mary's face when he walked through the door of his apartment, drifting to the state of his family, also, in his tired, darker moments, drifting to his last act, a violent act, on foreign soil. His youngest child had been ill and was now improving under the care of a physician. The other three had looked fine but were thin and lacked energy. He had found poor Mary emaciated and it was taking time for her to recover. She had smiled and broken down when he first walked in.

'I haven't cried one tear since you left. I saved them up for your return.'

He had dropped the two full bags of bread, fruit, meat and milk he had collected, and caught his wife as her legs gave way in their embrace. As he held Mary carefully, the children gathered silently beside them; his eldest daughter, Ruth, wrapped her arms round them both.

'It's alright now children, I'm home.'

The fire was unlit. Joe reached into his satchel for

two shillings and sent his eldest boy, also Joe, and Ruth to quickly fetch coal kindling and lighters.

'And bring some eggs and honey from Fletcher if you can.' He handed them another shilling.

'I'm fine Joe,' said Mary gaining composure. 'Just relieved to see you. What have you brought us?'

'Sit with me Mary, just a moment. It will be alright now. I have brought plenty of food and we have made a good profit.'

'I knew you would come back.'

The office was dusty, almost unused since he last sat at his desk. When was that? Eight, nine weeks ago? It seemed longer. There were three offices and a reception hall. James Lockhart had the largest, well-furnished room with an imposing desk. It was the only room with an outside window, a fine view to the north toward Calton Hill. Tom had had a smaller functional office and the clerks had a room with walls full of books and ledgers. Piles of notes, letters and papers sat on and around two large tables and a mishmash of stools and chairs.

The last day-ledger entry had been six weeks since. Joe was familiar with the ledger and the records of the trading transactions. Now he was trying to decipher the company's balance sheet. He could see that, after the loss of the ship, his father-in-law had, early on, made some effort to pay monies to names, whom he presumed were debtors. There were sales of furniture and various sundry goods. Cash in bank had been reduced to a negative number, but not a large one. Some outgoings were regular, one, a inconsiderable sum, was paid monthly to the asylum. Joe wondered if these were still maintained; he would have to contact the bank. A pile of unopened letters lay on Lockhart's desk, to which he added those he had picked up at the door. It would take time. Along with the company accounts, Joe had to account formally for the transactions and expenses of his trip to the Low Countries. He had funds at the moment, but his free use of them, even those used to feed his family, depended on concluding the transaction with his funder. He could not, at the moment, produce an exact tally for the purchase costs, never mind the sale.

Fortunately, during the voyage home, Ruud had switched back from being a youthful daydreamer to a reliable and attentive assistant. He had attended to the unloading, customs and portering of the crates to the company's quayside warehouse in Leith. He had spent days in careful inspection, and compiling an inventory, which he copied four times. Ruud extracted samples of each type of Delftware and wrote out a sheet for each type, with a description of the range, quality and source. Joe realised that Ruud had taken in, and understood, more than was apparent at the time.

Joe had written to Edward Clerk on his first day in the office and was disturbed that his reply took two weeks. Clerk was in London and he had written personally, expressing delight in the safe arrival of the porcelain and the indications of quality and quantity that Joe had given. Clerk was returning, travelling by boat, and would meet with Joe the following week. Joe was reassured; his optimism returned, and he pondered his next move.

He could pay the proceeds of the sale of the linen into the Lockhart Company's debt, extracting some expenses plus what should have been paid to his family while he was away. That would allow him to set up on his own. As Joseph Grieve, he had no status in the Edinburgh trading establishment. Edward Clerk was his singular sponsor. The company, despite its debt, still had a commercial presence, offices and warehousing. It had lists of contacts and valued traders, only a few, albeit important ones, had been left unpaid and in a state of dissatisfaction.

So far, he had not trusted himself to find James Lockhart in fear of his own reaction. Mary, now restored, was eating everything on her plate and anything her family left over. She said that James' reaction to her had been unnerving, the lack of recognition and agitation exacerbating his red-faced bluster. She did not know him well but, and Joe agreed, he had always been fair and straightforward with them. Dispassionate, yes, but a good employer. Joe was curious, but any concern for James and his family had dissipated when he came back to find the promise unfulfilled and his family in abject misery.

They were kept awake in the night with thoughts of what would have happened to them if Joe had not returned, or if he had been a few more weeks. Mary was a driven woman and she had sacrificed her own health for the children leaving herself incapable of seeking alternative sources of income or aid.

To stay within the company, he needed to be a part of it. James Lockhart was the majority partner and if there were others, Joe did not know. In fact, it may already have been sold or wound up. How would he know? He laughed at the thought. The reason he was sitting working there was because it was all he had known for a good number of years and because he had an office key.

It was amusing, but it made him think that he had to tread warily. He would approach the Company solicitors, Stuart & Denholm, they could deal with James, and he would better learn the situation. He wrote a short note, headed with the company name and title, requesting an audience with Mr Denholm, he signed it in his own name adding his title of Senior Clerk.

By the Monday of the following week, there was no reply. He knew this was the problem with trying to do business in Edinburgh, nothing was easy unless you were a *name*. Everything and everybody outside the known were treated with suspicion.

Edward Clerk returned to Edinburgh and Joseph was invited to a midweek luncheon with Edward and one of his staff. Joe was invited to bring a partner. There was only Ruud who had earned his place. Until then, Joe went through the papers in James' office, taking notes of information he thought may be useful. He moved into Tom's old office which still bore the stale aroma Tom's presence.

Momentarily, his mind left Edinburgh and went back to the day he was in Doortje's house, and sat on that chair. There were unopened letters and documents dealing with aspects of the fatal voyage of *The Reward*. Joe leafed through them prior to filing. There was a file with Edward Clerk's name; Joe picked it up with interest. He knew Edward Clerk was involved with the previous trade. His stomach lurched as he started to read about the insurance arrangement of the voyage of *The Reward*. There were copies of letters from James Lockhart to Edward Clerk and Edward's replies. James implied that Edward had some financial responsibility that had not been fulfilled. Edward's replies repeatedly stated that he was the broker and not the insurer and that Lockhart should deal with the insuring agency. Edward pointed out that he had also suffered a financial loss. In reading this, Joe became concerned. He did not know the details but had the impression that the insurer had not paid due compensation. He knew that Tom would have been thorough in his arrangements. The copies of James' letters were rambling to the point of incoherence. Joe's concern stretched to his current arrangement with Edward.

The lunch was in a private upstairs room of an inn on the High Street, down from the magistrate's court. Joe knew it as a place where advocates and burgesses commonly met. He had never been inside. Joe had Ruud trail down to Leith again, to make a second, smaller, box of samples for Edward to take with him, and he checked the agreement to see what negotiating room he had. He had drawn up a list of expenses he thought reasonable. Some expenses were up; some were down. The return shipping cost had been low for a vessel of that size and speed. In the late morning, Ruud loaded two crates on a cart, and they headed to the High Street. As they lugged the crates up the stair, Joe helping – he had not fully grasped the idea of being a man in charge yet – they were surprised to find Edward already there with his clerk, a man called Macdonnell. Macdonnell moved quickly to relieve Joe of his load. The room had a row of four mullioned windows overlooking the market, a long table and twelve chairs. Edward greeted Joe and Ruud warmly, shaking hands with both. A more personable salutation than Joe had previously received.

'What an adventure and a fortunate one according to your letter. May I suggest coffee as we look at what you have brought, then lunch? Negotiations are always improved by port.'

'By all means, sir.'

'I apologise for not meeting you earlier, my visit to London was unforeseen. I hope you were not inconvenienced.'

'Not at all, sir.'

An attendant who had appeared, disappeared back down the stair.

Joe continued, 'We have brought a large sample box to show you the full range and a smaller one for you to take with you. We have a detailed inventory. There were very few breakages and none of any import.'

Joe went on to explain his strategy in purchasing and that he had been guided by local advice. The quality of the porcelain had been assessed by a trusted expert he had hired. He had claimed for Grietje's expense. Ruud took the pieces out of the sample case, leaving the Royal Delft until last. Edward and his clerk took their time and looked carefully at each piece, passing a comment or two on occasion.

'Joseph, I am very pleased with your purchase. You have shown maturity in your decisions. I believe we can make a good price on the lower and medium quality, and the Royal, on the Royal we can make money.'

'Let us to lunch,' he patted Joe on the back, 'and tell us of the sights and the sounds, and the women perhaps!'

Joe and Ruud produced enough tales of interest: the canals, the soldiers and sailing on the *man o' war*, without mentioning Grietje, or the assault. They were served a hearty lunch of roast pork, potatoes and green vegetables, washed down with a dark claret.

Table cleared, the four men then sat with their tally books and lists to agree terms of payment. Edward started confidently.

'Joe, Ruud, you have the bills of sale...'

Ruud offered the three sheets, the receipts provided by the three potteries, which Edward passed to Macdonnell,

'...and details of expenses?'

Again, passed over the table.

'We have receipts for the major items.'

'The customs receipt?'

'I have the import document from the comptroller in Leith. There is no duty in Scotland for goods from Campveere.'

'The goods are from Delft?'

'Yes, we transferred the porcelain barge-to-ship at the dock. I notified the customs house and completed the log entry, but the officer was not very interested. It was the same the first time. I did not insist on any payment.'

'Joseph, I think we will work very well together.'

As Macdonnell started accounting and writing figures in his book, Edward continued,

'Joseph, we agreed twenty-five percent of profit plus reasonable expenses.'

Joe nodded.

'But we do not know what the profit is yet.'

'I would hope we can agree an estimate today.'

'Exactly.'

'I'll just check with Mac.'

Mac spoke quietly, Edward just making noises.

'Now, there is no problem with the expenses, you still have some cash in hand?'

'A little, it is on this sheet.'

'On the three ranges of pottery, Mac tells me we can expect twenty-five to forty percent margin for the lower and medium quality ware; these will go to dealers, unless Mac decides to set up shop. The Royal, he thinks we can sell directly to the fine houses. We may get sixty, eighty, one hundred percent profit. It will take a little more time.'

Joe was waiting for the bargaining or the catch. None came. He felt in retrospect his share should have been larger. He was in no position to ask for more. To an outsider he had been a high risk. Edward had gambled and won. Joe was not going to reveal the false receipt. He couldn't, it would cast doubt on the whole transaction. He endeavoured to do some good with it, as a gesture towards some kind of moral balancing act.

'Ah, you were expecting some barter?' asked Edward.

'I apologise, sir, I was. I would retain some of the good pottery if there were too much or it were not to your liking.'

'I will take it all, Joe, although I'm always open to offers above cost. My father told me when I started to trade, *"Do not beggar your neighbour when he is the source of your profit."* It was wise advice, which I have been far too late in the understanding. Now Mac, who you gather is a magician with figures, has come up with an estimated minimum margin for the inventory of... forty percent. He expects this to be higher, but it will give us a working figure until the sales are complete. Your share at twenty-five percent will give you this sum on receipt of the goods.'

Edward pushed a piece of paper across the table.

'Plus, the expenses, of course.'

Joe pushed the paper on to Ruud who got out his own tally book and worked through some figures. After a few minutes he nodded to Joe.

'That is acceptable.'

They stood to shake hands.

'You will provide sales receipts?'

'Of course. Now to the port,' and they sat to await the server.

'My question is Joe, Ruud, will we do this again?'

'You will not wait for the sale?'

'I do not disguise my confidence, no. If you would go tomorrow and double the amount, I would invest. But there is more to discuss on this, Joseph, we can meet again, within the next week or two?'

'Certainly, sir.'

The three drank to the toast of *future adventures*. They rose from their chairs at the bottom of the bottle.

'May I ask some advice, sir?'

'Go on.'

'I am not getting a response from Lockhart's lawyers. I wish to buy a share in the company.'

'Who are they?'

'Stuart & Denholm.'

'Ah yesterday's men. Just march in, Joe, march into their office. And sit down if they ignore you which, with your size, is unlikely.'

'Are you serious, sir?'

'Perfectly, and don't buy the company, buy the debt. Make a modest offer.'

'I thank you, sir.'

Joe didn't go back to the office, he went home and did something he had never done in his many years with Mary, he asked her out to dine.

'Don't be a daft lad, it is a waste of good money.'

'Mary, tonight you will come out with your husband.'

'But what about the bairns?'

'For one night, *they* can starve!'

As they sat at the table, later, too full to move, Mary sensed Joe had something on his mind.

'You don't need to tell me Joe. Just tell me how I'll manage with the bairns.'

'How do you know? I haven't...'

'I've known you too long, Joseph Grieve, and I will never stand in your way.'

'I will leave good money, for one, two years.'

'Not two years Joe, please.'

'No, no, two months only. I said that just in case, you know. Just the Low Countries again, on a good ship, in the summer. They say if you don't get on a sinking ship you never will.'

'Of course, you must go.'

The following Saturday, they went to Lady Yester's Kirk to attend a recital with their two middle children. It was a fine afternoon with only a slight chill in the shade. The vocal performances were moving and the music more uplifting than they usually heard in the church. Joe scanned the choirs and, with a start, nudged Mary only to be quietened. During a short break at a change of choirs,

'Mary, I think that is David Miller, do you see?'

'I hardly knew him.'

'I'm sure, Mary, he looks so like his father, we must try to see him later.'

'Is that wise, Joe?'

'I see no harm; I would like to know how the boy is doing. I feel an obligation for Tom's sake, if nothing else.'

'Well, husband, tread carefully.'

Joe met Ruud at the office early the next Monday.

'I think I can keep paying you, Ruud, if you will stay on.'

'So far as I may eat and sleep, I will stay. At the least until I buy you out.'

'I am trying to get a measure of the state of things here, Ruud. Mainly the money and the debt, but also to get a sense of the more successful business arrangements of the past. I think we may still learn from Tom's labours; God rest his soul. Look at the sourcing and cost of the goods from our previous trade. The more I look, I get the impression that Tom kept the business going without much support. My intention is to acquire and run this business.'

Later that morning, a small bundle of letters was delivered, three stood out, all conveyed by ship, two from Zeeland, and one from London. Joe slipped all three into his pocket, he would attend to them later.

Joe would tackle the lawyers as Edward Clerk suggested. He tidied himself up, the barber and a new suit. Arriving home, Mary barely recognised him; he had never been so shorn.

'You have to stand straight, Joe.'

'I'll hit my head.'

'Well, that may be a blessing.'

Joe knocked and went calmly into the offices of Stuart & Denholm. There were three clerks in the dark office; the one at a desk on a raised platform, looked up. Joe noticed two internal doors with nameplates, one Stuart, one Denholm.

'Mr Denholm, please.'

'The clerk looked at his journal, there is nothing in the book. You have an appointment, Mr...?'

'No, I would like to see Mr Denholm.'

'Sir, you need an appointment.'

'I have tried that,' and Joe moved toward the labelled door.

'Sir, you cannot...' The clerk rose from his desk.

Joe stopped and turned to look at him. The clerk stayed where he stood.

'Mr Denholm, Joseph Grieve, I have come to buy out James Lockhart, the merchant company.'

'Black!' Denholm barked.

The clerk had arrived at the door.

'Mr Denholm, I could not...'

Joe lifted a pile of papers from the chair at Denholm's desk, dropped them to the floor, and sat.

'I will buy Lockhart's, sir, you will attend to my business.'

'It's alright, Black, Mr...'

'Grieve.'

'Mr Grieve, this is most unusual.'

'That may be so, but it is an urgent matter, and in the interest of all parties.'

'It will take some time...'

'I believe not, sir. Here is a complete list of the monies owed according to the company, along with the names and offices of all concerned. And here is my offer.' He put a letter on the desk. 'I offer eight shillings on the pound.'

'Sir, I will need to...I don't think.'

'There is little chance of these good people getting any more. There are no assets to speak of. Indeed, it is generous under the circumstances.'

'Sir, if you give me time, I...'

'My offer will hold for one week. You have one week to find Mr Lockhart and get some sense out of him.'

'Sir, that is not possible.'

'One week, Denholm. I shall return to your office.' Joe got up and went to the door. Black was waiting there. As he walked through the anteroom, Joe noticed a wry smile from one of the other clerks.

'Thank you, Black.' Joe said, as Black, bowing slightly, opened the external door for him. 'I will return next week at the same time, please make an appointment for me with Mr Denholm.'

Joe strode down the street shoulders back, head high and smiled to himself, 'Thank you, Henry.' He acknowledged the influence of his mentor. He had no idea whether he had got away with it. He might arrive next week and find the City Guard waiting for him. He was glad he had tried. It was a good plan; there were other options for him.

Joe and Ruud spent the rest of the week in the office as if the business was already owned. Joe set Ruud the task of finding out the margins on exports to The Low Countries for a range of wares, starting with the records of Tom's earlier trades. Was it worth their while? He would await the meeting with Edward Clerk, but he expected to return to Delft the following month.

The weekend brought the visit to *Heriot's Hofpital* and a meeting with David Miller. It is not unusual for a boy to be like his father, but the painful loss of Tom, his absence in Joe's day-to-day life, in addition to Joe unexpectedly finding the boy in church, made their similarity acutely felt.

Joe had looked up to Tom despite being older. Tom's marriage to Margaret and his inclusion in the office had changed Joe's working life. He felt a strong liking for this boy on the cusp of manhood. His thoughts led him to recall his earlier conversation with David. David said there was a crate at the Lockhart's old rooms. He would send Ruud to investigate.

Joe wrote to Edward Clerk to request a meeting. If Edward would confirm his support, he would take the trip sooner. He needed to leave by September, or the timing of the return would increase Mary's unease.

A loud knock at the outside door and he heard it bang open.

A deep voice bellowed, 'Grieve, Joseph Grieve!'

Joe was on his own; he stuck his head out of Tom's office to look.

'Are you in such fortune now you don't answer my note?'

Joe's eyes met the familiar, effervescent face of Henry Egerton.

Joe shook Henry's hand, 'A note? of course, from Zeeland, I have left it in in my old jacket.'

'No matter, it was just to inform you of my visit to Edinburgh. I am now here and so are you.'

'It is very good to see you, sir.'

'Oh, stop that, *Henry* is just fine.'

Another banging and thumping at the door. Joe looked up to see the back of a man pulling a large, flat crate into the office. Beyond him, Ruud was pushing the other end.

'What on earth?' Joe's mind was so occupied these days. Never mind the note, he had forgotten what he had sent Ruud to do. He helped the two men move the crate into James Lockhart's office and dismissed the barrowman. They were all curious.

'Well done, Ruud. Do you know what it is?'

Ruud shook his head.

'Payment?'

'Two pounds and seven shillings, I thought...I have an old invoice, some papers and a receipt.'

'It's an expensive lucky dip,' said Joe.

'Well, let us open it then!' enthused Henry.

'Henry.' Ruud just noticing.

''tis I, Ruud. Hello!'

The papers were in Dutch, Ruud went to find a lever to open the crate. Joe looked at the papers and gave them to Henry.

'This is a well-timed arrival, Henry.'

'At your service.'

'The package is from the house of an art dealer, in Vaandelstrat, Delft.'

'There is nothing here,' interrupted Ruud, 'the bars are at the warehouse.'

'Ruud, can you go to the smithy and borrow something? Henry, I have nothing here, shall we repair to a coffee house? I know just the place.'

'Excellent.'

'Ruud, we will go to the inn where we lunched with Edward Clerk. Join us when you have found a tool.'

Joe and Henry walked up the High Street together, Henry still looking at the papers.

'Two paintings it seems, large, the dimensions are given. I recognise one of the artists' names.'

'Who is it addressed to?'

'Tom Miller, your lost colleague?'

'Yes...and the date?'

'Let me look, it is not clear.'

'Here we are.' They arrived at the inn.

The ground floor was full of men dressed in what could be described as professional clothing, in groups, two, three, four, around tables. Yet it was not noisy. There were papers on the tables and earnest discussion taking place, coffee more common than ale. They found a table at the back, which was being vacated. It was dark, but it had two candles and two more on the wall. The serving wench, young, plump, fair and pleasant, was there in an instant.

'Sirs?'

'Coffee, a pot, and what is to eat?'

Pottage or mutton pie, sir.'

'Pie, Henry?' Henry nodded. 'Three pies.'

'Three, sir?'

'And coffee.'

'Ah, I have a date on the customs sheet. January 1710.'

'After I had returned. Tom must have sent it.'

'To himself, not the company offices?'

'You have a point, Henry, or maybe two.'

'Anything else?'

'The letter is formal, to Tom, at this house address – Lawn Mercate, Edinbourg. Two paintings, as I said, ah, in oil, winter and nautical scenes. I'm very curious to see them now. You had no idea?'

'Nothing. Tom stayed to collect the paintings. I returned earlier. I think I told you, with the porcelain.'

'Yes, I remember.'

'I assumed any paintings were lost with him. I remember him saying he may buy some for himself, not just to trade.'

'So, this distinction may prescribe the ownership.'

'Yes, but the business of James Lockhart and the family accounts were not well separated. That venture was intended for Tom to obtain more autonomy, more independence from James and his family.'

'But not the wife?'

'Not as far as I know, I was not his confidant. Without any doubt, I trusted, admired and respected that man, but he kept his own counsel.'

'Past tense.'

'We must presume him lost.'

'Your tone of voice expresses a lack of conviction.'

'Ah Ruud, we have pie for you.' Ruud's eyes followed the rear quarters of the waitress which, by luck, brought him to their table. He put the cloth-wrapped bars under the table.

'I was concerned I would be taken for a robber.'

'What brings you to Scotland, Henry?' Joe changed the subject.

'Water and iron. I have a requirement for some large iron parts. Carron near Falkirk is making a name for fine mouldings in that business. And water, James Livingston of Callendar House, nearby I believe, wants to move some water. Too small a job for me, but he is a second cousin of a second cousin or some such, and he will likely host me well. I came by sea to Leith and could not pass you by.'

'It is very good to see you.'

'Is Falkirk far?'

'A day, I would take a boat upriver.'

'I'll ask for a room here then and depart early to-morrow. You two will dine tonight…at my expense, of course.'

'You are too generous, sir.'

Cleaning their plates, Joe paid the bill and they headed back to the business offices.

Joe held the crate and Ruud carefully prised along one edge. The long nails came clear and he repeated for all four corners. The paintings were wrapped in oilcloth and they lifted them out of the crate to place them on a cleared desk. They were large, bigger than the desk. In removing the outer cloth, it was easier to lay both on an edge. The two were individually wrapped. The frames were gold embossed and heavy. Henry found the nameplate to gain the orientation and bade Ruud wait, as he and Joe stood back, before Ruud pulled the inner soft cloth cover from the first painting.

'Winter Scene by Joos de Momper,' Henry announced.

It was an impressive, snow-covered landscape. Joe had no eye, but appreciated the detail, colour and the sheer size. He thought it pleasant to look at, unlike others he had seen; not that he had seen many. There were many small figures: men, women, children, skating, riding and walking. There were carts and horses, and a dog. It was an ordinary scene: a castle, a stream a bridge, and a few houses.

'Joe?'

'I like looking at it; only you know, Henry, does it

have value?'

Henry looked closer and carefully. He seemed to look at the paint itself.

'I have seen similar. They are becoming popular, yes. The new, large, estate houses desire works for their walls. Some works other than religious representation, tableaus of Greek Gods and family portraits.'

'A value?'

'I cannot say. We would need to get it south, to London and find an honest dealer.'

'Ten pounds, twenty?'

'Oh no, a few hundred, three, perhaps more.'

'Good God,' said Joe and Ruud whistled.

'And the next one, please, Ruud.'

The second painting, by Jan van Goyen, was a stunning view over water of a Dutch town, with yachts, boatmen and a large church in the background. It was clearly by a different hand. Henry said he had heard of the artist and that he thought he was well-known for his landscapes.

'I expect this will be worth more because of the name. These are both fine works. Do you know what was paid?'

'There is no record. Tom viewed and bought the paintings on his own, or at least, not with me. There were two dealers, and we do not have their names. In time, I may find out more of the paintings and what happened to him.'

'I will seek a room and rest, and shall we just return here later? We were well served.'

The three ate handsomely in the evening, talking over their earlier shared adventures in Delft. Ruud, under the influence of the claret, was in danger of becoming over familiar with the same serving girl. Joe sent him home, allowing Henry to talk with him about matters of business.

'Joseph, you seem well. The sale of the goods was it to your satisfaction?'

'Yes, my sponsor was pleased with the goods and there was no contention. I was recompensed on an estimated value and expect a further sum.'

'And the development of the business?'

'There is advantage in buying out the Lockhart business. Despite its current financial difficulty, the number of the company's debtors are few, and local. Its trading reputation still valued elsewhere. I have sought to buy the debt and hence control the business.'

'At book value?'

'No, eight shillings.'

'Excellent, and you would continue to trade with the Low Countries.'

'In the short term, yes. I remember your suggestion of investment.'

'Indeed, that is why I was keen to meet with you.'

'I suspect that I do not currently have sufficient funds to balance the debt and invest without further borrowing, which I am reluctant to do. I am interested in a partnership.'

'Do you have figures?'

'Not yet, I will have them in a few weeks.'

'I will come back this way on my return, let us see if we can find a basis for an agreement.'

'There is potentially another interested party.'

'Oh.'

'Edward Clerk. I think he is interested in importing more porcelain.'

'It would be ungentlemanly of me to enquire as to the details. But he would have taken a risk with you on your previous trade and presumably demanded a high return. That is not unreasonable. But let me say, that I am primarily interested in the business growth, not taking the profits out of the business at an early stage. I want to make that clear to you before you consider your options.'

'I appreciate that, Henry, thank you. I wish to return to Delft in the next month, as we promised our suppliers. If we agree terms are you able to commit before then?'

'If we have an agreement, I can arrange a draft on my return. Can you not borrow against the future trade?'

'It might be possible, but that is not the reason.'

'I won't ask.'

'I don't mind explaining. My family would have been destitute had I not returned when I did, and I have seen what happened to Tom's family. I had left their care in the hands of Lockhart and was badly let down. I will not let that happen again.'

'I see, so you cannot risk leaving debt should your God dessert you.'

'Exactly so.'

'I understand. I do have one other condition.'

'Yes?'

'I will sign the legal papers, but my interest and investment must remain anonymous. There is no subterfuge, I just prefer it that way.'

'You have my word, sir.'

'You are a good man, Joe.'

The two men sat in contemplation.

'Those paintings are valuable; they will help you.'

'Yes, but to whom do they belong?'

'Yes, I see. Let me share a cheerier tale before I take my leave. Shortly after you left, my travels took me back to Veere, and I sought out Grietje.'

'Ah, she is well?'

'Indeed, very well. I was curious to see her painting. She has been able to spend more time at her easel due to the payment she received from you. She has a fine hand and I was impressed enough to commission a portrait. It is not finished. I am due back. She said she has news for you and would write.'

'Oh, the letters. I had, I have letters, they were with yours, they were misplaced. I am well reminded. Did she say on what matter?'

'I could not prise it from her. She still does fine work for *Porceleyne Fles*.'

The serving girls were clearing the tables.

'Well, my friend, I must to bed...I will not approach that comely wench, but I may dream of her. I will send you notice of my return, if you would care to read it.'

'Of course, my apologies.'

As Joe walked home, he became concerned about the letters. They would still be in the pocket of his old suit. He then felt a slight sinking of the gut, as he could not remember when he last saw his old suit.

Mary was dozing by the fading fire in the stove. One candle lit their single room. The children were a sleeping raggle in the cabin bed.

'Mary, Mary, where is the old suit?

'Joe, I'm sleeping, the children, what time is it?'

'Sorry. Mary, what happened to the old suit?'

'What old, oh Joe, it was threadbare, I gave it to the

children for the tinker. They got a few pennies.'

'What, Mary, no.' Joe slumped in their other chair.

'It was of no use. You said we were fine for money now.'

'It's not that. It's, oh, never mind.'

Mary got up and went to stand by the stove.

'I saved the buttons.'

'Oh, Mary. It's not the money...'

'The buttons on the jacket...the lapel...the waist.' Mary reached for behind a wooden pot which sat on the beam above the fire.

'...and the buttons on *the pockets*.'

'Mary, the pockets!'

'Are these what you are looking for, Joseph Grieve?'

The chill of the next day's morning breeze prompted Joe to make arrangements for revisiting Delft the following month. He sent a note to Clerk suggesting a date for their meeting regarding the new trade. First, he would sit and read the bloody letters.

The first was from Henry and said all he now knew. The second, he thought the address was in Grietje's neat hand. The third was addressed to Tom, it was a spidery script. He opened Grietje's.

> *Dear Joe,*
> *I hope you well. I have to many news to writ*
> *in Englisch. I paint for Henry, he is funny*
> *and I do porcelain. But if you not mind,*
> *I ask about Tom and have news for speak*
> *only. I wish to do more work with you.*
> *Please let know if come.*
> *Grietje x*

He hadn't known what he expected. It was an agony

of brevity. Joe opened the last letter to find it more sub-stantial in content. It was to Tom from van Reit. At last the name he could not previously recall. He now had it and the address. It was dated late March and expressed regret that Tom had not come back to call on him. He understood that Tom may well have had other prior-ities. He asked for Tom to respond and requested that he visit, should he return to Delft. There was an unwrit-ten sadness between his words, although he would have had no more knowledge than Joe, at the time at least, of Tom's fate. These two missives removed any hesitation in Joe about his pending return.

Joe had asked Edward Clerk to come to the office in the morning. The only convenient day for Edward was the same day that Joe was due back at Lockhart's lawyers.

'Good to see you, Joseph, there is urgency? I do not have the full figures for the sale yet, but I can acquaint you with the progress.'

'It was not entirely that, sir. I wish to return to Delft next month and you expressed an interest.'

'Oh, that is good news,' Edward said hesitantly. 'A second trade would suit me; the porcelain has been well received. In regard of the funding, I would need to check with Mac as to the amount. Same terms?'

'Ah no, that is why I thought we should talk.'

'I thought you were pleased...'

'I was and I am grateful. Can I, however, propose a different arrangement, still to our mutual benefit?'

'Please do.'

'As I see it, I acquire the goods and manage the qual-ity, price and shipping. You have the market, manage the sales and delivery.'

'Yes.'

'My proposal is simple, we cover our own expenses and split the profit equally.'

'You do not need my banking?'

'I hope to use Lockhart. I aim to keep the business operating.'

'Shall we lunch while I consider your proposal? You asked me to the come to the office for a reason?'

'Ah yes, I am not used to this complexity in my life. If I may crave your indulgence, I have something to show, and I would value your opinion.'

'Again, please do.'

Joe was now using Lockhart's main office as his own. He excused himself to go to Tom's old office to fetch one of the paintings through to the lighter room.

'I have received two paintings. I thought you may be familiar with the market?' He turned the framed canvas toward Edward.

'Oh my, from the Netherlands?'

'Yes, a dealer in Delft.'

'You keep surprising me, Joe. It is for sale?'

'Potentially.'

'The owner?'

'At present...let us say, myself.'

Edward, as Henry had, took his time to look closely, and then stood back thoughtfully.

'I am not expert. It would sell, undoubtedly. But the price I cannot guess. Can you leave me with the details?'

'Of course, there is also a second.'

'Bring it in, Joe.'

'This is a good piece. Can I ask how much you paid?'

'In confidence?'

'Granted.'

'Two pounds and seven shillings.'

'What! I'm going to stick with you, Grieve, and I'll tell you one thing.'

'Sir.'

'I am never going to play cards with you.'

As they finished lunch, having agreed the deal, Edward would have all rights to the sale of the porcelain in England. Joe told Edward he had followed his advice with the lawyers. Duly fortified, he was going to revisit them presently to see if they acceded to his request.

'I know them of old. Would you care to have me accompany you? Now I have a vested interest in the outcome, I may be able to advise, should it prove necessary.'

Joe paid for the fare and they walked to the solicitors.

'Mr Grieve, oh, and Mr Clerk, I'll tell Mr Denholm you are here.'

'Thank you, Black.' They said in unison.

'Mr Grieve, Mr Clerk. Black do fetch another chair. You are together in this, may I ask?'

'Let us say I have an interest.' replied Edward.

'Mr Denholm, do you have progress regarding the debt?'

'Indeed, your offer of eight shillings in the pound has proved acceptable. There is a difference with your estimated figure, but it is not a significant one.'

'And the transfer of the company?'

'Mr Lockhart is not well, we, that is Stuart and Denholm, maintain the statutory authority and, in accordance with that duty, I do have one request.'

'Go on,' said Joe.

'There is a boy, you are aware of this.'

'Yes, in fact my wife and I visit him.'

'Ah, and there is a regular asylum bill, but this is not expected to continue for too much longer. The poor lady is not of good health. To help the family with these burdens, for the retention of the Lockhart name and the good will of the company, we suggest a ten percent shareholding to be retained by the family. This would pass to the boy eventually.'

'I intend the name of Lockhart and Grieve.'

'That would be most suitable. Is the condition acceptable to you, sir?'

Joe laughed to himself. *Sir!* He almost turned to look behind.

Edward whispered in his ear. 'Not a voting share and not immediately transferable. You must have first option to purchase back.'

Joe nodded and said the same to Denholm who nodded.

'Then we are agreed?'

Joe looked at Edward again who said it seemed reasonable under the circumstances. He then rose to shake hands with Denholm.

'You can draw up the papers within the week?'

'Ten days, I pray you, sir?'

'Ten days it is.'

Once back on the High Street, Edward, slapped Joe on the back. 'An ale, Mr Grieve, an ale is called for!'

The nearest inn was The Bell. Edward told Joe how well the pottery had been received and said that all three ranges were in demand. He suggested that Joe did not need to adjust the balance in the goods.

'You have the funds, no need for advance nor credit?'

'Thankfully, I am well placed. I cannot say more.'

Edward stood. 'A toast then, *to jugs, cups and bowls, long may they break!*'

Joseph extracted himself after the fourth beer.

CHAPTER 14

Kirkcaldy, Fife, Scotland 1733

Rosie turned too quickly in surprise and delight at hearing her friend's voice, and promptly fell backwards, over a tree root, onto her bottom.

'Adeline, you sit firm on that horse, and I can't stay on my feet!'

Jean pulled Rosie up as Adeline brought her leg over the saddle post and slid down the side of the horse, holding its rein. Adeline, hot faced and with a big smile, gave Rosie a prolonged hug before she was introduced to Jean.

'I think we may have met,' said Jean.

The three girls' conversation was light and restrained. Rosie and Adeline really wanted to be on their own to exchange serious gossip. That would have to wait. They walked on smartly keeping the marauding boys in front, in sight. The path narrowed as they reached open moorland which sloped downward towards trees and yet another small harbour with a single line of cottages.

'West Wemyss,' said Jean, 'we are going to stop there.'

'I'm hungry.'

'Rose, when are you not!' scolded Adeline.

Rosie noticed that the boys' play acting was as not chaotic as it seemed

'I've got the boys game! When you are killed you must lie still, until your leader comes to you, to tag you. You are then resurrected. A miracle cure. See the elder boy, John, is it? has all the younger ones in his army, and they get caught and killed easily by the other army. But John is too quick to be caught himself, and he runs around and brings his own back to life, killing some of the rebels on the way.'

'That actually sounds fun, could we join?' said Adeline.

'I wish we could. I want to be a boy sometimes,' Rosie added.

'I don't understand, I don't want to.'

'Jean, you could be...,' but Rosie couldn't think of anything.

The older group of boys ran out of sight and hid behind a hillock to the girls left. The younger ones, brought back to life, sat down with their leader. John, still standing, gave instructions like a real commander.

Adeline spotted another party coming up the hill from the front, 'Look.' Two men, one well-dressed, the other like a gamekeeper, and three boys walking ahead of them. The five, not part of the Oswald group, were coming up the hill towards John's sitting group of boys. The gamekeeper shouldered a gun and held two large hounds on leads. Dead rabbits and rooks were tied to his waistband.

The sitting boys spotted them and stood up. John lined them up and gave careful instruction. Then, at his command they charged down the hill at full pelt. Some stumbling and falling into the moorland heather as if they had been shot. There were yelling and shouting, 'Jacobites!' as they careered down the hill. The three boys, hesitated, looked at each other and yelled, 'Charge!' and ran up the hill toward them.

There was a great melee with lots of pushing and shoving and some very violent deaths. A third cry of, 'Charge!' came from the older group who emerged from behind the hillock and ran onward join the fray. The younger boys who remained standing turned to confront them as did the three new boys who had not yet got the point of dying easily.

In a few moments it was all over, all dead, complete devastation, a slaughtered field. The new three had finally got the game and fell dramatically like Bravehearts.

'That's enough now,' said the well-dressed man, picking up the smallest boy as they all began to rise in exhausted good humour. There was one grazed elbow and one sore knee.

Sir Peter and young Peter trotted on horseback down the path past Rosie and the girls, closely followed by the eldest Oswald boy, Jamie on his horse. Adeline mounted her mare with a great leap and a pull up, to lie on her front across the horse's back; she then swivelled both legs around its rear in a very unladylike manner, to end up sitting side-saddle. She had the horse quick-trot after the men before she was safely settled.

'Come on!' Rosie shouted to Jean, who responded with a negative shake of the head. Rosie, stopped, no, she was going. She raised her skirted dress and ran down the hill.

'Peter Higgs, by god!' The well-dressed man looked up. 'The cavalry behind the infantry. You are spending far too much time with the French.'

'Wemyss, nodded Peter, smiling, relieved that their host was in good humour.

'Are any of these your brood?'

'Just these two,' said Peter as he dismounted, and Adeline caught up.

'As yes, Master Peter and Adeline isn't it.'

'Your Lordship,' said young Peter. Adeline followed with a nod. As she dismounted, a breathless Rosie arrived at the same time as John who had sauntered down slope. Sir Peter gave Adeline his reins. Master Peter turned and Rosie quickly said,

'I'll take it,' and held his horse.

'And James Oswald,' Lord Wemyss continued.

Jamie also gave his reins to Rosie.

'M'lord,' said Jamie with a nod of the head.

'A decent flanking manoeuvre, John.'

'Yes, and by our adversary too.'

'And who is this?'

Rosie was now standing beside Adeline.

'This is Rose Miller, the daughter of our new schoolmaster.'

Adeline elbowed Rosie to make her curtsy.

'Ah, yes, I have heard.'

'Forgive our disturbance, Lord Wemyss, I was assured permission was sought,' said Jamie.

'Yes, yes, you are expected, although we were not anticipating an insurrection. I should have rolled out the canon. All we have prepared is soup.'

'That may be a greater defence from this rabble than canon,' Jamie replied, before sending John to round up the boys and take them down to the garden.

'The redoubtable Mrs Oswald wrote. We have provided some chairs for the ladies and a serving table in the garden. Her carriage has already arrived. Would that we could have a Prime Minster as forthright and determined as your grandmother, James.'

Jean had arrived and stood with Rosie and Adeline at the horses, near the men. The keeper had taken the hounds and gone on to the moor. As the men talked, Rosie asked Adeline softly, 'Who is he?'

'That is Lord Wemyss, he owns the land and the castle.'

All Rosie's attention had been on the boys, the men then the horses.

'What ca...?' She looked up. She was looking southeast from an oblique angle. Standing on the cliff edge, sun lit with a dark sea as the backcloth, was the biggest building she had seen in her life. Towered and crenelated, three, four stories high, three red sandstoned blocks, each four, or six windows wide, joined round towers and ended by a square one.

'Gosh.'

'These are fine beasts,' said Lord Wemyss as the men moved to examine the three Rigg horses held by Rosie and Adeline. Jamie Oswald explained that his had a sprained fetlock and they had a discussion on the condition and current form of the horses. Rosie just stood, content to listen. One of the horses kept pushing her from behind with its nose. The three Wemyss boys, muddied from their skirmish, approached and stood near the girls.

'Rose, this is David, Francis and Walpole,' said Adeline.

Rosie curtsied, 'And pray, good sirs, how many hath you killed in battle?'

The boys were not certain of the joke.

Jean looked around, 'Look.' The group turned to see a young man bounding over the heathered heath toward them.

'I think it's Master Smith,' said John.

'The military intelligence has arrived...conveniently well after the battle,' said Jamie, and they all laughed. Smith stopped when he realised they were looking toward him.

'Come Adam,' shouted John, 'you are the sole survivor of the massacre. You may claim your fair maiden!'

The girls squealed and Adam's face went bright red as he approached and nodded to Lord Wemyss.

'You will be glad to have a new schoolmaster,' said Sir Peter and Smith nodded again.

'I see the main battle group is approaching, I fear I must make my escape for my own safety,' said Wemyss responding to the sight of the others coming over and down the hill.

'Come boys.'

The three boys made to go but stopped, 'Father, can we please stay with the others?'

'May I leave them in your charge, John?'

John nodded. 'Of course, m'lord,' and Lord Wemyss withdrew. After a few steps, he turned around.

'Riggs, would you pay me call one afternoon, and bring the new schoolmaster.'

'It would be my pleasure.'

'And bring the two girls if you will, my girls could do with a bit of company.'

'Your Lordship,' nodded Sir Peter.

Jean left to join her family.

'David, can we water the horses,' Young Peter asked

the eldest Wemyss.

'At the stables, sire.'

'Adeline, would you walk the horses down for water. Then bring them to join us.'

John Oswald took his brother's horse, Adeline her own, and Peter, his father's. David Wemyss came to Rosie to take the fourth, but she shook her head and held her grip, moving to follow the others. David sent his younger brothers off with the rest of the boys and walked with Rosie and the horse. Smithy tagged along behind them. David and Smith were about her own age, she thought, but she was a good few inches taller. Rosie liked leading the horse and was surprised how compliant it was, given that she was unfamiliar.

'You are not from here.'

'I have come from Cupar, with my father.'

'With Sir Peter?'

'Adeline is my confidant.'

'Do you ride?'

'Yes, but not as well as Adeline.'

'She is sure in the saddle, for a girl. We saw her race up the pasture.'

'I can't ride side-saddle. I would fall off.'

'What do you do then?'

'I dress as a boy, in trews.'

That got Smith's attention, 'Are you not rebuked?'

'I make quite a good boy, no one notices.'

Smith smirked and David laughed.

'Do you have sisters?' Rosie asked David.

'Three and one more brother.'

'Well the house is big enough.' Sometimes Rosie wished she could stay quiet.

'Yes, if we play hide go seek it can last for months.

Actually, many of the rooms, and there are many, are unused. Where the ghosts live!' David then turned to Smith.

'Smith, what are you doing for school next, I believe you exhausted the last master?'

Smith trotted the few steps to catch them.

'There is a new master coming. He is more learn'ed than the last I hear.'

Rosie realised that they did not know who she was.

'He is here with the party...em.' Her confession was abbreviated as they arrived at the stables and took the horses to the trough.

The stable yard, enclosed on four side with two opposing entrances, was busy, other horses gaining harnesses and two carriages were being brought. Rosie took Peter's horse to where Mr Peter was standing.

'My horse is fond of you. She is a temperamental beast but she is calm with you.'

'She keeps nudging me. I think I smell of apples.'

The stable hand suggested they leave the horses with him; there was an enclosed paddock, and he would wipe them down.

The fourth Wemyss boy appeared, James, and they all walked to the lunch party.

'At last!' said Adeline grabbing her and pulling her back, 'I thought we'd never be alone!'

They walked at a snail's pace behind the others, except Smith who had moved on to other distractions.

'Rose, where are you staying?'

'At the Oswald's with my father.'

'For how long?'

'Until Tuesday, I think.'

'Oh, come and stay with us. We are at the Anderson's

there is lots of room.'

'There is a party, I have to be with my father.'

'I know we are going to that. Oh, please ask, even just for one night.'

'I will. I do really want to.'

'Then *you* will make it happen, Rose, you have that power!'

Rosie was very puzzled by some of the things that Adeline said to her these days.

'I will ask, of course. That Smith boy is a little odd?'

'I hardly know him. You would think he might be teased but the older boys respect him. He is very clever, apparently, and has a sharp wit. Though, you are never quite sure when he is being funny. He has no father and spends much time at the Oswald's with their boys.'

'There are so many boys.'

'*Beaucoup de choix.*'

'Adeline!' said Rosie, taking the meaning, despite the language.

'Bag a Wemyss and you will be a Lady'

'Stop it!' said Rosie. 'They are different though.'

'From what?'

'The boys at my father's school. They are...'

'*Civlisee?*'

'Well mannered.'

The girls arrived at the picnic.

'Ask your father!'

'I will, I'm hun....'

'Don't say it!'

Rosie went to find her father. The ladies were sitting and the gentlemen standing, near a long trestle table. There were two servants serving pie, meats, cheese bread and soup. He was trying to eat but still had the attentions of Mrs Oswald. Rosie thought Sir Peter was trying to rescue him. She went over, it was all school talk.

'Hello Rose, I hear you were nearly felled in battle,' said Mrs Oswald.

'We just watched. It was exciting.'

'No one hurt?'

'No, it was just play.'

'Too rough for developing ladies. I must circulate, David. We will talk more on this matter tomorrow?'

'Of course.'

'Have you been occupied, Rose?'

'Yes, father, Adeline is here.'

'I saw. Rose, this evening will be quiet and the cele-bration for Jamie Oswald's eighteenth birthday is to-morrow evening. I have to spend the day with Mrs Os-wald and visit the school building.'

'Do you wish me to come, father?'

'No, probably best not there are several issues that need to be dealt with.'

'Is there a problem, father?'

'Not really.' Then he thought he should include Rose more. 'There will only be two classrooms ready for the next school year. So, I have to sort out who, when and how the boys will be taught in them.'

'And the girls, father!'

'That is one of the problems to be solved.'

'I want to go to school, father.' The conversation was not going in a good direction, 'and I know you will sort it out,' she added with a smile.

'You will be taught, Rose, I promise.' He hoped he could keep it.

'Father, if you are busy tomorrow may I stay with

Adeline at John Anderson's, then you need not to worry of me.'

'Have you been invited?'

'Adeline asked me.'

'I think that is fine, but would you check with Sir Peter? John is not here.'

'Adeline said it will be fine.'

'I can't decide whether you two are angels or devils.'

'Father!'

Mr Peter standing on a chair banged the empty soup tureen with a metal ladle. It was too effective, there was immediate and total silence, followed by a few giggles from both adults and children.

'Forgive this interruption, I've been asked, to remind you that we must not overstay our welcome, and to ensure we get back to Dunnikier, in good time. I would like you to join in thanking Mrs Oswald and Lord Wemyss for this delightful exercise and picnic. To return you may walk the return journey with us or take one of the carriages that have been arranged. Ladies first and no children.'

That brought groans.

'My father and I look forward to seeing you again at Dunnikier tomorrow.' Peter then led the polite applause, repeating, 'Mrs Oswald and Lord Wemyss.'

John Oswald had found a good stick and attached a white napkin. Holding it aloft, he bellowed, 'To the flag, to arms!'

'That means surrender,' replied David Oswald.

'Never!' as the refuelled younger boys ran to their king and promptly left up the hill to plot an ambush.

Rosie, Adeline, Jamie and the two Peters walked to the stables as the ladies walked to find the carriages.

'Can you stay?'

'I have to ask your father.'

'Adeline, Rose can come but you must ask Jean Ramsay,' was Sir Peter's response.

'She is going back to Abbotshall with her family, she will return tomorrow evening.'

'That is fine, then.'

'*Merci papa!*'

Sir Peter and his son retrieved their horses, Adeline mounted hers. Jamie took the reins of his but instead of mounting beckoned Rose over. Without warning, he lifted her up to sit side-saddle.

'I will walk her,' he assured.

Rose wobbled then felt the motion. The four of them did not follow the armies but turned left out of the stables, down a short, steep track to find the sand. The horses went right down to the sea edge. Jamie said they just had to walk because of his horse's leg, but the other three charged into the surf. The water was shallow the sand firm the sea running out. Jamie' horse whinnied, snorted and bucked its head, not wanting to be left out. Stroking his neck, Jamie calmed him. Young Peter and Adeline charged along the beach in a few inches of water at the ebbing sea edge. Sir Peter trotted with occasional bursts of pace. Jamie's mare with Rosie on board neighed again in complaint, Jamie patting its rear firmly hope that she wouldn't buck Rosie off. Adeline and Mr Peter drew their steeds to a walk and then directed them to the water. They went deeper, Adeline's dress soaking up the water like a sponge. Sir Peter turned his and cantered back to join Jamie and Rosie. He walked his horse at their pace.

'Sir,' said Jamie in greeting.

'A notable date for you tomorrow, James, what are your ambitions?'

'I would hope to university, Sir, and then Europe, for a year perhaps before advocacy. It is not well to plan too far in these times.'

'It was ever thus, I think it is best to plan, but to prepare for other fortunes.'

'Have you travelled, Sir?'

'Indeed, and still do. And I wish I had started younger.'

'You find it of value?'

'The contradiction is that you learn more in regard of your own country when you are without it.'

He lost Rosie there. Rosie did not feel ignored, rather she felt grown now that these two men would talk openly within her ear.

Sir Peter continued, 'Do you have a university in mind?'

'I fancy the law, Sir, so I believe Edinburgh would suit.'

'For law, indeed, St Andrews for the ministry and Glasgow for merchants and thinkers.'

'Aberdeen, Sir?'

'Oh, they fish up there I think!' and they all laughed even Rosie who had no idea what it meant but he had made it sound funny.

'And what of *your* future, Miss Miller?' he said in false gravitas.

And that was the nearest Rosie came to falling during their return trip.

She thought awhile, 'I would like to teach, Sir!' and then added, 'but I would like a horse first.'

'Good for you, Rose, I believe that is possible, I have

heard there are female teachers in some of the parish schools. Would you not desire travel?'

'I fear, Sir, that is not my destiny.'

'Forgive my question Rose, but how many years are you?'

'Thirteen, this year, Sir.'

'In that case, if an old man may impart some advice.'

'Sir.'

'Do not limit your dreams, certainly not in youth.'

At the sound of fast hooves, they all looked to see Master Peter and Adeline galloping toward them.

'I worry that I may lose my brood before this afternoon is done,' said Sir Peter, under his breath.

On the panting arrival, from her saddle Adeline asked to take Jamie's horse's rein and lead Rosie back.

'Only at a walk,' said Jamie, with Sir Peter adding, 'Adeline,' firmly, in hope of obedience.

'We'll stay behind you.' Adeline replied submissively.

Rosie relaxed and looked around her. She could not yet take in this circumstance.

'Addie,' for this had become her diminutive, 'Can we please just walk the horses. I have never *ever* stepped on a beach.' Adeline dismounted, and Rosie slid off onto the firm wet sand. In the late afternoon, the two girls, each leading a horse, Jamie's mount calm now she had a companion, walked away from the men, to the edge of the sea. In Rosie's eyes it could have been the edge of the world. As they approached, they looked up to see their destination. A soft, warm mist rolled in on the water. The sun reddened the western sky. Waiting for them a high, golden castle sat on a cloud.

Back at Dunnikier, Rosie quickly packed her things and

they were allowed a gig to take them the few miles to the Anderson House. Adeline's horse tethered to the rear. David was happy that Rose was occupied, there was more to discuss with Mrs Oswald than he had anticipated. They had a supper together to talk through possibilities before going to Kirkcaldy the next day, where others, from the burgh council, would join them at the site of the school.

Mrs Oswald made it plain that if she and David could reach agreement on the major points, then the council would follow. David found Mrs Oswald to be open and clear. She was funding the building of the school, the master's house and the janitor's house. In exchange the council would fund the school stipends and maintain the buildings. Mrs Oswald confessed that she wished to employ David, yes, for the benefit of the community, but also for the benefit of her own boys - the Oswalds - along with the Adams and others from notable families, perhaps even the Wemyss. It was to be a grammar school. Several of the council members had voiced disagreement with this view. There was no other school for boys over ten years. Children needed a school to learn to read, write and practise arithmetic for the trades. Several acts of parliament were in place to enforce this requirement.

Kirkcaldy council funding, at that time, was not overly generous. The local economy was experiencing a dip due to a decline in overseas trade. An increase in the manufacturing provision promised to more than compensate for this loss in income and occupation, but it would take time. The manufacture, mainly of linen, was changing from home-based piecework to an industrial operation in small factories. The finished goods were in demand and could be readily sold at a profit. The council saw this as the source of future prosperity to the town. David agreed with the council's position of providing a general education, it must be a school for all. But he had taken the post primarily due to his own desire to teach the classics to the bright and able. From what he had understood of the boys he had met at Dunnikier, there was eight to twelve good boys, well capable of benefiting from a classical education, and keen to do so. Without this school they would be stuck with private tutors of an uncertain standard or sent off to Edinburgh each term.

Mrs Oswald made her point well, 'It is not just looking after my own brood, David. If we let these boys to Edinburgh, Dundee or Perth, they are unlikely to return. I would hope these boys will, in the coming years, support the growth here, in Kirkcaldy and Fife, and work for the people and our society. James, my eldest son, and indeed my late husband, have shown me what can be achieved by good and earnest men. Further, a grammar school will attract good families to our lands and the burgh.'

'We are in agreement on this,' said David.

'Aside that, I have been meaning to ask you, have you met our boy, Smith?' Mrs Oswald added.

'No, I know nothing of him.'

'I do not know him well, but I am well acquainted with this mother, Margaret Douglas. At first, he was thought a dreamer, but he has an unusual mind. When you talk with him, he is very engaging. He walks around apparently seeing the world as a complex puzzle, but one that can be solved – by himself. He stood out in the class which included my grandsons, and they are bright fellows. According to Mathew, he usually sat at the back not doing anything, to the annoyance of the doctor. But when questioned, he knew every answer, remembered every fact, solved every calculation; all without putting pen to paper. He astonished our boys and left the doctor exasperated. My point is, what would happen to the likes of him at Edinburgh's High School.'

David was intrigued.

Then there was issue of the inclusion of girls. David wanted girls taught in the school, Mrs Oswald agreed in principle but did not see how it could be made to work. The agreed they did not have to conclude on these decisions now. They only had to decide on the size, shape and scope of the school building.

These discussions were not as heated as David had feared. Mrs Oswald deferred to David's experience in matters of teaching and David understood, learning from his experience in Cupar, that pragmatism and compromise were necessary in dealing with the council in order to achieve a reasonable outcome.

'I accept your points, we must achieve your, our, aim and we must also cater for the town's general education. The lack of a good trade school is a problem, as we must make provision for the boys who would be apprenticed, and girls too, for employment in manufacturing.' He realised as he said it, he had the argument.

Mrs Oswald smiled, a rare event, in their debate, 'David Miller if you work hard to fill my objectives, I will work hard to fulfil yours. And now if you will forgive me, I must to bed.'

They shook hands warmly.

In the morning after breakfast, Mrs Oswald and David set off in an open carriage for Kirkcaldy. It was a short journey, barely a half hour walk. David was impressed by the site. High up above the harbour, a short walk from the parish church, good light from the south, with views to the Forth estuary. It was a good-sized plot, with yard space for outside activity. There were already wooden markers in the ground. A small janitor's house adjoined the school building and would sit at the gate. The master's house was of good size, positioned along the road off Kirk Wynd to the west of the school.

David paced out the ground. Lying north-to-south, two large classrooms were possible with a smaller room at the north end between the schoolrooms and the janitor's house. Each classroom sized for up to fifty pupils. The small room would have a connecting door, be book-shelved, and host a desk and several chairs. Two double door entrances for the schoolrooms and a smaller single door on the north gable. The building was to be raised high with large windows – to impress and inspire, if funds allow. 'Let us build for the future,' he said.

Mrs Oswald reserved a slight frown. Three council members attended, one took notes. They talked to each other and wore expressions which seemed to represent a spectrum of approval. As David and Mrs Oswald took the carriage back, David was buoyed by the prospect of the new school, 'I can solve any challenges in class arrangements with judicious timetabling. We are building, if it is approved, a good-sized functional school. Over time, it will adapt to its changing needs.

The older pupils may not have full days, but my experience is that this is welcomed by most, not least the pupils. It reduces fees and releases the children over twelve years for labour.'

'A grammar school needs a moto, something in Latin I think.'

'That ma'am, will not be a problem.' They travelled back to Dunnikier to rest before the evening.

There was so many people at the celebration, Rosie and Adeline found they could wander around the house as if they were invisible. They were overlong in dressing; there was no reception when they eventually appeared downstairs. They decided they were adult enough for the yellow sparkling wine, served in crystal glasses, which made Rosie's head spin. They mingled, saying hello and nodding to their father's friends and looked shyly down if they passed a boy of similar age. Jean sought them out and the three retreated to Rosie's room so they could talk unheard until the dinner bell.

There were two sittings and they almost missed their call. Then horror, the girls were to be seated around the table between the boys. As they stood at their chairs, Jamie's mother, Anna, whom Rosie had not met before, entered the room with Jamie. They walked around the table, shaking hands in introduction. Although they did not stay to dine with them, Jamie said he would join them later. As they left Adeline, she stuck out a foot to trip Jamie as he passed, almost sending him into his mother. He turned with a false, cross expression promising revenge. Adeline was all innocence, she was animated and enjoying herself.

Rosie sat between Mathew Oswald and an Adam Ferguson who, with his family, was visiting his uncle at

Raith House. Next to him was Frances Wemyss who was a younger sister of David. David Wemyss and John Oswald, who appeared to be close friends, sat together at the head of the table. Poor Jean, when she was seated became red faced and could neither eat nor get a word out. Adeline was to Rosie's left, on the other side of Mathew. Rosie expected the boys to lead a conversation but gave up waiting and began to tell Adam about the visit to Wemyss Castle, the horses and the fighting game. Mathew joined in, and the conversation livened up after that. She asked them about study and Adam Ferguson said he went to a parish school in a village called Logierait, much like the one in Cupar it seemed. Mathew said he would attend the new school. Rosie said she was to attend too. The boys did not believe her but did not press the point.

'Girls do not need to know Latin,' remarked Adam.

'*Ut credimus,*' replied Rosie, which led to a minute or two of silence before a change in subject to horses. She didn't actually know why she should study Latin either, but she trusted her own father more than...well more than god.

As the last dish was consumed, Jamie came back in. Mathew stood and asked the table to charge their glasses and raise them in a toast to his brother. Jamie gave a short speech of thanks and instructed the gentlemen to retire to the smoking room and the ladies to withdraw to the music room. He would now dine with his parents and their friends, then the room would be cleared for the dancing to start at half past nine.

Rosie, Adeline, Jean, and two other girls, Anne and Frances (Fanny) Wemyss, retired as requested. The girls sat and talked politely for a while and then decided to sing and play the piano. The Wemyss girls were very good and Jean was competent; Adeline was as entertaining as ever and they finished with a duet that she and Rosie had performed before. Rosie tried to avoid doing an entertainment on her own; she knew she wouldn't shine in this company. 'Rose, sing the rude song. I will accompany you.' demanded Adeline. The room's attention was now on her. A few moments' preparation with Adeline at the piano, she launched into the bawdy ballad. They clapped politely; Jean was amused but the other girls' reaction was hard to judge.

'But where do you learn this?'

Rosie could hide no more and told of her life in Cupar and helping Jess at the inn. Perversely, she thought, the girls were fascinated and kept asking questions. They thought it sounded far more fun than their overly-supervised, well-groomed lives. All girls then shared amusing stories from their families and childhood as the older ladies entered to join them in the room.

A howling from without broke the chatter, an extreme wail. Rose jumped and looked a bit feared. Spotting the others had not reacted she asked, 'What is that noise?'

'It's the piper Rose, for the dance,' said Anne.

Ann Oswald came in to summon them all through to the dining room. The table was cleared; the floor was bared. The chairs were placed around the perimeter of the room. A piper and two other players, a drum and a flute were set in one corner. It took some time for all the party to gather; the boys took a while to be extricated from their games elsewhere. It gave Rosie a chance to ask Adeline what was to happen, but Adeline was too distracted to give her any attention. She stood to the side with the other girls.

The flute player announced the dance and the men and boys proceeded to come over to the ladies and lead them on to the floor. The adults led the proceedings; Rosie saw the ladies prompting their sons. The boys came over, Rosie stood back and tried to hide. Mathew put out his hand and Rosie shook her head. He prompted again, and she said she can't. Mathew took his sister instead. The band started; it was loud, fast music, almost violent. Rosie could barely look. It looked fun but she didn't know what to do. Another dance and, embarrassed, she worked hard to suppress a tear. She looked up to see Smithy watching her. She hadn't noticed him until that point. A third dance was called.

'Would you dance with me please Miss Rose?'

The sound of that voice brought her such relief.

'Oh, father, I don't know what to do.'

'It is easy, Rose. I will tell you what to do. Just follow my steps as if you are my mirror.'

'I'll try father, if you will help.'

'Come and stand in line. First, we hold hands and walk four steps forward, then four steps back, in time to the music. We do that eight times. Then we hold both hands, facing each other and move up and down sideways, again eight times. The couple at the top will stop and make an arch, and we will all march through them. You will see.'

'Four steps forward, four steps and back?' she repeated.

'Yes.'

She danced twice with her father then Adeline pulled her away. It was a more difficult dance, but by then she did not feel the whole room was watching her. The next was then a skirling dance, where the girls and ladies were wildly spun around by the men. She watched in fascination, but also trying to learn and remember the steps. There were some near misses in the confined space. As the adults demanded a repeat from the piper, she found she was standing next to Mathew. Caught up in the excitement, Rosie finished an abandoned glass of wine that sat on a side table. She nudged him. Without even a glance sideways, he ignored her. She nudged him again, more firmly. Without turning his head, he said,

'Miss Rose, would you be requesting my pleasure?'

She looked shyly down.

Facing each other, he held her right hand in his left, his right hand at her waist, her left on his shoulder. They skipped sideways, to the left then the right, and spun round twice, then repeat. The music got louder and faster for the reel. Facing again, they held crossed hands, and Mathew spun Rose round and round on the dance floor like she was on fire.

She was.

CHAPTER 15

Delft & the Coast, Zeeland 1711

As the ship, one of seven that sailed in convoy across the North Sea, approached the now familiar dock at Campveere, Joe looked to the pier. He recognised one out of the many figures easily; the tall woman, wearing a green coat and dark red scarf, waving in expectation rather than recognition, for she had not known the name of his ship.

Ruud was not on board. Joe had set him to prepare a trade in other goods, coal, salt, linen, using Tom's old logbook of trades as a reference. He would get his chance of travel again soon. Joe made sure that one of them would always be in Scotland, on dry land. He had stored Tom's two paintings in their warehouse, in separate buildings in case of fire. At this time, they were his family's security. Henry and Ruud had sworn to ensure his family were looked after, in case of mishap. He had promised Mary two, three weeks at the most. He offered to send a message every other day. 'No, Joe, then I would worry if one did not arrive. Just send me a note when you can, if you wish or not. I will not worry.'

Joe waved back from the ship, she saw him now, her face alight. He had not brought goods to sell and he hoped the exporting trade would be straightforward, a duplicate of the last, double the quantity. He had written in advance to the potteries and expected to be well-received. Grietje had done some groundwork and visited the houses regarding the design and quality. He would hire local labour. As the leading partner in the company, he had been able to make prior arrangements with the Scottish trading bank. All that was required for him to do was complete the bargain. There were other matters that he now wished to follow up.

Grietje was at the end of the gangplank as he walked down. They met and greeted each other with an awkward clasp as she laughed.

'It is good to see you, Joe. Do you have to attend the ship?'

'No, I have my bag, and that is it. I will check in at the *Conciergerie* for a room.'

'Unless you need rest, let us walk there, and have coffee.'

'That is just what I need.'

'No limp?'

'No, I am fine now.'

'You know you are welcome to stay with me, Joe.'

'Thank you, I thought it best to spend time with other merchants. I have a lot to learn, still.'

'But you will come for supper?'

'Of course, thank you. Grietje, your English is good.'

'Ah yes, I have been practising hard...with all the Scotsmen!' she laughed.

The *Concierge* had a room for him. He left his bag and they went to the inn where they had hidden from the soldiers on Joe's earlier visit. Sitting, they ordered coffee, Joe asked for bread and smoked fish. He looked around. 'How times change, it is a different place.'

'A happier one, I hope. Do you want to talk of business first?'

'Just to check what we need to do. Then we can leave it until tomorrow. I will pay you for your days, Grietje.'

'Thank you. The money you left me made a difference in my life.'

'We could not have done it without you. Edward Clerk, our selling agent, was very pleased with what we brought him. My instructions are to continue to do the same. We make more money on the *Porceleyne Fles,* but it takes a bit longer to sell. He also says he can easily move large quantities of the cheapest porcelain through the markets.'

The coffee and food arrived, and Joe continued, 'I did not say much in the letter, but I have bought the business with the proceeds of the last trade and some additional investment. I still employ Ruud and work him very hard. It has taken forty years, but I suddenly find myself with ambition. I cannot account for it.'

'That is a good thing, Joe.'

'Maybe so, but there are many parts to play. I do not have them all. I am not Tom, but I gained much from working with him.'

Grietje laughed and reached over to straighten his collar. 'It takes all kinds.'

'I think Edinburgh can be stifling.'

'Sorry?'

'Oh, close, em, too many old families of merchants and lawyers.'

'I understand, *stifling.* I shall remember.'

'But I am determined to make it work, if I can, by trading overseas. Starting here. How have you been,

Grietje?'

'As I say, I have been able to paint, and our visits to *Porceleyne Fles* have helped their view of me. They pay me to do their fine work and they now allow me to design, not just copy.'

'I am glad for you.'

'Are you still thinking of your own designs?'

'Not my designs but finding designs for the English market. I cannot judge. If you can help, we can try this. Henry said the English potteries are aware of our market and will soon catch up.'

'That is exciting.'

Joe frowned slightly; he had inherited a Scotsman's reaction to enthusiasm which was hard to overcome.

'So, to Delft tomorrow?'

'No, I will have a day banking, and arranging the labour, portering and shipping and talking to other merchants. Delft the next day. Will you come?'

'Of course!'

'What is the quickest route with no baggage?

'Sail, with a good wind, on horse if not. I will go now and let you rest; you will come to supper at seven?'

'Thank you, yes.'

Grietje's room was tidier than he remembered, with a new padded chair and a small desk. Her painting area, near the window, took up more than half the floor. It was busy but not chaotic: stretched blank canvases; a paint mixing tray, pigment jars of colour, crayons, charcoal, cloths, a knife and paper. The table was incongruously clear, but Joe thought that was probably in expectation of his arrival. Meaty smells filled the room.

'Joe, you are looking smart.'

'I am not made for it.'

'Sit by the fire while I cook. I have a jug of ale.'

'Grietje, you have news that you could not write.'

'Yes, I hope you will not upset.'

'With you?'

'Yes, with what I have done and what I have learned. Grietje moved from the stove and pulled a loosely wrapped parcel out of a wall cupboard. She removed the paper and placed a satchel on the table in front of Joe. He recognised it, of course.

'I haven't opened it. I waited for you. It is Tom's isn't it?' The confirmation was already written on Joe's face. Joe went pale. Grietje put her hand on his shoulder.

'Joe, I am sorry, the shock.'

'Yes, but where...?'

Grietje saw that he needed a minute and went back to the stove. Joe didn't move to open it; he just sat. Joe was distant, after a few more minutes she pulled a chair and sat beside him.

'Have I done the wrong thing?' her hand on his arm.

Joe shook his head, 'No, no, sorry, just a... Where did you find it?'

'I went to the driver's house, Henrik, in the spring. It took a few visits before my knock was answered. An older lady, Henrik's widow, answered; she was kind and invited me inside. I think she was glad of the company. I said that I had a friend who was with her husband when he drowned. She was concerned for me. I told her Tom's name and said I was not his wife. She and Henrik had been married thirty-nine years.'

'Oh, god.'

'She made a warm, lemon drink and we sat. She asked of me and I told her more than I usually share. She bade me visit again, and I have done. It was just as I was leaving, half out the door, she said, 'Wait, I have forgotten. I have something,' in Dutch of course. And she went back inside and brought the satchel. She said it was found securely tied near where Henrik was found. She had looked inside; it was not her husband's; perhaps it was Tom's. She asked me to give it to his family.'

Joe still hadn't touched it.

'Shall we eat first and you can think about what to do?'

'Yes, and...and do you have wine?'

'Yes, of course. I don't have whisky though.'

Grietje filled two plates with a fine *hachee*. She served the dish with bread and cabbage. Joe drank the first glass of wine in one gulp. He was on his third when his plate was bared.

'Should I open it?' he asked.

'You ask me?'

Joe nodded.

'Yes, I think you should. There can be no harm in that.' Grietje cleared the table.

The leather of the satchel was stiff. He undid the two tied straps bound firmly round the front flap. He took out a familiar item, heavy, wrapped in oilcloth. It was Tom's pistol. Then the small wooden box which he knew held the rod, powder, balls and spark lighter. There was a large flat shape, also well wrapped. Joe took it out and put it on the table. A thick, flat leather pouch and a wrapped book followed along with something that used to be food, a few coins and lastly, a tattered, grey coloured letter. Grietje was trying not to show interest, to respect Joe's privacy.

'It is fine, Grietje, come and sit. It is a bag of curiosities.'

She brought the wine bottle, sat beside him, and filled both their glasses.

Joe paused. 'Does this make him dead, Grietje? I see now, I was holding a hope. I would not let go. That was the shock. He was never without this. Does this make him dead?' It was not a question to be answered.

'Do you know all this?' asked Grietje.

Pulling the flat book aside, 'This is his journal.'

'Leave that for now, Joe.'

'His money pouch.' He put that to one side also, left it closed, and picked up the bigger package.

'I do not know this.'

'Open that one, Joe.'

Joe took the package. It was well wrapped for the sea voyage.

'It is a small painting,' he said, lifting it free.

'Let me see. It's beautiful. A Dutch barge. He would take it as a keepsake?'

'I suppose.'

'What, Joe?'

'I haven't told you yet, but a few weeks ago I received another of Tom's packages, two large paintings. Nothing for nearly two years, then everything is Tom.'

'Is that not why you came?'

'Not only, but yes, you are right.'

Grietje picked up the pouch. Joe nodded. She pulled out the notes. They were not fresh, but neither were they torn nor discoloured, only slightly faded.

'There must be two hundred or more. Oh, Joe.'

'I didn't have the figures. He sold several cases of silver and then we came to Delft to buy paintings and pottery. He carried the full amount. When I got back to Edinburgh, I found there were many expenses left unpaid.'

'But whose money is it?'

'Well, it will belong to the business. Tom was acting for the business.'

'Joe, you bought the business?'

Joe answered slowly, just taking in his own answer. 'Yes, I have bought the business.' then he paused.

'Grietje, I, we, must go, get out.'

'Where to?'

'An inn, some life, I need to breathe. Is there somewhere busy, players, music and whisky?'

'At the dock, yes.'

'Will you come?'

'Yes. I will put the satchel back safely.'

Joe woke at first light and groaned. His head ached like it would fall if he moved. He was fully clothed, he didn't recognise the room. He looked round and saw Grietje's feet, she was lying beside him, also fully clothed, the other way round, fast asleep. He sank back, thirsty. Memory returning. There was music and reels in a tiny place, and whisky and whisky and whisky. Grietje moved and groaned, 'Water, please, water.' Her head was off the end of the bed.

'Do you want a trough or a cup?'

'Just water, please.'

Joe crawled through the rest of the day, brightening only after his third coffee house meeting. He set his mind to the task in hand, he would revisit the issue of Tom when he had time with Grietje in Delft. She had said the previous evening that she had more to tell. He talked to traders about business in general, but any query on specifics or prices was rebuffed. He kept quiet about his own business. He had brought scruffy clothes for travelling and put them on to speak to the locals who were waiting for the ships at the docks. A joke or two over shared tobacco gleaned more useful information than any from a fellow merchant. He got bankers' notes for the potteries and would not need to carry cash. He would also need, for security, to deposit the cash they had found in Tom's bag. He hadn't seen Grietje since she left his room before conversation in the morning and had a brief thought that she could just run off with the money. The thought did not worry him. At seven that evening, the aches of the previous night caught up with him; he ate lightly on his own and went to bed.

The knocking came from the door, his head was alright.

'Joe, Joe?' and the door opened.

'What time is it?'

'Just after five, there is a mail yacht at six. It will get us to Delft by sunset. Shall I bring the satchel or anything from it?'

'No, em, yes, bring the journal and the letter. Is the money safe?

'Only we know it's there.'

'Bring a quarter of it then, just in case.'

'I will be back in half an hour.' Grietje closed the door behind her.

It was a sleek yacht, like the one Ruud had taken when he left Delft. The coastal wind was from the south. There were two crew who were pleased to have passengers, well, Grietje anyway. They watched the sun rise over the land to the east. Joe took a turn at the helm when it was safe. He felt the yacht shift quickly at the slightest change. Porpoises appeared and disappeared at the bow, along with a larger fish, a small whale they said, which moved at a surprising pace for its size. Grietje had brought a feast that the four of them shared in the early afternoon. It was a speedy pleasure trip, contrasting their previous soporific journey on the barge. In the evening sun, they approached de Kolk basin at the end of the canal. Joe was still moved by the view of the towers, the walls and the single windmill at the southern port of Delft. Joe heard a voice, 'You could both run off with the money.' It was in his head. Disembarking, he said in a High Street preacher's voice, '*Thou shalt not yield to...*'

'Joe?'

'Oh sorry, that was not meant to be out loud. We need to find rooms.'

'No.'

'No?'

'Trust me.'

They were lightly loaded and took a route through the busier streets. As they walked across the market square, through the aroma of a street café, they looked to each other and took seats at a table with a view of the *stadhuis*. The top of the spire catching the glow of the sunset.

'Where are we going?' Joe asked.

'You will see, no hurry.'

'You said there was more to tell.'

'Yes, but nothing serious tonight. Let me tell you about Henry and his portrait. But do you not have a tale?'

'I am not a storyteller.'

'Joe!'

'Then I will tell you of Tom's boy.'

They ordered wine and food; it was a warm evening

for September.

'I don't think I have said much of him before. He would come to the office with Tom, occasionally. James Lockhart was, of course, his grandfather. He was, is, a tall, attractive child, looks very like his father, polite, a bit solitary, bookish. Not like my rabble. I didn't pay him much mind, even when Tom disappeared. Mary and I went to our church for a concert and I saw him in the choir. Well, I didn't at first, I saw Tom. I had time to think then about the boy, but more of what would Tom think or want. And I was concerned. I want the boy to do well and be looked after. He was under the care of the people who had let my family down badly. You know, Grietje, we went to him after the concert and it took him a moment to place me, but when he did, he cried.'

'Oh, Joe, was he alright?'

'Yes, he is fine. I think I know what he felt now. I guess it was like when you brought out Tom's bag.'

'And you say you cannot tell a story!'

The food arrived and they were quiet for a bit.

'He visits us now, once or twice a month and joins us for our family meal. My brood like him. He tells us all sorts of tales from Greek gods to school capers. When he does that he bursts into life and makes us all laugh. I will look after my own Grietje and I will look after that boy, not just for Tom's sake but because he does not have what my children have.'

'More wine?' Grietje offered.

'A small one, I, we, need clear heads tomorrow.'

As the warm air gave in to the evening mist, Grietje led the way out of the marketplace, along one main street to a tree-lined boulevard with fine houses and a canal running up the middle. Grietje stopped and walked up to one of the doors.

'Grietje?'

She knocked; an elderly lady let them in, but she did not attend to them. Grietje smiled as she led Joe upstairs.

'Grietje?'

She shook her head and laughed. There was one door on the first floor which she opened. They walked into a large, three-windowed, high-ceilinged room, well-furnished with a view over the canal.

'You have spent all the money!'

'I'm glad you joke, Joe. It is Henry's. I paint his portrait here. He has allowed me, and told me, to use it if I wish. It is just one floor and there is no maid.'

Joe flopped on a chair. 'It will do.'

'Joe, there is one bed. I can sleep in here. I know you love your wife.'

Joe sat quietly and didn't respond; he didn't know how. He had seen Tom and Doortje. He understood it better now. When you are in another land, are you another person? And their time was different, he had six years on Tom and Grietje more than ten on Doortje. It was not that the desire was not there; but he saw Grietje more as a cousin, a colleague a friend, a good friend. They had a future as such, a fruitful one. He could not betray Mary; he would be betraying his family; he would be betraying himself. His marriage was not Tom's; he was not Tom.

'I will make a warm Chinese drink for bed. Do you want to try?'

'Thank you, Grietje, yes. Why not?'

Joe's height made most beds uncomfortable, not this

one. He slept solidly, there was no intruding dream. In the morning, he woke late and turned to find Grietje sleeping beside him. He nudged her. She stretched, 'I'm sorry Joe, I came in earlier to see if you were awake and it looked so comfortable.'

'It is late now, I think.' Grietje added, 'Shall we find a place for bread and coffee and plan our day?'

They had sent notes to the three factories they had been to before, giving times for their intended visit. Joe went back to the port to reserve a barge, hoping to find the same men that he used before, while Grietje looked round the market traders to see what was selling. She bought some food for midday, wine and coffee. It was after two when the met back at Henry's rooms.

As they were finishing their coffee, Grietje said, 'Shall we look at the letter? And then we must find you a barber.'

Grietje had placed it in the front of the journal to keep it flat. She took it out.

'It has been wet,' said Joe. He carefully pulled two sheets from the envelope and tried to prise them apart. He looked at it closely.

'It is in Tom's hand. To Janssen, the lawyer. It's difficult, there are many unreadable words. It is thanking him for a dinner. Doortje was there. Janssen was going to forward two paintings. That's the paintings I now have. There is the dealer's name! Says he will visit van Reit before the voyage. Thanking him again. Will return next year. That is it, I think, in short.'

'He, Janssen, was unapproachable?'

'Yes, I wrote to him twice.'

'You never met him?'

'No, but there are other avenues now.'

'Hair and beard, short, you need to be smart tomorrow. I will buy meat for this evening, and something for myself, if you would advance me?'

'Grietje, I am so sorry, of course.'

'Try again, H-i-r-e-e-c-h-e-h.'

Joe tried, it defeated him.

'You know the fairie story, Hansel and...?'

'Gretel.'

'No, I don't like that, can you say Greta?'

'Of course, Greta.'

'Then that will do.'

'Short now!' she said pointing to his head.

'Yes, ma'am.'

Grietje made supper and Joe sat at a table by the window and went through the figures. He intended to buy some additional fine porcelain for his company to sell in Edinburgh. Clerk said he would double the previous trade for English markets. Based on their earlier trade Joe estimated best and worst prices for each of the potteries.

'Supper is ready. Shall we eat in this room?'

'Yes.'

'Do you want to look at the journal tonight?'

'No, I want to keep my business head. We can look another day. I also think I want to go to Monster again.'

All went to plan the next day. There was a dense mist, you could only see ten yards to the front and ten to the rear. It was eerily quiet, just the dull clopping of the trotting horse's hooves and the odd squawk of an ungrounded bird. It was a place between heaven and earth. Wrapped up in blankets in the open carriage, they did not dally. They were well received. *De Por-*

celeyne Fles, offered a light meal, which they accepted. After Grietje looked through the porcelain samples, Joe asked for a tour, paying interest to the details of the coating and firing process. Deals were struck, the prices were a little higher. Delivery to Campveere was arranged to arrive at the dock in three days' time. Joe had the name of the barge and its captain. They were back at the house by four.

'Shall I cook tonight, Joe?'

'No, I have shaken hands on three good deals we shall dine out.'

Over dinner Joe shared his plans for the following day.

'We have two more days here. Then I would like to be in Veere when they load the ship. I can check the goods there. I would go to Monster, tomorrow perhaps.'

'Joe, we should look at the journal. It might tell us something.'

'It is personal. It will be intrusive, a man's private journal. For the eyes of a wife or a child...'

'From what you have said, that is unlikely. '

'I would give it to the boy, David.'

'Look at the last few pages, that's all.'

'David?'

'Yes, you know they always called him *the boy*, even Tom most times. I won't. He is David.'

'He is a partner in the company, No?'

'Ha, yes, effectively.'

'So, he deserves that respect!'

'We will look to that when we return. We could visit the art dealer and try Janssen again, but I'm not sure we would find anything. We can see, if there is time. I think it maybe more important to visit van Reit.'

'I've forgotten who he is?'

'We stopped there on the trip with Tom. It was a cold, wet night and we came across his house as we sought shelter. The stables would have done, but he took us in, and he took to Tom; everybody took to Tom. Anyway, he sent a letter to Tom which I opened, I have it with me. It was after Tom disappeared, so I assume he knows or knew nothing of the circumstance, and I am duty bound to explain. He was a distinguished and pleasant fellow.'

'Will he remember you?'

'We dined together, so yes. He was old, seventy years at least, maybe eighty.'

Joe continued after a pause, 'It would mean going back to Veere overland by cart. I'll decide tomorrow and send a message.'

'Joe, I have something else to tell you. It may affect what you decide.' Grietje was serious.

'I went to Monster.'

'Oh, did you find anything?'

'I don't know. I was in Delft working on Henry's portrait and there were idle days, so on a *gril*?' Joe shrugged, Greitje continued, 'I just wanted to see where you had gone that day. I remembered the funny story of the name. I hope you do not mind.'

'You were not ill-intended, Greta. What did you see?'

'I went with a mind to paint, so I took canvas, easel and crayons. I set up with a view down the street toward the harbour. There were children playing nearby.'

'But you wouldn't know the house?'

'The children were curious, and we talked. I drew for nearly three hours. Some of the children sat on a grassy bank behind me. I was between the houses and the well. People walked by, they smiled and said hallo. Then a younger woman walked by, tall and fair, she did the same. One of the older children said, '*Hei Doortje.*'

'You saw her, but there is something else...'

'Joe, there was a child.'

'What?'

'She had a child, a baby, not walking age, the child sat on a sled.' Grietje paused.

Joe waited. 'It could be any...'

'The woman walked back, she stopped. We talked and she asked to look at my drawings, she said she might buy one.'

'Joe, I asked the baby's name.' Grietje took a breath, 'It was a girl. Doortje said she was named, Tomasine.'

'Greta, why did you not tell me?'

'I'm sorry. I thought it best to wait.'

Joe just sat quietly. He did not finish his plate. He shook his head when the serving girl asked if they wanted anything else. Grietje paid the bill and pulled him up and urged him out of the inn.

In the misty evening air, Joe said, 'You were right to wait, thank you.'

Grietje put her arm in his and they walked back to their rooms. 'And no whisky tonight!'

'One will not harm, Joe replied, 'Medicine.'

'There is a bottle in the rooms, I went shopping re-member. I thought one of us would need it at some time.'

'I don't know how I will manage this business with-out you.'

'Then don't,' she replied ambiguously.

After the first glass, Joe became more circumspect. 'It still might not be his.'

Grietje raised an eyebrow, 'Unlikely. Conceived before he left? Before he drown?'

'Well, after would be unusual,' remarked Joe. The whisky was having its effect.

'Why do you care so much, Joe?'

'He taught me so much, yet he learned from me too. We worked together for many years. That is the past, but this affects the b... David, could affect him. Tell me, Greta, did you think them poor? How was their dress?'

Their glasses were refilled.

'You would help them? You want to visit Doortje?'

Joe thought carefully. 'I would help, yes. I also want to know. To go back to Scotland and not know would leave it in my mind. For David's sake also.'

'You would tell him?'

'I don't know, not when he is young. But would he not have a right to know when he is older?'

'If you do not find out, you do not have that problem.'

'Hide from a truth?'

'I think we do that all the time.'

'You are too wise for me; I cannot think that way.'

'Or foolish,' she responded.

'Yes, that as well.'

'Joe, please do not become funny and handsome, you will break my heart!'

They both laughed and topped up their glasses.

They had a full day tomorrow and did not continue into the night. Joe went to his room and Grietje readied herself for sleep in the front room. After the whisky, Joe fell asleep quickly but was vaguely aware of another person climbing in the other side of the bed. They both slept peacefully.

A flock of geese flew overhead in the morning sky,

waking them both.

'It is a mystery to me how you can travel in your sleep.'

'Do you mind much? I find comfort in it.'

'No...I don't mind. I'm used to you now.'

'*Koffiehuis*?'

'Of course, and Monster.'

'A new day brings light,' Grietje replied.

'Take your crayons and easel again?'

'I can paint, yes, what will you do?'

'I will walk, perhaps, and I will visit Doortje. She said to write. I will deliver a message when we arrive.'

'You have a plan?'

Joe said nothing.

'Do you have the portrait of Henry here?'

'Yes, it's not finished.'

'May I see?'

'Of course.' Grietje took Joe through to a small room, off the bedroom, where she kept her paints and canvases. The portrait sat on an easel. She pulled Joe back from it and pulled the cover from it.

'Greta, that is wonderful.'

'Have I caught the likeness?'

'That is Henry!' Joe was stunned. 'It is not a likeness; this *is* him, the fun, the ebullience, the light, the life, it is Henry!'

'You talk too quick, Joe, I don't'...'

'It's wonderful.' Joe went to kiss her. She saw it coming and stopped him. 'Not a spark Joe, not a spark.'

Early the next morning, Joe hired a driver and cart, Grietje took her materials to paint, put them in a trunk and placed a small easel down beside it. She also packed water, bread, cheese and a bottle of wine.

'Do you need to write the note?'

'I have done it.'

They set off. They sat quietly.

'Around eighty years ago, a single spark from a torch started a fire in Delft. It was all wooden houses then. It burned to the ground. Many died, many badly injured and many more homeless; many families were ruined. It has taken eighty years to rebuild it. It was a single spark, Joe.'

'I understand. I'm sorry.'

'Don't be sorry, we enjoy what we have. We must be careful. We do not have eighty years.'

Joe returned her sad smile.

The journey took just short of two hours. It was light and cool when they arrived.

The driver took the trunk from the cart and Grietje set up her easel near to the place where she had sketched before, contriving a better view of the three houses. Joe told the driver to come back in three hours. Joe looked around, it was quiet, and he waited while Grietje set her things. She sat on the trunk, at the easel.

'I will drop off the message to Doortje. It simply says that I am in the area on business and I will call back at one after the noon. I apologised for the surprise. I will go for a walk along the coast. I will come back here for then.'

'That is fine, Joe. I am good here.'

'Will you keep an eye on the house?'

'I have to, it is in my painting.'

Joe walked close to the edge of the road near the houses. He walked up the steps to the door of the last house and pushed his message under. He did not hear any sounds or see any sign of life. It might all be a waste of time. He then walked out to the harbour and turned north along the coast. The only sounds were the lapping of the waves and the sweet chatter of groups of small, thin-beaked, long-legged wading birds. He thought again of Tom and their time together.

An hour and a half later, Grietje spotted Joe returning down the street. Grietje changed the drawing sheet. She had the company of two girls, sitting on the grass bank behind her.

'This is Lena and Benthe.'

Joe nodded and the girls ran off.

'Did you see anything?'

'Yes, please sit,' she said, pointing to the bank. She put her crayon down and turned to face him.

'How was your walk?'

'There is a calm beauty here. There were many flocks of small birds by the shore, chattering sweetly as they waded and dipped for food at the edge of the water.'

'*De kreet van der sand'ling*...the cry of the sand'ling,' Grietje reflected.

She continued. 'A short while after you left, Doortje came out, looked up and down the street and went back in. A little more time, then three came out, Doortje, holding the infant, and the other was a man.'

'You recognised him?'

'No, how could I. He was not as you describe. He looked older than you perhaps, grey hair. Slim, no beard, walked with a slight stoop. Not an old man though.'

'Not her father?'

'No, there is more.'

'Go on.'

'The girls arrived; they remembered me from the last

time. After a little time, Doortje came back. On her own, no child. She then went up and down the stairs carrying things to the shelter below the house. She is back in the house now.'

'She can see us from the window?'

'Not easily at this angle. When she walked back, she seemed *bezet*–' Joe did not know the word. '–busy with mind. But the girls said hallo to her, and she said hallo back using their names. She nodded at me. We spoke before, you remember?'

'Yes.'

'When she went back to the house, I spoke to the girls, *'Doortje's baby girl, Tomasine, is very pretty?'* And they smiled and said yes. I told them that I had a drawing for Doortje's husband, but I had forgotten his name. The girls looked at each other and they both said, *'David'* I asked if they knew him and they said yes, he was *'grappig, vreemd.'*

'Oh god,' said Joe, 'I feel too exposed here, shall we go to the inn. It's at the other end of the street near the harbour? Do we take the trunk?'

'No, it will be safe here, but I will take the drawings.'

Joe asked for two small tankards of ale without asking Grietje and they sat at the only table by the window. A fisherman, the only other customer, stood at the bar as if he was a fixture.

'It is too much of a coincidence, it must be.' Joe was deep in thought.

'Joe, I saw the three come out.' Grietje pulled a sheet out from her folded paper press.

'I see that is a lovely drawing, Greta. I can picture it now.'

'Joe, the three of them walked straight past me.'

She pulled out a second drawing.

'Oh god, oh my god, Tom. It's Tom.' Joe shook.

They finished their ale and Joe said he needed to walk. They walked south, past the harbour wall, along a grassy bank with the sea on one side and calmer water on the other. The small birds flew up, squawking, as Joe and Grietje's steps crunched on the gravelled top. The wind whistled through the reeds. There was a set of fishermen's crates which they used for a seat. Grietje produced the bread and cheese from her bag. They sat and ate in silence.

'Joe?'

'He's alive. Greta, he is alive.'

'Are you fine with that?'

'Yes, of course. I did not let go for a reason; he is alive. I felt it.'

'You want him back?'

'No, no, that is not my need. He lives, and if he chooses to live here, then that is what he chooses.'

'Will you meet with him?'

'I don't know. I do not think so. I don't need to. I will write to Doortje. That would be best. Do you have the money still?'

'Yes, I carry it. I will not tell where.'

'Good. This cheese is good!'

Grietje laughed, 'Your *maag.*' She pointed.

'Stomach. I want to write it now; do you have a pen?'

'No, we could try the inn.'

'Let us do that.'

> *Dear Doortje.*
> *I am sorry I did not return as I had hoped. Events overtook me. I wanted to let you know that Tom's son, David, is very*

well and we, Mary, the family and myself,
meet with him often. He is very bright, he
likes books, and is happy and full of life. I
shall see him though university, for that is
where he is bound. He shall not want for
anything. I have bought Lockhart's busi-
ness and it is now doing well. I know there
are secrets Doortje, and I shall keep them.
You have my word. They are yours, and
yours only, to reveal. If you need anything
please write to me at Lockhart & Grieve
or you can leave it care of the Concierge
in Veere. You have my confidence. I en-
close something to help. I hope you are not
offended. It is for the child.

> *with love,*
> *Joe*

'Greta, can I have the money you brought?'

'Yes, how much?'

'All of it.'

'I haven't counted.'

'It doesn't matter.'

Joe put the money in a fold with the letter and asked the driver to take it over to the house.

'Greta, could you also please leave the drawing for Doortje?'

'The one of Tom?'

'No, the one with the street. Just leave it at their door and put your name on it, if you do not mind.'

'You do not want to meet him?'

'No, I am happy with that. Let us go home.'

'Home, Joe?'

CHAPTER 16

Delft & Veere, Zeeland 1711

The cart driver lifted the trunk and the easel on the back of the cart, Joe and Grietje climbed on board and they left Monster and headed back to Delft. It cooled quickly during the journey and Grietje wrapped herself in a blanket and leaned into Joe.

'I *will* cook tonight Joe'

'I would enjoy that.'

'We need to buy wine.'

'I will go to the inn for a jug.'

Over supper, they revisited their strange day.

'I don't understand why you did not want to talk to him. Would he not be pleased to see you?' Grietje asked.

'I am very pleased to see him alive. During our journey back, I have thought much on this. Maybe one day, but knowing him as I do, I think he would have had great difficulty dealing with the situation he has been in: two women, two loves, two children.

From your description on seeing him today, it seems he has suffered from his physical experience. He did not drown. But how long was he in the water? How long did he wait for rescue? He has made a choice. In that situation, it would not have been easy. I think that if he, they, saw me, it may be my imaginings, but I think the questions and doubts would rekindle. I understand more now about his business and his family background. It was oppressive–'

'I don't know...'

Joe mimicked being smothered.

'*gesmoord.*'

'–Tom married up, and never quite felt he was good enough. He wanted to be accepted by his wife's family and their social circles, and perhaps even his wife. The business drive and social ambition were linked.'

'You are not his way?'

'No, I live at a lower level, their world does not attract me. I like my office job, the precision of accounting then going home to my family at six at evening. Yes, I wanted, want, more for them, but just an extra room, and new, rather than second-hand, clothes. When David visits, he comes in smart clothes. His school is like a palace, he is well-fed and provided for. He can bring us better food than we can buy. Yet his pleasure in being with us is clear. We talk when I walk back with him to the school.'

'You do not enjoy this world!' said Grietje opening her arms.

'Yes, of course, but I do not need rooms like Henry's or a carriage. I like Henry for who he is, not his wealth.'

'But the wealth gives him freedom and opportunity.'

'I'm just thinking through these things, Greta, I do not know these things; I do not have answers. I said before, I think you are too wise for me.'

Joe continued, 'I thought this money did not mean much to me, it doesn't. I find it funny that all this money has started pouring in, satchels, paintings, false invoices, excessive profits. I have done nothing! Edward Clerk thinks I'm some sort of lucky charm.'

'So do I!'

'Hah, that responsibility will beggar me. I will invest the money in the business, employ others, and benefit my family too - better rooms, running water, an education for my brood. But it will not last, it's a fluke–' Grietje frowned. '–sorry, em, it is just chance.'

'One that you must take, Joe.'

'I have learned from Tom's experience; we are only a day away from drowning.'

'Well, in Zeeland, that is true, always!'

'Speaking of water, I will to go see van Reit tomorrow. It will take an extra day. You do not need to come. It is a long and not very comfortable journey.'

'I will come, if you will have me.'

'An early start then.'

Grietje undressed in the front room after Joe had retired. She then went through to his room. Joe did not react when she got in beside him.

'Goode Nacht, Joseph.'

'I am getting too used to this, goodnight.'

As they neared van Reit's house, Joe realised they would likely pass the spot where Henrik drowned, and Tom survived; he knew naught of the horse. He did not know exactly the place. That did not stop him imagining it. Looking for residue, the cart, evidence of the crates of paintings. The road was raised but not by much. On one side the land looked dry and firm, cows were grazing, on the other, marsh with patches of water.

'One bloody drop of rain and we're turning around.'

'Sir?' said the driver.

'Sorry, I was just thinking, *denken*.'

Joe recognised the house, even though he had only seen it in the dark. The gates were open and by the time the cart stopped at the entrance, a footman or butler stood at the steps.

'Mr Grieve?'

'Yes, and *Mevouw*...'

'*van der Meer, Margrieta van der Meer*'

Joe looked at Grietje. He did not know her given name.

'Dr van Reit welcomes you. He is sorry that he is indisposed, but the cook has prepared a light meal and you may visit him in his chamber afterward.' The footman spoke impeccable English. He then repeated the message for Grietje.

The driver was instructed to go to the kitchen.

Joe nodded and they were relieved of their cloaks and taken into the dining room. Once the footman left, Grietje walked round the room and marvelled at the paintings. Joe, once again, remembered Tom and rejected his instinctive sense of loss, reminding himself that Tom was now alive. It would take time. But here, he must forget that. With van Reit he must act as if yesterday had not happened. He had given his word.

'Joe, for one born of, how you say, low-level, you have much up-level friends.'

They were quickly brought a jug of wine, a tureen of soup, and boards of cold meats, and cheese. They sat on their own with no maid.

'What did van Reit do?'

'I think he was a merchant and then became a collector?'

'Is he married?'

'No, he sadly misses his wife and he has no surviving

children.'

The footman, with unnerving timing, came in as they had finished and invited them upstairs.

'I'll go up Greta, I will see how he is, and tell him of Tom.'

Joe remembered the stairs. Van Riet's bedroom was bright, curtains open and blinds high, still more paintings. There was a faint smell of illness and something residual that may have been a herbal remedy.

'Joseph Grieve, how good to see you.'

Joe smiled and walked over to shake his hand.'

'Forgive my incapacity. I am weak but not uncomfortable.'

'I thought you may not recognise me.'

'In the street perhaps not, you look very smart, and well if I may say so.'

'Thank you. I have taken over the business from Tom and have come again to buy Delft porcelain. We have a good market in England.'

'I am glad. But what of Tom; he is not with you?'

'I'm sorry, sir, it is not good news.' Joe paused to let van Reit anticipate.

'I thought there was something wrong.'

'When we left you, all went well with the trade. Tom and I separated. He travelled by cart by night in a storm. A dyke gave and he was lost.'

'I was afraid of this. I am so sorry, Joseph. His family?'

'They have not fared well, but his boy, David is fine. I see him in fact, and I have pledged to look after him.'

'Such news. I live on in this state and young men die. I'm sure our maker has his reasons. I have spoken to Janssen about him. He had acquired some fine paintings–'

'I have recovered three.'

'–and a girl?'

'You know of the girl?'

'Only through Janssen. He said they were very close.'

'That is true, they became close.'

'Joseph, you look concerned.'

'Oh, nothing, the girl is fine. I have met her since.'

'That is not all my friend. I am sorry, age has few benefits, but it has some. Your senses fade, but you see people with greater clarity.'

'I am sworn.'

'Of course, I apologise. Would you tell me her name?'

'Yes, it's Doortje, Doortje Veenstra, I think. With her mother, she ran the boarding house in Delft where Tom and I stayed. I never saw a father.

'Thank you, Joe, for coming. And you are doing well?'

'I have stumbled upon good fortune. The business fell into debt - a ship was lost – but by trading Delft porcelain and some good advice and investment, I am now in a good position.'

'Excellent and you run it?'

'Yes, only recently. I know, it is a surprise to me too.'

'Tom believed in you more than you did yourself. He told me so. Did you know that?'

'We worked well together for many years, I considered him a friend.'

'And you miss him?'

'As I would a member of my family.'

'To the future, Joseph, I am sorry I cannot drink to it. And you have a girl with you today?'

'Yes, a woman, an artist. She advises my choice of porcelain.'

'Oh, my, she paints?'

'I am no judge, but very well I think.'

'Would she come up?'

'Of course, she has already admired your paintings. You are not tired, sir?'

'I can sleep later; I would like to meet her' He rang the bell.

Grietje and van Reit could have talked for a week.

Grietje noticed van Reit was fading, losing the thread, mumbling his words. She nudged Joe.

'Sir, we must go, we have overstayed.'

'I see, I see, you may...'

'We have to meet a ferry by six.'

'Ah.'

'Grietje, it has been such a pleasure. You travel this way?'

'I can, sir.'

'It would please an old man, if you would return.'

'It would give me great pleasure.'

'Perhaps, don't leave it too long. I don't know...' and he was asleep.

They departed quickly. Joe wanted to be at the ferryman's house before dark. They would stay there and cross first thing.

It was dark when they arrived. The cottage was small. The driver attended the horse and was left to sleep with the beast in the part of the cottage that was used as a stable. The ferryman said his wife was not well and he could not offer food. There was no other choice. The room was sparsely furnished. There was a cabin bed in the front room. Two upright wooden chairs were set by the lit fire and a small table against the back wall. The floor was stone-flagged and clean. The man said goodnight and disappeared up steps through a hatch in the ceiling. Joe and Grietje both removed their outer garments and Grietje pushed Joe in first.

'Greta, I can...'

'No, you can't. Get in.'

'I'm twice the size of...'

'That is your own fault.'

Grietje followed him in. With a lot of rustling and the odd bump to achieve a degree of comfort, Joe curled up facing the wall with Grietje behind him facing his back. Contact could not be avoided. They tried to sleep. Grietje put her hand round him, towards his chest. Restless moments passed.

'Joe, are you asleep?'

'No, I'm not restful.'

'Are you comfortable?'

'It's fine. It's just...'

Grietje moved her hand down. Joe was relieved to be able to sleep peacefully.

They arrived back at Veere in the late afternoon. Joe went to liaise with the local clerk, and he checked on the crates and the ship. The clerk was recommended by the Scottish Trading Bank; Joe found him to be efficient and reliable. There were more papers to sign and a tax form. Local knowledge had its penalty. He had split the load; the second was due to arrive at the same time the following week. The clerk assured him all was in hand. Grietje had gone back to her room. Joe followed later and collected the personal things he had not taken to Delft, plus the satchel, with the pistol, the painting and the rest of the money. They arranged to eat out in the evening.

They went to the *Toren Inn* at the harbour entrance. Kings and princes had dined there, Joe had been told. The room was rich, red tapestries and carpets, layer upon layer, portraits and mirrors on the dark panel walls, each lit by two candles. On every table a candelabra, silver plates, jugs, glassware and cutlery, white cloths and napkins. The ornately carved chairs had padded seats. It was Jacobean in nature as if, being out of reach on the pier, it had avoided the stark whitewashing of the reformation; a fashion more familiar to Joe than to Grietje. There was no ribaldry, just the murmur of the guests, subdued in conversation. Grietje arrived ten minutes late, looking different, causing Joe to stare when she walked through the room. She had put her hair up, donned a fashionable dress and had powder on her face. Joe knew to compliment her. The food was excellent, and the recommended bottle of red was a good accompaniment. Grietje was quiet throughout the meal. When they were served the cheese, Joe asked for another bottle and brought out an envelope which he handed to Grietje.

'What is this?'

'I employ you, Greta.' They were both getting used to the adopted name he used.

'Is that all?'

'You haven't opened it.'

'No, I mean is that all I am?'

'You know the answer to that.'

'I'm sorry, I'm just sad to see you go.'

'I am too.'

Grietje looked in the envelope. 'Joe, this is too much.'

'No, you provided four days' expert advice, food and accommodation.'

She laughed, 'Thank you then, it will set me free. Should I give Henry some?'

'I don't think he needs it. Besides I have more to ask of you?'

'You will come back?'

'Yes, all being well, but it will be late spring.'

'What do you want me to do?'

'I have a proposition.'

'What?'

'Ah the cheese, and this is a fine bottle. It goes well with this hard cheese, don't you think?'

'What!' she exclaimed, kicking him under the table.

'I need an artist for the business for three jobs, one small, two substantial.'

'Tell me more,' Grietje said, brightening.

'In Edinburgh.'

'Oh.'

'The first is straightforward. To continue getting a good price and sale for the porcelain, I need a catalogue. I know nothing about printing but, oddly, David has a printing press at his school, he knows the whole process. *De Porceleyne Fles* had a catalogue of all their designs. We looked at it. It was hand drawn.

'Yes, I did many of the drawings.'

'We, I, would like to print a catalogue for Edward, myself and others to take to trade. Presently, we show a few samples and sell to a limited number of traders and houses. I think we can do more and better deals.'

'Is it not expensive?'

'The printing is not, but the etching is. This is where you come in?'

'I am not cheap!'

'Well, name your price then?'

'What are the other jobs?'

'The second is to make drawings for new patterns, ones that the English and Scottish market might like.'

'They like the Chinese.'

'I know, but there will be competition and tastes change.'

'When did you get so clever?'

'I listen to people, Greta. Tom, Henry, Edward, even you.'

'And the third?'

'The two paintings that I, the business, have acquired. I would like you to see them, make copy sketches, and perhaps find a good buyer or at least the value.'

'Is that all, sir?'

'For now.'

'I would stay in Edinburgh?'

'Yes, I can readily find a studio and a room.'

'You are unsure?'

'Edinburgh is not Delft. Some aspects might not be easy for a foreign woman. You do not need to decide now. But I would like to know within a few weeks so I can make plans. If you do travel, you must be accompanied. Ships are not places for unaccompanied women. I would send Ruud or make some other arrangement.'

'You intend to change my life, Joseph.'

'Our friendship does not depend on this, I will come back if you stay here.'

'I need time to think.'

'Of course.'

They enjoyed the wine and the cheese.

'Will you visit van Reit? It is not an easy place to get

to.'

'Yes, *zeker*. I still go to Delft for *de Porceleyne Fles* and for Henry's portrait. I need to finish my work.'

'My ship leaves at four tomorrow.'

'In the morning?'

'Yes, at four bells to catch the tide.'

'Will you come back to my room?'

'I would like to stay up with you, by a fire and talk. I can sleep on the ship.'

'That is fine.'

Joe had bought a small painting of a sailing barge at sea, similar to the one they found in Tom's bag. He thought it must be good because of the price, the dealer would not move a penny. He gave it to Grietje, telling her not to open it until he had gone.

'*Dank u* Joe *heel veel*,' she said.

CHAPTER 17

Cupar, Fife, Scotland 1733

David taught his last at the parish school. Several of the boys brought small gifts and a few, those who had formed stronger bonds, were visibly upset. He had introduced the new master a few days earlier. The church council had approved of him. There would be more bible in their weekday classes, but he was an exacting teacher, not a cruel man. His god was forgiving, not vengeful.

The demands in Kirkcaldy had increased. The schoolmaster's house was not ready, nor was the school. John Anderson had offered accommodation for David and Rosie until they had their own.

Parting from Jessie and Cora was not easy, but the three were old enough now to see their destinies were diverging, and that the last summer of their carefree days was coming to an end. They had talked about it. Rosie saw that her future was undetermined. Cora would work on the farm, marry, children or not, she would work on the farm. The thought that she would marry someone other than a farmer was never considered. She didn't quite understand what other people did with their time. Jess would continue to work at the inn. She found it interesting and had thoughts of learning to do the accounts. More often, she dreamt of being whisked away by a stranger. For years it was a foreign prince, now any young man with property would merit her attention. She liked the sound of the lives of the girls in Kirkcaldy in the stories that Rosie had told. Cora preferred the stories of the tall horses and the beach. They teased Rosie about becoming a Lady. Rosie swore to come back to see them often and that they would come to stay when the new house was built. 'I will have my own room and bed.'

Then one day, three horse-drawn carts came and the schoolmaster and his daughter left. Many of the villagers brought gifts for their new house and for Rosie. Mrs Reid overly hugged Rosie and gave her a large, soft parcel, planting a kiss on her cheek. One of the boys had brought a book for David. Rosie noticed, as he looked at it, her father struggled for composure at that moment. Cora gave Rosie a cotton square with a horse and a farm embroidered on it. Jess gave her a lovely, small, polished, wooden box with brass fittings, a lock and a tiny key.

Rosie sat up front with the driver of the first cart and her father kept to the rear on his own horse. The wagon train moved away with the bystanders smiling and waving. Rosie smiled and cried at the same time, they turned south at the end of the street. Rosie sobbed quietly for a good while, until she was dry.

The Andersons had a fine newly built house; three floors with the entrance centred at the front, on the first floor, served by two external curved staircases, one on each side. Rosie and David were made welcome. Their household furnishings and goods were stored in an adjacent farm building and it was a short ride to the building site of the school. David worked most of the time. When not away at meetings, he made use of a small room and a desk John had prepared for him. The door was usually closed.

David and Rosie settled into the life of their temporary accommodation. John, like David, was often occupied and away for days at a time. On weekdays, he would dine alone or with David if he was there, and Sir Peter when he was visiting. Rosie was Rose in this house and she decided, on the move, to now be Rose. It seemed to best to her that she left Rosie in Cupar. At first, Rose was able to spend time with the Anderson girls, Catriona and Fiona. They were glad to have a new addition to the household. They encouraged Rose in her piano practice and singing, rehearsing new songs to perform for the adults at the weekends. Although Rose was a good bit younger than the two sisters, she was as tall and they all practised dancing. Rose always ended up being the boy. When Rose was on her own, she was allowed to read in John Anderson's library. The girls were well tutored. The only tutored class that Rose attended was embroidery; a skill at which she did not excel. She was allowed a pony, Bobby, but only in the enclosure. She practised her horsemanship and improved her stability in the side-saddle. Mrs Anderson would go to *afternoons* with Catriona and Fiona. Occasionally, Rose went with them. She became accustomed to being quiet and polite...and bored.

She became fond of the girls, Catriona especially. Rose woke up with a fright one night when she found her bed wet. She was terrified and started shaking when she lit a candle to find it was blood. She tried to clean it, but it only got worse. When she saw where the blood was coming from, it was Catriona she ran to. Catriona could not have been more comforting. She explained that this was normal, an affliction from god that women must bear. She found her a napkin, helped her wipe herself down and took her into her own bed. Rose was calming herself until Catriona explained it would happen every month. Catriona held her as she sobbed to sleep.

In the morning, Catriona told her what to do. Rose then went to deal with her bedding, but Catriona said for her not to worry, the chambermaid would deal with it. Later in the day, when Rose saw the housekeeper, Mrs McReidy, who she did not really know, Mrs McReidy called her, gave her some white napkins and a big hug.

On days when her father went into Kirkcaldy to meet with council members, or Pathheid to see Mrs Oswald, Rose would go with him and went for walks around what was to become her new home town. On warm days, it was the harbour and the sands that gave her the most pleasure. More often than not, on these occasions, she would come across Smithy also, apparently, on a solitary excursion. She chose to avoid contact and any awkwardness, unsure as to the social niceties. A child talking to another would not be blinked at, but a young woman and a young man... She was not sure what she was. She would sit on a rock on a quiet jetty which was rapidly becoming a favourite. She had brought crayons and paper and was trying to sketch a boat, when a voice she did not immediately recognise came from behind.

'Are you Adeline's friend?'

She turned to find Smithy.

'You were at Dunnikier, with the Oswalds, is it

Smithy?'

'The boys call me that. I prefer Adam.'

He twitched a bit then offered a hand to shake.

Rose took it, 'I'm Rose.'

He stood as Rose, still sitting, and turned on the rock to face him.

'Have you moved to Kirkcaldy?'

'I have come with the new schoolmaster, I am his daughter.'

Adam stood for a bit as if searching for something else to say, but he found nothing and turned and walked away. Rose watched him walk a few yards then turn and say, 'Goodbye.'

'Goodbye,' she replied. She had not been uncomfortable in their short interaction.

The whole Anderson household tangibly brightened when Sir Peter and Adeline came to visit and stay for two or three days. The men came out of their shells of gravitas. Whether this was due to a temporary release from their cares or the relief in sharing them, Rose did not know. The three men enjoyed getting the girls, dogs and horses out on the moors. The sisters were not as keen as Rose and Adeline. The men would disappear for hours to the smoking room after dinner and not join the women at all. When Adeline was there, Rose was included in more invitations from other houses. Rose was learning the poise, the conversation, the piano and singing and was comfortable but did not fully engage with it. She knew she was different. Even with the lovely cream dress Mrs Reid had gifted her, she had few suitable clothes. She appreciated the effort the girls and their maid made, to dress and prepare her for a visit or a party. She also knew that her future was soon to bring her a small house, no lady's maid, and no fine clothes. Rose remembered her father's words regarding their position at Dunnikier. She sensed the difference, even with Catriona and Fiona; she had to keep it in her head. She was not down with it. If her thoughts went in that direction, all she needed to do was remember Titch. If you were not Titch then, in a sense, you were rich. If she did allow herself one wish, it would be her own horse. She would still dream yet.

Adeline gave her no sense of estrangement. Adeline made no secret of their close friendship. When confined to the house Rose set herself to learning French as quickly as she could. Her sole motivation was so, with Adeline, she could have confidential conversations in the presence of others, well boys, actually. Adeline liked this and began to invent misunderstandings in English so as not to appear rude in company. This contrivance brought them great hilarity. Fiona joined in on occasion as her French was good.

One notable visit for Rose was to Wemyss Castle. She was not a tag-a-long on this occasion; her father was invited personally in the company of Sir Peter. She tried to deny the slight pleasure she felt when she saw that Fiona and Catriona were disappointed not to be included. The visit was not as Rose had thought it would be. The castle was vast, Rose tried not to be open-mouthed. She wanted to run though the long corridors as fast as she could. Many of the older rooms were tired. There were walls of removed pictures, a smell of damp pervaded some of the unused rooms, motes of dust in the corners; it was cold even though the day was at high sun. Not all the castle was careworn, one wing was newly built. The large south-facing reception rooms were the biggest rooms Rose had ever seen. They were light, airy and well furnished with large windows looking over the clifftop to the sea. The view was stunning and the Wemyss girls, Anne and Fanny, explained that the family lived in this part of the castle. Rose asked if there was a library and she was taken to a bibliophilic utopia. Galleried, with two-storeyed bookshelves accessed by a moving ladder on rails. The girls were surprised at her interest. They were served a light meal in a warm and comfortable dining room. The conversation was polite, Rose would have had difficulty if Adeline had not been there.

There was talk of their pending summer trips. The Wemyss girls were going to Europe this year and Adeline told them of the places she had visited. Rose remembered she had only recently found that France was not on the other side of the Firth of Forth; she was not telling that story. She could afford no such ambition. She was destined to lead a different life.

David Wemyss came in and greeted Rose and Adeline, who mischievously said, 'Rose is very interested in the library.'

'Well, let me take you there,' and offered his hand before Rose could explain she had already seen it. The others chattered as they left the room.

'We went in briefly.'

'Oh, would you like to see it again? I can show you some of the more interesting books.'

'Yes, very much.'

Nearly an hour later, it was Lord Wemyss who found them engrossed in a large atlas of the known world.

'There you are!'

Rose curtsied.

'When I heard you were with David, it narrowed the search.'

'I'm sorry m'lord,' said Rose.'

'Are you interested or is my son tiring you?'

'Not at all...tiring. I have a love of books, sir. I did not realise there were so many.'

'It is time for you to go now, but you must come back. Libraries are for reading not for dust. David makes good use of it; the others only *in extremis*. I hope one day to have the time myself.'

As they walked behind Lord Wemyss, David said kindly, 'You don't need to curtsy when it's informal.'

'Oh, thank you.'

'My father likes you. That is unusual.'

'Why do you think that?'

'He did not send a servant.'

'You are the schoolmaster's daughter?'

'Yes.' Rose could not judge why he asked the question. 'Will you attend the school?'

'I don't think so. I fear I am being sent to Winchester.'

'Oh, where is that?'

'In England, it's a bloody long way.' David did not seem happy with the prospect.

Once they had given their thanks and their farewells, the girls and their fathers sat in the landau for the journey back to the Andersons'. The men were engaged in their own conversation. Rose and Adeline could not talk openly, but Adeline kept thumping her.

'What? What!' said Rose as quietly as she could.

'You were away hours!' she exclaimed in a whisper.

'I was not,' rebuked Rose.

'Did he kiss you?'

'Adeline!' Rose shrieked aloud.

'Rose?' enquired her father.

'Sorry, father.'

Sir Peter said that they would collect their things and go on to Tarvit while they had light. It would be some time before they could return. Rose did not get the opportunity to share her confidences, before saying goodbye to her dearest friend.

A week later Catriona, Fiona and their mother started preparations for a sea voyage. They were heading to an estate near York, in England, to visit a relative. It would be at least six weeks until their return. Adeline was also away, to London Rose thought, and her world of companionship was shrinking.

She was happy in the house and was now under Mrs McReidy's overly attentive care. When Mrs McReidy found that Rose wandered the town and harbour alone, she became concerned.

'I'm sorry dear, you cannot walk unaccompanied in your dress.'

'Mrs McReidy?'

'You are a young lady now and it's best that you fit in.'

Mrs McReidy found a plain, full-length, black dress, with a white apron and a white head scarf. She had it were altered to fit, Rose. Rose also needed new shoes and was told to approach her father.

'Father, I look like a fishwife,' she complained, 'or a nun.'

'You should thank Mrs McReidy, Rose. She is correct, if you want to walk round the town, you cannot wear the dress clothes you wear in the houses.'

'Why not, father?'

'I am not going to explain this now. Let me say that it will make you fit in and you will be able to walk without hindrance.'

'In Cupar...'

'That was different, Rose. I said there will be many changes here that we must accept, and they would not all be to our liking.'

'Yes, father.'

When her father travelled into Kirkcaldy, she had gone to the town with him and she had visted the beach. Though it pained her to admit it, there were now fewer glances in her direction and she enjoyed this anonymity.

In the house, her time was spent in books, on the horse and at the piano. Mrs Oswald asked to see her when her father was at Dunnikier and he arranged the visit. Jean also invited her to visit once; it wasn't a great success. On fine days, sketching by the harbour and watching the boats was her favourite occupation and the market day at Kirkcaldy was much more exciting than the one in Cupar. For that, though, she had to be accompanied, usually by a maid or servant who would buy foodstuff and wares for the house. It was the rock though, that replaced the steps of the Mercate cross.

'I wouldn't have recognised you had it not been for you sitting on the rock and sketching.'

'Hello, Adam.'

'Sorry, I forget that part. Hello, Miss Rose.'

'Rose will do.'

'Why are you dressed like that?'

'I'm not sure. I'm supposed to fit in.'

'Odd.' Adam shrugged his shoulders. 'Can I see?'

'It's just the boats. I like drawing because it makes me look at things in different ways, I have no talent.'

'It's fine. You should see James Adam's drawings, he

has such a good hand. Do you remember him, he was at the party?'

'Oh, I think so.'

In the silence, Adam paused while turning to go, 'I'm going to walk along the beach to the harbour near the tower at Pathheid, would you like to come?'

'I have to meet my father at Dunnikier soon.'

'That is on the way.'

Rose saw no harm in it. Glad of some company, they set off.

Adam asked a lot of questions; it was like being dissected; factual ones, not, 'How do you feel? or, 'What do you think'? He was more interested in Adeline than herself, and she pretended that she did not know very much.

'How do you talk to her? She speaks only in French. Do you speak French?'

In time, she would get used to this. It was a typical Adam Smith dialogue. Rose laughed.

'*Oui.*'

'Say something else.' It was almost a demand.

Rose gave her practised Adeline impression, '*Je parle à mon ami en français. Comprenez-vous* ?'and ended with a big smile.

'Why is it funny?'

'She doesn't only speak French, she just pretends to.'

'Why?'

Rose was getting fed up now, 'because she's a girl.'

There was a lessening in his persistence.

'Where do you live, Adam?'

'A town house on the High Street. You will have walked past it. Near the market.'

'You don't have a horse?'

'No, actually I'm quite scared of them.'

Rose found that a strange admission from a boy. She thought boys were not meant to fear anything.

'That's only when you are not familiar with them.'

'Do you know any other languages?'

'Latin.'

'Latin, you speak Latin?'

'Speaking is not really possible because it is a dead language.'

Adam waited for more.

'We do not know how it was said. I can read and write it.'

'Because your father teaches school?'

'It helps.'

Dunnikier is up this way. I am meeting John, Mathew and Adam Ferguson, do you remember him?'

'Yes, we sat beside each other. Does he not live in the highlands?'

'Yes, he comes down here for part of the summer.'

At Dunnikier, Smithy ran up the few steps, opened the large door himself and entered, leaving Rose in his wake. They had caught the footman by surprise. Smithy continued up the stairs; Rose stopped in the hall.

'Miss?'

'Miss Rose Miller, I have come to see my father. He is with Mrs Oswald.'

'Ah, which Mrs Oswald.'

'Oh. Senior, Mrs Isobel, I think.'

'I shall tell him you are here.'

The footman left and came back a few moments later.

'Please come this way, Miss.'

He showed Rose into the drawing room.

'Hello, Rose, goodness, what are you wearing?'

'Hello, Mrs Oswald. I am instructed to wear this in town when I am on my own.'

'I did not realise we had become quite so Calvinist, David.'

'The housekeeper has been helpful.'

'She is very kind to me,' said Rose.

'What is it, Rose?'

'The boys, em, John and Mathew, are going for a walk, may I go with them?'

'Is it only boys?'

'Yes, father, but I will be fine. It is the Oswalds, Adam Ferguson and Smithy, I mean Adam Smith. I think they are heading to Wemyss.'

'You seem to know them well.' David looked to check with Mrs Oswald, who nodded. 'By all means, but they must escort you.'

'Thank you, father.'

'Rose, can you please send John in before you go.'

'Yes, ma'am.'

As Rose left, Mrs Oswald, continued, 'Is she in want of female company at the Andersons?'

'They have left to go abroad. Only John, myself and Rose are at home. It will be a few more weeks.'

'Well, she must come here. No girls in residence but the boys like her well enough. They have said as much to me.'

'You have asked?'

'Yes, even James said, *She is not dreary*,' and I think Mathew has a soft spot.'

'That would be very kind.'

The four boys arrived in the hall, three at pace and

James more composed.

'Rose, what are you wear...'

'I know, I know!' drawing breath, she continued, 'I am to take holy orders.'

Mathew and Adam Ferguson got her joke quickly and John followed. Smithy just looked puzzled.

'John, Mrs Oswald asked to see you before you leave.'

When he came back, he said, 'You will come with us, Rose?'

'It is all boys.'

'Come on, Rose, we will protect your honour!' exclaimed Mathew and they all trundled out.

John, Adam and Smithy walked on with Mathew and Rose behind.

'I'm glad you came. You might save us from one of Smithy's lectures.'

'Oh?'

'When he finds or thinks of something new, he has to tell us about it. He's fine really, and he doesn't do it all the time.'

Smithy overheard and fell back to join them.

'I try to understand things. Is that not why we're different?'

'Do you think we can understand everything?' asked Rose.

'That is my quest. I will understand everything!'

'Except women, you said once,' added Mathew.

'Yes, the only thing that is incapable of being understood with logic, is women.'

'I agree,' announced Rose, 'I am a mysterious, wild and magical creature,' and she skipped ahead to catch the others.

When she got there, 'Hello, I think you have entranced Mathew and puzzled Smithy,' said John.

'Smithy has eyes on things French.'

'Hah, yes that is true.'

They walked and rotated groups of two and three, talking of all sorts of things serious and silly. The boys would run and chase each other. Smithy did not wander off and became less intense with Rose. It was as if she had passed a test. She thought he may become tiresome, but he was never boring. She conversed with each of them and did not feel excluded. The group arrived at the small harbour. Two other boys came from the other direction to join them. They were David and Francis Wemyss and they had brought food and two bottles of ale.

'It's Rose. Hello,' David said, in surprise, 'what are you...'

'I have come to be a fishwife!'

David Wemyss did not understand the hilarity of the others.

They shared their food which Rosie welcomed, but she did not accept the offer of the shared bottle of ale. It was not really offered. Mathew looked at her when he had finished taking a sup and she shook her head. They did not sit long. The boys played tag and Smithy went to look at something on the ground near the bottom of a young tree. Rose joined him.

'What is it?'

'Ants,' he said, 'They appear to act in unison.'

Rose looked too, 'They will go up that tree. There, look.'

There were two lines of ants, one going up and one going down.

'What are they doing?' asked Smithy, more to himself than to Rose.

'I don't know, but I've seen it before. They don't do anything at the top, just turn around and go down. There will be a nest somewhere.' She looked to a flat stone on the sand in the direction of the matching ants. Lifting it, she said, 'Here.'

Smithy was looking when Francis arrived.

'Ants!' he said and jumped. Rose and Smithy laughed.

'Jacobite!' Smith accused.

Rose put the stone down. 'They will just rebuild it.'

'How do you know about ants?'

'I spent a lot of time in Cupar looking at the ground; there were a lot of ants.'

'We're going back now,' John called, and they bade goodbye to the Wemyss' boys and set off.

At Dunnikier, Mrs Oswald asked if Rose would like to stay for the two weeks until their house was ready.

'Thank you, Mrs Oswald. If the boys don't mind me.'

'Well you may be a curiosity to them, but to my mind, you are a good influence.'

'Father, the boys asked if you could give them something to do over the summer.'

'What sort of thing?'

'I don't know, lessons or bookwork.'

David thought awhile.

'I can give them something, yes.'

He looked to Mrs Oswald who gave an approving nod.

David and Rose returned to the Andersons' and Rose stayed one more night. She dined with her father, just the two of them which was rare these times.

'Rose, I know I am neglecting you. I am trying to

secure our future. You will let me know if anything troubles you unduly?'

'I understand, father. I will. I am fine.'

'You must miss Jess, Cora and Adeline, are you sure about all these boys?'

'Not absolutely, but they are interesting, and it is different. I am not troubled by it. I'm growing up, father.'

'I see, I think fathers are always last to notice.'

'Will you give them some work?'

'Yes, I have a device. You will find out along with them when I take you back tomorrow. Are you packed?'

'Yes, and I will pick some flowers from the garden for Mrs Mac if Mr Anderson will permit me.'

At Dunnikier, Rose was given a large guest room not on the same floor as the boys. David gathered the boys and Rose in the small drawing room. Adam Ferguson, Smithy and James, even though he was eighteen, were there too. David stood with his back to the window.

'Boys, I have work for you to do, and it will only be interesting and entertaining if you *do* the work. Do you understand this?' David looked and waited until every boy had nodded.

'I know you like battles, I have seen it with my own eyes. If you do not do the work, you will be uninformed; you will be ignorant, and you will die on the battlefield as a lost soul.

First, I will read a poem. I translated from a Greek fable, an allegorical tale. The poem is one thousand years old and tells of a bloody battle between the pigmies...the Greeks,' he whispered, 'and the Cranes... the Trojans.' 'There was no quarter given, no one was spared.'

There was a light titter from the boys, but he knew he had them interested.

Rose's father's voice changed. He was a player on a stage. He stood as if he was addressing a Roman legion. The sound was deep and round. He enunciated every word in its syllabic detail. His tone ranged from high in suspense to low in gravitas. He made it seem as if each word held a deeper meaning, which it often did.

'For he was born to wage against the Crane,
Eternal battles, and immortal Hate,
And dearly he repaid the wounds they lent.'

David fetched a long iron from the fireplace and held it aloft.

'When, Comet like, his dreadful blade he wav'd,
Before its Lightening flew to the blasted Foe,
Or in a moment loft, his power to Fly.
What Heaps of slaughter has it made!'

He moved, with his raised sword, towards Rose, who giggled.

'how oft Has the unfletched Infant fall'n before its Edge!
Alas! how oft has widow'd Strymon mourn'd,
Her husband and son's untimely fate.'

There was silence in the room.

'Now,' he continued in a lowered but still precise tone, 'I charge you *all*…with solving a *puzzle*… and telling *the story* of one of the *great* battles. *It - is - a - battle – of – the - Gods!'*

I will give you each a sheet and a book of poetry, with a poem about the battle which was written by the Romans in the original Latin. The sheet is an incomplete translation of the poem in English. Some of the words are still in Latin and some completely missing.

I do not give you the order of the sheets, but I will tell you that the poem starts in the book at the twenty-fourth page. Master Smith will hold the dictionary–' Rose walked over and gave the key book to him. '–and he will look up Latin words for you. The task is sim ple: you have to work out who the Gods are, where they are fighting, what happens during the battle, and who wins. You will then re-enact the battle for Mrs Oswald, your parents and myself, with quotations and speeches from the poem, in one week's time.' He paused and Rose handed out the sheets. 'It is a collaborative effort, not a competition. James and Rose know some Latin, they can help with the words. You will also write down any Latin word you learn and the English equivalent.' The boys gathered their bottles of ink, quills and paper and set to task.

Rose's two weeks passed in a moment. There was always activity: parties, visitors, horses, walks, dogs, picnics, with little breathing space in between. It had not been the solitary time she had anticipated. Too soon it was over. She was excited to move into the new house, but she would miss her band of brothers.

Term started at the new school, girls in one classroom, boys in the other. The girls were given enough arithmetic along with their reading, writing and needlework to be useful in accounting. All boys received some Latin, but they were bifurcated early on into apprentice boys and academic boys. For all David's principled argument for a grammar school education that included girls, there was demand only from one, his own. The apprentice boys left school each day at two and David continued with his classical scholars for a further four hours. Rose was included. She distracted no one, well not any more than usual. By late October, life for David and Rose found a satisfying routine, something that it had not held since the death of Janett. The Oswalds all attended the school, apart from James who had headed to university. David Wemyss had departed for Winchester, Adam Ferguson had gone back to Logierait. There were other bright boys to fill the class.

Smithy was a frequent visitor to the master's house. He got on well with David, challenged by the master's open questions. They had endless discussions on the balance of knowledge and belief, and compromises of principle in a personal and social context.

These issues disturbed Smithy's clinical, *perfect world*. He also spent more relaxed interludes with Rose. Rose said he could be 'Adam' now Master Ferguson had left for Logierait. Rose wondered if she was just a stepping-stone for him to meet with Adeline. Rose was not made to feel at all welcome when he took her to meet his mother in their small townhouse in the High Street. She sensed Adam's mother had greater ambitions for her son. Social differences became more important with age, she observed, not less. In school, however, they were all the same.

Her envy was for a horse, a stable and a paddock. These were conveniences to her friends, they were treasures to her. When she dreamed; it was of a house by the sea, with books and a guest room and a dining room. No handsome prince, not yet anyway.

Once a month, Adeline enlivened their weekends with a visit. Rose took to writing a personal journal for herself and letters to Adeline, Catriona, David Wemyss and Adam Ferguson. She had written to Cora and Jess but had received no reply from Cupar. She would travel back when the opportunity arose.

At the end of October, a sealed letter arrived for David. Rose brought it to him over supper in the evening.

'Father?'

'It is a piece of news from Edinburgh. My mother's father, James Lockhart, has died.'

'Oh, I'm sorry.'

'It is not important to us. I barely remember him. He has surprised us all by surviving his wife, daughter and my father, his son-in-law.'

'Who has written?'

'It is Joseph Grieve. You met him briefly at your mother's funeral.'

'I don't remember.'

'The intriguing thing is that he, Joseph, has asked to see me. After the funeral may be convenient, but at another time if not. He would travel here if I am unwilling to go.'

'Is it worrisome?'

'Hah,' David read on, 'Joseph thinks it may be of benefit, presumably from the legacy. I do have a fear it may be a debt.'

'Will you go?'

'Yes, I have to really. It was Joseph and his wife, Mary; they looked after me at school, not the Lockharts who had a troubled life.'

'You have never told me of this, father, may I ask why.'

'I don't want to bring it up now, Rose, I have lessons to prepare. But briefly, my father died when I was nine.

My mother took very ill. She was their only child, perhaps understandably, her parents attended her health. It was complicated by their business becoming bankrupt–'

'Father?'

'–loss of money. I was sent to school. It was a good school; I am the better for it. And I never saw them again.'

'I did not know, father. How sad.'

'It was a long time ago.'

'You never saw your mother?'

'No, she was terribly unwell, Rose. Please do not think ill of her.'

'I wondered why I had no grandparents, but I never wanted to ask. Your father died?'

'Yes, drowned, at sea, I think. It was not uncommon. It's getting late, Rose.' He smiled. 'It was a very long time ago and, as you see, I am now quite grown.'

'Can I come with you?'

He knew at the question, he was going, and so was his daughter.

'We will see.'

David spent the next few days making up work for his pupils. He found a monitor in the town, and the Doctor of the girls' class would oversee.

On Monday morning, along with Rose, they took the mail coach along the coast to Burntisland and expected to be back within the week. Rose was overexcited about the trip and sailing, David reminding her to be respectful, given the solemnity of the occasion. She felt her frequent use of the bucket on the boat was divine retribution. It was two hours to Leith.

As they disembarked, Rose's whole world now

seemed small. The people, the horses, the carts, the buildings, the smoke, the traders, a hundred Kirkcaldys, a thousand Cupars all in one place. Everything taller, wider, longer, smellier and noisier. There were many demanding a carriage and they had to wait. They had travelled light: linens, what they were wearing, plus a smart suit for David and two dresses for Rose, one dark one light. David had sent a message to Joseph but, by the time they left, had not received a reply. Having started early in the morning, it was mid-afternoon when they found the offices of Lockhart & Grieve.

David had come chiefly out of a sense of duty, but also with a slight concern of a financial threat. Joseph had said *benefit* in his letter. The last he had known of his grandfather's business was that it was being dismantled by the bailiffs. That was many years ago. He had not kept up with Joseph and Mary after university. There was an occasional card and the gift of a dress for Rose which arrived unannounced.

Until Janett's funeral, the last personal contact had been at his own wedding. A small affair, followed by a lunch with the Grieves and two friends, one from his university and one of Janett's old school friends.

David was thus circumspect when he and Rose arrived in Edinburgh. He had not accounted for the crashing waves of memory that hit his past shores as they left the carriage at the bottom of the Canongate and walked up the High Street. It was not his university days that came back, no, he was transformed back to the emotions of his schoolboy self. Momentarily, he became lost in it. His boys, the masters, Molly, the school meals, the smallpox outbreak, Daniel, oh, dear Daniel, what of him now.

'Father, father, father!'

He looked blank at her, 'Oh, Rose, I'm sorry.'

'Are you alright?'

'I was elsewhere. I was ten for a moment there.'

Rose feared to ask any more questions.

David thought, correctly, that the address on the letter was the same. He did not recognise the building. It was a different building. Three wide steps led to an imposing entrance. A large brass nameplate by the double door, Lockhart & Grieve. He and Rose were still in their travelling clothes. David regretted not changing. He gave his name to the uniformed doorman. He suspected Joseph had done well but he had not expected this. A boy was dispatched upstairs and they were invited to sit. Rose was wide-eyed and quiet, not nervous.

A tall, athletic older man, still with a full head of red hair arrived quickly down the stairwell.

'David, and Rose, how wonderful. I'm sorry it is a solemn occasion, but I am so pleased to see you both.'

Joe shook David's hand for an age and then, with outstretched arms, picked Rose up, lifting her two feet, two feet off the ground, 'and look at this beautiful creature!'

'Oh, I'm so sorry, I am rude and ill mannered.' He put her down and politely bowed while gently shaking her hand.

Rose's expression changed from alarm to amusement. She curtsied.

'If you can bear another journey, Mary has given me strict instructions to bring you straight to the house. You will stay with us?'

'We do not want to inconvenience you.'

'Nonsense, we have some grandchildren around, I think they are near your age,' he said, looking at Rose.

'That would be welcome, Joseph, thank you.'

It was a black, glossy, open carriage with two matching stallions that arrived immediately outside.

The doorman brought Joe's cloak and hat and took David and Rose's bag to the carriage.

'You have done well, Joe, all this?' said David gesturing toward the building.

'Not all. I manage it, yes. There are investors, the Clerk family and two others.'

Joe leant toward Rose. 'Your father remembers me in a two-room house in a damp close. I remember him as a naughty schoolboy who showed too much interest in my office girls.'

Rosie shrieked; she liked this monstrous man.

'But it is alright, because one of them was your lovely mother.'

Rose turned to her father, 'Really, really, father?'

David nodded and he fondly remembered Joe's quiet humour and good nature. He had grown as a person yet he still retained his youthful vigour. He must be well over sixty years now.

'It is not far. Please forgive this fancy carriage. We will use it for the journey to the funeral from the house, the day after tomorrow.'

'Where do you live, Joe?'

'Our new house is in Canon Mills. We have a good view up the hill to the town. The Leith water and the mill sit within our boundary. It is a colder situation than I would like.'

Outside the town they arrived at an elegant three storey house, with a short circular gravel drive. It was similar in design to John Anderson's; the main entrance being up an outside stair to the first floor. Mary had heard them approach and stood at the top of the stair with three curious children, one older girl and two younger, a boy and a girl of similar age. Rose kept her amusement hidden. These strange people treated her father as if he was a child. She knew they were of a far too open and affectionate nature for his liking. But, in this case, he did not seem to mind. She had caught him with a smile at their animation.

Inside, it was a beautiful house, decorated, not overly ornate, light and airy. It had a simplicity of style which was new to David; it had none of the cluttered stuffiness that branded the houses of many Scottish merchants. The furniture was elegant, thin-legged, made from light wood, decorated with marquetry inlay. There were seascapes on the walls and detailed townscapes of red-walled places David did not recognise. He saw later, in the dining room, paintings of simple domestic scenes.

David was cognisant of the prosperity it represented. Joe and Mary had been near paupers when he started school. With Rose he was taken into the drawing room and introductions were made. The twins were sent away to find their nanny and the older girl, Grace, asked Rose if she wanted to see her room. David was left with Joe and Mary.

Mary was in charge in the house, 'David we eat at seven hours, but do you need something now? Chinese tea and a slice of cake perhaps.'

'That would be most welcome.'

'I will send something up for Rose. Grace is well groomed unlike her grandfather. Rose will be fine. Has he been horrendous?'

'Yes, of course,' said David, making Joe roar.

'I married a quiet and serious man, you know, but when the grandchildren started to grow...I don't know what went wrong.'

David laughed.

'How is Rose, David? Is it over a year now? She must still be raw. And please tell us how you are.' It was a heartfelt question.

'It has been hard, Mary, thank you, but no harder than for others. I have been so busy with the new school that, thankfully, I have not had the time to dwell. As to Rose, she has low moments, but there is so much of her mother in her–'

'I can see that.'

'–she invests in life. She is bright and takes an interest in many things. We are lucky to have good people around us.'

'And the move to the new town...?'

'Was the right decision, there are many challenges. I think the loss would have been more harshly felt with daily reminders of her life in Cupar. We do not forget, of course. Rose must have her own life, unburdened. It is what Janett would expect.'

'She is a beautiful girl, so like Janett.'

'I am grateful for that.'

Joe took over, 'I know teaching is not well paid. Are you comfortable, David?'

'Oh, Joe,' his wife exclaimed, 'always money, you'd think he was Scottish.'

David found himself enjoying this company.

'We are fine. Let me ask a question, Joe.'

'By all means.'

David opened his arms. 'How? You were a thirty-odd year-old clerk! A good one by all account, but…'

'Chance and circumstance, in two words, David, in all sincerity, chance and circumstance. And I think now, that is all it ever is.'

'Oh, Joe, you have worked hard,' said Mary.

'So have the many.'

Mary took David to his room and they dined with Grace's parents, Grace, Rose and young Joe in the evening.

'This is young Joe,' Joe announced, at the entry of a red-headed man taller than himself, 'You remember our sickly child.'

The table talk was of old times. Rose, far from being bored was fascinated by these exagerated stories of her young father and mother. Rose slept with Grace, and the two girls insisted on going up to town, to the markets the following day. David was not given a choice. Joe said he wanted to meet with David in the afternoon and that the office would be a better place for the discussion. The funeral service and burial would follow, the day after, at Calton.

David was towed round traders and stalls in the town's morning air. The stench was unchanged. He observed the ability of the two girls, strangers two days ago, to get on as old friends. The girls found they had so much to share, Grace almost stunned by the fact that Rose not only went to school but sat in a class full of boys. David tried to interest Rose in places that were important to him in his youth, but today, dresses and giggling chatter were her preferred occupation. One that she did not, to a large degree, experience in Kirkcaldy.

He released them for a while, and sat in a long familiar coffee house where they would return to find him in an hour. He had his constant companion, a small volume of Roman oratory, but his mind wandered back to his earlier life, and then forward to what Joe's meeting was about. For an open person, Joe had been guarded about the reason for the meeting.

Mary collected the girls at the office and took them for a midday meal, and more shopping David suspected. Joe and David would eat in the small dining room in Lockhart & Grieve. The dining room and Joe's office were designed to impress and perhaps intimidate, David thought. Polished oak panels, a veneered table and matching chairs. Paintings of named merchant ships adorned the walls between the oil lamps. A platter of cheese, meats, bread and a cold pie was brought in along with a jug of light ale.

'Thank you, we will serve ourselves.'

'I feel I have been summoned to the schoolmaster's office.'

'I'm sorry, David, please help yourself and we can sit and talk. When you hear what I have to say, you will realise why we are better here.'

'Should I be worried, Joe?'

'Not at all. It's I that am in the position of discomfort.'

With lightly filled plates they sat facing each other.

'David, may I just talk for a bit?'

'By all means.'

'I know, that is I have information, from long ago that you have no knowledge of. With the death of James Lockhart, it is knowledge that you must now attain.'

'I do not see how...'

'If I may...'

'Of course.'

'There is a legacy.'

'I thought there was only debt.'

'Well, yes and no. That is the story I need to tell. When I first came back from Zeeland, and your father was lost, the company, Lockharts was in a very poor state. Not then but six months later, after a second more profitable venture, I started to look if anything could be saved. I found that your grandfather had accounting books I had never seen. The family's finances, his own and the company's were too much interlinked. There were attempts to resolve the situation, but the total debt was such that it was impossible. There was no regular source of income. His family's expenditure was still high. James Lockhart sold what he could. He then disappeared, refusing all contact. I did not see him again. Sorry, I digress. The company's books showed the company debt to be, well, manageable. I sought investors, bought the business debt, and took over the company.'

'I'll take a breath, and some pie, I'm getting there.'

David sat patiently.

Joe continued, 'I agreed to the Lockhart family retaining ten-percent of the company but I placed severe restriction on what they could do with it. They could not sell it, but they could spend income from it. The problem was that the family had great debt. Any money at all would just be used to fill a bottomless pit. This debt had been running for years, I doubt your father knew of it, or maybe he did, and he was trying to escape it, I don't know. Anyway, James was not well at this stage and his lawyers acted reasonably in the family's interest. Although I am not sure even *they* were acquainted with the whole situation. It was not in my interest to tell them.'

'Are you able to follow?' Joe paused for more pie and a sup of ale.

'Yes.'

'Your mother was in private care. For Tom's sake initially and then for yours. I paid for her upkeep until she passed, and I made sure that James and your grandmother had enough to live comfortably. None of them were aware of this, I did not want them to be. It was a private arrangement, an agreement between lawyers.'

'I thank you for that Joe, I had no idea.'

'Don't thank me yet.'

Joe continued, 'Remember, that the dividends on the Lockhart's ten percent were rolling up. The reason I kept it that way was to stop the family debtors getting a hold of the money. That could have put the family on the streets.'

'My university fees and stipend?'

'It was paid.'

'Oh Joe, I did not know. I am indebted.'

'No David, not yet. This is the difficult part.

'Tom, your father, had made money on his fateful trip to Zeeland. When I returned, almost a year later, after buying the company. I recovered a substantial amount of it.'

'But how?'

'I will leave that part to the dinner table, chance and circumstance. If you will still dine with us.'

'David, it was convenient for me at the time to treat that money as the company's. Your father was acting for the business. The business had underwritten the venture. The business was ruined because of the failure of the venture. I had bought the business. I was the legal owner.'

'But?'

'I think that a good proportion of that wealth was Tom's. I do not know. There are no books. Did he intend to bring it to his father-in-law? If so, it would have got lost in the family's debts. He may not have known that. Your father, remember, I was with him, I knew him, we talked. Your father wanted to break away. I sit here leading the life of your father. It is not my own.'

David, waited, trying to take it in.

'He died Joe. You could not...'

Joe took a draft and called for a bottle of whisky. David was about to speak but Joe put his hand up. There was still more.

'The consequence, the consequence is that with James Lockhart's death, well, I don't know if you know, but all debt is buried with the body.'

Joe paused again for David to catch up.

'The ten percent, with dividends rolled up over, what, more than ten years, which were invested, will be yours David. It is a not inconsiderable sum.'

David just sat. His first action was to pick up a piece of cheese. He stared ahead without seeing.

'You mean...'

'David, it is late in coming I know, but yes, you will. No, you *are* today, a man of considerable wealth.'

'It is too much to take in. I can't...'

'I understand. Can I suggest you take your leave? I will remain here. Come back any time before five.'

'And David!'

'Yes.'

'Do come back.'

'I will Joe, I will.'

David stood up with difficulty, his legs shaking. He left, forgetting his cloak and hat.

David walked down the mile to Holyrood. Turning right he headed over the moor and up the crags. He was not appropriately shod. He walked at such a pace up the slope, he was breathless. It was corporal punishment. He needed to think. He didn't want to think. He tired and turned at the top, down to the Cowgate. He looked to the church; he wasn't ready. He passed Joe's old rooms. St Giles, the Lockhart's Land. Through the *Grafe Mercate*, left at the West Port and through the oh-so familiar grounds of the school. How many times a young man paced this path. David walked through the town. David walked through his life. Calmer now, the clock at four hours and the half, he took the road back.

Quickly there, the doorman nodded for him to go straight up. Joe's office was opposite the dining room. He knocked and entered to find Joe at his desk. Joe stood.

'I'm glad to see you David, are you well?'

'It will take time Joe, as you can imagine. I can't think properly.' David paused. 'I will walk back to the house. I assume Mary has the girls.'

'Yes.'

'Joe?'

'Yes?'

David just looked.

'Oh, you are so like your father, David, he wouldn't have asked either. Enough, well enough...for a country house, and staff, and a town house and staff. You need not work again.'

'Thank you,' and David turned to leave.

'David, can I offer one more thing.' David waited. 'You don't *need* to take any or all of it. The fact of it can remain between us. It is under your authority. It can safely remain invested for some other future.'

'Thank you, Joe, that is exactly the dilemma which troubles me.'

David found Mary, Grace and Rose in the hall at the bottom of the stairs. Rose saw that something in her father was not right.

'Hello girls,' he managed, 'I am going to walk back to the house. I will see you there.'

'Father will I...'

'No, Rose, it is fine. I need to think. Do not worry.'

'Father, I have bought a dress. Mary said that it would be fine.'

'Oh Rose,' David moved to hold Rose in a clasp, kissing her on the head, he turned to leave, muttering, 'you could buy a hundred dresses.'

'Father, father!' The doorman closed the door behind David.

'What did he say?'

'Rose, he said, you can buy a pretty dress' Mary repeated firmly.

Rose frowned, and looked toward Grace, who was standing behind her mother, shaking her head.

David scolded himself into attending to the social evening with Joe's family. He was back at the house before the others arrived, talking of everyday matters with young Joe and Grace's father, Hugh. It helped David find firmer ground.

The girls skipped in with tales of their day. Rose had clearly enjoyed the afternoon and David suspected she had been spoilt. They all went upstairs to their rooms to refresh, coming down for dinner at a later hour.

The dinner was an informal occasion and it provided welcome and distracting conversation. Hugh was an advocate in Edinburgh. Joe's older boy worked for the company and was in the Americas. One of the company ships was due in from the Indies, always an eager anticipation. Its crew had been away for more than a year.

After the meal had begun, a woman entered, apologised for her tardiness and joined the table. Neither Joe nor Hugh rose and David, his back to the door, did not see her until she drew a chair and sat diagonally opposite him. The family was pleased to see her, the twins excited, and they exchanged pleasantries on her arrival. There were no introductions. It was as if, David thought, he was expected to know who she was, but he could not recall seeing her earlier. She looked younger than Joe, and had short dark hair, spoke with an unusual accent and wore a dark blue tunic rather than a dress. She was a familiar and behaved as a close member of the household. David noticed her hands were splattered with paint.

As David, Rose and Joe's family finished their meal and got up to leave the table, Joe said he would enjoy a glass of whisky and his pipe in the smoking room before bed, and that David was welcome to join him.

'But first David would you stay seated here for a moment and Rose would you come with me.'

The others bade them good night and retired.

After a good five minutes, Rose came back in alone-carrying a parcel. Ah, the dress, David thought, but Rose looked solemn. Rose placed the parcel on the table and sat down beside her father, before unwrapping it.

'Father, this is your father's bag, he had it with him when he was lost.'

She undid the leather straps and pulled out the lightly wrapped journal and the painting. Leaving them in front of him. She sat quietly.

David unwrapped the painting and then the journal. He opened the pages to see his father's writing. He put it back down and lowered his head to take in the smell of the satchel. David let a tear fall.

He opened his arms and turned to Rose, and in the corresponding movement, she leaned in to be held by him. She heard him sob but did not look up. Her father was crying, and so was she.

EPILOGUE

James Lockhart was an old man when he died. He had lost most of his friends and his professional reputation long since. Representatives of old family associations attended, as did burgesses who had prospered under Joseph's later management, lawyers, office holders from the kirk, and council members of the Merchant Company of Edinburgh. It was a dutiful attendance. The service was mercifully short: a few psalms, the minister spoke, *We are all sinners answerable only unto God,* and a eulogy delivered by a retired Lord Provost, who reminded the congregation of James' better days. In the procession to the burial ground, several mourners dropped away. The carriages were black, polished and unadorned; beggars demanded pennies when the procession passed. As the coffin was lowered into the grave, David stood with Joseph. The minister threw on the handful of earth.

Ashes to ashes dust to dust and it was over.

He was glad he had forbidden Rose to attend. He explored his own response; he was looking at the burial of a stranger not a man who had any meaning in his life.

David looked up and saw Joe's face turned white.

'Joseph are you alright. You do not look well. Joe?'

'Do you see there?' Joe said, pointing at a woman walking towards them.

'I see a woman walking this way. I do not recognise her.' She was young, fair, long-limbed and well dressed.

'Joe, you are being rude,' said David, as Joe continued to stare.

She smiled at Joe and then, as she neared, she turned her attention to David.

'It is David, David Miller?'

Her accent was foreign. Her speech hesitant, belying her elegant composure. David thought there was something familiar about her he couldn't place.

'Yes, I am sorry about Mr Grieve, and you are?'

'David, I am sorry for this surprise, I am Tomasine. I am your half-sister.'

ACKNOWLEDGEMENTS

In the writing and production of this book, I am indebted to many...

The patience of my wife, Christine, and daughter, Natalie, know no bounds. Not a word would have been written without the enthusiastic support and advice of Gavin @ UoE and the IYF gang (2019) namely, Neil, Eimear, Malcolm, Anna & Laura. The extreme tolerance and encouragement of my coffee buds: Rob, Zhamilya, Alan, Alicja, Pam and Alistair; all worth their weight in beans. The first readers: Nat, Diane, Ian and Chris. Last, and far from the least, the essential, invaluable detailed commentary & feedback from Aileen and Joanne.

TDB   25th May 2020

@DrTDB

BIBLIOGRAPHY

A History of Everyday Life in Scotland, E. Foyster & C Whatley, EUP 2010

The Scottish Revolution 1692-1746, N. Davidson Pluto Press 2003

Scottish Society 1707-1830, C.A. Whatley Manchester University Press 2000

Education in Edinburgh in the 18th Century, A. Law, University of London Press. 1965

The Scottish Staple at Veere, J. Davidson & A. Gray, Longmans 1909

An Economic History of Scotland in the 18th Century, H. Hamilton, Oxford 1963

The History of Scottish Education, J. Scotland, University of London Press. 1969

The History of Early Scottish Education, J. Edgar, James Thin, Edinburgh 1893

Education in Angus: A historical survey..., J.C. Jessop, University of London Press 1931

George Heriot's Hospital: memories of a modern monk being reminiscences of life in the Hospital, C.B. Gunn, Livingston (Edinburgh) 1863

Jinglin' Geordie's Legacy, B.R.W. Lockhart, John Donald Press 2003

The Royal High School, W.C.A. Ross, Oliver & Boyd 1934

Extracts from the Records of the Convention of Royal Burghs, (published by the Scottish Burgh Records Society, 1878-1918).

Testaments of Veere Residents Recorded in Edinburgh Commissary Court Registers, 1559-1732, National Archives of Scotland

Veer, Scotland Staple Port in Flanders: Shipping Records 18th Century, Dundee City Archives

Dutch Delftware, 1620-1850, J.D. van Dam, Waanders 1999

The Capital of the Mind, J. Buchan, Birlinn 2007

The Life of Adam Smith, I.S. Ross, Oxford University Press

Adam Smith, An Enlightened Life, N. Phillipson, Penguin UK 2011

Elcho of the '45, A. & D. Wemyss, The Saltire Society 2003

Printed in Great Britain
by Amazon